Elderkin Chronicles Volume I

I0649817

Heir of the Bindings

Elyse M Grasso

Superior Magpie Press

Ebook ISBN: 978-1-966887-00-3
Paper ISBN: 978-1-966887-01-0

Superior Magpie Press
300 Center Drive #G 399
Superior CO 80027
info@superiormagpiepress.com
https://superiormagpiepress.com

Table of Contents

Dedication

For my Mom and Aunt Irma
Finally, a Book

Wish you were here to see it

Heir of the Bindings

A Warning to Readers

In our world, the late 17th century on the Continent was not a gentle time or place. There were wars – civil and sectarian and otherwise – and plagues and famines.

Legal penalties were ferocious and often involved removing portions of the anatomy. So did medical care. Composers created great musical works assuming that castrato soloists would be available.

Slavery was legal everywhere but mostly found in cities and government installations.

Outside the cities, many jurisdictions still assumed that non-Nobles were serfs, bound to the land.

Women of all ranks and in most jurisdictions had even less control of their own persons and property than their male kin.

Most men of Noble rank found much of this – except, possibly, for the wars and famines and plagues – quite proper and convenient and satisfactory.

The world of the Chronicles is not as different as one might hope.

Heir of the Bindings

The Wolf, the Goat and the Cabbage

A man arrives at a river bank with a wolf, a goat and a cabbage.
He finds a very small boat with room for only himself and one of the
three things. If he leaves the wolf alone with the goat, the wolf will eat the
goat. If he leaves the goat alone with the cabbage, the goat will eat the
cabbage. How does he get all three of his charges across the river?

CHAPTER I: The Message

Wherein We Meet our Hero and Sad News Arrives

When the news came of his father's death in an overturned carriage on a country road, Franz-Karl was five years old as age was counted in the Kingdom of the Allemans, which preferred to be called the Holy Remoran Empire. Franz-Karl did not believe the news at first, when a palace official bustled into their apartments, struck a pose, and made the announcement.

He knew that the palace official – a middling Chamberlain called Ritter von Ostwald who claimed to be in charge of their wing of the Palace – was a fibber. Besides the many times the man had told them things that were not quite real, the Ritter did not properly fit into the shape of the World: he looked like someone had cut him out of a page and then pasted him back just a little out of place.

Besides, Franz-Karl knew that his papa hated carriages and wagons, and always rode horseback when he could.

But the Ritter von Ostwald (Ritter von und zu Ostwald, properly speaking – he was very fussy if he heard you say it the shorter way) handed Franz-Karl's Mama a sealed paper, and when she had opened it and read it tears began to drip down her face and she began to take off her jewelry. So Franz-Karl knew that she believed it. Or at least she believed the dead part. The Chamberlain said loudly that Papa had been seeing to his country estate when he died. Mama, who was Elderkin and never lied out-right, had said that Papa was running errands for His Imperial Excellency Papa's Father, but she did not say out loud that the Ritter was wrong. She just looked at him until he fidgeted and looked away, then left to fetch mourning cloth from the Palace storerooms.

Mama took off her necklaces and all her bracelets and rings – she even hung her signet on a white ribbon around her neck where it would be hidden by her clothes – and she replaced her earrings with studs that were made of bone or ivory: something dead. She sent her chief attendant, the Itron Gwenlian, to unpack the clothes that were made of dull cloth in the yellowish-brownish-gray that the Elderkin of Traventi called color-of-sorrow.

Mama even unwrapped her hair from around her head. By the time the color-of-sorrow clothes were brought, she had unbraided it to let it hang loose, with just two ties at her neck and waist to keep the long hair from going everywhere. Usually, when she was not being the Ambassador from Traventi, the warm brown braids were arranged so that the green streaks were folded inside. Now the green was just there. And there seemed to be a lot of green, more than Franz-Karl remembered.

The mourning clothes for Mama to wear every day had been cut with wide seam allowances, but stored un-stitched. Measuring and marking where the seams should go went quickly. The ritual garments to wear at the funeral had been stored since the last funeral with the seams already stitched. Mama put them on, decided that they fit well enough, and just left them on.

Small children did not have mourning clothes already prepared – neither Traventi's color-of-sorrow nor the black clothes the Allemans used – because that would be asking to have someone die while the clothes still fit them. So Nurse Rosa changed Franz-Karl and Philip-Augustus and little Sophie-Alexa into the plainest clothes they had until their mourning clothes could be made.

The Palace was Papa's family home, so there was supposed to be cloth in the storeroom so the proper clothes for the children could be sewn in time for the funeral. Traventine custom said that mourning clothes should not be fancy, and Allemanic custom did not officially disagree, so they would be quicker to make than most formal clothes. With enough people sewing all night, the clothes for all three children could be ready in time for the funeral.

Chamberlain von und zu Ostwald did not carry any cloth himself, of course. He was far too important to carry anything. He returned from the storerooms followed by four footmen, each carrying a few bolts of cloth, and some other Imperial officials. There was some color-of-sorrow cloth in the piles, but most of it was black.

There was an argument – mostly among the attendants and servants: the Chamberlain did not speak aloud, he just glared at people – about what color the children's mourning clothes should be. Of course. Mama's Elderkin attendants thought color-of-sorrow would be most proper, and the Imperial attendants wanted black, and the Palace servants who did most of the work wanted people to make up their minds so they would not get yelled at by the Chamberlain or blamed for causing delays. There were a lot more Imperial people, but Elderkin were famously patient and stubborn. The Palace servants shook their heads and spread out some of both colors of cloth ready to be cut. Mama pressed her fingers to her temples as if her head hurt.

According to the Marriage Contract between the Dukes of Traventi and the Lords of the Falkenburgs, Philip-Augustus was heir to Papa's titles and property in the Kingdom and Empire so he ended up with black mourning clothes. He agreed to one of the bolts of cloth from the choices that were offered, and the Chamberlain and some of the other senior attendants praised him extravagantly for it, but he made faces at them when they were looking the other way.

And then Chamberlain von Ostwald announced that since he was now the Count of Wolfsberg the clothes for Philip-Augustus should be made with breeches instead of the long, full-skirted robe customary for small children. Philip-Augustus made an even worse face at the Chamberlain's back, but he looked mostly pleased to be given grownup clothes. He was less pleased when they made him take all of his clothes off so that he could be measured all over.

Franz-Karl thought that it was all very well for Philip-Augustus to wear breeches for the very first time at their father's funeral. His brother did not have a tail – not even a flippy little goat tail buried in the skirts of his robe like Franz-Karl's – and had no need to worry about people like the Chamberlain being mean about Elderkin if they noticed.

Mama and Itron Gwenlian had sorted through the bolts of cloth from the storeroom and found some cloth that was completely black: not all streaked with other colors like most of what the Imperial people called black, and that was the one that Philip-Augustus had chosen. The thread chosen for sewing the seams was more the color of the stripes on apple-blossoms than plain black, but at least it all matched, and seams did not show much.

The Ritter von und zu Ostwald had made a huge fuss about black clothes for Philip-Augustus, but that did not stop him from complaining about how expensive the good black cloth was once it was chosen. Franz-Karl's Mama looked at him, and said in the style of Remoran used by diplomats, "Master Chamberlain, the expense of dressing my children is no concern of the Imperial and Royal Authorities. It will be supplied by my own household resources and the late Count's, in accordance with the Marriage Contract." She sounded very tired, and her hand clenched where it was resting on some of the color-of-sorrow cloth.

The Chamberlain bowed stiffly, and said nothing. He was carefully looking at the other bolts of black cloth, not at the table with the color-of-sorrow cloth spread out on it, as if not looking at it could make it not be there.

Sophie-Alexa ended up with black mourning clothes because the bolt of good black cloth was meant for a full grown man's suit, not to make clothes for a seven year old boy, and breeches needed even less cloth than the full skirt of a child's robe. When the suit for Philip-Augustus had been cut out of the good black cloth, there was just enough left for his little sister's mourning robe. People were already sewing the clothes for Philip-Augustus, piece by piece, and they started Sophie-Alexa's as soon as the cloth was cut.

Even though she was tired and sad, Mama still insisted that the mourning clothes should be respectfully plain. When the Chamberlain brought out some pieces of black lace for Sophie-Alexa's collar and cuffs, Mama ignored them. Gwenlian said something about profanation and disrespect for Heaven and the Dead that sounded even more rude in Allemanic than it would have been in Elderic: two Allemanic ladies-in-waiting who were helping with the sewing turned pale and looked twitchy. The Palace servants quickly hid the pieces of lace under some of the other bolts of cloth and pretended they had not heard.

Ritter von und zu Ostwald tried to suggest that for the Dowager Countess of Wolfsberg, black might be more appropriate than her own mourning garments of color-of-sorrow that had come from Traventi in her wedding chests, but he never quite finished the sentence.

Franz-Karl's Mama interrupted firmly, still in the Remoran used by diplomats. "I am called Silvia di Armorius, Recognized Heiress in my own right to the Sovereign Duchy of the Elderkin of Traventi and a Binder and full Notary of the Elderkin, and I shall dress properly and respectfully for my husband's funeral. We have already mentioned the Marriage Contract once this day. Shall we now invoke the Advocates and Justices? Or the ancient customs of the Elderkin?"

Everyone in the room could see that she was becoming annoyed enough to do something memorable: there was a spot of red showing on each tan cheek and her long hair was spreading out beyond its bindings and getting crackly. The room was starting to smell a little like lightning.

Chamberlain von und zu Ostwald bowed stiffly. He tried to make a polite answer in Remoran but he got lost in the formal clauses, and his accent was regrettable. Looking around a little desperately, he saw Franz-Karl standing by the table with the bolts of cloth, pointed at him rudely, said bluntly, in Allemanic, "That child shall wear black like the others."

Franz-Karl answered in Remoran, "I cannot. The cloth they wear is used up." He pulled a bolt of color-of-sorrow out of the pile that matched the thread and weave of the plain black cloth, and added, "This is the nearest match."

Three people started cutting out his clothes before the Chamberlain could do more than take a breath preparing to complain. Itron Gwenlian threaded a needle from a bobbin of color-of-sorrow and opened a box of the bone buttons that went with mourning clothes. Franz-Karl sighed. With the hemming begun piece-wise before the robe was fully assembled, he would need to tread carefully while wearing it.

He had chosen color-of-sorrow partly so his Mama would not be alone wearing the color, and partly because the remaining bolts of black cloth were all horrible in look or feel or both, no two the same, and none of them truly black. Also, being honest in Heaven's light, he chose it partly because it would annoy the Chamberlain who was being mean to his Mama.

The Chamberlain glared at him: round-pupiled blue eyes drowning in the whites, snug against the narrow bridge of a narrow nose. Eyes that clearly did not work well. The so-called black clothes Chamberlain Ritter von und zu Ostwald was wearing were the best proof Franz-Karl had ever seen that Worldfolk were partly color-blind.

To his Elderkin eyes the garments were not plain black, but streaked and splotched with the colors that the Elderic tongue called 'forge' and 'apple-stripe' and 'heaven-bright' and Allemanic had no names for at all. The black cloth offered for Franz-Karl's clothes was even worse than what the Chamberlain was wearing, as if something nasty had happened to each bolt while it was in the dyer's vat. The lengths of color-of-sorrow cloth were all evenly dyed the same dull shade of color-of-sorrow, but the dye probably came from Traventi, and it was hard to get that muddy, middling color wrong.

Chamberlain von und zu Ostwald was not happy that everything had not gone his way. He scowled at the color-of-sorrow cloth and made a huffing noise and said, "Oh, very well. It is not as if any of these children are Initiates who could attend the full rites. Perhaps they should not come to the mortuary chapel, either."

Franz-Karl's Mama did not bother arguing about whether her children would attend the funeral to say goodbye to Papa. She did not send to His Excellency or the Hierophants, either, or talk about the Marriage Contract. She just said, "The children will attend their Father's funeral as required by due respect for the Household Guardians." She repeated it four times, then added "I call upon Heaven and the Living World to witness that the children of Leon-Alexander paying their proper respects is a thing that is Bound and shall happen."

The Chamberlain winced at the mention of the Household Guardians.

Franz-Karl shivered in a wind that did not ruffle a single candle flame nor thread of cloth in the room. He could not remember his Mama speaking a Binding before. Not in public like this. The stories and chronicles all agreed that when an Elderkin Binder made a promise or signed a contract... or said something four times with the right words... anyone who went against it would suffer so long as they tried to defy the Binding. So Franz-Karl did not worry that the Allemanic officials would block him from the funeral: the Chamberlain and those who served him would obey what his Mama said, or else Heaven and the Living World would make them.

That did not stop some people from wanting to argue, as if even four times might not be enough for a real Binding, but the Chamberlain had sense enough to go away and take the others with him. Mama's hair had not gotten any less crackly after she made the Binding.

There were lots of stories about what happened when Elderkin decided to be memorable.

Franz-Karl's Mama ignored the remaining Imperial attendants, and fetched her own scissors and needles and other sewing tools to join the group of people sewing. She was going to sew most of Sophie-Alexa's robe herself.

Once the grownups were all busy working on the new clothes, Franz-Karl slipped out of the Wolfsberg apartments and went down the servants' stairs and across the courtyard to the stable where his Papa's horses usually lived. He was not supposed to leave the apartments alone, but he was too twitchy to stay still. Sneaking turned out to work even better without Philip-Augustus, who had been captured by his tutor. Franz-Karl was careful not to look anyone he passed in the eyes – being small helped – and did not move when anyone was looking in his general direction.

He went by way of the kitchen to get some treats for the animals. The kitchen was easy. Marna the baker and Frieda the nice cook were both sitting in chairs, at the same time, crying, and Clothilde the mean cook was on the far side of the room sort of quietly yelling at some of the kitchen maids and scullions. No one had attention to spare to notice him.

All of their horses were in the stable except his Papa's most favorite horse, and the one that was usually ridden by Ernst, Papa's aide. The Chamberlain had not mentioned Ernst, but Franz-Karl thought that meant he was probably dead, too. There were too many people crying.

Two horses that he knew had gone on the trip with his Papa were in the stable, and none of the carriage horses were missing or injured, and all of the horses were upset. Some of them were even too upset to want treats, which was more upset than he thought quiet horses could be. His Papa's carriage – the only carriage his Papa was usually willing to ride in – was sitting in the carriage barn beside the stable without a scratch on it.

Franz Karl nodded. "Fibbers," he said to the horses, and to the Living World. "Sloppy fibbers."

When he returned to their rooms, he found his mother searching for him frantically. She hugged him so hard she nearly squeezed the breath out of him. "Where have you been, my love?"

"Giving our horses treats," Franz-Karl explained reasonably, in Elderic. "Brownie and Blaze are missing, but Smoke and Red are in the stable, and the carriage is not broken, not even scratched. Those people talking about Papa –" He waved indignantly toward the central block of the Palace. "They aren't just fibbers, they are bad at being fibbers."

His Mama took a deep breath and asked quietly, "Franz-Karl, how did you get from here to the stables and back?"

"I walked, of course."

"Did no one notice you?"

"Well, I was careful not to look anyone in the eyes, naturally..." He looked up into his Mama's Elderkin 'goat eyes': beautiful golden-hazel eyes that clearly showed the broad oblong pupils, and showed only tiny triangles of white at the corners. People in the Palace said that Mama's eyes were too far apart and creepy, but Franz-Karl thought they were beautiful and brave. His own eyes were sneaky 'cow eyes': such a dark brown that the shape of the pupils were hard to see even though they were just as broad as his Mama's, and the bridge of his nose was narrower, so that his eyes were closer together.

"Dear Heaven bear witness." His Mama shook her head slightly and sighed. "And you haven't even begun losing your baby teeth! I had hoped we might have another year before you needed to deal with Gifts and Bindings... Very well, my love. Thank you for the news you bring, but please stay close to me this next while. And don't speak of this to anyone else, not even to your brother."

"Philip-Augustus is a blabbermouth," Franz-Karl agreed calmly.

She smiled sadly and tapped his nose with a fingertip. "We are not all born old and open-eyed, my love. He does well enough for a child two years older than you in the flesh."

As they walked out into the reception room of their apartments, Franz-Karl noticed one of the Imperial Chamberlain's favorite assistants standing nearby. The man had seldom served as an attendant in their apartments because he always made a fuss about wearing extra badges blessed at the cathedral – he said that Mama's Papa once turned one of his relatives into a newt. Franz-Karl was glad that he usually stayed away: for some reason worrying about being a newt did not stop him from trying to poke or trip the children every chance he got, or make them look bad.

"Mama? If I have Gifts and Bindings coming in, will I start turning mean people into newts soon?" Franz-Karl asked in Allemanic. He was glad to see the man look worried. Maybe he would keep too far away to trip people.

Mama looked up toward the ceiling and then back down at Franz-Karl. She said firmly, and loudly enough for the assistant Chamberlain to hear clearly, "No, Franz-Karl. You will not be able to turn people into newts until you are grown up. Elderkin children are not allowed to use Gifts and Bindings against people. The Child Blessings will prevent it from happening by accident, so there is no need to worry."

INTERLUDE I: The White Hall

An Account of Sanctuaries and Delays

When he was teaching in the world before the long decades of the Sectarian Wars, the Great Teacher Pristinus de Millau announced that the accumulated treasures and ornamentation of the ancient shrines and sanctuaries were evidence of corruption, and hazardous to men's souls. Other Reformist Teachers had agreed, to varying degrees, and by the time the Wars subsided most of the shrines and sanctuaries and even the cathedrals in the Emperor's territories nearest the Northern Sea had been stripped and purified, and their traditional rites were superseded by the newer Reformist formulas.

The Sectarian battles had been over for more than a generation, but many of the common people in the territories that remained traditionally Ecclesialist still referred to the northerners as 'god-robbers'... and often by worse titles.

The Archduchy of the Eastlands – the Emperor's home territory and the site of his capitol – was far from a northern territory, no more so in spirit than in geography. The local people of all ranks largely remained enthusiastically Ecclesialist in their observances, and their holy places continued to be richly ornamented and somewhat cluttered by the votive offerings they and their ancestors had provided to the gods. Since they found the old sanctuaries distasteful, His Excellency had allowed the northern lords who served him and owed him fealty to construct gathering places where they could observe their own rites.

The funeral of the late Grand Duke, Prince Leon-Alexander would – of course – take place in the capital city of Karnburg, in the cathedral's mortuary chapel and crypt, not in the rural district where he had died. His Excellency graciously invited all of his nobles present in Karnburg to attend, even though the rites were, technically, a familial matter. It was not an invitation that could be safely ignored or declined by anyone who owed fealty or service to the Elected King of the Allemans, or to the Archduke of the Eastlands, or to the Overlord of the Falkenburg Domains, or to the uncrowned Holy Emperor of the Remorans or to any of the other positions held by His Excellency.

The Pristinist lords from the northern provinces gathered in their White Hall to fortify themselves for their entry into the corrupting precincts of the cathedral. Some of the lesser men who would accompany them looked worried – some of the serfs and other servile members of the party looked terrified – but the Highborn, assured by their wealth and power of Heaven's favor, remained properly serene.

The Highest Born lords present in the city were the last to join the Session. The Prince-Elector of Bremerhaven arrived promptly at the time that had been arranged, with his attendants around him, and took the seat prepared for him, notable not for richness of materials but for being one of the few in the Hall.

The Margraff-Elector of Ansbach arrived rather late, even though the temporary White Hall was situated within the bounds of his city estate, reachable by stepping through a door. He left the lowest-born of his attendants waiting outside the Gate of Purity, but the room was crowded once he and his followers had joined those already inside. He paused to allow the some of those subordinate lords to bow over his hand – the Ritter von und zu Ostwald among them – but finally seated himself in the central chair and flicked a hand toward the officiants.

Despite the lateness of the hour, the black-robed Teacher did not limit the length or number of his selected readings on duty and rank and purity. The white-robed Preacher's answering exegesis did not in any way lack proper thoroughness, and if anything, he spoke with even less speed and more consideration than usual. Those present who were most hesitant to enter the cathedral's maw were greatly reassured by the

Discourse, but by the time the Session completed, there was no time for the Lords Elector to consult together.

The men who had been summoned to the cathedral needed to walk with unseemly haste, but they arrived at the mortuary chapel before the bells began to toll. On a few occasions their way was cleared somewhat violently by their attendants. They paused for a breath outside the cathedral porch.

The Margraff-Elector's voice was properly calm. "I shall have the beast-born whelp properly Silenced and yoked to my will soon enough."

"You doubt the acting Archduke will watch after the False Heir?" His colleague was less winded, and more worried.

"I spoke of the changeling..." The Margraff-Elector flicked a hand at his attendants, who opened the cathedral door, bowing deeply as the Electors passed.

They found the Prince-Elector of Magdoberg was before them, and already bowing over the hands of Their Excellencies. Reinhard von Bernberg was a northern lord and technically a Reformist, but he observed the looser teachings of Demetrius Harfner rather than adhering to the precepts of Pristinus. He was accompanied by his wife – even in such a public place – and the Princess of Magdoberg was presenting a corpse-candle – intricately carved in the antique style – to Her Excellency.

The Prince-Elector of Bremerhaven joined the group gathered before Their Excellencies, but the Margraff-Elector of Ansbach looked away from the trappings of womens' feeble rites.

CHAPTER II: The Funeral

Wherein the World Pays Attention

There was arguing at the funeral. It was whispery arguing in the corners that did not want to admit it was happening, but it was happening anyway. It was very rude to Papa for people to be arguing in the funeral chapel, and rude to the cathedral they were standing in and the High Gods who might be watching. Sometimes people remembered, and the arguing got quieter, but then it bubbled up again.

Franz-Karl's Mama did not let anyone else hold Sophie-Alexa while they waited for the rites to begin, but kept her in her own arms. But she let Franz-Karl stand by himself in the place where the priests had told them to stand while she stepped aside to talk to their Excellencies and the Hierophants and the acting Archduke for a moment, while they were getting things ready.

Philip-Augustus was standing nearby. He had inherited enough of their father's fairness that in his new, black, grownup clothes, he looked like a perfect little Allemanic lord in mourning. He was scowling – Franz-Karl could see that he was trying very hard not to cry – and he flinched when anyone came near. After a few tries the more fluttery little old ladies let him alone, but a soldier from Wolfsberg stayed nearby.

Franz-Karl kept hearing the arguing whispers while he was trying to say his prayers and look at the beautifully carved corpse-candles that Mama and Her Excellency His Grandma and Papa's sisters had set up to light Papa's way to the Halls of Judgment. Franz-Karl could see that the hard shape of the coffin was covered by the funeral cloth, so he was a little worried that Papa might not be able to see the guiding lights. He took a small step nearer to the red groove on the floor that marked the holy boundary around where the coffin was, trying to see better. The boundary-marker torches did not give much light because they were not ordinary torches with big fires on the ends: they were glass sculptures full of expensive imported olive oil with wicks floating in them.

The Margraff-Elector of Ansbach walked over, heels clicking, and stood between Franz-Karl and the bier, blocking his view and the lights, and looming over him. He was facing Franz-Karl and there was not enough room for him to stand a polite distance from both Franz-Karl and the red line: his heels were almost touching the line. A group of his attendants had followed him in a clump that trailed away like the tail of a peacock, but at least they were spread toward the foot end of the coffin, not the head. One of the attendants, at the Margraff-Elector's elbow, was muttering what was probably a prayer: his Remoran was terrible, and Franz-Karl could not hear most of the words. The rest did not say prayers or do anything proper: they just stood and stared at the Margraff-Elector, blocking the people who were supposed to be near the coffin from finishing the preparations.

Franz-Karl thought the Margraff-Elector must be a worse fibber than the Chamberlain: his edges fit his space in the Living World so badly that Franz-Karl wondered how he did not fall out of it into the World Beyond, the way demons did if demon-hunters shoved them hard enough. He tried to ignore the huge fib crossing the man's forehead like a bruise-colored caterpillar, scattering smaller fibs that seemed to be afraid of it.

Somehow, not fitting in the world made the Margraff-Elector's clothes even worse. Franz-Karl wondered if there was no one who cared to tell the man what he wore? Or no one who dared? Or had they tried and not been listened to? Most of the attendants were wearing the Margraff-Elector's colors, and most of them had metal collars or cuffs or medallions to show that they were serfs or slaves and their fancy clothes were their Lord's, not their own, so they probably were not listened to.

Franz-Karl was pretty sure the supposed-to-be-black clothes the Margraff-Elector himself was wearing were made by someone who could see all the colors that had Elderic names, very clearly, and that person did not like the Margraff-Elector at all. He did not think that anyone could manage something that nasty without being able to see what they were doing. The front of the Margraff-Elector's breeches – which were about all Franz-Karl could see without craning his neck, since the Margraff-Elector was standing so close – showed colored streaks that were arranged in what even a five-year-old knew was a very rude pattern, and he had serious suspicions about the markings on the coat and waistcoat. The marks were clear and never overlapped, and there seemed to be very little empty space between the patterns they made. Some of the patterns made Franz-Karl's eyes want to flinch away.

The Margraff-Elector was a grownup and a very important person in the Empire and the Privy Councils, so Franz-Karl could not tell him to go away, or even turn his own back or close his eyes. The man started to make a speech that was too loud. He was trying to be fancy in a church, so he started out speaking Remoran... more or less. He stumbled over one of the irregular verbs, made a mean face, and switched to Court Allemanic with a strong Northern accent. The attendant did not stop muttering in bad Remoran, even while his master was speaking.

The Elector's speech pretended to be telling Franz-Karl that the Margraff-Elector was sorry that his Papa was dead, but it was partly aimed at the people standing nearby, not at Franz-Karl: some of the words were the wrong shape, and sort of leaned toward the other people.

The part of the speech that was aimed at Franz-Karl was mostly talking about how Papa had died, and telling fibs about it. He said things like "we all know that..." a lot, and shadows like old bruises chased each other across his face like ripples across water. The Allemanic sentences were shaped so that if Franz-Karl said anything polite – or even just nodded – he would be agreeing with the fibs. But if people thought he was being rude, they would say even more mean things about his Mama than usual, and Papa was in the coffin, not standing ready to stop the mean people. He opened his eyes very wide as if he might be impressed by the Margraff-Elector's words instead of his clothes, and stared up at a button on the Margraff-Elector's waistcoat. He did not think there was anything sneaky or dangerous about the buttons: they were tapered discs carved from shiny black stone and nearly as plain as the buttons Philip-Augustus was wearing.

All of the fibs started to make Franz-Karl's skin feel sort of prickly and squirmy, and it got hard to breathe. He hoped the Margraff-Elector would stop talking, but he just kept on and on, in sentences that sort of circled around, and circled around, until Franz-Karl thought he could feel the lies piled up around him like sticky spider silk, ready to wrap around him and trap him forever and suck him dry if he moved wrong.

Franz-Karl remembered an old story about a Knight and a River-Maiden, and breaking a trap woven of lies by telling the Living World thirteen true things about itself. There was a poem in the Elderic version of the story. He moved two steps to the side, so the Margraff-Elector was not blocking his view of the head end of the coffin, bowed to his Papa, and began to sing the otter-maiden's Elderic rhyme to the tune of an Allemanic children's prayer that had the same shape. "These things stand true within the Living Walls..." Thirteen more lines telling thirteen true things about the World... and when he sang the last line, the lies tangled around him shriveled as if they had been salted.

There was a weight of someone or something watching the chapel that had not been there before.

Franz-Karl turned to the Margraff-Elector, bowed politely – it would have been the bow to someone he outranked if Franz-Karl was taller – and said in his best, clear Court Allemanic, "I hope the owner of the carriage was not badly injured."

That statement both ran against the pattern of the Margraff-Elector's fibs, and was completely a fourteenth true thing. It was also what some people called an Elderkin truth: true in more than one way. Because if the carriage owner was innocent, Franz-Karl hoped he was very well, and if he was guilty in the matter of Papa's death, Franz-Karl hoped the carriage-owner was as dead as his Papa.

The Margraff-Elector made a choking sound, very clear in the silence. Franz-Karl looked way up to meet pale, pale, angry eyes that had pupils that were, very slightly, not quite round. Eyes that were framed by ash-blond eyelashes and eyebrows that were almost invisible against the man's pale skin. He bowed again to the Margraff-Elector, still very careful of their ranks and status in the present ceremony.

The Margraff-Elector winced, flicked the fingers of one hand toward the praying attendant and reached toward Franz-Karl with the other. The weight of watching shifted very slightly, and a glass boundary torch behind the Margraff-Elector shivered into splinters and oil. It was near enough to splash his coat, but not to do worse damage. The attendant was less fortunate and was doused rather thoroughly. He stepped back hastily from one of the wicks that landed in a puddle of oil and kept burning. The other wicks landed on bare floor tiles and guttered out.

Cathedral servants hurried to clean up the mess and replace the torch and take away the oil-dripping attendant. The Margraff-Elector's other attendants made a huge fuss about the oil splashes on the coat, and two of them went running to fetch a clean coat, while he went off to one side to wait with his other attendants gathered close around him so that no one would see the stains while they waited. Several bystanders talked about how lucky it was that the area around the coffin had not been consecrated for the ritual yet.

Franz-Karl was careful to keep the long skirts of his robe out of the spilled oil when he walked away to stand beside His Excellency His Grandpa and Her Excellency His Grandma. He used a family bow to his Imperial and Royal grandparents, not a court bow. Her Excellency His Grandma took his hand and gave it a little squeeze, and held it even after Franz-Karl's Mama came to stand beside them. They all waited together for the torch to be replaced so that the important parts of the ceremony could begin.

Philip-Augustus, the new Count of Wolfsberg, came to stand on Franz-Karl's other side and hold his other hand. His hand was cold and damp, but he did not do anything annoying, just held on.

The Margraff-Elector of Ansbach did not follow Franz-Karl to their Excellencies, not even to greet them with a proper bow, which he should have done. Not even after his servants returned with a clean coat and he shrugged into it. Their Excellencies had been in the chapel since before the Margraff-Elector started talking to Franz-Karl, but he had not greeted them yet, and his Excellency was the Margraff-Elector's liege lord. There were rules. Even for Margraff-Electors.

When the great cathedral bells rang, just before the official singing and recitations were supposed to start, His Serene Grace the acting Archduke Uncle Helm-Friedrich lifted the cloth on the bier aside and cut locks of hair for members of the family to keep in their Household shrines. Then he put the cloth back and poured a few drops of wine into the Blood Trench – the red groove on the floor around the coffin – while priests and choirs sang prayers to set the coffin apart from the Living World. Franz-Karl was relieved to see that the wooden lid was not on the coffin yet, so it would not block the candlelight during the ceremonies.

There needed to be a lot of locks of hair for the memorials, because His Excellency had a lot of relatives. Some of the Reformist half of the Allemans that were mad at the Holy See in Remora did not keep proper Household shrines any more, and the Court mostly tried to ignore sisters' children, which Franz-Karl thought was stupid. But there still needed to be a lot of locks of hair for the memorials, so some of the locks set aside for more distant relatives ended up kind of skinny.

Her Excellency Franz-Karl's Grandma had four children... well, three now that Papa was gone... but her daughters had married foreign rulers and lived far away. Franz-Karl had never met them, or any of his cousins that were their children. The sisters' locks of the hair would be sent to them along with official death notices carried by diplomatic couriers.

His Imperial Excellency Franz-Karl's Grandpa had his own younger sister Sophia-Augusta living in the Palace, and his children from his first marriage to her Late Excellency – Helm-Friedrich and Erminia and Gertrude – lived in various wings of the Palace buildings when they came to the City of Karnburg.

His Serene Grace the Acting Archduke Uncle Helm-Friedrich's family were all at the funeral, including his wife and two sons and two daughters, and a daughter-in-law, and a grandson, Friedrich-Karl, who was older than Sophie-Alexa: nearly Franz-Karl's age. Friedrich-Karl already loved music more than anything, so it was a little sad that he would someday get stuck being a lord and giving people orders and running the Privy Councils, like his grandpa acting Archduke Uncle Helm-Friedrich.

Her Royal Highness Aunt Queen Gertrude had gone away when she married and come home after being widowed, like Her Serene Highness Sophie-Augusta. Her Serene Highness Grand Duchess Aunt Erminia was not very serene: she spent most of her time in the Palace even though her husband and son were usually far away at their estates in the provinces: they were too far away to attend the funeral, but she was present. Gossipy people said mean things about both of the imperial princesses, but they were Papa's half-sisters, and they were in the chapel, and Uncle Helm-Friedrich made sure they received locks of hair.

His Serene Grace the Acting Archduke Uncle Helm-Friedrich made sure Mama and Philip-Augustus and Franz-Karl and Sophie-Alexa each got a good lock of the hair (Mama held Sophie-Alexa's so it would not get lost.) He even gave them an extra lock of hair to send to the Household shrine in the House on the Rock in Traventi.

That started the whispers again, but His Serene Grace the acting Archduke Uncle Helm-Friedrich was good at staring at people very calmly. Besides, there was probably something in the Marriage Contract about it. It seemed to Franz-Karl that whenever people in the Palace were annoyed about things and Traventi was mentioned, his parents' Marriage Contract was mixed up in it somehow.

With all of the locks of hair handed out or set aside for the couriers, and the cloth put back over the coffin, the main part of the funeral started. Papa was the son of the Imperial Lord of the Falkenburg Domains and Elected King of the Allemans and the Archduke of the Eastlands, so it was an important funeral. The Arch-Hierophants were in charge of the rites – since the rites were happening in their cathedral – but there were other priests and priestesses doing things, too, and three choirs chanting responses, and the deepest toned bells rang sometimes, and the cathedral organ played low, sad notes that shook your bones and teeth.

It was very beautiful, and even the public parts of the rites were very, very long. Then at the end the coffin and corpse candles were carried away down into the crypt by the clergy, and some of the grownups who were both Initiates and close family went with them for the holiest part of the rites. Their Excellencies and Franz-Karl's Mama, went, of course, and His Serene Grace the acting Archduke Uncle Helm-Friedrich, even though he was only a half-brother.

Most of the people who had attended the public rites followed the coffin out into the main part of the cathedral during the Transition to the Crypt but continued walking out of the cathedral into air that was less full of incense and sadness. Franz-Karl and Philip-Augustus and Sophie-Alexa waited with their aunts and various attendants in the cathedral's vestibule.

Some of the highest ranked people at court also remained in the vestibule with their attendants, waiting for their Excellencies. Franz-Karl would have been happier if the Margraff-Elector of Ausbach was not one of them. He felt itchy where those pale, pale eyes were looking at him, even though he did not turn to look.

Franz-Karl took advantage of the wait to look around at the public parts of the cathedral – at least, the ones he could see without walking away from his companions. He paid attention to where Margraff-Elector was without looking straight at him, but Elderkin eyes were useful for that sort of thing: he could see a little farther to the sides than round-eyed, narrow-nosed folk expected. The darkness of his coweyes was also useful: people did not always know where he was looking.

The first time the Margraff-Elector beckoned to him – which he had no right or authority to do in that time and place – Franz-Karl's nose was pointing far enough to one side that he felt no need to notice the movement, even though he saw it. That odd weight of attention, which had largely faded during the funeral rites, suddenly became heavier again.

At the time of the second attempt to summon him, Franz-Karl ignored it again. He was looking carefully at a section of fresco that someone had sloshed untidily with whitewash. From the bits of the picture that remained visible around the edges, he was almost certain that it had showed either a planting or harvest festival, such as any non-Initiate might attend, so he did not see why they had covered it. There were pictures in the Palace much rowdier than these seemed to be. Even if there was a good reason to cover the painting, the workmen should at least have done a tidier job.

The Margraff-Elector huffed in annoyance and flicked a hand at one of his collared attendants, one who carried the Margraff-Elector's fancy lace-trimmed gloves in one hand and a long, ornate rod or staff of office in the other – it was finely carved but did not look sturdy enough to support a grownup's weight while they walked. The glove-bearer began to cross the vestibule toward the Imperial party.

Franz-Karl turned to face the man as he approached. He certainly did not want a possible enemy at his back or flank. He was rummaging through his memories of old stories and chronicles for grownup words to use. It was written in many places, mostly in Elderic: "Words are the weapons of the Elderkin."

The glove-bearer stopped well beyond arms' reach. "Come with me, changeling brat." His tone was as harsh as his words, and his accent spoke strongly of the Northern seacoast. There were gasps from behind Franz-Karl.

Ah. Petronello and Damaris. And 'brat' definitely crossed the line of courtesy. 'Changeling' might be worse. Franz-Karl asked calmly, translating from poetic Remoran into proper Court Allemanic and enunciating clearly, "Who are you addressing, sir? I see my parents' faces in every mirror. Their ranks are well-attested ... and their Marriage Contract is notorious." The gasps behind him were replaced by chuckles: at least two different women and a man.

The Northerner's face turned from pale to purple and he moved a step closer to Franz-Karl, rapping the metal-shod tip of the rod on the tile floor. "Thou shalt come with me, my lord –" the 'my lord' was a sneer that matched the vulgar familiarity of the demand better in its tone than in its words. "– and that right soon." The weight of attention in the area increased again.

Franz-Karl did not exactly choose to use the Defiance of Karrenius, but he found himself translating its words. "Heaven and the Living World may bear witness: I do not answer to you, nor to your master. No more than my father before me." Something snapped like a harp-string breaking between the glove-bearer and the Margraff-Elector. The looming attention was ... pleased.

The glove-bearer turned darker purple and raised his rod high. It came down in what should have been a full strength blow on Franz-Karl's right shoulder, but just as it touched the fabric of his coat the rod was transformed into a burst of sparkling dust and a sheaf of long, soft fibers better suited to being spun off on a distaff than to any more martial purpose. The man staggered forward, then hastily back, turning deathly pale.

Franz-Karl felt his lungs emptied and refusing to fill for a moment. He gasped and wheezed, trying to fill them.

There were gasps from the witnesses – both the Imperial party and the others in various parts of the vestibule – and words were spoken that should NOT have been used in that way inside a holy sanctuary. Not even in the public areas. Perhaps especially not in the public areas... even Franz-Karl heard rumors about what some Initiates did during the private rites.

Two of Her Royal Highness Aunt Queen Gertrude's attendants were hard-looking men wearing dramatic, colorful clothing and empty scabbards that would hold their weapons once they left the cathedral. The older man stepped forward beside Franz-Karl and took a knee to bring their heads nearer the same level. "Is your lordship injured?" he asked gently in accented Allemanic.

"No. I... I think I'm all right," Franz-Karl managed. He was still wheezing a little.

As the man stood up, he squeezed Franz-Karl's shoulder, the one the rod had been aimed at before it fell apart. It was a very brave thing to do – braver than Franz-Karl could have managed if things were reversed – and kind as well. Franz-Karl was feeling very frightened and alone at that moment, and it helped to have a grownup take up a guard position behind him.

The vestibule was very quiet for the rest of the time until their Excellencies and the rest of the funeral party returned from the crypt. No one spoke, and people even seemed to be breathing more quietly than usual. No one at all met Franz-Karl's eyes, not even Philip-Augustus. The Margraff-Elector completely turned his back on the Imperial party, which was contrary to protocol, but a great relief to Franz-Karl.

The gossip and discussions began as people passed though the great doors of the cathedral and moved out under the open sky. And away from Franz-Karl.

CHAPTER III: A Promise with the World

Wherein Precautions are Taken

The funeral supper was going to be the first time Franz-Karl attended a proper grownup dinner, outside their own apartments, that was not just a family gathering. His Mama changed her mind three times about whether he should attend the meal with her and Philip-Augustus, or stay in their apartments with Nurse Rosa and Sophie-Alexa.

Finally, a while before they needed to leave their apartments to go to the reception hall where the supper would be held, his Mama brought him into their Household Shrine, and lit the Lamp and put incense on the Altar, and put clean water and salt into the bowls. She sat down on the floor beside him and looked at him very seriously.

Franz-Karl remembered the Margraff-Elector's sticky lies and the glove-bearer's rod. The light of the Lamp blurred as his eyes filled with tears. "I didn't mean to do any anything bad at Papa's funeral," he said in Remoran, sniffing a little.

Mama hugged him and wiped his eyes with her handkerchief. "You did not do anything wrong at all, Franz-Karl. I assure you. You did very, very well, when grown men were behaving very badly." She sighed, and continued in Elderic. "Small children in Traventi are protected because everyone abides by the Laws within the Blessings. Things are different outside the Gates of Air, and some things are already becoming more different and dangerous with your Father taken from us. I believe that you will be safer when you are inside the Palace but not in our rooms if the Living World is watching after you."

Then she surprised him by asking "Franz-Karl, do you know the Hospitality Rules for Hosts and Guests?" in very formal Elderic.

Franz-Karl thought carefully. You needed to tell the truth as much as possible when you said things in front of the Altar and the Lamp and the Ancestors. Hospitality was something important and holy. And usually something grownups took care of. "Maybe not all of the rules," he finally answered carefully. "Some stories talk about different ones or say them different ways. I cannot say that I have seen or heard a list." He hoped he got the verbs right: Elderic had some complicated verb forms that Allemanic and Remoran lacked, especially when you were talking about rules and promises and holy things. And Truth.

He thought his Mama would have smiled if she was less sad and worried. "If I tell you the Rules I care about for now, will you make a Holy Promise to me and the Living World that you will try to follow them?"

Franz-Karl wanted very much to please his Mama and he also wanted very much to go to his Papa's funeral supper like a grownup member of the family. His Papa's picture on the shrine had been moved from the section for the living family to the section for the dead, and was already looking strange to him: like someone out of a story, not someone who hugged him just a few days ago. The picture was a good likeness, but its eyes would be that one shade of green forever, not his Papa's hazel-green that was never the same two minutes together. Part of a lock of hair had already been braided and pressed into the carvings of the picture frame. Franz-Karl swallowed hard, twice, because the first time did not get the lump out of his throat.

He wanted to agree, but "Holy Promises are important! What if I don't know? Or a mean grownup tries to trick me? Or make me do something bad." The mean people at the funeral had been scary. And even in their family apartments sometimes people from the greater Palace came in who tried to get him to do things that were stupid or wrong so that he would be laughed at or punished. Maybe that stupid assistant Chamberlain who wore all the badges would be at the dinner, trying to make him spill the soup. And he was sure the Margraff-Elector would be at the dinner, probably with his glove-bearer... or someone else even worse. He got a little shivery when he thought about the Margraff-Elector.

"That is why we will make it a Holy Promise: a contract for you with Heaven and the Living World. Part of the World's side of the contract will be to make it harder for you to do the wrong thing by accident or because of trickery, and to help you know what the right thing to do is."

"Will it hurt?"

His Mama said carefully, "The Living World is much larger than we are. If it gives you a path down a hill and you try to fight it and go uphill instead, you may get hurt. And it all flows better if you pay attention and don't try to make the Living World do all the work. But making the promise doesn't hurt, and the World will not be unkind to you on purpose just because of the Promise."

"Have you made a Promise with the Living World?" He was not sure he wanted something as big as the World pushing him around, any more than he wanted the Margraff-Elector doing it. But having the Living World on his side, pushing the Margraff-Elector around, might not be a bad thing.

"I have made a similar promise, and your brother Philip-Augustus made one last year. Most people in the Duchy have made similar promises, but usually not until they are older than you are now and lose their first baby tooth." Philip-Augustus was two years older and had grownup teeth on the bottom and the top, both, so Franz-Karl would be catching up.

Franz-Karl sat for a moment, waiting for the ideas in his head to stop sort of spinning around each other and settle into thoughts. Finally he said, "I will make the promise, I guess..." No. This needed one of the strange Elderic verb forms, so he repeated more definitely: "I will make the promise." He continued, remembering the stories, "What are the rules? And what do I need to do to seal it?" Sealing and witnessing promises to make them real was very important in all the old stories, and he was sure a Holy Promise witnessed by the Altar and the Ancestors would need something special.

"I will manage the sealing, but only if you agree." Again, he thought that his Mama would have smiled if she was less sad. "So ... The main rule is that anyone who willingly crosses the boundary and Threshold of a House and accepts one of the forms of Welcome is either a Guest or Kin or in Service to the House. They are held within the Household, to be sheltered and fed by it, and allowed to leave when they choose, and they help support and defend the House and each other. Someone who crosses the threshold by force or by trickery, without seeking or accepting honest Hospitality, is an enemy who may be attacked, but people who are part of the same Household do not attack each other or allow someone held within the Household to be dragged back out across the Threshold or attacked from outside. A proper Host also does not drag anyone in across the threshold unwilling, nor stop a Guest from leaving. Will you honor the Household Boundary and Threshold and the Forms of Welcome as Host and Guest and Kinsman?"

"I agree to honor the Threshold and Boundary and the Forms of Welcome for Households and those they hold, as Host and Guest and Kinsman," Franz-Karl said after thinking about it for a moment, and sorting out the verbs in both his Mama's speech and his own answer, and comparing them to speeches in the old stories he loved.

His Mama added a piece of incense to the Altar. "Sharing food and drink is the strongest sign of the connection among Family and Guests and those in Service within a Household. If someone is sick or parched or starving they can be given special food or drink as medicine, and accept it. But otherwise offering food or drink that is made specially for a particular person and not offered to others, or requiring someone to eat food that is only made for them, may cut them apart from the House and proper fellowship, or else bind them in ways contrary to honest hospitality. Those who have promised to follow the House Rules do not prepare or serve food that cuts people off or binds them, nor do they eat food outside the offerings of hospitality and fellowship unless they need it as medicine, even when they are outside the Threshold."

"I agree to only seek and accept food and drink that are the offerings of hospitality and fellowship, or medicine at great need," Franz-Karl said. Food was important, and could be used as a weapon or a defense or a trap. People in the stories had to be very careful about food – there were five different stories about pomegranate seeds and at least seven about apples where the fruits were variously required, forbidden, safe, dangerous, beneficial, or meaningless distractions, and even salad could be tricky – and the phrase 'medicine at great need' occurred in some strange places in the stories. His Mama took a few grains of salt from the offering bowl and placed them on his tongue.

She took a deep breath, but spoke gently. "Elderkin are the children of those Manifesting from the World Beyond as well as children of the Living World, and our words Bind us beyond the bindings of flesh. Until you are both an Initiate and an adult, you rest within the Boundary of the Household Shrine and the guardians of the Lines," she swept out both hands in a gesture that made the Lamp and the incense flare, producing strange flickers of reflections in the tokens arrayed on the memorial panels of the shrine. "You will not cross that Household Boundary to pledge obedience or service to any single person, mortal or divine, or loyalty to any group other than Traventi as a whole, or the Lineages of your parents and grandparents whose Shrine bears witness now, not until you are grown and Initiated and reach your majority."

Thinking about oaths ... was worrying: half the old stories in Elderic warned against taking oaths of fealty or promising service, especially by accident, since such things were often traps for Elderkin. The story of the river-maiden and the wicked Knight was just one of many.

Franz-Karl thought of sticky lies and did not just say that he agreed, he figured out the proper binding forms of the verbs before he repeated carefully, using all his grandparents' lineages so none of the ancestors would feel left out, "I, Franz-Karl, of the Lines of Falkenburg and Armorius and Leonstein and Capradaventi, will not pledge obedience or service to any single person, mortal or divine, or loyalty to any group other than Traventi as a whole, or my Lineages whose Shrine and Guardians bear witness now, until I am grown and Initiated and reach my majority." He remembered an old formula for casting out traitors, and thought the inversion would fit well. "Nor shall I willingly place myself outside the boundary of House and Kin and Line." That last bit seemed to echo strangely in the small room.

His Mama looked startled, but said nothing. She just dipped her hand into the bowl of water and flicked some of it at him. The droplets tickled.

Franz-Karl was surprised when his Mama did not continue with any more rules: he knew that most Bound contracts and promises were arranged to have four sections. Stopping after Thresholds and Food and Oaths was like a too short staircase.

His Mama wrote a fancier version of what he had agreed to, with official words wrapped around all of his own words, and watched him sign his name with green ink when he had read it. Then she signed it herself and sealed it with her signet ring, with sparkly green wax melted with a flame borrowed from the Lamp. Then she burned the Bound contract, so that the Living World could keep it safe, and nothing material could meddle with it.

Sealing the promise did not hurt at all. It felt sort of warm and cuddly, and he thought that he could feel the Living World looking at him in a way that reminded him of the cathedral. Looking at him must be strange, since he was inside the Living World: it would be like trying to see a speck of bone inside of one of your fingers without cutting it open.

CHAPTER IV: The Funeral Supper

Wherein Our Hero is Assigned a Task

When they arrived at the banquet hall that was being used for the funeral supper, the Palace Master of Ceremonies had Mama and Philip-Augustus announced by their names and titles. That included giving Papa's title of Count of Wolfsberg to Philip-Augustus, which still sounded strange. The Master of Ceremonies did not mention Franz-Karl at all, or look directly at him, though the announcer winked at him.

The Master of Ceremonies himself led Franz-Karl and Philip-Augustus and their Mama to chairs that had been prepared for them at the high table. There was already stuff that looked like food on the plates on the high table – it was arranged in very elegant patterns – and stuff that looked like drink in the glasses, but nothing smelled right and it all looked fake, like pictures of food instead of real food. And none of it was hot that should be hot or cold that should be cold. Franz-Karl's Mama just sat back in her chair looking straight ahead, with her hands folded in her lap, so Franz-Karl did the same thing. Philip-Augustus leaned away from the table, but he twisted in his chair to look at His Excellency their Grandpa, who was sitting next to him.

Her Excellency Franz-Karl's Grandma, sitting on the other side of His Excellency, called the Chief Steward and ordered the fake food taken away from in front of herself and His Excellency, and acting Archduke Uncle Helm-Friedrich and his family, and Franz-Karl's Papa's family.

Her Royal Highness Aunt Queen Gertrude, at one end of the high table, spoke up to add herself and her companion to the list for replacement food: she was so extremely polite about the quality of the food in front of her that everyone knew she was being sarcastic. The stones used to construct the Palace probably knew that she was being sarcastic.

Her Serene Highness Grand Duchess Aunt Erminia, at the other end of the table, just fidgeted with her cutlery and did not say anything. She was looking at the Margraff-Elector and some other Electors at the next table, not at her own family beside her at the high table.

The Steward started to explain that replacing most of the food at the high table would cause an unseemly delay, but Her Excellency called the food that was already on the high table 'table decorations' and said firmly that the high table was ready for the real food. Everyone at the high table (even Her Serene Highness Aunt Erminia) were all served fresh drinks that were ladled from a large punchbowl and fresh, hot real food that was served from large fancy platters and bowls. A few things got dropped because the servers were in such a hurry, but it was only some of the decorations, not the real food.

The other people, sitting at the lower tables, acted like their fake food was real and delicious, even though most of it was cold except the parts that were supposed to be. Even the food at the high table was nearer medium rather than hot: Franz-Karl wondered how far the banquet table was from the kitchen in the Main Palace.

At the end of the funeral supper, His Excellency stood up and announced that besides being the landed Count of Wolfsberg, Philip-Augustus von Falkenburg was now an Imperial Grand Duke, and Franz-Karl and Sophie-Alexa were a Grand Duke and Grand Duchess.

Franz-Karl's Mama stood and bowed to His Excellency and then to His Serene Grace the acting Archduke Uncle Helm-Friedrich, then sat down again.

Then Philip-Augustus also stood and bowed. Then he pronounced the formal oath of fealty as Count of Wolfsberg to His

Excellency their Grandfather as Overlord of the Falkenburg Domains – within the Lines in the Household Shrine. He did not mention any of his Excellency's other titles, just bowed again and sat down.

Franz-Karl was wondering whether he should get down from his chair and bow also when His Serene Grace the acting Archduke stood and announced that Grand Duke Franz-Karl would convey the memorial token of the death of his father the late Imperial Grand Duke Leon-Alexander (that would be the lock of hair) to the Grand Duke's family shrine at the House on the Rock in the Sovereign Duchy of Traventi. And furthermore the Grand Duke would remain in Traventi for the summer as the honored Guest of his Grandmother, Her Reverend Grace the Duchess Adriana of the Elderkin in Traventi.

Franz-Karl was very surprised to hear that he would be traveling to Traventi. He thought, from a twitch of her lips, that his Mama was surprised by the announcement, but not by the journey. Philip-Augustus seemed surprised by everything, and not very pleased. He was pretty sure Philip-Augustus would have kicked him under the table if they were sitting next to each other, so it was a good thing that their Mama was between them.

The arguments that followed the announcement of Franz-Karl's errand were not whispers, though they were mostly framed as very polite questions, not statements or demands.

Some members of the Privy councils from the the Falkenburg Domains got rather loud about asking whether it was wise for an imperial grandchild in the male line to leave the palace, especially with a prince of the line so newly dead. Franz-Karl wondered whether they believed the story about the carriage.

Lords from some parts of the Allemanic territories – a lot of them were sitting near the Margraff-Elector – asked whether a woman should be properly counted as a guardian of anyone, supposed monarch or not. They tended to avoid using the title of the monarch of Traventi, even the wrong one that was customary at the Imperial Court. In Traventi, Her Reverend Grace Adriana's title was Duke – because she ruled in her own right – but the Northern lords avoided even calling her a Duchess.

There were other Lords who agreed with both groups, and some others, especially Hierophants, who seemed to be upset for different reasons entirely.

Franz-Karl thought this fuss was surprising for three reasons. First, because the noisiest complaints – or most pointed questions – about an Imperial Grandchild leaving were coming from the councilors who always said the meanest things about Franz-Karl's parents' Marriage Contract.

Second: because his Serene Grace the acting Archduke Helm-Friedrich was usually in charge of the meetings of the Privy Councils. The councilors were not supposed to come this close to yelling at him in front of witnesses, and were usually more careful about it.

And third: a few of the lesser lords came much too close to saying out loud that the Elderkin might not take proper care of a guest. Using 'honored guest' in the announcement was already somewhat rude if you translated it into Elderic. All of the stories and history chronicles in Elderic and Allemanic and Remoran agreed that saying out loud that you thought Elderkin would harm a guest was just asking for bad luck. The Allemanic stories leaned toward the sort of bad luck that had people being turned in to something slimy, sometimes with gills, while the Elderic chronicles leaned toward barn fires and sunken merchant ships, or all the wine and beer turning into something smelly and undrinkable. A few stories and chronicles, especially the older Remoran ones, talked about old wars starting, and people dying unexpectedly.

The oddest thing was that in all this arguing, they were not arguing about Franz-Karl. Or at least, no one except His Serene Grace the acting Archduke Uncle Helm-Friedrich ever mentioned Franz-Karl's name or title. It was all 'Imperial grandchild' this , or 'the late Prince's son' that, or, even, once, 'the Count of Wolfsberg's brother'. And the Margraff-Elector did not say anything at all. He just sat, and listened, and did not look at Franz-Karl. But sometimes he nodded at someone at one of the lower tables, and that person would be the next to speak.

People were moving beyond noisy toward fierce when his Imperial Excellency Franz-Karl's Grandpapa stood up again. Everyone hushed, especially one lord who had just pounded his fist on the table, and was suddenly looking as if someone had farted and he was wondering who it could possibly be.

His Excellency did not raise his voice. He did not need to. "The Marriage Contract between the House of Falkenburg and Her Highness the Dowager Grand Duchess Silvia, Childe of Traventi, specifies that the Traventine authorities are responsible for dealing with any unexpected

Elderkin manifestations within the borders of the Falkenburg Holdings. We assume that they will hold to their side of the agreement, as we will hold to ours."

So. This journey was about what happened in the cathedral.

His Imperial Excellency bowed slightly toward Franz-Karl. "May Heaven grant you a safe journey, my dear boy. Kindly present my warmest greetings to your Grandmother, her Reverend Grace Adriana."

Franz-Karl slid down from his chair and returned the bow properly, with a bow that was a compromise between a court bow and a family one. He did not try to climb back up into his seat until His Excellency His Grandpa sat down, and he did not try to say anything. No matter what he said, some of the grownups who had been arguing would find a reason to be angry about it.

Kings and Emperors did not have their words written into the shape of the World like Elderkin Binders, but they came close: sensible people did not argue to their face. At least two privy councilors were left opening and closing their mouths silently, like fish.

The Margraff-Elector looked like he had bitten into a lemon, and it might be rotten inside. His fingers kept moving as though he wanted to grab something and hold it tight.

INTERLUDE II: The Inner Chamber

An Account of Conflicting Funeral Rites

After they left the funeral dinner and the Palace, the Margraff-Elector and some of his associates returned to the White Hall of the Pristinists for their own celebration of the death of Leon-Alexander von Falkenburg, son of their overlord His Excellency Friedrich-Augustus von Falkenburg, Holy Emperor of the Remorans, King of the Allemans, and Archduke of the Eastlands.

By ancient tradition, full funeral rites were not complete until the next rising of the Unconquered Sun, and Leon-Alexander's absence from the Living World would not be completed until then, but the Outer Rites that were open to all comers ended after the Funeral Supper.

It was expected that close kinsmen and allies of the deceased who were Initiates and could enter the Inner Sanctuaries would return to the mortuary chapel for the Inner Rites at midnight, and again at dawn, while others who had paid their respects in the Outer Sanctuary – or even taken part in the Outer Rites – would get an unbroken night's sleep.

The Pristinist lords and their associates were not the late Prince's close kin, and far from being his allies, and they were even farther from being Initiates of the Sanctuary. They gathered in their own place to purge the contamination from being too close to the Ecclesialist

Sanctuary and its rites, and in this case the possible contagion of beast-born mischief as well. Both the cathedral rites and the funeral banquet were... suspect.

The gathering in the White Hall was subdued.

The Purgation was held in the Outer Hall, a room with plain, whitewashed walls that had once been an elegant, richly decorated ballroom in the Karnburg residence of the Margraff-Electors of Ansbach. The Teacher's texts were a bit sparse and not quite on point: his preparations had not expected such an awakening as the congregation had encountered. The Preacher had not been present at the cathedral, of course. His Discourse did not mention spilled lamp oil or a destroyed Rod of Office, even though such events would have been treated as dire portents meriting extreme purgation if they had involved anyone less Highborn than the Margraff-Elector. The nearest mention to the uncanny events at the mortuary chapel was a reference to the unholy alliances of the Falkenburgs and a slight expansion of the usual speech deploring the unwelcome existence and abominable terms of the Traventine Marriage Contract.

After the Purgation, the Teacher retired to his study and the lesser folk dispersed to their various tasks and duties, or to one waiting room or another. The unfortunate glove-bearer was gone, of course, his place already filled by another. He was not mentioned during the Purgation and would not be seen or mentioned again among the faithful. The Remoran-speaking slave was kept elsewhere, lest Purgation might dull his usefulness.

The Highborn and those who served them most closely gathered in the adjoining Inner Hall.

The Inner Hall was furnished even more sparsely than the Outer Hall, with only a single lectern and four straight-backed plain wooden chairs with arms, their backs graduated in size. The three chairs with the tallest backs stood near the center of the room, while the lowest was usually set in a corner and heaped with books and papers. The room's light came from tall, floor-standing candelabras: the solid panels of the window shutters were kept closed and latched so that the light of the Sun never entered. The walls and ceiling were not whitewashed but covered with a coating that was as hard and gleaming as mother of pearl. The men who gathered there huddled together like conspirators in the center of the room: the room had been chosen for the symbolic ratios of its dimensions, not its usefulness for music or oratory, and the hard shell of walls and ceiling and shutters made things worse, so loud voices were echoed and distorted and soft voices vanished into silence at any distance.

The Margraff-Elector of Ansbach sat in the First Chair, surrounded by those he directly commanded in strict order of rank. The Prince-Elector of Bremerhaven sat in the Third Chair, surrounded by his own associates. The Second Chair was left empty, but the Count of Norderstedt, serving as proxy for the lord of his home province, rested one hand on its back and his allies were arrayed around him.

The fourth and smallest group of men were gathered more loosely, but there was a hollow place in their cluster that might have held the Fourth chair if it had not been banished to the corner. Courtiers outside the Inner Hall believed that these men served the Prince-Elector of Magdoberg, despite being Pristinists when he was not.

The Preacher stood by the lectern and tried not to lean on it too openly. Most of the rest of the men in the room stood, but a few slaves and serfs knelt ready to attend the whims of their freeborn masters and tried very hard not to look suspiciously interested in the discussion. There were – of course – no females in the room, ever; and absolutely none of the beast-born, not even as chained and collared slaves.

In accordance with the prescriptions of Pristinus de Millau, the first voices heard in the discussion were those of the lowest ranked free men present and no records were kept of who among the lesser folk said what. But those early voices fell silent as higher ranked men voiced opinions, and those higher ranked men were, perhaps, less patient listeners than Pristinus had hoped. The Conversation narrowed quickly until the only active speakers were the two Electors, the Count, the Preacher, a General (a General of the Allemanic Imperial Army – not the Falkenburg Imperial Army which was larger and generally better equipped – and certainly not a General of the Army of the Eastlands), and a senior Justice of the Allemanic Kingdom. The rest of those present awaited their tasks, the free as much as the servile.

The first few comments carefully avoiding references to the beast-born and only indirectly mentioned His Excellency. The third voice suggested that with the Prince dead, the Empire would do well to repudiate the Marriage Contract with Traventi entirely. Many of those in the room seemed to approve the idea, though none said so clearly.

The Justice sighed and pinched the properly narrow bridge of his nose. "Will you also cast aside all Imperial claims to the lands and wealth of Traventl?" He spoke with the weariness of frequent repetition.

The room subsided with a sort of wordless grumble. The Count answered, "That space in the map has been a pebble in the Empire's shoe since before great Karl was crowned in Remora. Throw away the Duchy and the Kingdom will shred you like a pack of wolves. Beast-born or no beast-born."

The Preacher asked, "Could we raise a cry of sacrilege against the beast-born, for what happened today?"

"Only if you want the Margraff-Elector torn apart by the local commons and consigned to the elements, or else bled out on Leon-Alexander's tomb," the Prince-Elector said. "Or perhaps to renew the Wars of Piety. Before the Funeral Supper was finished, there were already petitions posted on the doors of the Cathedral and the Rathaus. Some acclaim the late Prince as a saint, protecting his honor and his orphaned child even after his own death. Some others preach a summons to Holy War because the High Gods have rebuked misbehavior within their precincts." Several listeners winced.

"They will not." The Margraff-Electors voice managed the calm that was suitable for one of the Highborn, except for a hint of a question, just at the end.

"Half the people in the funeral chapel believe that you set your foot on the Blood Trench, and all of them will swear that you were between the brat and the lamp that broke." The Prince-Elector shrugged. "I cannot bear witness, myself. I was facing His Excellency, as was my duty, and did not look until after it broke."

"That part is, at least, nearly plausible," the Justice said. "The rumors I have heard about the cathedral vestibule are nearly gibberish. The one thing they seem to agree on is that whatever happened did not happen on consecrated ground. That should spare us their War against Impiety. It may even spare us having this White Hall burned down around our heads, like the three before it. I recommend some future circumspection until tempers have time to settle: remember that the Eastlands are not the North."

The Prince-Elector shrugged, "I left the cathedral as soon as the rites allowed. I agree, the rumors seem unlikely."

"Nonetheless, with the Prince gone, I shall have that changeling brat Silenced and leashed to my service before he is much older," the Margraff-Elector said calmly. "I'd have him now if he had worn the cloth prepared for him. Ostwald?"

Ritter von und zu Ostwald bowed deeply where he stood at the edge of the group attending the Margraff-Elector. "I was instructed to see that the new Count of Wolfsberg and his sister wore black to the funeral, and the other as well, if possible. The Count and the girl wore black to the funeral, and I argued for the other until their beast-born dam's hair was dripping sparks like a lit fuse. Much more and the room would have caught fire or the matter would be referred to her Excellency... or both." He paused, then added the formal finish for a passage of Pristinist discourse: "Let others speak for their share in the matter."

"Yet I will have him," the Margraff-Elector repeated serenely.

The General said, "Well, the roads are long between Karnburg and Traventi, and much may happen to those that travel them."

The Preacher's face was untroubled and his voice was calm, with a slight touch of satisfaction. "As we see from the fate of Leon-Alexander, in accordance with the texts: not all of those who set their foot on the road shall return."

The General's nod was nearly a bow. "As for whatever will happen, best that it should happen before the brat passes beyond the Gates of Air into the witch-lands. What passes those gates rarely returns unchanged, and rarely for the better."

"I have plans," the Margraff-Elector said.

"As have I," the Prince-Elector said, "One or both of us may succeed." Unlike his colleague, he looked very slightly worried.

CHAPTER V: Plans and Seals

Wherein There Are Many Preparations and Farewells

Before Franz-Karl could travel to the Duchy of Traventi, there was a lot of planning and packing that needed to happen. More clothes needed to be made for him, too. Even with everything being very plainly styled and made in color-of-sorrow, a Prince's clothes for a funeral feast were different from the clothes for every day matters, and those were different from the clothes for traveling. There were layers of clothes needed for traveling in different kinds of weather, even though the year was rising toward summer.

Chamberlain von und zu Ostwald complained a great deal. All cloth was expensive, and color-of-sorrow, being rare in the Palace and city, was thus more costly. He tried to push the expense onto Traventi or Wolfsberg, but their Excellencies and the acting Archduke insisted that the Palace would bear the full cost of Franz-Karl's journey.

There were shoes and boots needed as well. Roland, who was his Mama's chief male Elderkin attendant, was also an Elderkin Cobbler every bit as skilled as the ones in the old tales. Roland made Franz-Karl Elderkin shoes and boots for his journey that were suited to Elderkin feet: the first shoes and boots that belonged to Franz-Karl without being remade from ones worn by his brother first.

When everything seemed planned, it turned out that there was one final problem about the clothes for traveling. Part of the journey would be made on riverboats and part would be riding on horses or mules. Regardless of whether Franz-Karl would ride pillion behind an adult or on his own donkey or pony, no one thought that a child's skirts would be appropriate for riding. That meant that Franz-Karl's traveling clothes would include breeches.

Franz-Karl was not pleased at the idea of wearing breeches. They would not make managing his tail impossible: he had a little goat tail, not a long swishy tail like a horse or cow. Breeches were cut full at the back so that people could sit down without splitting the cloth, and then covered by the long skirts of the waistcoat and coat. But he was gloomily certain that breeches were going to be uncomfortable. Probably in ways that could not be fixed once the journey was well advanced.

Philip-Augustus was even less pleased about the breeches – he was already not happy that Franz-Karl was having the adventure of a journey and he was not, and the matter of the breeches for Franz-Karl just set a feather on top of all the changes and upheavals for him. Mama finally decided that she and Philip-Augustus and Sophie-Alexa would spend part of the summer at one of the estates that now belonged to Philip-Augustus. Not the distant one that Papa had supposedly been visiting, of course.

The plan for the rest of the family to travel a short distance from the Palace caused almost as many arguments among the Palace officials as the plan to send Franz-Karl all the way to Traventi, which seemed strange. The districts near Karnburg were supposed to be safe, and nobles visiting their estates was a common thing, especially during the warmer months.

Somewhere in the middle of all the arguments, someone decided that Franz-Karl needed to take a huge pile of lessons set by his brother's tutor to Traventi with him, even though he was really too young to have a tutor of his own. Poor Meister van Diesen was so busy putting together the package of texts and instructions in grammar and logic and rhetoric that he worked through the night more than once. Then some messages came from some of the authorities in the Palace – Chamberlain von und zu Ostwald seemed very annoyed – and Meister van Diesen had to change some of the lessons and lost even more sleep trying arrange things properly without ignoring his regular job of teaching Philip-Augustus, while preparing for the family's visit to the estate besides.

In the end, the packs intended for three different mules needed to be adjusted so things would balance properly, even though there was only one package of lessons added to the pile of luggage. The mules were even grumpier than Philip-Augustus, so it was important for the packs to balance.

Franz-Karl's Mama had explained that it was a long journey from the Palace in Karnburg to the Duchy of the Elderkin in Traventi, so you needed to be careful not to leave anything important behind. Even if you turned around when you got there and came straight back, you would be gone more than a month. Going, you had a choice of horses and carts, which were slow, or river barges moving against the current and usually against the wind, which were just as slow or slower, but they carried more. And there were mountains in the way, so that you could not travel in a straight line from Karnburg to Traventi. There were not really any good choices. Coming back would be a little faster because you could move with the wind and current on some of the watery parts of the route.

After some arguments – of course – it had been decided that Franz-Karl would travel with an Elderkin diplomatic courier called Claudius, who had cats' eyes, and marmalade hair complete with stripes. Franz-Karl had seen diplomatic pouches of various sizes delivered to his mother, and wondered if they also came in people-size... or perhaps they would attach a wax seal on a ribbon to his collar.

It turned out that he did not have an attached seal, nor did his clothing, but every single piece of luggage was marked with the seals of the Duchy of Traventi and the Falkenburg Domains. And the Kingdom of the Allemans, which sometimes claimed to also be the Remoran Empire. And there were even seals for the Archduchy of the Eastlands, which was His Excellency Franz-Karl's Grandpapa's actual inherited Falkenburg title: parts of the Archduchy were outside the borders of the Kingdom on the map, so the Eastlands seal was included just in case, even though they were not supposed to travel in that direction.

It was probably no wonder that grownups were confused all the time. Traventi was its own single place, but people in places that answered to His Excellency Franz-Karl's Grandpapa might not be sure of where they were or what the rules were, or who they were supposed to be compared to the people they were talking to.

Some of the smaller pieces of luggage hardly had room for all of the seals. And there was a lot of luggage. Besides the usual documents and official business Claudius needed to carry, and the package of lessons, there was all of Franz-Karl's new clothing for every possible formal and informal occasion for several months, with extras to allow for growth, and more extras to allow for destruction and even more extras because there were certain events and religious rites where one should not (or was forbidden to) wear mourning colors because it might cause bad luck. There were also official gifts from the Empire (or Kingdom or Archduchy) to the Duchy and less formal gifts from His Excellency and Her Excellency and various other relatives on Franz-Karl's Papa's side to Her Grace the Reverend Duchess Adriana and various other relatives on Franz-Karl's Mama's side. And some presents from Franz-Karl's Mama to her Mama and some of their relatives. And every trunk and bale and parcel had all of the seals.

On the day they finally set out, Franz-Karl noticed Imperial seals embroidered on the saddle-cloths of the pack mules, and briefly collapsed in a fit of giggles. He did not try to explain: it was too early in the morning. He did try to avoid looking at the saddle-cloths until they were all safely away from the Palace. When he explained the joke later, when they stopped for their midday meal, Claudius just smiled thinly, but some of the others in their party agreed that all the seals were funny.

Claudius had two clerks and some guards, and servants to tend the luggage and animals and take care of meals and laundry, but they were a very small group that were traveling together compared to the merchant caravans that usually traveled along the greater roads. Franz-Karl had been to family picnics in the gardens inside the Palace walls that involved more servants and attendants than this whole long journey from the Palace in Karnburg to Traventi, but when they were starting out the familiar stable yard seemed very crowded and as they began to move the column of horses and mules seemed to stretch out longer than the distance from the stable yard to the Palace's main gate.

Just before they left the stable yard, Claudius performed a rite at the center of the group of people and animals. Then he turned and bowed and asked Franz-Karl whether he knew how to share Manifest weight.

Franz-Karl answered, "Share? Like when the stories say that people used the formula that begins 'Let us join our Gifts together'? Mama says I'm too young to learn that one ..." But he felt a sort of click in his bones and the edges of the stable yard went wavery as if seen through heat haze. Two mules turned their heads to look at him, one of the muleteers said something that was probably rude in a language Franz-Karl did not know, and Claudius turned pale and took two steps back before bowing again, very deeply. The animal Franz-Karl was mounted on did not seem upset, which was a very good thing. He was more perched on its top than gripping the animal with his legs.

Claudius mounted the horse he would use for the first bit of the journey and led the way out of the stable yard toward the main gate of the Palace. When the riders reached the Palace Gate, everything stopped, because Franz-Karl's family were waiting to say one more goodbye and wish him luck for the journey.

His Excellency was not among them: His Excellency rarely went as far as the Palace gates unless it was required for a formal rite like his son's funeral, and the entourage that accompanied him to the gates would probably have outnumbered everyone else at the gates including the animals in the pack train. There were some complicated rules wrapped around the King of the Allemans, and the Falkenburg Domains were so huge that their Lord was always very busy. Franz-Karl had been summoned to his Excellency's study the night before for a farewell audience that lasted nearly five minutes before it was interrupted by three councilors and a courier.

On the way back from His Excellency, Franz-Karl had visited the kitchen to say goodbye to the people and the Hearth, and he had said goodbye to the cats and dogs while he ate some of his breakfast. But there were still more goodbyes to say.

Acting Archduke Uncle Helm-Friedrich lifted Franz-Karl down from the mule he was perched on, so that his feet would be on the ground while people said farewell and exchanged blessings. Franz-Karl took off his hat: there were going to be grownups kissing him.

Her Excellency his Grandmother kissed Franz-Karl's forehead and hung a medallion of the Protector of Travelers around his neck.

Her Royal Highness Aunt Queen Gertrude kissed him and told him to have fun and to pay attention to the new things around him, while her companion handed him an embroidered pouch full of small hard knobbly things and told him very quietly that if he ate only two pieces of sugar candy each day, the pouch's contents should last until he reached Traventi. Her Highness' male attendants had weapons in their scabbards, since they were outdoors and not in a church, and saluted Franz-Karl magnificently.

Philip-Augustus hugged Franz-Karl and gave him the proper kinsman's kiss of farewell on his cheek. He also punched Franz-Karl in the shoulder. Hard. Franz-Karl bowed to a kinsman.

Franz-Karl's Mama knelt beside him and hugged him hard. When she began to say the prayer of leave-taking in Elderic, Sophie-Alexa suddenly squirmed down out of Nurse Rosa's arms, and grabbed Franz-Karl's coat with both fists, saying, "No. Don't go away. No. No," over and over again. She was speaking loudly but not screaming, and there were tears and snot streaming down her face.

Franz-Karl's mother moved her arms so that she was hugging them both, and said soothing things in both Elderic and Allemanic, but Sophie-Alexa did not seem to hear.

Franz-Karl said, "Sophie-Alexa, I'll come back," several times, in various languages, until she finally looked up at him. "I will come back." That was Elderic, with a very emphatic verb form.

"No." Her fists twisted where they were grasping the fabric of his coat, and her repeated words were sounding more like hiccups.

"Sophie-Alexa, I promise. I will come back... like in the story: we'll be together again even if the Threshold stands between... right? I promise!"

She finally nodded briefly and loosened her grip on his coat. Slightly.

His Mama had gasped when he mentioned the Threshold. When he looked at her she seemed surprised – or frightened – but she handed him one of her handkerchiefs and he used it to wipe his sister's face before handing the sticky cloth to Nurse Rosa.

Mama kept hugging both of them while she said the whole prayer of leave-taking. Sophie-Alexa flinched at every phrase, but her grip on Franz-Karl's coat loosened and at the end she whispered along with the words of closing and she was holding her Mother's sleeve instead of her brother's coat.

And then Uncle Helm-Friedrich lifted him back onto the mule he had been perched on, with a quick hug on the way, and wished him well. Franz-Karl put his hat back on, and the procession continued out of the Palace Gate.

Just before he passed through the gate, Franz-Karl looked back across the grounds and gardens at the long gray stone blocks of the Palace wings, under their darker slate roofs. They were leaving on a day that was sunny, at least at the time they made their start, so the many windows of the upper floors were sparkling in the sunlight despite looking a bit hazy. The walls around the Palace grounds – which were not quite tall or thick enough to give a determined army much trouble – were also gray, and had respectably elaborate defenses at the gates.

Philip-Augustus could explain the details and purpose of the Palace defenses at great length. Franz-Karl just found them annoying to pass through. At least pack mules had fewer problems than carts might have. And all of those seals were probably helping.

The road between the Palace Gate and the water gate of the city of Karnburg was busy and in need of repairs: the mules had to tread carefully to avoid ruts and missing cobbles and passers-by.

The City Walls – Philip-Augustus could talk all morning about those – were absolutely intended to stop an army: they had stopped one when Franz-Karl's Papa was young, and they had not had time to be surpassed by improvements in cannons. They were tall and thick (and mostly gray) and had very strong, complex gate defenses with three separate gates that could be closed along the path into the city. There were even gates and forts around the places where a looping channel of the great river came near the city. There were stellated earthworks against the outer sides of the walls – large mounds of dirt that were meant to deflect or absorb cannonballs and protect the stone walls. The long mounds were covered with turf, so they were green, with occasional weedy flowers, instead of the gray of the rest of the defenses. Somehow the haze in Franz-Karl's vision did not prevent seeing distant things.

Heir of the Bindings

CHAPTER VI: Journey to the West

Wherein There Is an Abundance of Rain and Travel

The river that ran past and through the city of Karnburg was not the river that flowed near the Duchy of Traventi. The two rivers could not even carry boats anywhere near each other: their headwaters were on different sides of a lumpy patch of mountains. Franz-Karl had seen the map.

A little after midday, several hours after they left the Palace, Claudius ordered the party's banners folded up and put away. A while after that, they turned off the Great Road and went down to a wharf by the river, where a plain-looking barge was moored. All of the packages and luggage and supplies were taken off the horses and mules and carried onto the barge, where the things not needed for use on the journey were piled up and covered with a cloth that might once have been a sail, and the rest were stowed in various nooks and crannies. All of the horses and mules went away except one team waiting on the tow-path, with the barge's tow-rope ready to be attached to their harness and a pair of armed men to look after them.

The barge was crowded, but everyone managed to find places to sit and stand and sleep. Franz-Karl had his own private nook, which felt odd – he had always shared a room with servants or his brother or both –

but the bargemen were openly twitchy in his presence and Claudius and the other ranking members in the party were carefully, distantly, polite.

The travelers rode the barge west up the Daonas river for days and days, almost until it could not carry the barge any more. The journey was slow: there was always at least one armed man walking with the team on the towpath with no problem keeping up. But at least the current never pushed them backward. During the hours of darkness, they stopped and moored to some wharf, or occasionally just to the riverbank with stakes pounded in. Every day near midday the team on the tow-path changed: when Franz-Karl asked, the Bargemaster said that matters were arranged so that the animals were usually pulling the barge toward their home stable. If it was a market day nearby when the team changed, some of the less ... remarkable looking ... servants and guards would buy fresh bread and replenish other supplies.

They left the barge at a city – Franz-Karl only ever saw the outside of its walls and was not sure of its name: Claudius and his men were not chatty when they were busy. All of the luggage was carried onto a wharf on the riverbank and counted three times, and checked off on a list, and all the seals were checked. Then it was all loaded back onto mules – except two packs set aside because their seals were not trusted – along with more supplies for the journey. The Falkenburg banners were unfolded so that people on the road would know they traveled on His Excellency's business.

The pack mule train slogged south for several days on an old Remoran Road that went over a mountain pass that Claudius said was annoying rather than dangerous at this time in the season.

Franz-Karl was given a donkey to ride, or maybe it was a very small mule: it was grumpy and opinionated either way, and riding in breeches with a tail stuffed into them was... annoying... besides. He refused to allow it a stronger word. There was a trick to riding with his tail in a good position. He did not always manage it, though he did improve over time, and he certainly had plenty of time to practice. It was especially annoying when the tail was as rain-soaked and wet as the rest of him. The fur got all squishy.

After a while the Road turned even more west to cross the Raenos River using a ferry just downstream from an ancient, ruined bridge. From there it went south – upstream – beside the River until they finally approached the stretch of the Raenos that formed part of the border between the Archduchy of the Eastlands (which was on the west side of the river) and the Sovereign Duchy of the Elderkin in Traventi.

The east border of Traventi was closer on the map to Karnburg than the city where they left the barge, but no one traveled that way except pigeons carrying messages. There were mountains and glaciers along the eastern length of Traventi, and no useful passes that anyone admitted to. The travelers were aiming for the western border of the Duchy for lack of a better option.

It was a long, slow, and mostly boring journey south. Too often, it was also very soggy: on the river boat they had roofs of wood or canvas between them and the rains, but on the roads they just got dripped on or poured on, depending on the weather's moods.

There had been occasional market towns and small cities along the banks of the Daonas and lower Raenos, but there were fewer as they traveled south along the Old Road. In between the markets, the larger estates and smaller villages had been set away from the river in case of floods, and were set away from the road in case of ... well, probably mostly in case of large groups of armed men traveling fast and escorting artillery: the past century had been uncomfortably busy, even in this remote southwestern region of the Falkenburg Eastlands domain. One of the older guards told some scary stories in the evenings by the fire.

The Eastlands' borders had changed more due to marriages than due to violence in recent generations, but not for lack of people trying. At least, most of the estates and villages they passed were inhabited, this year, and most of the farmlands were cultivated, if occasionally overly soggy. Claudius said that nothing seemed parched, or flooded enough to threaten famine, and he seemed pleased about that.

It was difficult for Franz-Karl to see much of the distant settlements they passed. On soggy days they seemed draped by mist, and on sunny days they were partly veiled by heat haze.

The road surface was terrible, especially once they left the ancient Remoran route. Claudius had frowned when they reached the northernmost turnoff toward Traventi: he looked down both forks of the road, blinking the rain out of his eyes, and muttered something unflattering about cow-paths. He did a divination three times to decide whether to stay on the Via and try one of the more southern approaches to the Duchy instead, but decided to take the shorter route. It had started raining too hard for him to manage a fourth divination.

Franz-Karl thought the World might be grumpy at being asked a question it had already answered more than once. He could feel something get more twitchy the second time Claudius cast his tiles, and even worse the third time. It was getting harder to see very far from their trail, too, but that might be just the rain.

An hour later Claudius grumbled that he had made the wrong choice, but by then it was too late to choose differently. They continued along the path they had chosen.

While traveling along the rivers and the main roads, their guards and Falkenburg banners had been enough to deter any brigands who noticed them, but the people living along this lesser road were more brave, or more desperate, or less impressed by the Falkenburg banners: this was a long way from Karnburg, and not even very close to the seat of His Excellency's vassal, the Landgraff who held the Upper Raenos.

Ragged looking people holding various sharp tools stepped out into the road ahead of the travelers and more came out behind them, blocking the way both forward and back. The guards whose muskets were loaded and primed pointed them at the ragged people, while the rest of the guards started loading their muskets with fresh dry powder that was more likely to fire despite the rain.

The weight of attention that Franz-Karl had first noticed at the funeral had eased during most of their journey, but now he could feel the full weight of it again, heavier than ever. Even though the season was rising toward summer, the rain suddenly felt icy, and he began shivering enough that his teeth chattered.

Claudius' senior clerk stood beside Franz-Karl, and called him by name. Not 'my lord' or 'sir': his name. The man looked him in the eyes, wincing slightly, and told him very firmly that he had no need to be frightened or concerned. The weight of attention lessened... but not entirely. The shivering also lessened, but also not entirely. The clerk took a careful step back and out of the line between Franz-Karl and the people blocking the road in front of them. Their outlines seemed fuzzy in the mist and rain.

Claudius muttered something in a disgusted sort of voice, pulled a lumpy, egg-sized metal thing out of a pocket, and twisted part of it. There was a sound like a stick snapping. A large image of a Traventine banner appeared in the air above his head. It looked the same, like a flat piece of cloth up in the air, no matter what direction you looked at it from, in a way that no material banner could manage. The falling rain did not seem to notice it, passing through as if nothing was there.

The people blocking the road grumbled loudly, but moved aside, making rude gestures and signs against the evil eye as they went. The guards did not unload any of their muskets and kept them pointed at the local people while the pack train slowly slogged past them. Most of the weight of attention Franz-Karl was feeling turned elsewhere, and he stopped shivering, but the banner made his eyes itch if he looked at it too long.

The road itself continued to get worse. Franz-Karl stopped wondering why they did not use a cart or two for some of their luggage and supplies. Instead, he wondered how the local Eastlands nobles supplied their estates and collected their taxes. Carts needed roads without holes and ruts that would break their wheels and axles. Or risk drowning the entire cart and the hitch that pulled it, in a few places. It did not help that rain had been pouring down on them for two days, so the ruts were turning into streams and there were places in the roadbed that looked ready to start producing pond-lilies and frogs at any moment.

Finally, at the end of a too long, too wet day, the so-called road brought them back to the Raenos, and the crossing to the Duchy of Traventi.

Near the north end of the the Traventine border there were a pair of villages, one on each side of the Raenos River, connected by a bridge, that were together just marked on the maps as the Traventi Crossing.

The approaches to the bridge on the Eastlands side were crowded by small, worn looking houses and blocked by a small fortress-like barrier with stone walls that had metal spikes on top and gates that could be barred. The Landgraff's guards opened the barrier for them, grudgingly, demanding fees for the service. Claudius clucked his tongue, but paid rather than argue. The guards looked hungry and the few other people they saw looked even hungrier.

When their party rode through the barrier, Franz-Karl could see that it was separate from the bridge – there was a least a foot wide gap between the stone of the bridge and any of the fortress's worked stones. The style of stonework in the bridge was different from the fortress, too.

When all of his mount's hooves had crossed between the end pillars of the bridge, off the road's mud and onto the bridge paving,

Franz-Karl felt something change. For a moment he thought that the stone of the bridge had gone slippery in the rain, but his donkey did not seem worried or upset.

The Traventi Crossing village on the Traventi side was set well back from the river. There were no visible barriers on that side of the bridge, just an empty area where travelers (even wagons, if they somehow arrived there) could decide whether to continue east into the village, or turn onto a well-maintained road, wide enough for carts or carriages, that went south at a respectful distance from the river.

The party traveling from Karnburg paused long enough for Claudius to recite a short verse before they turned south into more rain but suddenly, less mist. Franz-Karl felt that click in his bones again. He gasped, looked up, and got a face full of rain that made him sputter, but his whole body felt... lighter. The feeling of being watched was almost entirely gone.

"Just a little farther to go," Claudius said. He had never been so cheerful before.

Claudius and Franz-Karl and the clerks and guards and all the rest of the baggage train continued their journey south until they reached the mouth of a small river, the Elde, that flowed out of the main valley of Traventi into the Raenos. The cart road crossed it by a bridge that was wider than the Traventi Crossing Bridge across the Raenos, and much fancier, though the carvings on these end-pillars were just dim, swirling shapes in the rain.

The road divided again south of the bridge, with one branch continuing south along the Raenos and the other turning uphill beside the Elde. There were clusters of buildings on both sides of the stream, but none of them were very near the Bridge, or the Raenos, or the Elde. The River Elde was carrying quite a lot of water but was even less useful for boats than the Raenos' headwaters: besides being smaller, it was swift and turbulent. The chronicles and lesson-books said the lower Elde was very good for watermills if they were built between the steepest bits, but mills needed to be built strong: the water gathered speed and power on the slopes, and there was a lot of water during the Thaw.

Franz-Karl was keeping his head tipped down so that the rain would run off his hood and cloak, so most of what he could see was water and mud and a very grumpy donkey. There were no docks or piers visible through the rain when he tried to peek, or mills, either, or anything else of that sort.

One of the mules needed its packs adjusted, so the travelers paused briefly after crossing the Elde Bridge, but it was not a good time or place to stop for food or anything else. The rain was still falling with determination (and possibly a grudge). The wind was also quite grumpy, but undecided about which way it was coming from.

Franz-Karl was bundled into a hooded, waxed cloak that was much too large for him – the hood went over his hat, brim and all, with plenty of room to spare – and mounted on a smallish donkey that was only a little too large for him and seemed glad to be sharing the cloak. Claudius and a few of the most important bits of luggage were on two large mules – Claudius was leading the one he was not riding, and leading Franz-Karl's donkey, too. There were some muleteers in charge of the rest of the mules and luggage following behind them, with the clerks and guards and servants.

Claudius took Franz-Karl and the special mule and two of the mounted guards, and left the rest of the pack-train to straggle behind with the muleteers while they moved ahead in the rain, slightly faster, up the hill beside the Elde. It was a zigzag path which was not sure whether it wanted to be a road, a stream or a mud slide, though most of it seemed to be cobbled somewhere under the heavy sheet of rainwater. At the top of the steep slope the road improved a lot, or at least the water stayed more in the ditches beside the road, instead of flowing across the paving stones. There was not much level land between the place where the road flattened out and the steep mountain slopes rising on either side of the river, but the valley widened quickly once they moved out onto the flat.

After a few miles they turned back north and recrossed the Elde over a very fancy stone bridge in something like the Remoran style, with a span much longer than the water flowing in the stream was wide. The river channel below was not narrow, but the mud and tumbled debris along the banks showed that it had recently been even wider. The rain seemed to be doing its best now to replace the snow-melt that had recently passed downstream: looking down, Franz-Karl could see some of the debris at the edges being drowned by deepening water.

On the north side of the bridge, safely away from the river, they approached the Ceremonial Gateway and Threshold of the House on the Rock. The Gateway was built in a very antique style: instead of an arch crossing the road it had a triangular pediment full of brightly painted sculptures – like the front of a temple – and the gateposts were classical pillars with colorfully painted trim. When Franz-Karl tried to look up to see what the sculptures in the pediment were, he got a face full of cold rain that poured into his hood and dripped down inside his collar. Looking at the figures would need to wait.

There was no physical barrier visible in the Gateway, not even a change in the road's pavement where it passed between the gateposts. There was a barrier stretching out to either side of the Gateway, but it was not a stone defensive wall: it was a 'laid' hedge of densely woven, living, blooming thorn-bushes. Some distance off to each side the hedge sort of reared itself up into arches that were crossed at the bottom by quite respectable farmer's gates, suitable for keeping in cattle and sheep and horses... and goats if they were feeling law abiding. It was not a barrier that seemed worried about invading armies. At all. And nothing about it was gray, not even in the rain.

Beyond the Gateway and the hedge (which rejected capitalization as much as the City Wall at Karnburg demanded it) the House on the Rock spread broad and mostly low, with a taller section off to the right, and another off to the left, and a third straight ahead beyond nearer, lower buildings that faced the Gateway. There were towers, no two alike, but they poked upward from the middles of built-up places like church towers, and seemed useless for defense. Philip-Augustus would disapprove, probably loudly.

Even in the gloom of the late afternoon rain, it was clear that the House on the Rock was as colorful as its Gateway. The roofs were done in several colors of tile in patches and patterns and full out mosaics, and posts and beams and doors and window-frames were picked out in red or green or blue or ocher-yellow – or actual gold leaf – on light warm-colored stone, or occasionally, plaster.

Most of the towers had different colored lamps on top, like the lamps that topped holy sanctuaries in Karnburg. In the gloom of the rainy afternoon, and with the Sun already nearing the distant western peaks, the lamps had already been lit. They cast smears of light out into the rain, which was trying hard to drown the light, if not the lamps.

There were even some lit windows and doorways showing in the walls of the buildings of the settlement that faced the hedge and the river. Some of the lighted doorways opened into fenced cattle-pens or stableyards, but none of them showed signs of fortifications. It was very different from the walled and guarded Palace inside the mightily walled city of Karnburg. The House on the Rock was very brave.

The tallest tower was straight ahead of the travelers, just beyond the nearest low roofs as they looked along the paved road that led from the bridge across the Elde and through the Gateway. It had a broad flat top level that extended out beyond the lower levels on all ... six sides? ... eight sides? (it was hard to tell in the gusty, darkening rain). Instead of a single large lamp on its top, it had smaller lamps hanging from the bottom corners of the top level.

A handful of people cloaked and hooded against the downpour met the travelers at the Gateway. They said, "Welcome home, Claudius. Welcome four times, child of the House!"

Franz-Karl answered, "May peace abide among the peaceful," which was not the correct response, but at least not insulting. He was too wet and chilly and tired to think straight, and people in the old stories were seldom welcomed as Children of the House. Something about blessings?

The welcoming party unloaded the special luggage, and took the donkey and mules away to one of the livestock gates. The two guards went with them.

Franz-Karl passed through the Gateway of the House on the Rock for the first time on foot. Claudius escorted him along the Processional Way, past a large old-fashioned Altar with a serious Blood Trench around it, to the formal Threshold of the House. There was a porch in front of the door with another pediment and pillars – like the Gateway but smaller – and two wings of the house reached the front edge of the porch on each side, so the door was set back in a niche and well sheltered from the wind and rain. There were carved stone torch symbols on each side of the door, under the shelter of the porch.

Claudius grasped Franz-Karl's wrist and guided his hand to touch a golden mark in the center of the complex vine-pattern carved on the door. There was a sound like a bell, but sweeter and more lingering than most bells Franz-Karl was used to: a hum rather than a clang. The door opened and her Reverend Grace the Duke his Grandmother stepped out and knelt to hug him, then picked him up bodily and carried him across the Threshold saying in Elderic, "Welcome to peace and safety and plenty and kinship under this roof! Welcome, child of the House! Welcome! And Four Times Welcome!"

When Franz-Karl was well past any danger of stumbling at the Threshold, his Grandmother set him down, saying, "Here, let me look at you, Child." Her Elderic sounded a little different than his mother's but their voices were very similar, and the words were just... home. His mother had said 'Here, let me look at you, child' when he put on his sorrow-colored clothes for the first time, and when he was dressed for the start of his journey, and so many times before. He was starting to shiver in the warmth of the house and suspected he looked half-drowned, but he knew that she would not care. He had started crying from tiredness and ... everything... and he was sure she would not mind that either, even if she noticed through all of the rest of the dripping wetness.

Her Grace His Grandmother offered him all of the special Guest tokens: water and fire and wine and bread and cheese and meat and salt, as if he was someone in an old story. He remembered the proper responses this time. It helped that she used the formula for a newly arrived kinsman. The full rites were described in the old stories more often than hasty greetings fit for a child of the house arriving in pouring rain.

The Duke his Grandmother shared a small glass of sweet, watered wine with him and let him choose from a tray of delicious, warm guest morsels – aogreamana – made from the other holy items, and he could feel the warmth of the room wrapping around him and see the fire in the Guest Hearth. They exchanged the proper oaths of Peace formally, followed by the second sip and bite. So now he was a proper Guest according to the ancient rules, just as if he was a grownup arriving on some important errand in an old tale.

That reminded him that there was one task that should not wait. Franz-Karl fumbled in the layers of his clothing and brought out the small package containing the lock of his father's hair. He checked carefully to make sure it was the one meant for the House-on-the-Rock's shrine, not his personal keepsake – which he had kept in a different pocket – before he held it out with both hands. He found that he could not speak.

Her Grace his Grandmother received it formally with both hands, and bowed, and said in Allemanic, "Your father Leon-Alexander was a good and honest and kind man, and a clever one. The Living World is poorer for his loss." She repeated it in Elderic, with a twist in the verbs that marked it as a statement of fact rather than opinion, and the words echoed off walls that were larger than the room. Franz-Karl was tired enough that the edges of things were getting a little uncertain in his eyes and ears. He thought the weight of attention was back, too.

Her Grace smiled a little when Franz-Karl flinched at the echo and said in Elderic, it seemed mostly to herself, "It seems we are not before time. Well, tomorrow is no doubt soon enough."

CHAPTER VII: The House on the Rock

Wherein Our Hero Explores a New Place

Franz-Karl awakened early on the day after his arrival, partly because of the daylight coming through the window – which was glazed but not shuttered – and partly because there was a large orange cat lying halfway on top of him and his arm was becoming the prickly sort of not-numb. He managed to politely squirm out from under the cat and got up to search for the chamber-pot, and more clothes than the nightshirt he was wearing.

He did not remember the room at all. He remembered arriving at the House. He remembered a warm bath in the laundry cauldron with an odd-looking laundress making the familiar jokes about child soup, followed by a wonderfully hot meal – mostly soup and delightful fresh-baked bread – full of nearly unfamiliar flavors, and introductions to several members of the household. He did not remember being undressed and put to bed – except for his Grandmother's kiss – and wondered whether the neatly stacked luggage against the wall had arrived before or after he had arrived in the room himself.

There was nothing he needed to do, at least, not until after breakfast. After all those days and weeks of wet and weary travel, his official errand for His Excellency had been finished the previous evening, less than an hour after he crossed the Threshold. There was a pile of lessons somewhere in the pile of luggage, but those could wait a little.

It was still raining, though not as fiercely as the day before, and the wind was quieter and less variable. The room was a little damp, and too chilly to be standing about in a nightshirt, even one that was so long it touched the floor. He recognized a pack that held some clean stockings and bracchae and his last shirt that was clean after the journey and tugged it out from the bottom of a stack without pulling the whole lot down on him. He opened three different chests before he found a clean, dry suit in the color-of-sorrow and some shoes that were suitable for indoors, and a bone-colored hat that had not been completely wrecked by travel and rain. Franz-Karl remembered Nurse Rosa fretting about the mountains being cold even in summer and chose the warmer waistcoat of the two he found to wear under his coat. He did not bother trying to battle his hair: not in this damp.

He hoped whatever attendants they assigned to look after him and his things would be nice. There were two alcoves behind curtains, one at each end of the room, both with proper beds, not just pallets on the floor, and each with its own washstand and chest, so at least those tending him might not have harsh or mean spirited treatment to sour their moods. The alcoves even had their own windows, glazed and shuttered against the weather, and unlit candles waiting for use.

The furniture in the uninhabited alcove was as fine as the furniture in the main room – the pieces were not battered castoffs – and he assumed the occupied alcove was similarly furnished. He was very careful not to awaken the woman who was sleeping there. He almost remembered her from the previous evening: he thought he remembered broad-pupiled goats' eyes in a human shade of blue, and one of three names of Remoran heritage, not Allemanic or Elderic... but he did not know who she answered to.

Servants might be nice or mean, but mostly they were busy. Attendants had rank and titles, and people they answered to. And who they answered to mattered. Philip-Augustus said that a mean attendant who answered to one of the Falkenburg Households was worse than a nice one who answered to the Chamberlains. But Philip-Augustus could not see fibs, not even if they were really awful.

Franz-Karl did not see any fibs on the sleeping woman, but he did not know whether he could see that people were fibbers when they were asleep. The people who slept in their family suite in the Palace were not fibbers. He turned away from the alcove.

The washstand was made for a grownup, and the ewer was large and heavy. It was also very full, which made it even heavier. He stood on a pack and managed tip it enough to splash a little water into the basin. It was not enough to wash thoroughly, but it was enough to wet his face and hands before he said his morning prayers. And he had just had a complete bath last evening.

Since there was not anyone awake to tell him not to, Franz-Karl left the room quietly and began to explore. The door opened onto a passageway with pillars and railings on one side that overlooked a garden courtyard. At one end there was a rather steep, ornamented staircase going down toward the main entrance of the House. There seemed to be only the one, not one fine stair and a plainer one for the servants, unless it was very well hidden. The Household Shrine was on the way to the entrance, so he paused to say "Blessed morning" to his Papa and the other Ancestors and Guardians. Then he turned back, to go into the House on the Rock, not out of it.

The House was not made of long ranges of rooms and hallways with gardens outside, like the Palace in Karnburg. It was a cluster of courtyards and plazas of various sizes, all joined together like a group of bubbles with smaller ones huddled around and between the larger ones. The walls and narrow buildings that bordered the open spaces were pierced by gates and doors, sometimes at the corners of the courtyards, sometimes in the center of a wall. Sometimes a corner door in a small colonnade opened into the center of a wall of a larger neighbor.

He avoided doors – even empty doorways – that were marked with paired torches and other emblems and images of the two-faced Guardian of Gateways. He especially avoided one ornate door that looked like it included a compact Ceremonial Gateway, pediment and all. There were plenty of places to explore without crossing Boundaries and Thresholds or intruding in some stranger's Household.

The ground floors of the buildings had part of their depth taken up by colonnades that wrapped around the open spaces on three sides, or sometimes on all four. It was possible to walk a long way without getting wet or snowed on or whatever, but without exactly being indoors. On hot sunny days, assuming there were any, the colonnades might also provide welcome shade. On days that were cold but clear, the plazas would catch the sunlight: their walls were mostly lower on the south.

All of the walls and ceilings were decorated, at least with patterns and borders, and often with more. He did not see many oil paintings like the ones in some parts of the Palace. It was mostly all frescoes and mosaics – he recognized scenes from old stories, and wondered whether some of the odder people portrayed were authentic Elderkin, or made-up creations. The floors at ground level were all stone or tile or mosaic, but some of the upper levels had floors made of wood. Some of the upper floors were sort of like mosaics made of wood, which undoubtedly had its own name, but Franz-Karl did not know it in Allemanic or Elderic or Remoran. He would need to ask someone.

The most amazing thing was that the courtyards were all different, not at all regimented or uniform. There were themes in the decorations: grapes and grapevines were very common, sometimes in places where one would not expect them, and there were fountains and wells and narrow stone-lined ditches that were managing not to overflow in the rain as they carried the water somewhere. But any greater pattern was unclear, at the least: a mostly paved space opened into a formal garden, which was followed by one planted with things that were almost certainly early season cabbages, along with other tiny plants that Franz-Karl suspected would probably also grow into food. And in the paved court beyond that, something large was being built of wood and metal, though at the moment it was mostly covered with tarps, along with various piles of materials and tools.

There were some people moving through the colonnades despite the early hour. They smiled and nodded at Franz-Karl and wished him 'Blessed morning' in Elderic, and some of the men touched a forefinger to their forehead or hat brim in something that might have been very distant kin to a salute. But no one fussed at him and no one failed to notice him, where people in the Palace in Karnburg nearly always did one or the other.

Some of the people, working in pairs, were hanging wreaths and garlands of flowers and branches on the walls beneath the colonnades where they would be protected from the weight of rain and wind. Franz-Karl knew that just because he was traveling, time did not stop in the world, but even counting three times, he could not make the days of travel add up to this being May Eve. But people in the Palace would say that he was six, now. That was stranger than the people, and they were quite strange.

Some of the grownups he passed had horns. Most looked like goat horns, but some were more like cows or sheep, and some were curved or twisty like nothing Franz-Karl had seen before. There was also one man who had feathers instead of hair, and amazing eyebrows that started as tiny feathers by his nose and ended as a long iridescent plume on each side trailing back along the sides of his head.

The man with feathers was bareheaded. In the Palace, respectable people did not go outdoors – or even out of their apartments – without wearing something on their heads. But it was hard to judge what would count as outdoors in the House on the Rock. Some of the people with horns just wore their horns plain or decorated, while others wore soft caps or kerchiefs. People with neither horns nor feathers generally had something.

Some of the people in the House were walking around barefoot, or wearing shoes that revealed they did not have regular human feet. That was almost more surprising than the horns or feathers. Franz-Karl had been taught very strictly not to go barefoot in the Palace if anyone outside his Mama's Household might see. Some people made a fuss about Elderkin feet.

There were two people with tails that showed outside their clothes, but that was no great surprise after seeing so many people walking barefoot. Seeing those tails made his own tail sort of restless.

None of the people showed shadow marks or other marks from fibbing. None of them at all. That was almost stranger than seeing people with horns or tails or feathers. There were a very few whose edges looked a little strange.

A few of the people were moving heavy or bulky things using small carts pulled by goats or donkeys that fit in the passages on the dry side of the columns. The cartwheels were all bound with cloth or leather, not iron, so they were quiet and did not scratch or scuff the pavements. One woman was leading a tiny donkey, almost hidden by a huge load of kindling, that almost seemed to be tiptoeing across the tile floor. Franz-Karl wondered whether the animals wore indoor shoes on the patterned floors, just as the people did.

Franz-Karl walked around the colonnade of a library then down a flight of stairs to a formal garden of the 'sculptures and trimmed box hedges' sort (though these statues were all brightly painted, unlike the ones in the Karnburg Palace that stood around looking like ghosts). When he opened the next door, two goats tried to push their way through. Fortunately, they were very small goats, so after several chaotic minutes Franz-Karl managed to close the door with the goats, and himself, on their own proper side of it, not on the library side. Goats in a library seemed like a very bad idea.

There were more goats in this courtyard, both babies and grown ones. The fountain in the center was a faun playing a double flute with water coming out of the flute instead of music, as good or better than the sculptures cluttering the Palace gardens and corridors. The pose was not a recent style: it was either very old, or a very good copy. The paint had not been refreshed lately, but it was not left as boring, plain stone. The flute and the faun's horns were gilded, and much of the rest was colored. There were just some bare, scuffed spots where the goats had rubbed against it. Or jumped on it: there was a baby goat standing on a grown one under the colonnade off to one side, and there were scuffed spots on the faun's shoulders.

There were a few grownup goats standing near the fountain in the rain, looking annoyed, but most of them were standing or lying in the colonnade, where there was a thick layer of mostly dryish straw bedding. There were some feeding troughs along the wall near where Franz-Karl was standing, and a double gate or door in the center of the left hand wall that had its top halves open to show where a small pasture – or possibly a very large grassy courtyard – was being rained on.

On the side of the colonnade opposite Franz-Karl, some of the grown-up goats were taking turns walking up ramps onto tables to be milked by two women wearing kerchiefs. The first two little goats were still complaining about not being allowed into the library, and testing whether Franz-Karl's clothes were good to eat.

One of the women looked up from pouring a bucket of milk through a strainer into a large jug to see what the fuss was about. The dairywoman set down the empty bucket and walked straight across the rainy courtyard to shoo the little goats back to their mothers and rescue Franz-Karl's cuffs and buttons and shoe buckles.

Franz-Karl said, "Blessed morning. That was very helpful," in Elderic. There were rules about saying 'Thank you' to Elderkin, complicated rules. Statements of fact were safer and usually more polite.

"My honor. And blessed morning to you as well. Would you like a cup of milk?"

"Milk would be a fine thing."

She filled a cup with milk ladled out of the jug and took a sip before she offered it to him. "Here, Child of Sorrow, may this bring health."

The other woman looked up and said sharply, "Tsk, Gwenned. No need to set an ill word on the boy."

It was not an unreasonable title for a boy wearing color-of-sorrow. Franz-Karl said carefully, in Elderic "I think my father dead and myself carrying but seven years is plenty of sorrow." He suspected he'd gotten at least one of the verbs wrong: it was early and Elderic verbs went so strange once you stopped talking about purely physical things. At least he had remembered the age counting difference.

The woman who was not Gwenned was eager to push the sorrow into the past. "That is true and worth saying four times."

Franz-Karl finished the milk and handed the cup back to Gwenned, so that she could put it somewhere safe from goats. "That was very fine. I should go back. They will be serving the meal soon." Sharing names was one way of giving thanks safely, so he added, "I am called Franz-Karl."

"And I am called Markia," Not-Gwenned answered. "Do you know your way?"

"The eating place is between the two towers that are like mushrooms, I think."

She laughed. "Ah. So it is. The tall one with the flat top is the Tower for Looking at Stars. The one with the dome and pillars on top is the Tower of the Breezes. Here, try this way..." She led him to a door in the wall opposite the pasture gate, fending off goats. It opened on a rose garden courtyard he had not yet visited, but he could see the tall, flat tower not far away, and the other off to one side.

He arrived at the door of the eating room at precisely the time appointed for the meal.

.

CHAPTER VIII: More Promises

Wherein Our Hero Becomes a Sworn Notary

After breakfast, her Grace the Reverend Duke his Grandmother took Franz-Karl into the Household Shrine and showed him where she had put his father's hair in a people-shaped jar inside the lower part of the section of the shrine that remembered the dead. They knelt together and prayed for his father's Journey, though it had surely been completed before Franz-Karl's own arrival in Traventi.

Unlike the journey from Karnburg to Traventi, the Journey from the Living World to the Halls of Judgment was said to be measured in days, not weeks. Franz-Karl wondered whether souls got rained on while they traveled to the Halls of Judgment. Probably only if they liked rain, he decided, or perhaps it was a part of being tested.

Afterward, they went to Her Grace's study and Her Grace the Reverend Duke his Grandmother began to talk about Elderkin things. Franz-Karl listened very carefully, partly because she was speaking Elderic and not avoiding the hard verbs.

"You have heard of the Manifest, of course," she began.

Franz-Karl nodded. "Yes, Your Grace", he said quietly. Everyone knew about the Manifest. He listened even more carefully. His Mama said that when they told stories in the shrine that you had heard many times before, you needed to pay extra attention in case there were parts you had not noticed before. Sometimes there were bits that were hiding. Franz-Karl thought that talking about the Manifest was probably the same kind of thing as church stories.

"The Timeless Ones come from outside the walls of the Living World," Her Grace said, "and they are made of stuff like words and poetry and meanings the way things in the Living World are made of stone and flesh and wood and water and air. When they come into the World they put on bodies the way we put on clothes, so that they can talk to the Worldfolk and handle the things that are in the World. When they are here, we call them Manifest Ancient Ones or sometimes the Manifest Blessed Ones. Or sometimes daemons. Or Demons if they are being very rude."

Franz-Karl nodded again to show he was listening. There were turning out to be some very big new pieces of story, and they were going in a good direction. He had never liked it when people like the Ritter von und zu Ostwald said that Elderkin were demons. Elderkin were born people and demons... were not. At least, the demons in stories did not act much like people. Demons being unblessed Manifest made more sense, somehow.

Her Grace His Grandmother continued, "Sometimes the bodies that Manifest Ancient Ones wear to walk in the World are so cleverly made that they can make babies with the Worldfolk that are properly part of the World. Elderkin are people born into the World who have some Worldfolk ancestors and some ancestors that were Manifest, not born."

That part was mostly not new.

"The Manifest walk heavy in the world because they come from outside. Their weight burdens the world a little, in a way that the Living World notices and pays attention to, and it sort of stretches itself to make room for them. Because their true nature is something like words and poetry, things the Manifest say can get tangled in the World, and reshape it, and change things. Sometimes they do it on purpose, sometimes it just happens, when the World is making room. Sometimes the changes make an awful mess, because the Timeless Ones are from Outside, and don't always completely understand how the Living World is properly shaped."

Franz-Karl remembered thinking about the World trying to see inside itself. "Does the Living World completely understand the Manifest?"

"That is an excellent question." Her Grace smiled at him. "Very likely it does not... nor do Elderkin, nor Worldfolk, completely understand the Manifest, either. Elderkin inherit some of the heaviness of the Manifest Ancient Ones. Elderkin with a Manifest Grandparent or Great Grandparent – or someone with a lot of Manifest ancestors farther back that add together to make enough Manifest weight – can make just as much of a mess as any Manifest Ancient One, because it turns out that flesh-born people don't understand the World very well either." She smiled again. "And the Living World seems not to entirely understand even the people that are part of it."

Franz-Karl thought about some of the people in the Palace who never understood very plain, simple things. "Does the mess ever get worse than in the scary stories?"

"Yes. Sometimes much worse." She looked up at something hung on the wall of memorials with an expression he did not understand, then looked back at Franz-Karl before she continued. "We call the changes that happen to the World that stick 'Bindings' and the flesh-born people who can make the changes all by themselves are sometimes called 'Binders.' Sometimes people say 'blessings' to mean bindings that are intended to help and 'curses' to mean bindings that are meant to hurt or break things, but that is not very useful because sometimes the results are not what the Binder wanted, and other times you need to break something in order to be helpful." Franz-Karl nodded: this was complicated but not confusing.

She continued. "It is very rude – and usually wicked – to put a Binding on someone else that will change them, or stop them from doing things that they could otherwise do, especially if you do it without asking or warning or giving them a choice. If you are very careful, putting a Binding on yourself can be a way to learn something complicated more quickly or to avoid making mistakes."

"Oh! Like the Binding Mama helped me put on myself."

Her Grace looked at him for a long moment, with a very blank expression. Then, speaking very carefully and precisely and quietly, she asked him to tell her about the Binding.

Franz-Karl told her about the funeral and the Holy Promise, and how the World turned the sneaky, mean food into table ornaments to help keep the family at the high table safe. He mentioned that the Margraff-Elector was mean and rude at the funeral, but did not try to explain the cage of lies: he was not sure what to say. It sounded stupid in Remoran or Allemanic, and he did not know if there were words in Elderic that would be better. He did not know words for what had happened to the glove-bearer's rod either, but described what had happened as well as he could: that was too scary to leave out. As he spoke, Her Grace looked more and more serious, and her hair sparked a little.

When he finished, his Grandmother said, "Dear Heaven and all the saints," in a way that sounded like praying, not swearing. "Well, that explains the Archduke's urgency..." She took a deep breath and said, "In the Duchy of the Elderkin here in Traventi it is customary for heavy Binders to create Bindings on themselves to make it easier to do things safely, and harder for bad Bindings to happen by accident. That keeps the World around them safer for them and for everyone else."

She seemed to be expecting an answer, so Franz-Karl said, "That sounds very... useful?"

Her Grace the Reverend Duke his Grandmother picked up two long pieces of parchment – one written on, one blank – and handed them to Franz-Karl. She spoke in Allemanic, then repeated everything in Elderic. He was a little surprised that she did not use Remoran instead of Allemanic: his Mama and Papa would have used Remoran. "This is a list of agreements that various people have made with the World to help it to know when it should pay attention to what they say and when it should ignore them because they are joking or telling stories or playing pretend. There are also rules for doing some complicated things safely. Please read them and decide: do you think any of them are agreements that you would like to make with the World now? If you do, copy them so that you can make the Bindings yourself: I am just a bystander in this, not even properly a witness. You do not need to make any choices at all now, if you do not want to, or you don't understand the writing, or you don't see any agreements that you like. And you can come back later as often as you want to add more, if a time comes when you decide that they would be useful. But once an agreement is made, it cannot be unmade, so do not be too hasty in making your choices."

The page with writing on it looked very odd. The words were written in Elderic: grown-up Elderic with the complicated verb forms and what was called esoteric noun agreement, and they were written using Elderic letters. But the paragraphs and words were written in a sort of fake Remoran style, with spaces between the words, and line breaks, and all of the words moving left to right and all of the letters facing the same way. All but the shortest agreements were chopped into little separate pieces by line breaks instead of being whole connected things. That did not look right at all: not if the agreements were supposed to be whole.

Franz-Karl frowned at the pages and asked for the pen and ink. He copied out the first few agreements he wanted in the proper Elderic style he had seen in the old chronicles on his Mama's bookshelf: with raised dots between the words and vertical lines instead of periods, and the words and letters inside each paragraph running ox-wise back and forth, so the sentences were all continuous, never broken. He was especially careful writing the letters that did not happen in Allemanic and Remoran. Some of them were sneaky on the return lines, with shapes that were not quite mirror images of the advancing shapes.

The first few agreements were easy and sensible:

'something he knew was a lie would not ever make a binding',

'bindings for agreements or witnessing would only happen if he signed and sealed a document, or spoke the proper words either four times for most things, or three times for wills and weddings and some other ancient ceremonies',

'he would not sign any paper he had not read or did not understand, or knew was a lie, and he could not be forced to sign'

'he could not be part of a binding agreement he did not agree with, but he could bear witness to bind an agreement he thought was stupid'.

That one was part of the first cluster of choices, all written together in a group, using larger letters than the agreements that followed, but Franz-Karl read it a couple of times silently, and once aloud, and looked at Her Grace the Reverend Duke his Grandmother before he dipped his pen to copy it. "Really?"

"You need not bear witness just because someone asks, and you should never lend your weight to something you think is truly wicked, but sometimes you may be ... witnessing that a promise happened more than the thing that was promised," she suggested.

Franz-Karl thought, then snickered. "We can say 'Yes, the Baron's will truly gives 500 gold marks to his monkey', and we don't need to decide whether it is good or sensible for the monkey to get 500 gold marks instead of the Baron's cousin?"

She laughed. "Yes. Precisely. Was there a Baron with a monkey at the Palace?"

"I never met the old Baron – or the monkey – but the cousin was an officer in the Palace guard before he inherited the Barony. He got the title and the estate, but the monkey got most of the gold. I saw the captain a few times. He complained a lot, and forgot things... I think the monkey is probably smarter and not nearly as mean."

He added the rule to his paper and looked at what he had written, then back at the chopped up text he was copying from. There were two words trying to pretend they belonged to the previous sentence. He wrote them clearly on their own line, with the fancy capital to show it was a fresh paragraph.

"Do you know what that says?" Her Grace the Duke His Grandmother asked in Allemanic, keeping her voice very even and quiet.

Franz-Karl considered. He was remembering a grownup conversation, and translating words about meanings would be... no. Just, no. Safer to use the words he had heard, or something close to them. He answered carefully in Remoran, trying to remember. "Papa says... said... a motto using words with more than one meaning is like a coin with two sides, or a die with six or eight or twenty, that is still one coin or one die. The common Remoran translation of Traventi's motto is 'Choice Without End', but the Old Elderic 'choice' was the same word as for a contract or promise... or a Binding? The root of the verb is an action of ending or going away, but the form marks it as a false or impossible action... So, 'contracts are permanent' and 'there is no last choice'... and maybe 'choosing can't be prevented'. Is that right?" The feeling of attention being paid was suddenly very heavy. He coughed, and took a deep breath.

Her Grace the Duke answered in Elderic, not quite as old as the version in the motto. "Well enough." She was still being very careful.

"If I choose this, no one can stop me from making choices? Not even you or Mama or the Margraff-Elector or Philip-Augustus or His Excellency?" Modern Elderic and very careful of the verb forms.

"That is correct." Modern Elderic with no room allowed for uncertainty.

He looked from her face to the paper he had written. "Can I sign and seal this much before I continue? To say that I am deciding this? This much is Bound?"

"Certainly." She smiled. Not a 'hidden joke' smile. A 'something good is happening' smile.

He signed his full name in the Remoran style, Falx Franciscocarolus, feeling the watching weight shift its balance with every stroke of the pen. Her Grace heated green wax for the seal, then handed him a signet to use. He squished the wax with the carved stone while it was still warm and soft, then looked at the picture the ring had made. It showed the goats and grapes and four-pillared house-on-a-rock of the Duchy's great seal (fortunately, they were right side up: he would need to be more careful about that), but there was a compass star added in the center. He knew that his Mama's personal signet had a crescent moon with the points touching between the goats, and Her Grace the Duke had a Sun-in-Glory. He thought this signet was beautiful. It was very comfortable to hold.

"Is this mine?" Franz-Karl was hopeful, but did not want to be rude and assume. It might be a signet the House kept for guests to use. The Palace had some things like that: foreign guests could use them while they visited, but not take them home with them.

"Yes. Dear heart, it is yours." Her Grace his Grandmother even had a plain ribbon ready for the signet, so that he could wear it around his neck and tuck it inside the color-of-sorrow clothing he wore. Even if he had not been in mourning and avoiding the display of ornaments, he would have needed the ribbon: the signet was a grownup's ring, not made for the small hand of a seven-year old.

Franz-Karl was very glad to have his own signet. His brother Philip-Augustus had gotten a signet for his seventh birthday (in the Allemanic age count) which showed a version of their father's device, but all the little details of the wolf's head and oak branch had just left the wax looking messy. Philip-Augustus owned all of Papa's things now, so he was using Papa's signet, which at least was less messy. Franz-Karl's own new ring had left a nice crisp image and not taken any of the wax with it when he lifted it away. He petted the ring before he turned back to the papers.

The next group of agreements had to do with marking the boundaries between talking about facts and agreements, and things like stories and word games and make believe. They used a lot of the hard verb conjugations, and even some sneaky noun declensions. Knowing that Elderkin words could really change the World, it made sense that formal Elderic had ways to say that what you were saying about the future was probably false, but that did not make the verbs easier to understand or use. Sometimes if he sort of let his thoughts go soft, he knew what a sentence or paragraph meant even when he did not quite follow what the words said, but that was not helping much now, when he needed to be clear and precise. So he had to keep poking at the paragraphs and discussing them with Her Grace. Once he finally saw the pattern, the rules for what he was supposed to do and what the Living World was asked to do were not really very complicated, just a bit finicky.

He copied all of those agreements, and a few of the next group, which were about how not to put Bindings by accident on people and and other living things, and on the World itself, or not making Bindings even on purpose unless you were very sure you needed to. He was not sure he wanted to know what most of the agreements he did not copy and sign for in that group were talking about. Some of them made him feel very creepy: it seemed better not to poke at them. So he went ahead and signed and sealed the ones that felt right and ignored the rest. The weight of attention managed to be lighter without being more distant.

There was a list of a handful of agreements that were variations of saying that promises of permanent, unending loyalty or obedience or… bodily access? … were never real and Binding. Half the time, when they were not complaining about the things the Marriage Contract required them to do, people in the Palace and the Privy Councils complained about Traventine limits on oaths of fealty and service and subordination. Franz-Karl guessed agreements from this list were what they were complaining about. Considering who disliked them, and the mean things they said about Elderkin, he was in favor. These would be the Bindings that helped keep you from finding yourself enslaved to whatever fool got his hands on a particular ring or lamp or tinderbox or whatever… dangers that the old Elderic stories and chronicles often warned about, and some people in the Palace wanted very much.

There were five choices, beginning with the strictest, which was marked 'suitable for hermits and anchorites', and ending with a version that allowed some kinds of oaths of obedience, that was marked 'risky'.

The middle choice was marked 'generally suitable for daily life'. Franz-Karl remembered the pale, pale, angry eyes of the Margraff-Elector and hands wanting to grab him. And his brother's angry blue goats' eyes, whenever Philip-Augustus did not get his way. He thought that protections suitable for daily life in the House on the Rock might not be enough outside Traventi's Gates of Air.

The second choice was marked 'Others can advise, but your words and actions are your choice and responsibility' and its words looked a lot like the Binding his Mama had given him – except not ending at his majority – so he chose that one. His memory of the cage of lies had faded during the many days since the funeral, but for just a moment he clearly remembered the feeling as it shriveled away.

Her Grace the Reverend Duke His Grandmother looked surprised by his choice. But she smiled when she helped him melt the wax for signing and sealing the second bunch of agreements.

There were several groups of agreements that he skipped entirely because they seemed to be aimed at grownups in certain professions or crafts, or talked about the World in ways that did not make sense to him at all.

Her Grace the Reverend Duke his Grandmother was very fair about letting him make up his own mind. She explained a few things when he asked, but did not urge him toward or away from any particular agreements. She did remind him several times that he could wait to decide on some things until he was older. (Like Philip-Augustus, he thought.) And she was careful to say important things in both Allemanic and Elderic, and a few times in Remoran as well.

The final large group of rules had to do with law courts and creating contracts and witnessing agreements among groups of people: things like who counted as Parties to a contract, who counted as Witnesses, and who were just bystanders. Two of the example agreements looked very strange until Franz-Karl realized that of course the Living World knew what was happening everywhere inside itself, so you probably needed to remind it that people could not see or hear through solid walls to Witness things. Some of the others were a bit like number puzzles or riddles, or that thing about crossing a river with a wolf, a goat and a cabbage that never explained why you needed to bring the wolf.

He chose two groups of the agreements about witnesses and such – ones that seemed likely to work together – copying them carefully onto his page and signing and sealing each group. One group was mostly contracts and the other was mostly law courts and puzzles.

Before he signed that fourth section of agreements, her Grace the Reverend Duke his Grandmother asked, "Franz-Karl, are you quite sure of all of these?"

"Of course, your Grace my Grandma. Mama reads to us out of the old chronicles and the Lives of the Notaries almost every night. And I read some myself, too. The Frog General was my favorite dead relative before Papa died, so I know Witnesses and Contracts are important. Most of these rules are just... sensible. But these five agreements I'm skipping –" He pointed to them with the dry end of the pen. "These have all been trouble-makers forever, according to the chronicles, so why are they still on the list for people to choose?"

"Some people think they are important, others disagree." Her Grace his Grandmother was not laughing at him, but he could tell that she thought something was funny. Perhaps she was laughing at the people who liked those rules.

Franz-Karl frowned at the page. "If they are important, someone needs to write them better to get rid of the traps." He looked at the document he had written and tapped the first place he had used his new signet with the dry end of the pen. "I can't Bind things I don't understand, so if I don't truly understand these, something will happen in the World to stop me from signing. I have seen Mama say things four times, dealing with the Palace officials. When she is really serious and sparks come out of her braids, people trying to go contrary are like rocks trying to fall upward."

Nothing did happen to stop him from signing the final set of agreements he had chosen. Since he had signed them in groups, there were three more signatures after the first one, and four patches of green wax on the paper in all. That seemed right: it harmonized with the 'saying things four times' rule.

After Franz-Karl signed the parchment for the final time and pressed his signet into the warm wax he put the signet away inside his clothes. He was very glad it was nearly time for the mid-day meal. Making promise-bindings – choices – had left him as hungry as if he had been running around all morning, or climbing things and jumping up and down.

Her Grace the Reverend Duke his Grandmother put the signed parchment away in a locked chest for safekeeping. "You have accepted enough of the Notary bindings for your name to be added to the official list of fully sworn Notaries. We will attend to the list in a few days, at the Duchy Council meeting."

"Thank you, your Grace my Grandma." He started to turn away, then turned back to face her and asked as casually as he could manage, "Philip-Augustus has a signet. Is he a fully sworn Notary, too?"

"No, Philip-Augustus is not a full Notary. Not yet. When your Mama showed him the list, he only chose a few bindings – and not all of the first group. He still needs to grow into things a bit, but small bindings were starting to happen around him, and he has a temper, so your Mama thought it best to offer. Sometimes just knowing about the list helps people think about what they should do." She smiled and leaned toward him as if she was sharing a joke. "Saying that a grownup in the Duchy is 'just a Binder' is very rude because it suggests the person is not careful or not really safe, or taking responsibility. People with the Manifest weight to be Binders are properly styled 'Notaries' outside the Duchy if they are sworn to fair witnessing, partly because talking about Binders makes Worldfolk ... twitchy."

"I don't think there are any Binders in the Palace, or Notaries either. Not our kind of Notaries. There are lots of other lawyers and advocates in Karnburg, though."

"Your Mama is a full Notary, of course, and there are a few other free Binders in Karnburg who don't make a fuss about it, besides the few Elderkin who are Bound slaves." She looked sad, but took a deep breath and continued. "But having so few makes it a little riskier to make a new Notary there because there is no one to take precautions and provide an anchor. The official rules of the Palace do not allow your Mother to have any Binders in her Household, and very few heavily Gifted Elderkin." Her Grace his Grandmother sounded annoyed. "She only has that much because we insisted on it as part of the Marriage Contract and would not let it drop."

"Can they make me stay away from Mama because I am a Binder? Or Philip-Augustus if they decide he is one? Or Sophie-Alexa?"

He shivered, remembering the surprise announcement about his journey, and how that was tangled in the Marriage Contract.

Her Grace the Duke His Grandma put an arm around him. "They may try, if they do not read the Contract carefully and consider how the sections connect. We had some clever, careful people involved in the writing."

Franz-Karl nodded uncertainly. He hoped being a Notary would be more help than trouble. He could think of some people at the Palace who would stir up trouble even if there did not need to be any.

His Grandmother smiled. "Are there any other questions that trouble you in all this?"

He thought for a moment. Better to know how big the mess might get...

"Yes. Binders and Notaries are important, and Contracts and Witnessing. But some of the stories and chronicles talk about contracts written into the World by groups of Elderkin who are not Binders. Is that real?"

"Yes." Her Grace took a couple of deep breaths. Her free hand sketched something in the air and then made a sort of weighing gesture. "When the right ... shapes of words ... are used and there is a certain weight of Manifest heritage bearing witness, a contract or promise can become Bound and anchored into the shape of the Living World. The World does not much care whether the weight is all in one body, so long as all the people carrying it agree very, very thoroughly, and they are asking for a thing the World understands. So if a group of Elderkin agree on something and add up to enough weight, their words can bend the World. Elderkin can also add their weight to someone who doesn't have enough Manifest weight for a Binding by bearing witness to a promise."

"Oh! That's why Binders are Notaries. So they can lean on the contracts to help seal them!"

"Yes. We also very commonly know when we are lied to, so for a Notary to be willing to bear witness is not a small or meaningless thing."

Franz-Karl nodded again, making it a minor bow. It was probably part of fibbers not fitting in the World. He might need to pay attention a little differently when people spoke in front of him, if he was going to be officially Witnessing things, but the Bindings he had just acquired should help him avoid being tricked.

CHAPTER IX: A Town on the Rock

Wherein Our Hero Views the Town of the Elderkin

Later that afternoon, after she had taken care of some official matters and sent out several pigeons in different directions, her Grace the Reverend Duke his Grandmother showed Franz-Karl some of the notable public areas within the House on the Rock.

They stayed under roofs because it was still raining, but that was not a problem in the House, where everything was connected. That was why it was called a House, not a town. There were no empty gaps where you needed to run across an open space getting rained on, as long as you did not insist on taking the very shortest path. They moved from one colonnade to another on the ground level or through sequences of balconies and chambers in the upper levels and things changed with every doorway they passed, and around every corner.

The sovereign Duke and her grandson walked together with only a pair of attendants to fetch and carry, and people they met smiled and bowed, and offered greetings, and occasionally paused to share bits of gossip with their Duke, without any great formality.

The people they met addressed Franz-Karl as Childe of the Elderkin. That was a little strange: Reverend Childe of Traventi was his mother's proper title as heir to the Duke, according to the Palace Master of Protocol, but Franz-Karl had no official title in Traventi, as far as he knew. According to the Marriage Contract, Philip-Augustus was Papa's heir, but the rules for Mama's heir were different: Philip-Augustus would not inherit the Duchy automatically.

There were people in the Palace who hated that so much that they could not talk about it, even though the Kingship of the Allemans was also supposedly passed by election, not inheritance. Franz-Karl's Papa had laughed about that more than once. Of course, his Excellency was about the twelfth Falkenburg in a row to hold the Kingship, so it was hard to say what the rules really were. Grownups in the Palace talked about rules that were supposed to be ancient and permanent, and then did not follow them at all.

The House on the Rock was shaped a bit like a three-leafed clover, with the Processional Way as a stem leading out to the South past the Altar and across the Duke's Bridge over the Elde, where it turned into the Market Road.

The central area where the lobes joined together, under and around the Tower for Watching Stars, held the Ducal Court and Council Chambers, some formal reception rooms, and such governmental offices as the Elderkin bothered with: the Duchy numbered its people in tens of thousands, not hundreds of thousands, much less millions, so they did not need many people involved in governing, and many of the government people spent much of their time about their own private matters.

There was an ancient open-air theater carved into a hillside northwest of the House that could hold most of the Duchy's populace. Besides entertainments – Traventi remembered the original music of many ancient tragedies and comedies, besides newer pieces – the Stone Theater was occasionally used for other religious gatherings, and for votes of the full Council of the Duchy's People. There were some things the Council of Traventi was not supposed to do unless the people agreed by voting. The people in Traventi were almost all Elderkin, even though most of them were not heavy enough to be Binders and Notaries or bind contracts alone. But they could still Bind things in groups. If enough of them thought the Duke's Council was doing something wrong, or stupid, things could get very messy while the Living World decided who to listen to.

The northern leaf of the clover, around the Tower of the Breezes, was mostly full of the ducal household and places for lodging and entertaining official guests. But there was no real separation between areas that would be part of the citadel or palace in other cities, and those that would be part of the town, or even part of the countryside. The courtyard with the goats and the flute-player fountain was part of the Ducal residence, out at the northern edge where the structures of the House were fraying into farmland.

The eastern and western leaves of the clover included a variety of craft halls and workshops and schools and shrines, and the homes of those who worked in them and in the government offices. The House on the Rock was not quite a city – except for being the largest settlement in Traventi and having a cathedral – but it was a respectable, prosperous market town by any reckoning.

Franz-Karl remembered from his Mama's lessons that the exports of the Duchy were like the great seal. The seal was goats, grapes, and a house on a rock, so the exports were cheese, wine, and crafted things that were mostly made by the townsfolk of the House. There were a few blacksmiths and woodcarvers and potters and such elsewhere in the Duchy, but they worked more for their neighbors than for trade. The House on the Rock was a very rich market town because some of the crafted things could not be copied anywhere else, so they were very valuable outside of Traventi: they required Elderkin Gifts for the crafting, or materials that had been tuned or polished by Elderkin Gifts.

The western end of the House had a large, roundish market square with merchant shops and craft workshops around the square and in the colonnades and courtyards on all sides. On the north side of the square, a Shrine to Saint Victoria and All the Saints with a proper amber Lamp on its roof shared a clock tower with a Guildshall even taller and wider than the church. There was a Lamp on the clock tower as large as the one on the Shrine, but enclosed in blue glass instead of holy amber.

The market's fountain held a brilliantly colored statue of winged Victory on her chariot holding a green laurel wreath. Her horses were four different colors, and her wings were rainbow-colored. Her hair and robe were gilded.

At the opposite end of the House on the Rock was the Great Shrine of Saints Clement and Sophia, the Duchy's cathedral. The amber

Lamp on its bell tower was the first bit of the house on the Rock to be touched by the Sun's rays each morning.

The cathedral grounds opened onto a second market square, which was actually almost square: at least it had four corners. The Cathedral Square also had three separate fountains with brightly colored statuary depicting legendary battles of human warriors with inhuman beings. It was not entirely clear who was winning the battles, or who you were supposed to root for in the encounters, but that may have been because the rain was playing tricks on Franz-Karl's eyes. Some of the human warriors may not have been entirely human, either, not even for loose Elderkin values of human.

Franz-Karl thought the cathedral in the House on the Rock was impressive, even though he had grown up in Karnburg Palace and had been inside Karnburg cathedral. It was tall, below the bell tower, and long from east to west, with several Holy Shrines clustered along the south side like nursing kittens. The north side of the main cathedral was snug against a lump of the mountainside, so people could walk into the choir loft without climbing stairs.

The people decorating inside of the basilica of Saints Clement and Sophia had not stopped until there was no longer any place to put more twining and spiraling patterns, and the materials they used made the Karnburg builders look stingy. The May Day wreaths and garlands hanging everywhere just added to the richness.

There were stained glass windows, and frescoes on some of the walls and the ceilings of Traventi's cathedral, just as in Karnburg, but the ornamentation that framed them was far more vine-y than geometric. There were heads and tails and feet of animals that showed in places among the interlaced spiral motifs, but if the interlaced patterns were animals, they had extremely strange bodies and a peculiar lack of straight bones.

There was a large triptych in stained glass at the back of the sanctuary beyond the incense altar: the Transubstantiation flanked by the Nativity and the Bargain. Franz-Karl could only peek at it though the gilded, filigree gate in the chancel screen that kept out non-Initiates, but he looked at it for a long time before he finally asked, quietly because they were in a church, "Your Grace my Grandmother, is there a reason the colors are only wrong on one side?"

She smiled and led him out into a colonnade around an herb garden that was probably an actual cloister before asking, "Which side had colors that looked wrong to you, Childe?"

"The Bargain."

His grandmother's eyes widened. "Indeed? And can you tell me when the colors of the World changed around you, to bring it to the colors you now see?"

"No, Your Grace, the colors of the World don't change!" He stopped walking, looked up at her and added less certainly, "Do they?"

"Dear Heaven." She pinched the broad top of her nose between her eyebrows, took a long breath and let it out slowly.

"Is it... is it ... bad?" Franz-Karl's voice came out as little more than a whisper. In the Palace, things that were different or unexpected were usually bad, especially when there were Elderkin involved.

Her Grace turned quickly, knelt beside him and hugged him as hard as she had when he first arrived, leaning her forehead against his. "Ah, no, dear child. It is nothing bad at all! I promise you four times it is not! It is just a surprising thing. Some people who carry Gifts from our Manifest ancestors see colors differently than Worldfolk or people who carry different Gifts, and the artists made a joke about the different colors when they created the windows. But most people don't see the extra colors until their Gifts come in, and you are very young for that."

"Oh." He looked away, then back at her. "Do the colors I see tell you which Gifts I will have?"

"No. The First Speakers and Dukes of Traventi have been marrying heavy Elderkin who arrived here – wherever they came from, and whatever their Gifts might be – since before the city of Remora was two thatched huts on the riverbank. Our heritage is so mixed up that there is no telling what will pop out of the stew when things get stirred up in a new generation."

Franz-Karl giggled. "Might be an apple, might be an onion?" he suggested.

"Precisely." Her Grace His Grandmother agreed.

There were proverbs about apples and onions being different, but Franz-Karl privately thought they went together very well when they were both cooked with pork.

INTERLUDE III: News of Arrival

An Account of a Private Discussion

How can an imperial cavalcade be lost to view?" The Preacher was wringing his hands and pacing, not standing peacefully at his lectern in the Inner Hall of the Pristinists. It was fortunate that there were only a few witnesses to his distress and lack of confidence. The Select among the Pristinists were supposed to have no need for anything but serene confidence.

It was early on a morning nearly three weeks after the death of Prince Leon-Alexander, and only a few men of the Pristinist faction were gathered in the Inner Hall. Besides the Preacher, the room held only the Margraff-Elector of Ansbach, the Prince-Elector of Bremerhaven, and the General of the Army of the Empire. Even the Teacher was elsewhere. They were attended only by a handful of their most trusted subordinates, none of them secretaries or scribes. Even without the Preacher's fretting, this discussion was not for the ears of outsiders, or even for the lesser-born who gathered in the White Hall.

"There are plenty of proverbs about the folly of chasing Elderkin." The General was looking at the lectern, not at the Preacher. "Either the changeling brat is gone for good – and the court is well rid of him – or he will turn up again." He sighed. "No doubt to our sorrow."

The General had eaten at Leon-Alexander's table a few times, and carried worrying memories of the three beast-born children in the Prince's household.

"The brat carries his fate with him." The Margraff-Elector of Ansbach was seated quietly in the First Chair. He spoke calmly, but one of his hands gripped the chair's arm tightly enough to whiten his knuckles. "Once all three brats are properly silenced, bridled and broken to service, they will be our foes' sorrow. Not ours."

"And until then the demon-born wretch is left rampaging around the countryside at will!" The Preacher caught himself, took a couple of deep breaths, and walked over to stand – too close – facing the General. "Shouldn't you at least have people looking for them?"

The General did not step back. "We of the Confraternity know that the brats are a delusion, but His Excellency still counts them as kin. Setting soldiers to search for the Archduke's kin within the borders of the Eastlands, unasked? That would lead to official questions. Most likely rather pointed ones." He tapped the hilt of one of the blades he wore.

"You lack men you trust?" The Prince-Elector of Bremerhaven, in the Second Chair, was relaxed and seemed amused.

The General turned to face him. "Honest soldiers can't travel the roads without being noticed and gossiped about, even if we had them. But the Army of the Empire has no full companies of Pristinists this far south! More than half of our men and officers are Harfnerans or Ecclesialists, or worse. And even the mixed companies are well outnumbered in the camps near Karnburg: most local garrisons and nearly all of the quartermasters are Imperial Army or Archducal Forces, not part of Army of the Empire. Unexpected troop movements will not go unnoticed or unquestioned."

The Margraff-Elector flicked a hand. "Yes. Yes. And even without military... complications, we don't want our own interest in the brats to lead others at court to suspect their value."

"Or to wonder what we plan." The Prince-Elector looked straight at his colleague. "It is less than a month since Leon-Alexander's funeral, and half the gossip in the city still blames Your Serene Highness – not the beast-born – for that mess in the cathedral."

The Margraff-Elector was already sitting stiffly erect in the hard wooden chair: he could not straighten any farther, though he tried. "The common dregs of this city are beneath our notice."

"Is that why Your Serene Highness has 'God-Robber' and two signs against the evil eye chalked on your gate at the moment?" The General's tone was casual, and he did not look toward his superior as he spoke.. which was an offense in itself.

Before the Margraff-Elector replied, there was a soft tap on the wall panel that hid the servants' entrance to the Inner Hall. After a pause, there was a second, softer tap.

The lowest ranked of the subordinates in attendance rose to his feet, strode to the panel and opened it, to revel a kneeling slave holding out a folded paper sealed with wax. The attendant examined the seals carefully, then used a penknife to scrape the wax off the paper, making sure that it fell outside the Hall before the panel was closed.

The attendant rejoined the cluster of principles in the center of the room and knelt before the Margraff-Elector. "A message from the Arch-Hierophant at the cathedral."

"Read it," the Margraff-Elector snapped.

The attendant unfolded the paper, holding it by the edges. "It says: 'The Dowager Countess of Wolfsberg has paid for thank offerings of fire and music for the safe arrival of her younger son at the border of Traventi.'"

The General, personally, opened the main door – the one that led to the White Hall – and gave some quiet orders to one of the men waiting there. "They made good time, given the season," he said as he returned to the center of the room.

"No rider brought that news," the Prince-Elector said.

"Traventi has the best pigeons on the continent. They can't be caught and retrained, and if you breed from them, the newly-fledged young fly back to the witch-realm at their first chance."

"No matter," the Margraff-Elector said calmly. "Once the brats are ours, and the dam and grand-dam culled, the rest of the witch-realm will serve our convenience soon enough. From the landholders down to the pigeons." He shifted slightly in the hard chair. "In the mean time, we have little cause for concern because one small creature has passed a border into a monstrous wilderness."

The other men in the Room waited in proper silence as the Preacher walked over to the Fourth Chair, with its pile of documents, and searched for one specific text. Before he found it, there was a tap at the main door.

The General received a paper from one of his men, and held it out at arm's length to read it: highborn Pristinists naturally had no need for spectacles. "Word from the Palace. It seems that contrary to the assurances of the Landgraff of the Upper Raenos, the northern approach to the Traventine border is not impassable." The Prince-Elector made an annoyed sound, deep in his throat. The General continued, "The party transporting Leon-Alexander's brat crossed the bridge at Traventi Crossing late yesterday. There has been no time for any more detailed news to reach Karnburg."

CHAPTER X: Family Breakfast

Wherein Our Hero Meets Far Too Many Relatives

The next morning Franz-Karl awakened early again. His dreams had been strange, but it was not only that. The windows were propped open, since the rain had finally faded, and there was a humming in the air, fading slowly. The sound strengthened again, and he realized that being midway between Saint Victoria's clock and Saints Clement and Sophia's bells, he could hear both.

He was sorry to be missing the morning rites, but May Morning was one of the times color-of-sorrow was not allowed, and it was too soon after the funeral for him to wear other colors. Her Grace the Reverend Duke his Grandmother had said there would be a moderately formal family breakfast later this morning where he could properly wear mourning clothes. He listened to the bells and distant echoes of pipes and singing, and decided he was no longer sleepy. The orange cat moved into the center of the warm spot in the bed as he left it.

It took longer to find the right clothes to wear because everything had been unpacked and rearranged by the attendant, Amalia – her position was Tirewoman, but he was still not sure of her rank or who she answered to – who was sleeping soundly in the curtained alcove at the bedroom end of the room. She had returned from the May Eve rites long after midnight.

He eventually got himself dressed without waking her. He had gotten used to dressing himself at home instead of waiting to be dressed because Nurse Rosa was usually busy with Sophie-Alexa – who was still just little – and Philip-Augustus – who was a fussy peacock – and his Mama's household had fewer attendants than it needed, or the household of an Imperial Prince would be expected to have. The plainness of mourning clothes made dressing himself even easier than it would have been... before... though his hair was as uncooperative as usual. He tied it back with a strip of color-of sorrow ribbon and did not struggle with it.

He did not go wandering far, because of the warning about the moderately formal family breakfast. In the Palace that would mean only two trumpeters being noisily out of tune at people with aching heads, and only four tables of courtiers besides the high table. He did not think the House on the Rock leaned toward trumpeters at breakfast (though his Papa had sometimes teased his Mama about bagpipes. He swallowed hard, remembering Papa would not tease her any more). But it would not do to be late to a meal that was any kind of formal at all. People would say rude things about his Mama.

After greeting his Papa and the rest of the Household Shrine, Franz-Karl found his way to the library by the goats' dairy, which had a chair with stuffed cushions and an illuminated and illustrated copy of the Lives of the Notaries. It included some stories that were not in his Mama's copy, which was a fun surprise. Some things people did in the stories made more sense now that he knew the list of Notary bindings and what some of the rules were, but the new stories talked about Gifts more than Bindings, which tangled up in his head with the colors in the cathedral windows. All of the colors in the illustrations seemed to be the right ones for his eyes, though the illuminated letters, and the people and animals in the margins, used whatever colors the painters thought were pretty, or maybe whatever ink was handy.

He arrived at the dining room door at precisely the moment that was appointed for breakfast, just as he had the day before. Her Grace the Reverend Duke his Grandmother saw him enter the anteroom, and looked amused.

His attendant the Tirewoman Amalia was not amused at all. She was standing facing her Grace the Reverend Duke his Grandmother with her back to the door, and waving her hands and speaking very quickly and much more loudly than the Palace would think appropriate for a servant addressing a Duke. Or an attendant, either. Amalia finished "... and now he is lost!" just as Franz-Karl walked up behind her and said "Blessed morning" politely. Amalia jumped and gasped and whirled to face him. "You!"

Franz-Karl bowed slightly and said carefully in Elderic, "There is 'lost' when you yourself do not know where you are, and 'lost' when other people cannot find you because you are not in an expected place where you were not even told to be. I believe my timely arrival shows that I had not lost myself."

'Timely arrival' was a phrase in one of the stories he had been reading, and he was quite proud of it. He turn to Her Grace, made a bow to a senior family member, and continued, "Is it even possible to lose oneself in this House provided there is neither heavy fog nor snow filling the air? As long as the mountains and towers are visible, how can one be lost?"

Franz-Karl had spent his whole life in a place where more than half of the servants were his mother's enemies. He did not wish to make an enemy of Amalia, but he also had no wish to begin his visit in Traventi by being bullied when he had done nothing wrong.

Amalia sputtered. "Even so..."

The Duke did not quite laugh, but her lips twitched and she gave a little cough. She said firmly, "As the Honorable Notary rightly pointed out –" Amalia flinched at the word Notary and moved back half a step. "His Honor's arrival was timely, and we are now delaying the others at their meal. I will speak with you later, Amalia."

She turned and led Franz-Karl into a larger dining room than the two of them had used the previous day. It was surprisingly full given that his Mama had neither brothers nor sisters – some people in the Palace thought that lack was important enough to mention it a lot. It turned out that Her Grace the Reverend Duke had a living sister, Countess Cecilia, who had two daughters, who each had children, some older than Franz-Karl, some younger. There were some more distant kinfolk present as well.

The Imperial Palace authorities ignored all these relatives because they were kin to the Duke through the female line, even though the Duke was female herself, and so was her Heir. Highborn Allemanic rules about patriarchal lineage and inheritance and primogeniture were a little excessive even compared to the rules of the classical Remorans, which were already extensive. They would have been annoyed by the Duke's relatives even if they had noticed them. The Master of Protocol would have had three fits.

Both of the boy cousins were children of Cecilia's younger daughter. There were also two husbands at the table, but Franz-Karl was not sure which of the ladies they belonged to: he thought, perhaps, Cecilia and one of her daughters, but no one was mentioning family or lineage names or titles or styles or anything, so it was all a bit confusing.

The Priest and Priestess of the Shrine of Saint Victoria were also at the meal, with the Priestess's little boy. The Priest and Priestess, Lucian and Lucia, were twins, and they were children of Franz-Karl's Mama's father's sister, who lived somewhere in Traventi's North Valley, so they were also cousins of a sort. Lucia's little boy, Apollon, was about the same age as Franz-Karl's sister Sophie-Alexa, and a little older than the youngest of the other cousins.

In all, counting Franz-Karl and Apollon, there were eleven or twelve children in the room, depending on whether the oldest cousin counted as a grownup. The room did not need trumpets to be noisy enough to make some of the grownups wince, including the Tirewoman Amalia, but Franz-Karl thought that it was a comfortable sort of noise. The room was small enough and softened by draperies enough that cheerfully raised voices did not echo. Much.

The grownups were kind to Franz-Karl and the children were friendly and interested to meet a new relative. They spoke quickly and sometimes several at the same time. Franz-Karl was able to follow most of what was said in Elderic – except for some grownup things he probably was not expected to understand.

But his own slow, careful responses made gaps in the conversation. They also got him giggled at by the smaller children, but mostly not in a mean way. Nevertheless, his cousin Morgan, the oldest one at the table who was not a grownup, told the others they were being rude and should apologize. That caused wide eyes and stammering:

apologies were almost trickier than saying 'thank you' for Elderkin, and being told you were rude to a guest was a shameful thing, even for a child.

Franz-Karl said, honestly, that he had not minded. He did not add that they had not been nearly as annoying as his brother in a bossy mood.

His cousin Helena, who seemed about Philip-Augustus's age, had not giggled. She leaned toward Franz-Karl after the others apologized and said very quietly, "I think the way you talk is very pretty. You sound like someone in a story." She told him what was in some of the dishes he did not recognize and asked about the foods that were served at the Palace.

After breakfast Apollon and the other child smaller than Franz-Karl were taken away by their parents. Morgan and Helena invited him to join the older cousins and some other children in a game in one of the courtyards, since the rain had stopped, though the skies were still clouded. Morgan said that merely threatened rain was no reason to stay indoors in Traventi, or no one would ever go out. The cousins said that one of their usual playmates had gone away to visit relatives in the countryside for the festival, which was at least partly a true thing and a great kindness that Franz-Karl saw no need to question.

Franz-Karl wondered whether he should change his coat to a more sturdy one, but Her Grace told him to go and play: his plain mourning clothes lacked lace or other embellishments that might be damaged during the game. He had put his hat back on after eating.

Before the game began, Morgan explained the rules to Franz-Karl. Twice.

Franz-Karl sighed. He would prefer not to be thought of as a lack-wit. He asked, "Do you know any Remoran?" which was slightly insulting since any educated person in this whole quarter of the globe knew some Remoran. Then he repeated the rules Morgan had listed, but in Remoran.

He wondered whether Morgan would be angry – Philip-Augustus would have been, and he was several years younger than Morgan – but his cousin laughed, and answered carefully, "Yes, truly, I have some Remoran, but less than yourself has of either Remoran or Elderic, it seems. I should not wish to try much extempore translation outside the borders of my lesson books." He switched back to Elderic and added, "And none of us has any Allemanic at all, so you are well ahead of us all, there."

There were nods of agreement all through the group. Morgan's younger brother, Dion, glanced toward the grownups, looked away, and asked in a low voice, "Do you know any bad words in Allemanic, Franz-Karl?"

This he could manage in Elderic, but he knew there were probably grownups listening. There were always grownups listening in the Palace even if you did not always see them. Franz-Karl put on a very bland tone and expression, and nodded, but said in Elderic, "How could I possibly learn such things? Grownups are not supposed to speak so in the presence of highborn children." But he nodded 'yes'.

That led to answering nods, and grins and snickers, and the game began in a friendly mood.

Running around with balls and sticks and no need to think about more than his aim and the rules was a surprisingly restful thing after too much time spent thinking about grownup matters. He was too small and too unpracticed to be very good at the games, but no one got angry or made fun of him for that. They explained things and showed him some of the special tricks and tactics that made it easier to win, or at least harder to lose.

CHAPTER XI: Messy Lessons

Wherein Our Hero Confronts the Trivia

After the midday meal, there were more ceremonies where the color-of-sorrow was not allowed, and Franz-Karl was ready to be quiet for a while and away from strangers, so he returned to his room. He unpacked the pile of lesson papers that he had been given by Philip-Augustus' tutor, Meister van Diesen, with so much fuss. Amalia had buried that pack under a pile of emptied ones, so it took him a while to find the papers. There were not enough cushions for him to sit high enough in the chair at the worktable, so as he unwrapped the package he set the pile on his bed. At least he could reach that.

And in Traventi he could take off his shoes so as not to muss the bedcover when he climbed onto it to look at them. That felt scary, even though he had seen Elderkin walking barefoot out in public and he was still wearing his stockings. His head knew there was no reason not to take off his shoes in Traventi, but the pit of his stomach did not quite agree.

He settled on the bed, and sighed, and, since no one was there to see, let his shoulders droop. There were such a lot of papers, and in all honesty, the writing of the Meister was scratchy and full of contractions and abbreviations and nearly impossible to read. And half the ink used had been weak, besides. He remembered poor Meister van Diesen losing sleep to write out the lessons for him, and felt a little guilty at his own grumpiness.

That did not make the handwriting any better or the ink any darker. Or the papers any fewer. There were streaks of the nameless colors on some of the pages, not spills or spatters but nothing that looked like patterns he recognized.

The pages were not even marked or arranged in any kind of sequence, they were just all jumbled together. That was not the fault of anyone in Traventi, since Franz-Karl had unsealed the package himself, but he was sure the people in the Palace who ordered the lessons would not agree.

The people who had arranged for the lessons had not sent a tutor with him because they said he was two years too young to have or need a tutor, by the usual Allemanic reckoning. But some how he was old enough to be given lessons. How did they expect him to do the lessons they set for him when he did not have a tutor?

Franz-Karl knew the answer to that question, without needing a tutor to tell him.

The people who had insisted that he should bring these papers all the way from Karnburg expected that he would forget about them, or be unable to finish the tasks. And then, when he returned to Karnburg with the lessons lost or not done – even though he was too small for them – people would stand around in the Palace and say mean things about him, and vile things about his Mama, and rude things to Philip-Augustus. People would talk about what a savage, uncivilized place Traventi was, even though it was famous for its Archive that General Rano once said was already old when Remora was two huts on a riverbank and the she-wolf was a pup. (The Remorans did not like that, but they had just lost a battle.)

Franz-Karl stirred that pile of messy papers with one hand, scattering the top of the pile, then stopped. He pulled a paper out of the middle of the mess that looked very familiar.

Franz-Karl had never had a tutor, but he had shared a room for the better part of a year with a beginning student who did have a tutor. Philip-Augustus had complained more than once that the three initial branches of learning – the Trivia – should not be called Grammar, Logic, and Rhetoric, but repetition, recitation and memorization instead. Franz-Karl had seen plenty of his brother's papers spread about in their room, and listened to many hours of repetitions and recitations of his brother's lessons. The paper he had found demanded conjugation, from memory, of Meister van Diesen's three most favorite irregular Remoran verbs.

Franz-Karl began to sort the large pile of papers into four smaller piles. One pile for the papers that were least legible and comprehensible – it was smaller than he had feared, but some of the pages were truly awful. One pile for papers that were clearly, or very likely, grammar lessons. One pile for lessons in the terms and procedures used in logic and formal proofs. And there was a small pile for rhetoric that consisted of a few famous speeches to be memorized.

There was also a long list of passages in books to be looked up and memorized to prepare for proper training in rhetoric, so that added to the rhetoric pile. Franz-Karl was sure the list had been created partly in the hope that some or all of the books on the list would not be available in Traventi. Some of the required texts were only available as fragments in the Allemanic territories, or as copies that famous Scholars argued about. He hoped the Traventine Archivists had better examples that would let him make ... kind ... updates to the list, and generously offer to arrange for the Allemanic Scholars to send people to Traventi to write out copies of the better versions.

Franz-Karl decided that his next task needed to be making clean, legible copies of the lesson papers that were comprehensible before he began to write his answers. He quickly counted the sheets of paper and guessed at the amount of ink that he would need to make the copies, and wrote a note in Elderic for the House staff. Then he went back to the library to read more of the Lives of the Notaries. He took the reading list with him, in case the household library might contain some of the volumes he needed.

Reading and memorizing was not a task that worried him. Not at all.

CHAPTER XII: The Council of Traventi

Wherein Our Hero Meets a Sphinx and Is Introduced to a Council Session

After the evening meal, Her Grace his Grandmother introduced Franz-Karl to a new Tirewoman who would look after his room and his things, and answer to him, now that he was a full Notary. Olivia seemed older than Amalia – which did not mean much when Elderkin were involved – and was much less taut and fretful. Before he went to sleep, he gave her the note about the paper and ink for his lessons, and she showed him a safe place to keep his Allemanic and Remoran lessons and papers and the books he would use, and a shelf for the few toys that had traveled with him all the way from the Palace. Olivia put a large earthenware turtle that must have been heated by the fire into his bed while he was saying his evening prayers, so that that the sheets were cozy and warm and dry when he got in, not damp from the humid evening air. The orange cat settled herself partly on Franz-Karl and partly on the lump in the blankets that covered the turtle.

Olivia also set out some clean clothes for the next day. It was a little hard to tell, with everything being plain and color-of-sorrow, but he thought the clothes she selected for him were more formal than anything he had worn for the past few days: even more formal than the family breakfast clothes. The coat was nearly as stiff as the one he had worn to his father's funeral supper – but less hastily made – and he thought there was silk in the dull cloth of the waistcoat. Franz-Karl wondered what a formal breakfast that was not all family would turn out to be like. He hoped there would still not be trumpeters. Or bagpipes, either.

When the bells awakened Franz-Karl, he found that the Sun was shining brightly for the first time since he had crossed the Raenos into the lands of Traventi. There were little drops of water that had not dried yet all over everything, sparkling in the sunlight, and when he slid out from under the cat and looked out the window, he thought he could see part of a rainbow over in the west behind the one of the lower towers. He dressed hastily and washed and said his prayers – Olivia appeared in her dressing-gown with her hair mostly down, to pour the water for him – and hurried out to get a better look at the rainbow before it faded.

He walked through the middles of three of the garden courtyards trying to keep the rainbow in sight, careful to stay on the paved paths and avoid puddles because he was wearing house shoes and good clothes. The rainbow was extremely impressive once there was no tower sticking up in front of it: it was a double one and very bright and clear in the mountain air.

Walking farther toward the northwest edge of the House, nearly as far as the Stone Theater, Franz-Karl arrived at a large enclosure full of trees. When he went through its gate he discovered that it was an orchard: he could see the tiny baby fruits growing on the lowest branches. There was a line of beehives along the far wall of the orchard, toward the mountain, and flowering plants and bushes had been planted among the trees to keep the bees busy now that most of the trees carried their tiny fruits instead of blossoms.

He followed the paved path around the corner of the L-shaped orchard and saw a living, breathing person walking toward him on the path that looked like she might be a Winged Sphinx. Woman's head? Yes. Except for the golden cats' eyes, which were just properly Elderkin. Eagle wings? Yes. Lion's body? Well... she was very much a cat, but tawny gold colored with small inky rosettes, so apparently this was a leopard sphinx instead of a lion sphinx. (Franz-Karl knew the difference: the Imperial Menagerie included a pair of lions and an elderly and somewhat decrepit leopard. There was even a sad, restless cheetah, which had spots that were entirely different than the leopard's rosettes. Many artists got that wrong.)

The Sphinx wore her hair up, in a complicated pattern of braids, and the person who did the braiding had made interesting patterns with the black streaks in her tawny hair. The braids were held in place by sparkling hairpins and she was also wearing earrings and necklaces, including a signet ring on a ribbon.

Franz-Karl made a deep bow and said in his best Elderic, "Blessed morning, Blessed One. I hope you are well today." And then he asked her a famous riddle whose answer was 'an orchard'.

She said the answer properly, with a rhyming couplet and a tag, then continued, "I am not one of the Blessed, Dear Childe. In this time and place I am properly styled Reverend Count, but you may call me 'Great Aunt Adrasteia'." Then she asked him a famous riddle whose answer was 'Bees'.

Franz-Karl said the answering couplet and tag before he bowed and said, "Thank you, Great Aunt Adrasteia. I am not sure how I am properly styled in this time and place, but you may call me Franz-Karl."

"I am glad to meet you at last, Franz-Karl. Come, walk beside me to Her Grace Duke Adriana's dining table." She settled her wings a little more tightly to her sides so there would be room for them both on the paved path.

The World went a bit strange when Franz-Karl was close to Reverend Count Great Aunt Adrasteia. Even though she stepped as lightly as any other cat, he kept expecting to see deep footprints on the path, as if she was walking in freshly fallen snow. The strangeness got worse when they arrived at the dining room and her Grace the Reverend Duke his Grandmother and Great Aunt Adrasteia hugged each other. He started gasping a little, as if the air in the room was no longer doing its job.

The strangeness eased when the two ladies stepped apart, but increased again when they sat on either side of him at the table. Her Grace the Reverend Duke his Grandmother said, "Hmm" and moved to the other side of the wide table so that she was facing Franz-Karl and Reverend Count Great Aunt Adrasteia instead of sitting beside them. She told Franz-Karl to move to the chair she had used at first, so there was more space between him and Reverend Count Great Aunt Adrasteia. Breathing became easier.

When they were walking from the orchard Franz-Karl had wondered how the Sphinx would manage at the breakfast table, but that was not the sort of thing you could ask about politely unless you were the host. It turned out that Great Aunt Adrasteia used a dining couch in the antique style instead of a chair. When the food was served her hands? front paws? were shaped like eagle's talons, even though they had definitely been cat's paws when they were walking through the gardens together. Most of the cooked food that was not soup was served on skewers, with sauces that were sticky rather than drippy.

The breakfast was very nice, but most of the conversation was gossip about people Franz-Karl did not know. Quite a lot of the rest was a discussion of what the spring floods had done to the Duchy's roads and fields. Reverend Count Great Aunt Adrasteia described this year's floods as "emphatic, but not out of the ordinary". After traveling for days and days and days on rutted, partly-washed-out roads all the way from Karnburg, Franz-Karl hoped he never had to deal with a flood the Sphinx considered out of the ordinary.

When they were walking from the dining room to the room in the Tower for Looking at Stars that was used for council meetings, Reverend Count Great Aunt Adrasteia had cat's paws again. The Sphinx stepped out into one of the courtyards briefly and gave her wings a good flap, then folded them neatly. Franz-Karl was not at all sure that her flight feathers had been the same length when she was flapping as they had been at the breakfast table or after she folded her wings. Her body seemed bulkier, too, for a moment, and then more slender, as if the strength for flapping was put away when it was not needed. She had said that she was not one of the Manifest – who some stories described as only material by courtesy – but he very much wondered what she was. There did not seem to be much material in the mix.

The Speakers' Chamber – the room used for Duchy Council meetings – was on the second level above the ground in the Tower for Looking at the Stars, up a flight of fancy stairs from the Tax Office's door. There was a rule about not storing books or documents at ground level.

Reverend Count Great Aunt Adrasteia showed Franz-Karl around the council chambers while Her Grace His Grandmother discussed things with the people arranging the room for the Council meeting. The Speakers' Chamber took up most of that level in the

Tower, but there were small rooms along one side for private matters, and storage, and places for servants and attendants to wait who were not allowed into the council chamber during the meetings. The recent archives and records of the council's past business were kept in the next two levels upward, and when the Duke and her companions arrived at the chamber door, several people were still carrying piles of books and papers down into the Speakers' Chamber in case they were needed during the meeting.

The fancier of the two waiting rooms was also used for people from outside the tower who wanted to bear witness about something in person, or present complaints or petitions. That room was only used on the first day of a council session if there was an imminent threat of war or something equally urgent.

The plainer waiting room had chairs and tables and a few eating couches, and a table loaded with drinks and aogreamana, and another larger table with a complicated game called Dragons' Teeth – a bit like dominoes crossed with divination cards – that Reverend Count Great Aunt Adrasteia said had been running since before Franz-Karl's Mama was born, and was sometimes used by the council for quick auguries about the state of the world.

In the center of the Speakers' Chamber there were three fancy tables arranged in a U, with a fancy dining couch and twelve matching fancy chairs – with seat cushions and arms and high backs – arranged around the outside of the U. There were three more dining couches pushed against the back wall out of the way, with two more of the fancy chairs. There were some plainer chairs along the sides of the room. At the front of the room between the door and the open side of the U there were four small tables with piles of papers and scrolls and codices on them, and men and women in advocates' robes and stoles and silly squashed hats fussing at them. There was also a table with inkwells and paper and chairs set up for scribes and secretaries to write down what was said, for the archives.

Two of the small tables had two advocates each. One had two advocates and a young assistant wearing plainer robes and no stole (but she still had the silly hat). The fourth table had two advocates, a stole-less young man, a boy wearing even plainer robes and a plain cap who would have been eleven or twelve if he was Karnburger Worldfolk, and a huge pile of documents including one scroll that insisted on falling on the floor no matter where they tried putting it. The boy finally picked it up and stuck it into one of the wide sleeves of his robe.

Reverend Count Great Aunt Adrasteia stretched out on the dining couch. Her Grace the Reverend Duke sat in the chair opposite the opening of the U, with a small bell and a sheathed dagger on the table in front of her. Other people began to come into the room and sit down around the table. When the councilors were all seated, there were seven men and six women (counting Great Aunt Adrasteia as one of the women) sitting around the main table, and other women at the lesser tables.

In Karnburg there would have been no women permitted in the room at all: Franz-Karl was glad to see that Traventi was more polite and less wasteful. At meetings of the Privy Councils in the Imperial Palace where women were not allowed even as witnesses or spectators, his Mama used to send his Papa to get official attention for Traventine concerns. Now those problems would probably be piled on top of everything else Acting Archduke Uncle Helm-Friedrich had to worry about. Franz-Karl's vision went blurry for a moment, but tears did not quite start to drip down his face.

Franz-Karl was given one of the chairs along the sides of the room to sit in, next to a little writing table that was too high for Franz-Karl to use even if he wanted to write something. The advocates' boy came over and gave him a thick cushion to sit on, then sat in the chair next to his, sharing the little table. The other advocates also sat in chairs at the sides of the room, and the scribes were taking their places at the writing table.

"I'm Willy," the boy said very softly

"Franz-Karl." With a slight, neutral bow.

The Chamber's double doors were closed and the Great Seal was pressed into a splodge of wax where they joined. The air in the room thumped strangely even though two of the windows were open. Franz-Karl could feel attention being paid from elsewhere.

The Duke rang the bell and the scribe sitting in the center took the roll of the names and purposes of the people present, so they could be recorded properly for the Archives.

They began with Adriana, Notary and Duke of the Elderkin of Traventi and First Speaker of the Council, followed by Adrasteia, Notary and Count of the South Valley. Franz-Karl was surprised that the Notary part seemed more important than Noble rank, but remembered that Notary meant Binder and warned that a person was mighty in the World, and likely dangerous. There were two male Count-and-Notaries in the Council, but one had sent a different Notary, also male, as his proxy.

The Chief Justice of Traventi was both a Notary, which made sense, and a woman, which would have been a terrible scandal in the Karnburg justice courts. Franz-Karl was not sure which people in Karnburg would be cranky about the female Hierophant of the Cathedral being a Notary when the male Hierophant was not, but he was sure it would be a problem.

All of the Council Notaries had features like metallic eyes or elaborate horns or feathers that would get them mobbed if they tried to walk down any street in Karnburg.

The rest of the Councilors were not Notaries. The Archivist of the famous Archive and the Praetor of the Borderers and three tribunes elected to speak for the populace – one was a woman – were less fancy looking than the Notaries. But Franz-Karl was a little surprised that the Guildsmaster of Traventi, another woman, was not announced as one of the Notaries. She looked like a rosy, little, wrinkled apple-doll with wispy white hair, but had smallish goat horns, and her eyes were an inhuman shade of brilliant leaf green that clearly showed the horizontal pupils of goats' eyes. If he had met her in Karnburg, Franz-Karl would have thought she must be very old.

After he finished listing the councilors, the secretary recorded the other people in the council chamber. He was Hieronymus, and neither he nor his assistants seemed to be Notaries or Binders. Most of the others in the room were Notaries: the eight people with stoles said they were Advocates and Notaries, and named the places they resided, and their two companions were Observers and Notaries.

Willy was a Wilfried, not a Wilhelm, and was also an Observer, but not a Notary, it seemed. Franz-Karl was marked down as Falx Franciscocarolus, Observer. Hieronymus the secretary bowed to him gravely and two of the councilors on his side of the U, Tribune Ursula and Aurelian the Praefect, turned in their chairs to look at him and nod politely.

The secretary consulted a list on a wax tablet. "There are two new full Notaries to be added to the List today." He took out a parchment with a purple wax seal on it and handed it to the

Guildsmaster, who was sitting at one end of the U. She read it and passed it on. When it had traveled all of the way around the tables to the Praetor, and all of the Councilors had looked at it, the secretary placed it on the table with the huge pile of documents, where Willy had been working earlier. It took three tries before it would stay where it was put.

Duke Adriana rang the bell and said "It is claimed that Wilfried of the line of Rothfel is a Notary and fully sworn according to law and custom. Does anyone challenge?" and waited. She repeated that a second and a third time. After the third wait, she rang the bell, and said, "I say a fourth time that the Honorable Wilfried is a full Notary, and so he is, and so he will be, and he shall be added to the List of Sworn Notaries of Traventi."

Franz-Karl felt shivery when the secretary took out his parchment with the four green wax seals. He was suddenly certain that one of the Councilors would reject him as too little or too foreign or too... something. But nothing special happened as the parchment went around except that Count Severin turned and bowed slightly to Franz-Karl after examining his parchment: the Count's tall, elaborate horns made even a small nod very impressive. He thought that Chief Justice Laurentina might be happy or amused by the promises he had chosen: she tapped two of them with a fingertip.

Franz-Karl let out his breath with a quiet whoosh when her Grace the Reverend Duke his Grandmother announced that the Honorable Falx Franciscocarolus was a full Notary and should be added to the List.

The two lesser scribes brought documents for Willy and Franz-Karl to read and sign and seal, using their own signets with very pale yellow wax. The documents were contracts with the Council that promised that as Observers they would not talk about council matters that were declared secret except with others who were present and already knew about them. There were specific exceptions spelled out, including if you decided after you had heard something that it should not be kept secret after all. You were supposed to notify the members of the council before you talked about it with anyone else, but even Franz-Karl could see the loop-holes in that. For one thing, it did not specify how long before talking you needed to notify the Council. Or how to do the notification: nailing a notice to the council chamber door would probably work, even if all of the councilors were at the other end of Traventi. Or the other end of the Mothersea.

Once the actual Council meeting started, Franz-Karl was fascinated. He had always loved the old stories and chronicles, as much or more for all of the rules and categories and how all the pieces fit together to make things work than for the battles and wonders. The Council's work was beautifully complicated, like the guts of a city clock that had faces and hands on all four sides, and planets and constellations and dancing puppets as well. (He had been very impressed by the Guildshall clock at Saint Victoria's square.)

Traventi was very small in both extent and population, but it was nearer three thousand years old than two thousand. While it had paid tribute to Remora for a few centuries for the privilege of being left alone, its traditions had never been disrupted by a conquest, or a serious invasion... or a bad fire or flood in the Archives, either. There had been a long time for things to be added to their procedures for governing, and there was little sign that they had ever discarded any that already existed.

There were at least four kinds of land tenure outside the House on the Rock's hedge and at least three more inside the hedge. People could pay taxes and fees in all sorts of ways, including various kinds of corvee labor which counted differently depending on how difficult it was to find someone else who could do it. There were some important tasks that only one Elderkin knew how to do or was able to do. Or only a single Lineage. Assigning values in those cases never satisfied anyone, and there were bounties for anyone who could devise ways to match or replace certain tasks. Everyone else in the room, even Willie, groaned when one craftsman's name was mentioned.

The Secretary and the Archivist sometimes had to remind the Councilors of which rules applied to the current question. It was not clear what rules applied to arguments about which rules applied, but those were less common than one might expect, considering how complicated things were. Everyone around the Council tables seemed to know how things were supposed to go.

There were topics where the Duke was just the thirteenth vote in the Council, topics where the Duke counted double, topics where the Duke did not vote, and a few topics where the Duke did not vote but had the option of over-ruling all twelve of the other Councilors.

The Praefect was sort of military – there were centurions reporting to him. He and his Borderers were responsible for some aspects of the House on the Rock, and some aspects of the borders, including collecting fees and tariffs, and for arresting evil-doers other than Notaries and other Binders, and helping people deal with bogles. The Duke and Landed Counts handled criminal Binders and Demons and managed something called the Gates of Air which were important defenses for the Duchy as a whole, and they were each responsible for one of the four Quarters of Traventi.

The three tribunes seemed to be friendly personally, or at least polite, but in Council discussions they rarely agreed. Even when two of them agreed on a question, it was rarely the same two that had agreed on the previous one. It was not clear who else was in their various factions, (Franz-Karl had not lived in a Palace for six years without learning about factions) but Guildsmaster Mathilda frequently sided with Tribune Ursula. Praefect Aurelian agreed with Tribune Constans more than half the time, but did not seem happy about it.

People were very polite to Tribune Ulrich, but Franz-Karl thought that Ulrich only pretended to be polite back. Ulrich was one of the handful of people in Traventi whose edges seemed not quite right, and there were very faint shadows on his face that might be left from long-ago fibs. Once when Ulrich was making a speech and looking the other way, the Praetor made an old gesture that meant 'count your change', but he did it below the table. Franz-Karl was the only one short enough to see it: even Willie was too tall.

The four small tables with their piles of documents corresponded to the Quarters of the Duchy, which were not at all equally sized, neither by area nor populace. The tables with two Advocates each were for the North and South Valleys. The table with two Advocates and an Observer held documents about the Home Quarter of the central valley, including the House on the Rock, with a middling amount of territory and by far the largest populace.

The fourth table, where Willy was still struggling with the unruly scroll, represented the portion of the Central valley that was across the bridge from the Ceremonial Gate of the House on the Rock. The Quarter Across the Water had such a huge pile of documents because it had several streams that had changed their courses during the spring floods, many resulting contested field boundaries, and a handful of contested wills.

There was also a dispute about the ownership of something called Hallan's Tor that might have started as a contested will a few generations ago but seemed to be viewed as more of a customary entertainment by most people in the council chamber. After listening to the discussion, where all of the arguments were backwards from what you would expect, Franz-Karl guessed that there was some reason no one wanted to own or be responsible for Hallan's Tor. He wondered what Hallan's Tor was, and what was wrong with it.

The only things everyone in the room seemed to agree on were that the major roads needed repairs or improvement, the waterways needed work, and doing either of those things would cost too much.

It was gloriously complex. And even with all of the complexities, it made sense in a way that the overlapping councils and jurisdictions in the Palace did not. Everything under Palace authority seemed to be trying to be three or more things at once, while Traventi seemed to want each thing to be its own specific self. Even Hallan's Tor, whatever it was.

CHAPTER XIII: New Notaries

Wherein our Hero Learns a New Style of Writing, and a Meal and Gossip Are Shared

When the Council adjourned for the midday meal, Franz-Karl helped Willy sort the documents that would no longer be needed because they had already been dealt with, and hand them over to the Archivists for storage.

"This was not necessary, your Honor."

"I thought we agreed I am called Franz-Karl? Anyway, you are a 'Your Honor', too. Where does this one go?"

"Uh. Here, Franz-Karl. See? They go by category, then date, then the most important person in the matter, if you can figure out who that is."

"This style of writing is truly excellent." Franz-Karl said as they finished. "Both clear and elegant. I think it would be a fine thing to have a sample page so that I can practice it."

There was an annoying style of Remoran writing where the word 'minimum' was just a row of thick vertical lines with a couple of hovering dots and nearly invisible connections at the bottom of the u and the tops of the n and m's. It looked impressive, especially when written carefully in fancy inks, but it was difficult to read any text you were not already well acquainted with. Meister van Diesen's awful handwriting tried to imitate that style, when things were going well. But it was not consistent enough to do it well, and he trimmed his pen nibs wrong.

Willy's Elderic Chancery script was just the opposite: the letters looked like they belonged together, but the letter-forms had brave swooshy curves in places that emphasized the differences between them, so you always knew which letter you were looking at.

Willy got a pen and ink and a blank parchment offcut and began to write quickly. "These are the fancy Capitals for the beginnings of paragraphs, and these are the capitals for the forward row, and the return row, and the small letters for the forward row and the return row. These are contractions of the fifteen commonest prepositions and postpositions and these are the small versions that can be used for the same groups of letters inside words."

"How do you decide when to use the contractions?"

"Always use the contractions for the actual prepositions except when beginning sentences or paragraphs. Avoid using the contraction at the beginning of a larger word, especially at the beginning of a sentence or paragraph. It's sloppy to run a short word around the pivot and there are places in long words that are better for the pivot than others. Writing tighter or looser can move the pivot a little, but choosing between a contraction and writing out the letters individually lets you move things farther, so you need to plan ahead. Here – "

He wrote a quick paragraph with wrong use of contractions and very bad pivoting, lightly drew a large X across it in red ink, then wrote the same paragraph properly. The example paragraph included the equivalents of Remoran punctuation marks like commas, colons and semi-colons, and had question marks and quotation marks on both forward and return rows to show the proper positioning.

"And when a word ends at the pivot, the dot-between drops so that it it sits between the rows, and we draw it larger."

"Ah, this is marvelous! I'm sure it will be very helpful." Franz-Karl placed the page on the chair he had been using. "Now we should probably hurry to the dining room before the grownups eat all of the best things." He was already thinking about ways to use a curvier, more open style of lettering when he copied out his lessons, even though they were Remoran, not Elderic. Words were so important for Notaries:

writing things you could not read clearly afterward might even be dangerous.

The room used for casual meals during Council sessions was on the level below the meeting room, across the landing from the Tax Office, with the final cooking done on the same level behind a partition with hatches to pass things through. The low-ceilinged ground floor below the dining room was not used for much: Willy said that there was no record nor rumor that the river had ever managed to flood the central part of the House on the Rock – that was why it was built on the rock – but no one in Traventi left things they cared about less than a yard above ground unless they were well up a mountainside. Not even kitchens and storerooms.

The meal was arranged in proper, hospitable Elderkin style. There was no high table and lower tables, just several similar tables arranged around a central brazier left unlit on this summer day. There were secretaries and observers and archive clerks and even some servants mixed in among the councilors seated at the tables.

The conversation was general, in between chewing and drinking, but Franz-Karl could see that there were groups that were friendlier or more comfortable with each other among the larger company. The Notaries sat at separate tables, or on opposite ends of a single table, but that was because the World went funny if they clumped together too much.

Everyone kept a respectful distance from the Reverend Count Great Aunt Adrasteia – she shared a table with some of the servants – but that did not stop anyone from laughing and joking and gossiping with her. Her Reverence knew wonderful stories and gossip about everywhere and everyone, and told them well. She even knew gossip about things that had happened in Karnburg after Franz-Karl began his journey.

She said that Franz-Karl's Mama and brother and sister were well, and he felt a little knot of worry untie itself in his chest.

Tribune Ulrich was goat-eyed, and never looked straight on at any of the nobles or other Notaries, watching them out of the sides of his eyes instead, while he spoke mainly with the other Tribunes and Guildsmaster and Praetor. His answers to Notaries were usually polite but very brief, except when he was trying to flatter Chief Justice Laurentina. He was sarcastic to people who were not Councilors. The faint fib-shadows on his face showed clearer in the sunny dining room, but he was not fibbing now, as far as Franz-Karl could tell.

When the meal was almost done and people were doing more drinking than eating and much more chatting than either, Franz-Karl finally could not resist asking, "Your Reverence Great Aunt Adrasteia, please ignore this question if it is rude, but were you born a sphinx?"

She saluted him with her wine cup. "No, Franz-Karl. I was born in the Duchy so my mother had the benefit of all of the Child Blessings that were known then. They did not entirely work, so she died bearing me. But I was born with the shape of a Worldfolk child – more or less – just as you were."

"Did you decide to be a Sphinx?"

"Ah, yes." She smiled. "With enough experience and weight of Manifest heritage, shape is a matter of will, not destiny. After trying some other shapes, I found this one comfortable for daily use. Being human shaped had gotten boring after the first thousand years."

Tribune Ulrich snorted, and shifted in his chair so that he was looking even less at the sphinx. Franz-Karl suspected he was still watching her with the side of one eye.

'The first thousand years...' Franz-Karl thought about the old chronicles and some of the names that appeared in them. "Great Aunt Adrasteia, are you the same Adrasteia that was the granddaughter of Gaius Antonius Drusus Igniculo?"

Tribune Ulrich looked positively smug and took a sip from his wine glass. He clearly thought Franz-Karl was being a silly little child, who would learn better when he grew older. Franz-Karl knew that look very well. It was as annoying in Traventi as it was in the Palace in Karnburg, even though it did not necessarily involve fibbing.

The Reverend Count Great Aunt Adrasteia touched her signet, where it hung on its cord, and said cheerfully, "Why yes, Franz-Karl, I am that same Antonia Adrasteia." Tribune Ulrich's jaw dropped and he turned very pale. A sworn Notary did not – could not – make that kind of statement as a joke without immediately saying that it was a joke. So it had to be true.

Franz-Karl continued, "If it would not make you sad, Great Aunt Adrasteia... at some convenient time... Would you tell me more about your family and the Frog General and the others?"

"Yes, Franz-Karl, I think I would like that. We should plan to meet later in the summer, when we are not busy with Council matters."

"That would be a wonderful thing."

If Tribune Ulrich's jaw dropped any further, it would fall off.

Secretary Hieronymus mentioned that the Sun was not delaying His journey, and the piles of papers in the meeting room were not growing smaller while people chatted. Hierophant Silvian raised a full glass in both hands while he recited the final blessing on the meal, and Hierophant Emilia recited the response while feeding a small bit of bread to the flame that heated one of the serving dishes. There was a bustle as people finished their last drinks and nibbles and gathered themselves up to go back to the council session.

The afternoon council session was much like the morning, but with a long discussion about the Duchy's borders instead of some of the arguments about field boundaries. The Landgraff of the Upper Raenos – the Falkenburg district on the other side of the river – was not doing his share to tend the roads and river crossings. It was hard to imagine that people would just ignore the roads and crossings while they fell apart, but after the mess he had seen during his journey Franz-Karl still wondered.

CHAPTER XIV: A Household of His Own

Wherein Our Hero Acquires a Companion

On his fourth morning at the House on the Rock, Franz-Karl took a map of the Duchy from the library and climbed to the top of the Tower for Watching the Stars. The map had crosshatching to indicate the various kinds of property ownership outside the hedge, and he wanted to see whether the kinds of landholding showed on the land as well as on the map. Comparing the land he could see to the map, he decided that grain fields seen from a distance just looked like grain fields, but the gardens and vineyards and orchards, and even entire villages, were laid out differently depending on the property ownership and taxation rules that governed them.

Looking nearer the tower, he tried to recognize the parts of the House that he had visited. The churches and market squares were easy, of course. He recognized the goats' place and the orchard with the bees, and that gave him some of the courtyards he had passed through going to and from them just by remembering his route and judging what things might look like from above.

The thing that was being built out of metal and wood had its tarp off now that the rain had stopped, and people were working on it.

But he still could not tell what it was going to be. He would need to visit it in the sunlight at ground level, and possibly ask someone.

He was moving to the west side of the tower when a pigeon flew down, landed beside him and pecked at his shoe. When he moved away the pigeon followed and tried to land on his wrist that was holding the map.

Franz-Karl tried to shoo it away. That might have worked better if he had known which of the other towers held the dovecote, so that he could shoo the bird toward its home. In the end, he let it sit on his sleeve while he carried it to the dining room. His grandmother and Great Aunt would not be there so early, but it would be embarrassing if a hawk – or, considering that this was Traventi, possibly something fire-breathing – arrived to eat the pigeon before he showed it to the grownups. The capsule tied to the bird's leg might get lost. Or swallowed along with the pigeon.

Carrying the pigeon down the stairs without letting it mess on the map was a little tricky. He finally managed to get the map roughly folded and stuffed it inside his coat.

When he reached the small dining room he asked a servant laying the table what to do. The man fetched a very plain tray – little more than a sheet of metal covered by a rag – with a pile of grain and a small bowl of water on it. The pigeon drank, then ate, but it would not stay on the tray unless Franz-Karl stayed within arm's reach. It would let him pet it gently if he stayed beside it, but would flutter after him if he moved away.

The pigeon did not want to be anywhere near Reverend Count Great Aunt Adrasteia when she arrived. Whenever she moved, it hid on the opposite side of Franz-Karl. It would have been funny if he had not been worried that it would poop on something precious.

The pigeon did not hide from her Grace the Reverend Duke his Grandmother, but Franz-Karl had to hold it while she took the capsule off its leg. Then it flew to the windowsill farthest from Great Aunt Adrasteia. Franz-Karl opened the window and the pigeon went out and flew away toward a smaller tower near Saint Victoria's clock.

When her Grace the Reverend Duke his Grandmother unrolled the strip of paper that was in the capsule, it came out much longer than should have fit in such a small capsule. She read the message and frowned, then showed it to Great Aunt Adrasteia.

"So the Landgraff across the river has his head up his ass again," Count Great Aunt Adrasteia said. "Not exactly news... Interfering with trade, contrary to the Contract and treaties, and damaging the roads he needs for his own governance! What does he think he's doing? Has he forgotten the previous lot?"

"Mama said once that she did not understand why someone so scared of Elderkin wanted a province on our border so badly," Franz-Karl offered. "He spent a lot of money on the court case to get the lands instead of his nephew. Some people said he lied in court, but he is one of the Chancellor's friends and an ally of the Margraff-Elector, so the judge did not question him very strictly."

The tip of Great Aunt Adrasteia's tail twitched. "Oh, lied in court, did he?"

"My Papa thought he did. I heard him say so to acting-Archduke Uncle Helm-Friedrich and Aunt Queen Gertrude."

The Sphinx made a noise that was very odd to be coming out of a human woman's face.

Her Grace the Reverend Duke his Grandmother said firmly, "This is a matter for the full council, Great Aunt Adrasteia... Franz-Karl, would you like to attend the council again? Or would you prefer to find some of your cousins to play with?"

"I'll come to the council, if I may." He took the map out of his coat and tried to straighten it. "I was looking at the land to see what village-held and land-held holdings look like when the pigeon came."

The Sphinx made an odd noise that was half a chuckle and half a purr.

Her Grace his Grandmother took the map from him, shook it sharply, and it returned to its original folds, without extraneous creases.

The three of them walked to the Council chamber together, just as they had the previous day.

The morning Council session was fascinating, and it was interesting to hear the other side of some of the same problems that the factions in the Palace always complained about to his Mama and Papa. (Always used to complain about.) With proposed solutions just as far away from usefulness, in many cases: he could almost hear his Mama sigh. (And his Papa's comments.)

Franz-Karl had to listen carefully to the councilors to understand some things the grownups were talking about. Most of the complaints were about things that had happened in the past century, and he never bothered much with chronicles that were that recent. The chronicles in the Palace mostly reported the Allemanic versions of things – even though they were written in Remoran – and at least half the time they were fibbing. Sometimes they were fibbing so much the ink did not want to sit still on the pages. He thought he should try to look at the Traventine chronicles for those years: if Notaries sworn and Bound to the truth wrote the histories, at least the words might sit still on the page for him to read them.

When the council was nearly ready to resume after the midday meal, her Grace the Reverend Duke his Grandmother asked Franz-Karl to join her in her study.

There was a young man waiting for them in the study, sitting in one of the side chairs and reading a small book, with a tricorn hat resting on a table beside him. He stood up, set the book aside, and bowed politely when they entered. He was very tall and quite broad across the shoulders, but he moved in a way that suggested he was not fully grown into his bones, and maybe the bones were not finished growing, either. His clothes were well-made and not old, but fit in a way that suggested the tailors were having trouble keeping up: too loose or too tight or too short in odd places. Acting Archduke Uncle Helm-Friedrich's younger sons moved like that, and had clothes that fit like those, too, when they were growing tall all at once.

The young man's close-cropped hair and beard were absolutely black and he had Elderkin cow-eyes – so dark you did not notice the horizontal pupils, with very small white areas in the corners – but his skin was light enough that even the places where his hat had not shaded his face were fairer-skinned than Franz-Karl.

His features might have been described as striking, in Karnburg, but never as handsome: the dark eyes faced forward – mostly – but they were too well separated for a Worldfolk face, leaving room for a nose that was broader and flatter across its top than the human triangle. From the side, his jaw and profile were a little too long and hinted faintly at a muzzle.

Her Grace His Grandmother bowed to the young man slightly, then turned to Franz-Karl and said, "Since you are now a fully sworn Notary, you will need someone to look after your papers and such, and you should not be wandering around unattended like some craftsman's apprentice. Fritzel speaks, reads and writes Remoran and Allemanic as well as Elderic, so he will be able to assist you in any of the languages, but I have asked him to prefer speaking to you in Elderic, so that you will become more practiced and comfortable in conversation. If you suit well together, he will travel back to the Palace with you in the autumn as part of your household."

"That would be a fine thing, Your Grace my Grandmother," Franz-Karl said. "But you know the Palace has all those stupid rules…"

Her Grace smiled a smile that someone was not going to enjoy. "I know of no documents nor decrees touching on the composition of my grandson's household," she answered calmly, though a couple of sparks dripped from the end of her braid. "And I do not believe their Excellencies or acting Archduke Helm-Friedrich will deny you a proper attendant. If the Palace officials cause problems about Fritzel, both of you may return here. If the palace officials try to separate you, you will not allow it. You are a full Notary of the Elderkin, and not to be bullied by Worldfolk servants." After a moment she added, "If they are not satisfied with someone as Gifted as Fritzel, I am sure we can find a reason to propose adding full Binders and Notaries to your Household instead."

Fritzel smiled a smile that someone would enjoy even less than Her Grace's, and cocked his head slightly.

Her Grace the Duke took out a parchment from the pile on her worktable and gave it to Fritzel to read, and to sign if he agreed to the terms. He signed, and she signed and sealed it: using her personal signet, not the great seal of the Duchy of Traventi.

Her Grace the Reverend Duke his Grandmother showed Franz-Karl the contract they had signed and she had sealed. It said in formal Elderic that the job of Friedrich of the lineage of Boukolyos and rank of Tiarna, was to travel with Franz-Karl, of the lines of the Falkenburgs and of the Dukes of Traventi, and be an attendant in his household. Friedrich of the Boukolyos was to assist him, and speak Elderic with him most of the time, and to look after him and any papers he handled as Notary. The Tiarna's salary and equipment would be paid for from Duke Adriana's personal household funds: that would limit opportunities for official meddling from either the Traventine or the Imperial councils. (The contract was not quite that blunt, but it came close.)

A final note mentioned, as an example of the limits of responsibility of the attendant's position, that Friedrich Boukolyos was expected to fish Franz-Karl out of the duck pond if he fell in, but not necessarily to prevent him falling in, because it was not fair to set a task on a mortal that might exceed the capabilities of the Manifest Blessed, nor to expect one of the Gifted to overrule a Notary's choices.

Franz-Karl thought that note was a little unfair. He did not think he had ever done anything to suggest he was likely to end up in the duck pond. On the other hand, her Grace had probably heard about Philip-Augustus and the duck pond at the Palace, and perhaps she feared ill luck about water might run in the family. He had to admit, after the things he had seen in these past few days, even including the days when it had been too rainy to go outdoors, there were few signs that this would be a boring summer. There might come a time when it would seem sensible to be in the duck pond.

He looked up at the tall young man, then bowed moderately. It was not the mere nod appropriate to a servant: he gave the proper bow to a minor noble attending on him. He added his own signature and seal as Witness to the contract. "Welcome to my household, Tiarna Boukolyos."

"I am honored by the welcome, Your Honor. But I am generally called Fritzel," the young man answered. His voice was very deep, with an undertone that struck the bones rather than the ears.

"And between us, in private, I am called Franz-Karl."

Fritzel looked cheerful and friendly, but very different from people in Karnburg. . Looking at the cow-eyes and the lines of the neck and jaw and temples, he thought that he would not be surprised if Fritzel had relatives with bull's horns: the stories said that there were plenty of people in the Duchy descended from the Blessed Lord of the Labyrinth and it was hard to imagine a more likely example for that line.

Fritzel looked at his new lord, then dropped to one knee so that his eyes would be more on a level with Franz-Karl's. "Do you know how to swim, your Honor?"

"Uh, No?"

"Neither do I. But when one of the mighty says you may be going to fall in the duck pond, it seems wise to take precautions. I'll find someone to teach us both."

"That sounds like fun."

Fritzel shook his head slightly, and one shoulder twitched in a tiny hint of a shrug. "I doubt that, Your Honor. All the streams in Traventi are fed by melt from the snowfields and glaciers, and the streams feed the ponds. The water stays cold enough to freeze your parts off even in high summer." Fritzel did not sound worried or angry about it. He was just accepting the shape of the World.

Fritzel moved into the attendant's alcove at the other end of Franz-Karl's room from Olivia's. He had two chests besides the one already there, and a sack of things that went into the chest that belonged to the House, and some fancy boots and a big coat and hat that did not fit into any of the chests, and a small crate containing some books and a very fine lamp, and a pen stand, and a few other useful things.

He set a candle and offering dish and holy image on a shelf in the corner, to make a tiny Shrine, then nicked his little finger and touched the drop of blood to the offering dish, saying, "Well, now I'm home."

After a quiet conversation with Olivia, and a few of the people who served the House, Fritzel sorted through the piles of packs that had come with Franz-Karl on his journey. The empty ones were taken away to a store room to wait until they were needed for the journey back to Karnburg. The others were set on a rack of shelves that was brought in, instead of being piled on each other.

Franz-Karl thought the new arrangement looked very fine: it made the apartment look like a place someone lived, not a traveler's way-station. But Fritzel frowned at the shelves, and moved things around until Franz-Karl's toys and books and the papers and ink for his lessons were all on lower shelves where he could reach them easily.

There were also three new packs with small locks, for storing different kinds of official papers, that were placed in easy reach for them both, and a strongbox with heavy sides and a very serious lock that went under Fritzel's bed at the other end from the chamberpot. Fritzel suggested that Franz-Karl should tell the strongbox to make itself inconspicuous, and seemed satisfied by the result.

The next morning, when Franz-Karl got up early as usual, Fritzel came out of his cubicle – fully dressed and ready for the day – while Franz-Karl himself was still fastening the many button of his waistcoat. Franz-Karl was sorry for disturbing his aide: disturbing people before the morning bells was rude.

Fritzel shrugged one shoulder, said cheerfully, "At least Your Honor doesn't need to be milked", and turned to the washstand to pour water from the ewer into the basin.

After they had both washed their faces and hands properly and said their morning prayers, Fritzel held up a comb and asked, "May I?"

Franz-Karl waved him to a chair and stood in front of it with his back turned toward the comb. He braced himself: he had been sort of fake-combing his hair since Karnburg, leaving the visible surface almost presentable and the underneath parts a tangled mess, so this was going to hurt.

He was surprised when the hair combing did not hurt at all. His Mama and Itron Gwenlian were the only ones who could usually manage that, and they were both all the way back in Karnburg. His Papa had combed Franz-Karl's hair sometimes, less successfully, but he was even farther away.

Fritzel worked slowly and gently, teasing loose the tangles and untwisting the tendrils. As the expectation of pain faded, Franz-Karl said, "Your own hair is short..."

"I don't have human hair, " Fritzel said cheerfully. "I have a bull's pelt. Gets a bit scruffy at shedding season, but if I get a good barber to sculpt the beard and shape the edges a bit, it looks well enough most of the time."

After all of Franz-Karl's hair was loose and smooth (but already trying twist back into witch-locks) Fritzel divided it into small sections and folded them into a braid that started above Franz-Karl's forehead and went all the way back to the color-of sorrow hair-ribbon. When he held a mirror to show the result, Franz-Karl saw that the green streaks were showing in a sort of pattern, like a tree growing up from the mud of the ribbon. Not identical on the two sides, since the streaks were not, but balanced.

"Oh! That looks wonderful!" He turned and tipped his head, looking at the effect in the mirror. "But it won't stay," he finished sadly.

"That braid'll hold horses' manes, that are stiffer than any hair Your Honor has. And I'll carry a comb in my pocket. If Your Honor's hair starts having opinions, we can remind it where to sit..."

They both put on their coats and hats and left their rooms.

Fritzel stayed out in the passageway while Franz-Karl was greeting his Papa and the others in the Household Shrine: they were not his ancestors and relatives, after all. When Franz-Karl left the Shrine, Fritzel said quietly, "Your Da's lack leaves a sad gap in the world."

"You met him?"

"Not proper met: he'll not have known my face or name. When my folks came Across the River for the Wedding Contract Vote, and the feast after, I was older than you are now but not grown, and neither heir nor Notary."

"Ah. He was one of the few foreigners present, and you were one among hundreds."

"I remember Grand Duke Leon-Alexander had a fine laugh... And when he danced with your Ma, it was like they'd danced together since birth or longer."

Franz-Karl remembered his parents dancing like that... never again. He did not quite start sobbing, but his eyes filled with tears and spilled over. Fritzel took a knee, put an arm around Franz-Karl's shoulders, and handed him a handkerchief. When time passed and the quiet weeping did not, he picked up Franz-Karl and carried him back to their rooms.

Olivia was in the main room, dressed for the day. She took a step toward them when Fritzel entered carrying Franz-Karl. "Is he ill?"

Fritzel shook his head. "Nah. Just sad."

"Of course."

She brought a wet cloth to wipe Franz-Karl's face, when he was ready, and a cup of water for him to drink.

They all went to breakfast together, Franz-Karl and the whole two people of his household. The Count of Wolfsberg had more people, but they were all outside the Palace and did not eat meals with Philip-Augustus or share his table properly.

As Franz-Karl was finishing his meal, Hieronymus the Council Secretary approached their table, flanked by two of his assistants. He gave Franz-Karl a document written on fine parchment and sealed with the Great Seal of Traventi and announced loudly that the Notary Franz-Karl of the lines of Falkenburg, Capradaventi, Leonstein and Armorius was requested to present himself before the Duke and Council of Traventi. No one cheered, but there was that sort of feeling in the crowded dining room.

Heir of the Bindings

CHAPTER XV: Recognition

Wherein the Populace Choose and Our Hero acquires a New Title

The Council was already in session when Franz-Karl was ushered in, and Fritzel and Olivia came in with him. Fritzel was duly sworn as an Observer, which he would need to be to handle Franz-Karl's official papers, when Franz-Karl had official papers to handle. Olivia took a lesser oath about confidential matters. They both sat in Observers' seats along the walls.

Franz-Karl was given a fancy chair that matched the ones the Councilors used, but placed so that he was facing the council and had his back to the secretaries. He was glad that he was wearing his best coat, and that Fritzel had fixed his hair so that no one could say he looked like a ragamuffin.

After formally asking to speak to the Council, Her Grace the Duke stood beside Franz-Karl, facing the council tables and announced, "According to the fourth section of the Marriage Contract between my daughter Silvia and Leon-Alexander von Falkenburg, the first child of that marriage to become a fully sworn Notary should be presented promptly to the Council and People of Traventi for Recognition as Silvia's Heir in matters pertaining to our Line and to the Duchy. I now present my grandson, the Honorable Notary Franz-Karl, as a candidate for Recognition as required by custom and the Wedding Contract."

Franz-Karl's first thought was that Philip-Augustus would be angry.

His second thought was that there were a bunch of nobles at His Excellency's Court who would be absolutely furious to have their scheming disrupted. Folding Traventi into the minor Falkenburg holding of Wolfsberg, as they had planned and bragged about, was not going to work as well if the inheritance of Traventi did not go through the same person as the County of Wolfsberg. He was not surprised when none of the Traventine councilors argued against recommending him to the people for Recognition: a chance of having a future Duke of their very own instead of sharing their First Speaker as someone else's Count, sworn to a foreign loyalty, was not something they would throw away.

Some of Franz-Karl's choices when he took the Notary oaths would make the Traventine Council even happier... and the Karnburg courtiers even angrier if they knew about them.

The Council held a formal vote, which was recorded as passing thirteen to none with six Notaries present and voting. The secretary Hieronymus announced that the Council of Traventi officially agreed that Franz-Karl, being a fully sworn Notary and the child of Silvia and Leon-Alexander, was fully qualified to inherit the position of Duke, and recommended that he should be presented to the populace to be Recognized as next in line to inherit the position of Duke after the Reverend Childe Silvia. Several copies of the announcement were written and signed and sealed by Hieronymus and all of the Councilors.

The Council vote was followed by a procession. Her Grace put on more regalia than Franz-Karl had seen her wear before. The dagger from the Speaker's table went into a jeweled sheath at her waist, and there were bracelets, and a necklace supporting a heavy pendant, and a jeweled belt, and a wreath on her head that looked like grape leaves and grapes but was made of gold and silver and jewels and enamel.

The wax seal on the chamber door was broken, formally, using the Duke's dagger, and a piper waiting outside began to play a cheerful tune when the door was opened. Her Grace the Duke took Franz-Karl by the hand and led him out of the room. Adrasteia walked behind them and everyone one else in the room followed her. Franz-Karl's own people, Fritzel and Olivia, were ahead of everyone except the Councilors and

Hieronymus. They all followed the piper down the stairs to the ground level of the tower, then out through the courtyards and walkways of the House on the Rock, out to the Stone Theater on the mountain slope. The few people they passed joined onto the end of the procession.

The curved rows of seats of the Stone Theater were very full of people. That explained why the passageways of the House were so empty, but the people from the House would not come near filling the Theater. Franz-Karl wondered where all of the rest of those people had come from. Traventi was small, but not so small as all that, and its people were scattered in the mountain valleys. Some of them must have begun traveling almost as soon as he was made a Notary.

He had seen reports that the theater could hold about twenty thousand people, while the entire population of Traventi was said to be barely more than twenty-five thousand even if you counted toothless babies. Most of Traventi was here.

He wondered suddenly why 'toothless' mattered for inclusion in the count instead of age: it was always toothless babies that were set apart in the descriptions of populations in the chronicles. It gave him something to think about other than how many people were looking at him.

Even with the Notaries and other Binders spread through the crowd as evenly as possibly, the shape of the Living World trembled beneath the assembled Manifest weight of so many Elderkin. Sound carried unevenly, like a banner rippling in a strong breeze. The air above the crowd was filled with moving patches of rainbows, as if the bright Sun shone on a mass of huge bubbles that were invisible except for those colored gleams.

Franz-Karl was glad to stand near Her Grace the Duke His Grandmother on the stage, which at least felt solid under his feet. Her Reverence Count Adrasteia stood at the far left end of the stage and His Reverence Count Severin stood at the far right, and it seemed that the World might split itself if they moved any closer.

The Piper played a fanfare that was echoed by trumpets. The crowd, which had been humming like a beehive, went completely silent while Her Grace the Duke made the proposal of Recognition and reported the Council's recommendation. The theater looked enormous from the stage, and the people in the topmost row looked tiny through the rippling light.

Secretary Hieronymus stepped forward, rapped a staff on the stage, and announced that the votes of the Councilors would be all counted as 'in favor', including all of the Notaries. That led to some oohs and aahs from the audience. No one answered an invitation to contest the proposal for the vote. No one answered the second or third invitation either.

The voting took most of the afternoon. The crowd sounded a bit like a happy beehive again while it was happening: there was a lot of murmuring and movement in the crowd as things were sorted out. Once it became clear that the proposal would pass, long rolls of parchment began to move out of the crowd and onto the stage: people who had approved of the proposal signed to bear witness to their choice and Bind the decision into the shape of the Living World. Notaries applied their seals to the list as well as signing. The people who had voted against Recognition signed different rolls recording that. And there were several copies of everything: Franz-Karl was not sure how many.

Franz-Karl thought that he could tell when the vote officially tipped into passage: the whole World steadied, and the shifting rainbows... stiffened, was the only word he could find for it, though it was not really correct. Neither rainbows nor soap bubbles were stiff.

When the voting was done, even though rolls of parchment were still being shuffled around for people to sign and seal, the Chief Justice and the Archivist of Traventi and the Secretary of the Council reported the results. Four fifths of the enrolled voters of the populace were present or voting by proxy, more than the two thirds needed for a quorum in the present matter. Of the votes cast, nineteen in twenty – less five – favored Recognition. That nineteen in twenty included all of the Notaries and other Binders that were present for the vote, and Count Valens and a few other Binders and Notaries that had voted by proxy: all of the adult Binders known to be in the Duchy had supported Recognition.

There was not much regalia for the Heir of an Heir, and most of the pieces in the treasury were not appropriate for someone who was not yet Initiated and whose Father was only a few weeks dead. Her Grace displayed a bracelet and ear-rings and a pendant to Franz-Karl and to the people in the theater seats, then set them back in a casket. She took out a chain of links of dark iron supporting carved white ivy leaves, and held it up. The crowd filling the rows of seats that spread up the hillside became quieter. Watching. Witnessing.

Hieronymus, as the Council's Secretary, explained that there was no fixed oath for a second Heir. There were several traditional formulas for accepting agreements and contracts, and a new Notary being added to the Recognized line of succession usually used one of them. Franz-Karl glanced at the list of examples Hieronymus held out, but none of them looked... right... and when he looked at the bone-carved ivy leaves and the people sitting above him, he knew what words he wanted to say: they were much older and plainer than any that the Secretary was offering. He stepped onto the colored stone that marked the spot on the stage where his voice would be heard the best.

"I am Franz-Karl." Not 'I am called', no mention of lineages... The crowd went so silent that many of them must have been holding their breaths. "Before Heaven and the Living World and those assembled here to Witness, I say that I shall guard the peace of Traventi and the freedom of the Elderkin however I may, with Flesh or Voice or Gift or Binding, for whatever time is given to me." It was the old Defender's Oath, from the ancient days when the Duke and the First Speaker of the Council were still two separate people, and the old chronicles said that it neither transmitted nor claimed authority. Maximianus Rano, the Frog General, would have pronounced most of the words differently, so many centuries ago, but they were the same words that bound and supported him when he broke Remora's hold on Traventi.

There was a crack of thunder that echoed from the nearby mountainsides, despite the cloudless sky. Her Grace the Duke Adriana looped the iron chain over his hair so that he was wearing a wreath of ivy leaves, but her hands shook as she did it. Franz-Karl shivered, too: the Crown of Ivy and Iron was mentioned in some old and terrible stories. It fitted well with the ancient oath.

The musicians produced a very loud fanfare and the spectators roared a response that made the World tremble again. When he looked from side to side of the great mass of Witnesses, Franz-Karl noticed in the edge of his vision that there was a streak of a tear on the cheek of Reverend Count Great Aunt Adrasteia, and she had reared up and spread her wings.

Fritzel appeared, comb in hand, to tweak a few tendrils of Franz-Karl's hair back into place, re-tie the hair tie, and add a couple of pins to anchor the Ivy and Iron more firmly to the braids. Franz-Karl thought it would not be fair to complain about some of his hair having opinions after a time when the sky and mountainside and most of the people of Traventi had been so excited.

While they waited for the last copies of the voting register to be signed and gathered from the crowd, Her Grace his Grandmother explained to Franz-Karl that the Elderkin of Traventi mistrusted unanimous votes by large numbers of people, so nineteen in twenty was the legal maximum for such a vote, with the additional five votes left as a margin for error. The customary ways of balancing the voting results were too complex to be managed under the compulsion of Bindings: things would get snarled.

There could not really be a secret vote when Bindings were involved: sealed Bindings were inscribed into the structure of the World for anyone to read who had the Gift. But if the vote had failed, there would be no Binding, and therefore no inerasable record of how anyone had voted: only the fact of the vote and the summary of the count would be kept in the archives.

Nineteen in twenty of four fifths of the adult citizens in the Duchy made for a huge number of people signing the scrolls as formal witnesses of the official decree of Recognition. The signing lasted well into the evening and only finished so quickly because there were customary ways to hasten the process. As people finished signing the various copies of the Registers, they moved out from the Stone Theater and prepared for feasting and dancing in the squares and courtyards of the House on the Rock.

Reporting the vote to anyone not present in the House on the Rock in Traventi would take days or weeks. Several copies of the announcement of Recognition with the summary of the vote results would be sent out and posted in various parts of the Duchy, with each copy carrying the Great Seal of Traventi in bright green wax. More copies would be set aside to be sent to various neighboring governments, many of whose leaders or monarchs were Franz-Karl's relatives, including – of course – several for various people and offices in the Imperial Palace at Karnburg. One of the Karnburg copies would include a copy of the full list of formal witnesses – partly on the theory that burying the Allemanic and Falkenburg councils in parchment would make it harder for them to challenge the results – but most of the foreign announcements were signed by the Councilors and just included the summary of the Popular vote.

Franz-Karl thought that there were officials in the Palace who might benefit from seeing the World tremble under the weight of thousands of Elderkin. Assuming they noticed anything more than a sunny summer day: noticing the weight of the populace of Traventi might be like seeing the colors that only had Elderic names.

That evening there was a huge banquet to celebrate Franz-Karl's official Recognition as a Childe of Traventi, with tables set up throughout the House on the Rock in its greatest extent, and food and drink for everyone involved in the vote. There were even bagpipes at the feast, which turned out to be far more tuneful than the trumpets used at Palace banquets. Drums were drums, wherever you were. Unfortunately.

Mid-way between sunset and midnight, before the festivities had begun to subside, a messenger wearing a cloak of the color-of-sorrow approached the Duke and bowed deeply, and even more deeply to Franz-Karl. She said, "Theodore the Potter, whose name appears on the rolls of Witnesses, has died of his age and infirmity. By the Binding of Maximianus Rano, the vote and oath-taking are now a fixed and unchangeable part of the Affairs of Traventi."

Franz-Karl signed himself and bowed to the messenger, feeling the Iron and Ivy shift on his head with the movement. "May his spirit find safe and speedy passage to the Halls of Judgment." He shivered a little: the Recognition was done and sealed, in this world and the next.

CHAPTER XVI: A Revealing Walk

Wherein the Nature of Electors Is Discussed

After the Council session ended and his new regalia were packed away into the strongbox under Fritzel's bed, Franz-Karl's life in the House on the Rock settled into a different pattern.

Each day he and Fritzel walked together through the colonnades near the Duke's Residence in the early morning quiet, returning to the small dining room for breakfast. They played hiding-and-hunting games, occasionally, and learned that Franz-Karl could keep people from noticing Fritzel, provided the two of them were careful not to make a fuss. On the other hand, Fritzel could always see or find Franz-Karl, even if he was inside or under something or behind a closed door, unless Franz-Karl tried very hard to prevent him. But for the first few days Fritzel thought their games were fun: he did not think they were important.

One morning, when they were walking back to breakfast after a session of the hiding game that had gone very well but taken them farther from the breakfast room than on previous mornings, Fritzel asked how the food in the Palace compared to food in Traventi. So Franz-Karl told him about the fake food. Fritzel seemed angry when he finished, but not at him, so he continued with the story about the Margraff-Elector and the trap of lies and the thirteen true things. After thinking hard about it, he even told about the glove-bearer's rod, which was almost scarier than the trap of lies. Finding the right words in Elderic was harder than it might have been in Remoran.

If Fritzel ended up coming to the Palace at the end of the summer – and Franz-Karl was already hoping very much that he would – he needed to know about these things.

Fritzel kept walking a little way, then asked, "What's this important Margraff fellow the Elector of?"

"Well, nothing, really."

Fritzel stopped and looked at him. "Seriously?"

"I know that sounds stupid, but… " Franz-Karl waved his hands in a shooing motion, and sighed. "Look you: the Falkenburg Archduchy of the Eastlands mostly passes by ordinary inheritance, but with some fussy rules about the male line. But the Kingdom of the Allemans that still tries to call itself the Holy Remoran Empire is different. The Kingdom of the Allemans is supposed to pass by election, not inheritance, but it isn't a vote of everybody, like it is here, or even a vote of all of the High Born. There are only six High Nobles and three Hierophants from important cities that are members of the College of Electors. But His Excellency my Grandfather was elected when he was … twenty? … twenty-four? Something like that. And he is old now as Worldfolk see things: his Excellency's eldest son, Helm-Friedrich, is a grandfather. And the Hierophant-Electors and Prince-Electors that voted for him were mostly old themselves. No one living now in the Kingdom of the Allemans with the title of Elector has ever Elected anyone or anything. And the Margraff-Elector is the youngest of the lot."

Fritzel looked impressed, but not in a good way.

Franz-Karl added, "And besides all that, even though the Kingship is not supposed to be inherited, the previous several Kings were all Falkenburgs like my Grandfather. And not even unexpected Falkenburgs, mostly, even when the World might have been better if the Electors had at least chosen a different Falkenburg. So I'm not sure how much actual electing got done."

"Huh. Sounds like you could replace these Electors with puppets from a clock tower and no one would notice."

"Don't be silly. Of course people would notice. The puppets would be prettier. And much, much cheaper to maintain. The Electors receive huge amounts of authority and wealth."

"For having a title that does nothing?"

Franz-Karl turned his hands palm upward. "The College of Electors officially advises the King about some things. The Princely Electors are also members of the College of Princes, so I think maybe they get two chances to yell about things, where the other advisors get one. I don't think that His Excellency my Grandfather does much that they don't agree to. The Kingdom has a College of Cities, too, but I'm not sure anyone listens to them at all. All the official meetings of the Colleges happen in Konigsberg, and His Excellency hasn't visited there since before I was born."

Fritzel shook his head slowly. "Sounds a proper tangle. My Gran always says the Lowlands are full of lies and illusions, but I thought that was just tales. Still... Surely the fellow did not really intend to claim a falsehood?"

Franz-Karl groped for words and did not find them, certainly not in Elderic. Elderkin who lied outright or broke promises damaged themselves – better to cut yourself with a knife than a lie, the stories said – and the greater their Manifest heritage, the greater the damage. Describing the way things worked at the Imperial Court was just... beyond what he could manage for someone who had never been out of Traventi...

He was so tired of people telling him that he was young and confused when he tried to tell them true things. Traventi was better for that sort of thing, but the Palace in Karnburg set the bar so low it needed a ditch dug for it.

He remembered an old story from the chronicles and pulled on the ribbon around his neck to bring his signet out from inside his clothes, then breathed on it and buffed it on the fabric of his coat. "I am called Franz-Karl von Falkenburg, a full Notary of the Elderkin of Traventi. If my Father Leon-Alexander did *not* die of deliberate malice, may the Living World let lightning strike the arch of that gateway." He pointed at the gate, then repeated the invocation a second, third and fourth time. When nothing happened for four long breaths after the fourth invocation, he added, "If my Father Leon-Alexander was honest and loyal to my Grandfather and my Uncle Helm-Friedrich, may the Living World let lightning strike the arch of that gateway."

It was not much of a lightning bolt: just a big blue-white spark and a crack like an unusually loud bull-whip. But it happened, almost before he finished speaking, as if the Living World was eager to be helpful and bear witness. It left a dark mark on the stonework, so there was no doubt it had happened.

Franz-Karl looked up at Fritzel. "Do I need to continue?" He tried to keep his voice steady, as if he had completely expected that to work. Somehow that tiny lightning bolt was more surprising than the World trembling during the Recognition voting. Franz-Karl had not been the one making the Living World tremble.

Fritzel did not answer Franz-Karl, exactly. He suggested to two specific Saints that they perform acts that... were extremely rude and would require truly remarkable limberness... even if one of the Saints happened to be a Glove of one of the High Gods and therefore not constrained by concerns for time and distance.

Franz-Karl was not sure whether to be shocked, but decided that if someone was going to blaspheme, they might as well be thorough about it. He took a couple of breaths to get past the urge to giggle – or possibly scream – because now he had the Living World's witness that his father was murdered: he himself was not just confused or unjustly suspicious – and asked again as steadily as he could manage, "Shall I continue?"

In the stories, more repetitions of the request often led to greater demonstrations by the World. Franz-Karl was not sure he wanted to see what would happen if he asked for another sign.

"No, Your Honor, I think that was enough and more." Fritzel laughed a bit shakily, and they continued on toward breakfast. But it was after that conversation that their early morning games began to include closed doors and such. And they also played at devising hidden ways of signaling to each other.

INTERLUDE IV: News from the West

Wherein an Imperial Audience Reveals Surprises

Two weeks after Franz-Karl arrived in Traventi, messengers and parcels from Traventi reached the Palace in Karnburg, after a journey by day and night that involved frequent changes of and left some of the horses unfit for hard use thereafter. A few of the messages were delivered directly to Silvia, Childe of Traventi and Dowager Countess of Wolfsberg, but most went to the staff of the acting Archduke, Helm-Friedrich, on behalf of His Excellency, Friedrich-Augustus, King of the Allemans, Elected Emperor of the Remorans and Archduke of the Falkenburg Eastlands. Among other titles and holdings.

Many of the high Nobility were dispersed to their provinces and estates for the season. An Imperial audience was decreed for four days later to allow some of those within reach time to return to Court for the occasion. Even with the delay, most of those attending would be his Excellency's Eastlands vassals and a few Allemanic officials who resided in Karnburg and attended at Court: the rest of the Allemanic territories were too far away.

The Margraff-Elector was residing in Karnburg, as usual, not in his far northern province of Ansbach, so he was one of the exceptions. He arrived at the assembly wearing an austere suit of dark gray brocade –

dark enough to display his Highborn pallor but not dark enough to suggest mourning or commerce – that drew the eye in the glittering crowd, since it had black silk braid instead of gold at the collar and hem and down the front around the buttons and buttonholes. His waistcoat was embroidered only in black and white. He arrived at the out-of-season gathering just before the appointed time instead of waiting to make a disruptive entrance, eyed the number of chairs of state arranged on the low dais, and frowned.

When the Grand Duchess Erminia arrived, the Margraff-Elector ignored her to such an extent that the princess and her companions needed to walk around him. Pristinus' writings deplored a married woman straying so far from her husband's hand, even to be under her father's roof, holding that her father or brother should thrash her and ship her back to her proper place. The Margraff-Elector could not dispute with his sworn liege about a household matter, so he treated the woman as invisible. It was a compromise that satisfied no one, but the Margraff-Elector had just enough rank and influence for the breach of protocol to be tolerated.

He stepped aside and bowed very slightly when the Dowager Queen of the Magyars moved toward her place on the dais. A childless widow maintained by her husband's family under her father's roof fulfilled the strictest outline of respectability – though she spent far too much time in public view – and the maintenance included a company of Hussars who tended to ... remonstrate... with what they viewed as excessive disrespect.

His Excellency and His Serene Highness the acting Archduke both arrived accompanied by their wives, so everyone pretended that the Margraff-Elector's bows when they took their places at the center of the dais included the ladies.

When the Elderkin Dowager Countess of Wolfsberg entered the audience chamber, she was wearing the same dull mud-color she had adopted at the time of her husband's death, but the two small blond children with Falkenburg features who flanked her were dressed in proper mourning black. She was accompanied by two attendants of her own inhuman kind wearing mud-colored sashes, and several Palace servants carrying burdens and wearing black sashes. The Margraff-Elector hastily stepped well back from any chance of contamination by the 'beast-born'. He did not look toward them, but only toward His Excellency and His Serene Highness.

After the Traventine Princess and her companions had formally bowed to the Imperial party on the dais, the servants stacked their parcels in a tidy pyramid at the edge of the dais and retired to positions along the chamber's walls and near the doors.

Silvia of Traventi's male attendant opened a document bearing a large wax seal, displayed it to the dais and then to the rest of the room. He announced in a loud, clear voice, "The Duke and Council and Populace of Traventi send greetings to His Excellency Friedrich-Augustus von Falkenburg, Archduke of the Falkenburg Eastlands, and to his servants. The problem of the eruption of Elderkin Gifts within the Falkenburg territories has been examined, in accordance with the contracts and treaties between the sovereign realms. The youth Franz-Karl of the lines of Falkenburg, Capradaventi, Leonstein and Armorius has been fully sworn to the service of Truth and is now a Notary of Traventi and presents no undue hazard to himself or those around him." He closed the document and held it out toward no one in particular.

The Master of Protocol grasped it before it could fall. He beckoned hastily toward a minor official in the Allemanic Office of State, but the Chief Justice of the Falkenburg Eastlands stepped forward and plucked the document from his hand. "Your Eminence!" the Master tried to protest.

The elderly jurist was a minor Duke in his own right: a Falkenburg vassal holding territory outside the ancient border of the Allemanic Kingdom that was smaller than many counties. He was seldom inclined to accept backtalk from minor functionaries of lesser formal rank. He bowed to His Imperial Excellency and the acting Archduke of the Eastlands, then said blandly, "By ancient custom and recent treaties, the Notaries of Traventi are accredited as advocates before the courts of the Eastlands. One of my clerks will see to updating our rolls."

The acting Archduke pinched the bridge of his nose with one hand and waved the other hand at the Elderkin man serving as spokesman for Traventi.

A second, somewhat larger document with a number of seals was produced. "In accordance with ancient custom, and the explicit requirements of the Wedding Contract between Silvia of Traventi and Leon-Alexander of the Falkenburg Domains and their respective families, the Duke and Council of Traventi have Recommended the Honorable Notary Franz-Karl von Falkenburg to the Populace of Traventi for addition to the list of heirs for the Duchy following immediately after the Reverend Childe Silvia, heir to the current Duke. The Council vote in favor was unanimous and included the votes of all of the Notaries present."

The Margraff-Elector pivoted to stare directly at the Traventine spokesman. More than half the people of rank in the audience chamber began talking all at once... and many of them were unhappy. The Margraff-Elector looked at the Chief Justice of the Eastlands, who was reaching for the document, and demanded, "Can those beast-born wretches *do* that? That changeling brat is *not* Leon-Alexander's heir."

The judicial Duke shared an overlord with the Margraff-Elector, but saw no particular reason to show greater deference to a foreign Noble who was barely half his age – and a heretic to boot – than he had been offered. "The Council of Traventi are required to 'do that' by the terms of the Wedding Contract. As soon as any child of Leon-Alexander and Silvia achieves the status of Notary, the child must be proposed as Silvia's heir for the duchy." The Justice paused a moment, assumed a formal pose for delivering a judgment then finished, "The Council and People of Traventi have fulfilled their contract, as Elderkin must. Everyone knows that, and law courts on both sides of the Gates of Air acknowledge it."

The noise in the audience chamber was increasing. His Excellency flicked a hand and said, "Silence". When everyone had turned to face him, and bowed, he gestured to the Elderkin spokesman. "Continue."

The Traventine messenger bowed – not very deeply: the Duke of Traventi was a *sovereign* Duke answering to no overlord – and opened another document which he held in one hand while he indicated the pile of parcels with the other. "The Populace of Traventi in full assembly agreed that the Honorable Notary Franz-Karl should be Recognized as next after Her Reverence Sylvia in the line of heirs to the position of Duke. This report – " he lifted it higher, "provides an accounting and summary of the voting, and a notice that the death of one Theodore the Potter has sealed the vote. These –" with a wave at the neat heap of parcels, "contain signs or signatures of all those who voted to approve the Recognition, with seals from those whose rank warrants them." The spokesman handed the final document to the Chief Justice, made another very slight bow toward His Excellency and the acting Archduke, and rejoined the Dowager Countess and her children and attendant.

His Excellency spoke in a voice that filled the room despite its apparent gentleness. "Childe Silvia, I hope you will accept our congratulations on this promotion of your and Leon-Alexander's son Franz-Karl."

She answered in a demure voice that was equally room-filling: in Traventi it was not only princes that were taught rhetoric in all its forms. "It is all very gratifying, Your Excellency. I hope that the absence of female voices in the announcement fulfilled your ritual requirements?"

"It did." His Excellency answered warmly.

"Of a certainty," the acting Archduke agreed. His voice was only a little louder than His Excellency's but it carried a force fit to rattle teeth. His gaze passed over the room, pausing rather pointedly as he met the eyes of some of the courtiers and functionaries.

The Dowager Countess and her companions bowed gracefully, then turned and left the audience chamber, leaving the documents and parcels behind them. They were followed by those seated on the dais in reverse order of their arrival.

The Margraff-Elector was next in precedence of those present after the Imperial family, at least among the Allemanic Nobles. He refused to be preceded by purely Falkenburg vassals like the Duke-Justice. But he could pause only briefly before he followed the various Imperial parties out of the audience chamber. He hastily directed some of his attendants and hangers-on to summon the Ritter von und zu Ostwald and other Pristinists who were Palace functionaries to attend him at his home the next day.

CHAPTER XVII: Summer Scenes in Traventi

Wherein Our Hero Learns Many Things

After breakfast, depending on the weather, Franz-Karl sometimes worked on the pile of lessons he had been given, either copying the instructions out into readable form or writing answers to the ones he had already written out. He set aside the lessons that were incomprehensible and worked on the rest as they came to his hand. His studies progressed, but in an order that resembled no syllabus ever devised.

Fritzel helped find the texts he needed, and signed and dated the answers, providing grownup witness that various tasks were performed from memory without looking at crib sheets. He also helped decipher some of the messier lessons, but there were some sheets where neither of them could do more than guess at the intent of the tutor's writing.

Other times Franz-Karl read in the libraries or archives, or met with his cousins in some parlor or courtyard for games, or lessons in music and dancing. Often, Fritzel stayed nearby: he read while Franz-Karl read or studied, and helped referee some of the games. When Fritzel was busy about his own affairs, Olivia would stay nearby, or sometimes one of the servants of the House would be summoned so that a Notary and Heir of the Line was not left unattended.

Fritzel joined in some of the music and dancing. He was a reasonable partner for Franz-Karl's oldest cousin, Andrea, being the same sort of newly-adult age – though much taller: Andrea was not short, but Fritzel was taller than most people Franz-Karl had ever seen, even in Traventi, provided you ignored the height of horns and such. He played a stringed, bowed instrument called a lira and already knew the tunes and steps for many of the dances, and could sing words that went with the tunes. Some tunes had different words depending on the time of year, or how polite you were trying to be, and Fritzel seemed to know all of them, even the rude ones. Sometimes, especially the rude ones. The cousins all approved of Fritzel, though some of their parents were a little doubtful.

After the mid-day meal, for the first week and more, Franz-Karl and Fritzel went out from the Duke's Residence into the more distant, town-like sections of the House on the Rock. If it was a market day, they explored whichever market was active. If it was not a market day, they visited shops or workshops.

Twice or thrice each week they sat in the back of the public lecture hall near the cathedral (there was only the one lecture hall) and listened to formal discourses by one of the members of the Scholas, or sometimes debates between pairs or groups of Scholars.

Traventi was too small to support a College, much less a University, but it did have a few resident Scholars who took on student-apprentices. A few of the Scholars were loosely attached to the cathedral and primarily cared about educating prospective priests and priestesses, but there was a second group that were more independent and spent much of their time discussing things like Abstract Philosophy or Natural Philosophy, and whether there was a difference, and where Elderkin and the Manifest fit into the structure and pattern of the World.

Fritzel wrote lots of notes of the lectures, filling wax tablets and scraps of paper, and occasionally even offcuts of parchment. Franz-Karl did not understand many of the discussions – some were noisy enough to be arguments, not just debates. But he thought that the demonstrations of dissections, and the new optics with prisms and lenses, were very impressive. So was the telescope recently installed on top of the Tower for Looking at Stars. He drew pictures in his wax tablets during the lectures, or wrote down words that were new or surprising.

Not all of the scholars' attempted demonstrations succeeded, which was sometimes amusing and other times worrying. At least twice the failures might have been dangerous in a place lacking people with useful Gifts and a willingness to act quickly. One of the most energetic 'debates' was about whether there was a way to tell whether a particular demonstration could be performed by Worldfolk without Elderkin aid. Some of the debaters started to provide practical demonstrations of what they were talking about, until someone important stopped them: Franz-Karl thought she was a Master Scholar, but the Free Scholars did not dress in any special way, so it was hard to tell.

Some of the younger scholars came to the Ducal Residence to spend evenings talking with Fritzel, or play chess or other games. A few became interested in sorting out the puzzle of Franz-Karl's mixed up lessons. Eventually, even the scholar Maestra Diotima, and Marcus, the Chief Archivist and Historian of Traventi got involved.

Since most of the Notarial oaths that Franz-Karl had chosen were connected to contracts and Witnessing, he and Fritzel visited the Courts of Law on a few occasions, but only when they were invited to observe by the Justice and Advocates. Traventi was afflicted by what was called the Curse of Rano, which made amending agreements in Traventi tricky at the best of times: to change a Bound contract you needed all of the original signers and witnesses to agree. If some of them were dead or missing, (like Theodore the Potter, after the Recognition Vote) you were out of luck for amending things, and the Bound agreement was permanently part of the landscape underlying any future negotiations. The weight of extra Binders bearing witness would cause extra anchors, so having an unexpected Notary turn up at random could cause ferocious complications in future dealings with contracts that had expected the ordinary sort of witnesses: even ordinary Elderkin Witnesses. It would be rude for a sworn Notary to go into the Law Courts unasked, especially a Notary who was going to be living far away in Karnburg in a few months' time.

Franz-Karl and Fritzel dined with Justice Laurentina after each law court session they observed, and she encouraged Franz-Karl to ask questions about the ceremonies and procedures as well as the decisions that were made. That was almost better than being able to sit in the council sessions. Franz-Karl had a lot of questions, and learned the answers well enough that as Harvest approached he was allowed to serve as presiding Notary in a few small matters, with a regular Justice observing in case things turned tricky.

They also sat several times with Maestro Petros. Maestro Petros was an elderly Notary who had a quirk of mind that stopped him from reading written texts, but he had more knowledge of the subtleties of spoken contracts and Bindings than any three other people in the Duchy combined. Franz-Karl suspected that Maestro Petros also knew more gossip than any three people: at least about people living in or near the House on the Rock – if not the Duchy as a whole – any time during the past three generations. Sitting with Maestro Petros beside the Saint Victoria fountain on market day and watching him deal with market disputes was extremely educational, but not always in ways some people back at the Palace would have approved of. Her Grace his Grandmother laughed when Franz-Karl mentioned Maestro Petros, and sent the old Notary her regards.

Most nights before Franz-Karl went to sleep, he listened to bedtime stories that were not in any of the books. Usually it was Fritzel telling the stories, but sometimes it was Olivia. Once, on the Eve of a Festival, they told a story together and did all of the voices between them. Occasionally, Her Reverend Grace the Duke His Grandmother came to sit beside his bed and tell him old stories of their ancestors that were rarely shared with outsiders.

Twining around all of this learning about Traventi: the dancing and games and libraries and scholars and law courts and markets and stories, there were always the formal lessons in the Trivia that had been sent with Franz-Karl on the journey from Karnburg. He used a style of writing that was quick and clear – like a Remoran version of the Elderic script that Willie had show him at the Council session – and was very glad that he was good at memorizing things.

He sometimes thought about an old story about a bird that had to peck at a mountain until the mountain was gone. But as the summer progressed, the pile of completed lessons grew taller and the piles of unfinished lessons grew shorter.

INTERLUDE V: An Inhospitable Chamber

Wherein Layers of Conspiracies Are Discussed

The Margraff-Elector had closed the doors between the public and residential sections of his city estate and the portion that served as the White Hall for the Pristinist community. He expected to be discussing matters that were no concern of the Teacher and the Preacher. The Teacher merely shrugged and returned to his rooms at the one Reformist college that was tolerated at the city's University. The Preacher, who lived in a pair of rooms just outside the White Hall, found it more inconvenient: with the house doors locked his servant could not visit the estate's kitchens, and neither of them could go out into the city.

The room where Horst-Konrad received the men he had summoned was called the study, but was not arranged to support study. The one chair was not designed for comfort, and there were only two books visible: ostentatiously displayed, but without labels on their spines or covers and far out of easy reach of the person seated in that chair. If there were other books or papers present, they were hidden away in cabinets and cupboards that were kept carefully locked, and in most cases bolted to the walls. The inkstand on one corner of the desk or worktable was spotless and held a single pen and a full inkwell. On the opposite corner of the desk a polished silver tray bore three unlabeled decanters of clear cut glass holding variously colored liquids, and a single small, matching goblet. On a third corner of the desk there was a gavel resting on a hollow wooden box, tuned to resonate. The walls were white. The furniture was made of dark woods transported from distant lands.

It was not a general gathering: the men who had been summoned stood in an antechamber, uncomfortably silent, until they were summoned into the Margraff-Elector's presence individually, or in pairs, or – just once – in a group of three. No food or drink was offered to those waiting, nor was there a single spark of flame in the antechamber. These were not men who discussed policy with someone of the Margraff-Elector's rank: these were men who received orders – always phrased as suggestions – and went away to obey them.

The suggestions they received were very carefully phrased. No one, of course, would disobey orders delivered with the authority of His Excellency, or His Royal Grace the acting Archduke, and within the Palace Her Excellency was the ritually established Mistress.

But it was the responsibility of the Imperial family's faithful servants to safeguard Imperial time and goods and wealth and honor. Surely no honorable servant could justify setting the convenience – or needs – of the beast-born above those of His Excellency's proper, human subjects and servants. Not when there were better – more righteous – uses for such wealth and goods and labor and attention.

These were faithful followers of the Pristinist teachings that set Elderkin somewhere below livestock in the proper hierarchy of the world. Most of the men eagerly accepted the offered license to obstruct and inconvenience the affairs of what was now generally called the Traventine Household: no longer Grand Duke Leon-Alexander's.

One or two, who served in offices headed by non-Pristinist officials, seemed worried by the suggested disobedience. The Margraff-Elector did not press them. Neither was in a position that mattered much. The northern Pristinists had been influencing appointments for years to ensure that people they trusted held most useful positions of authority in the Palace. The more they succeeded, the easier it became to go further: proof that Heaven smiled on their efforts.

The group of three who faced the Margraff-Elector together included the chamberlain Ritter von und zu Ostwald, the Master of Protocol of the Palace, and a minor official from the office charged with managing the Imperial Privy Purse. These three were higher born than the rest (though still far beneath the Margraff-Elector) so their discussion with him nearly approached the form of a conversation. They each, once or twice, offered comments that were not responses to direct questions.

Their first problem was the lands and wealth associated with the county of Wolfsberg, which had been designated for the support of the new Count and his mother and siblings. The teachings of Pristinus de Millau assured his followers that females provided their male progeny with shelter and sustenance without contributing to their inheritable traits, only molding their surfaces. But a generation hosted in beast-born females and stamped with their corruption had no place among the Select of Heaven. The boy's features allowed no argument that Philip-Augustus was not Leon-Alexander's son. But, since he lacked a human mother, the full rules of patriarchy and primogeniture might not count him as legitimate, making him a False Heir.

Fortunately, the False Heir was still a decade from his majority, and His Excellency was old. If the formal transfer of the Wolfsberg rights could be delayed, and His Excellency were to die before Philip-Augustus was of age, the matter might resolve itself. The Wolfsberg title and property could reasonably transfer to a member of Helm-Friedrich's less polluted line. In either case, steps would need to be taken to ensure the beast-born witch's female spawn did not marry into and corrupt any properly human Highborn lineage.

They all agreed that if Philip-Augustus was not a useful tool to bring Traventi into the imperial protection of Wolfsberg, there was no compelling reason for him to get any benefit of the imperial inheritance at all.

"Of course," the Master of Protocol said, thoughtfully, "the Changeling Brat is in the Traventi Ducal line now, but he is even younger than the False heir, and small children sometimes fail to thrive, no matter how promising their beginnings... if the False Heir can also be added to the Ducal line, even though he follows his brother, the original plan may still work. No need to be too hasty in the matter of the Wolfsberg properties, or too public in challenging the False Heir during his Grandfather's reign. We don't want the old man to issue another Edict on Inheritance."

All four men shuddered: the great territorial princes had been spared, but the last sputter of the Sectarian Wars had been a loss of temper by His Excellency's late father that had disordered the estates and domains of the Reformist North and disrupted marriage negotiations of long standing. Inheritances and holdings of the middling nobility in the North had been reshuffled to suit the preference of the late King of the Allemans, with enforcement that in one instance had involved gelding knives, and in another, an extra-judicial executioner's ax. His Excellency Friedrich-Augustus was far more amenable to persuasion than his late father had been, to the great relief of his vassals, but Helm-Friedrich, who was now acting Archduke, showed worrying signs of inheriting a bit of his Grandfather's stubbornness.

Ritter von und zu Ostwald had spent more time in the presence of the three beast-born brats than any of the others. He reminded them that if they wished to hold the original plan for Traventi and Wolfsberg in reserve, it would be vital that the False Heir should be properly constrained to obedience, and possibly the Changeling Brat as well.

"Proper discipline and an appropriate choice of tutors and lessons should suffice," the Margraff-Elector said, with a slight but real smile that his companions found profoundly worrying. None of them dared ask what he meant.

With the flow of the Wolfsberg funds temporarily disrupted, financial support for the False Heir and the Dowager Countess, Childe Silvia of Traventi would then depend on the Imperial Privy Purse. The Purser assured the others that no directions had been given about dispersing those funds, since it was assumed the the Wolfsberg treasury was accessible to the Traventine Household. On the contrary, since the household was no longer supporting a Prince busy about his father's business, and Silvia's entourage was now even smaller than envisioned in the original Wedding Contract, there had been a careful directive about reducing the flow of funds in that direction.

There was no office in the Allemanic and Falkenburg governments that would notice or report any excessive reduction of the Traventine Household to anyone in authority. There was no authority with a responsibility to take notice, and those offices that came nearest the matter were directed by Pristinists, who would naturally ignore the complaints of lesser beings like women and beast-born.

The kitchen at the north end of West Palace served the beast-born-infested Residence and catered to their bizarre rules for meal service. It answered to the staff of Her Excellency in her role as Mistress of the Palace, and there was no hope of Purging the ancient abomination of a woman with authority over men any time soon. Chamberlain von und zu Ostwald warned that sudden changes to the kitchen's staff and activities would draw the attention of Her Excellency's excessively diligent attendants. But the quality and quantity of the supplies (and workers) provided might be gradually diminished and the relevant funds safely diverted to less sacrilegious uses. That was all they could manage for the present.

After the Palace officials had agreed to their path forward and taken their leave, the Margraff-Elector paused for a midday meal that owed more to expensive imported ingredients than to the currently flourishing local crops. Horst-Konrad von Neumark returned to his study for an interview that involved the Margraff-Elector himself seated behind his desk, and Meister van Diesen, tutor to Philip-Augustus, on his knees in front of it.

The tutor kept his eyes decently lowered, and his hands at his sides, but his body was straight, his voice was calm – though tired – and he did not flinch when the Margraff-Elector's tone sharpened. Though certainly no Ecclesialist, as a Harfneran he was less impressed by rank and hierarchy than a Pristinist would have been.

The Margraff-Elector gazed at him for a long moment before demanding, "Well, scholar, how do your tasks progress?"

"Your Serene Highness may rest assured that the Count of Wolfsberg is progressing with gratifying speed both through the formal lesson plan and the less formal and more important lessons about the proper beliefs and behavior of an Imperial Prince. He rarely refers to the customs of his mother's people, these days, but is polite and properly biddable according to his age when dealing with those in authority over him."

Horst-Konrad snorted in a most undignified fashion. "Beast-born brats not yet thoroughly broken to service are incapable of learning or politeness. That is both doctrine *and* common knowledge."

"Then why provide one with a tutor, Highness?"

The Margraff-Elector's jaw dropped – very briefly – with the shock of being questioned. "Their Excellencies required a tutor for the creature they insist on treating as a grandchild. We had hoped that you would show some resistance to the wretched thing's deceits. Have a care that it does not lure you to your destruction: body and soul."

"As Your Serene Highness commands." The man bowed by bending at the waist, not by prostrating himself. The Margraff-Elector tapped a finger on a paper with an account of the ongoing unsuccessful search for a more amenable, Pristinist tutor willing to work with a beast-born brat... and refrained from summoning his servants to have the fool whipped.

"You were also instructed to provide lessons for the younger brat..." A snap of fingers directed the tutor to continue.

"The lessons for the younger Traventine boy –" the Margraff-Elector glared, but did not correct the term, "were prepared precisely according to the extremely detailed instructions given to me by Your Serene Highness's servants. Despite the lack of advance notice or sufficient time for the tasks. First, the usual series of instructions and lesson texts were ... adjusted... with the addition of the various required phrases progressing through the sequence. Next, certain lesson pages that contained designated phrases were anointed using brushes dipped in the various colorless liquids provided, in the patterns specified. And finally, the three additional lessons that were provided were copied by my hand onto the sheets of treated paper that I was given using the special inks, allowed to dry without blotting, and inserted in the required locations in the succession of pages."

The Margraff-Elector held a letter from servants in his pay who had carefully watched the tutor during his labors and had not reported any deviations from the complicated instructions the man had been given. Despite his uneasiness, there was no evidence that the Changeling Brat had received anything but what Horst-Konrad's servants had devised for him. He cast it down on the desktop in unseemly annoyance.

The Margraff-Elector sent the tutor away, but remained unsatisfied. He poured a small amount of a clear liqueur with colored specks floating in it, and sipped at it while he thought. Finally, he sent a summons to his kennel-master, and one household clerk whose skills – carefully hidden from the Preacher – ran more to secret writings and forbidden wisdom than to account books.

During the time before they arrived, he walked to a plain, locked cupboard, firmly attached to the wall in the corner of the study farthest from his desk. Unlocked and opened, the cupboard interior revealed patterns in five colors, including metallic silver and gold, all over the inside walls and doors, exceedingly carefully applied so that the patterns would form a continuous cage when the doors were closed.

There were three books stuffed haphazardly into the bottom of the cupboard, a lumpy object shrouded in pure black silk on the next shelf up, and fifteen objects carefully arranged on the upper cupboard shelves. Some of the talismans were precious in their materials and crafting, others might have been culled from some midden. Three were utensils that might have been gathered from any workshop or kitchen.

The Margraff-Elector reached out his hand, but drew it back without touching any of the objects. Useful as they were, talismans carried beast-born contamination, so faithful Pristinists were enjoined to avoid such things. Horst-Konrad took a slim, battered volume from the bottom shelf of the cupboard and placed it on his desk face down, so that the three alchemical symbols on its cover were hidden. He closed the cupboard door but did not lock it while the book was out of it.

When they arrived, the clerk entered the room and knelt, crouched and huddled, on the same spot before the desk that the tutor had recently occupied. His garments were worn and showed a few ink stains, but were intact – not ragged – and he wore a badge of indentured servitude with six unbroken tabs remaining pinned to one lapel.

The kennel-master knelt in the doorway, with his knees just outside the formal boundary of the threshold: he carried even more contamination than the talismans, but had the advantage that he could be given spoken orders from a distance. He wore a slave's iron collar, and barely enough cloth for decency, and his skin showed marks that came from neither blades nor burns nor ink.

The Margraff-Elector questioned the clerk first, reviewing the design and creation of the trap for the Changeling Brat from the beginning, when they selected the text that would provide the structure and instructions from the three books and five fragments they had available. Everything seemed plausible and complete, but then, they could hardly review their preparations with someone more experienced.

On the one hand, despite the clearly pious intent of the act, the imperial courts were unpleasantly likely to view the creation of a demon trap as treason when the intended target was publicly acknowledged as the Emperor's kin, so the Margraff-Elector could not openly seek assistance. And on the other hand, experienced demon hunters were able to charge exorbitant fees, even for advice, because so few survived to be counted as experienced. Successful, surviving captors of demons – rather than dispellers of demons – were even rarer and accordingly even more expensive.

Pristinist texts did not entirely prohibit the use of demon traps, but they included dire warnings against them. Public involvement in such disreputable matters was far beneath the dignity of a Prince-Elector of the Kingdom of the Allemans. So he kept the matter private.

The Highborn Pristinist and his tame hedge-wizard reviewed all of their steps and choices, and came to the same conclusions as five times before. All of the instructions given to the tutor and the demands given to the kennel-master and his charges strictly followed the directions in the manual they had employed.

The Margraff-Elector finally sighed and sent the man away. If there were any flaws in their contrivance, they were weeks past any point where they could make adjustments except to the portion that remained in Karnburg, and that remained as flawless at they could make it and safely stored in its protective cover until its time came. He poured a larger portion of the glittery liqueur.

He gazed at the kennel-master for a long moment, then tapped the cover of the book from the cupboard. "Could They have conspired together to disrupt my plans?

The slave scratched one of the marks on his skin. "Not conspired..." he said, finally. His Allemanic was abominable and gave little hint of what his native tongue might have been. "Them beasts in t' kennels get no sight or sound each t' other, and the three that was tasked with t' work come out on separate days entire, with t' other beasts an' workings safe locked away." The Margraff-Elector leaned back a little in his hard chair, but straightened when the kennel-master added, "Did seem number 'leven was mebbe a bit pleased with hisself. Kind o' smug."

"You did not think to report it?" Horst-Konrad snapped.

"Report to who? And when? Your Serene Highness an' his wizard took away t' goods w'out askin' for a report."

"But it obeyed the instructions..."

"I give 'em the stuff an' tools and spoke the exact words I was gave to speak. Din't see none of them make a move that warn't required, nor leave none out... But..." He shrugged, and scratched again, somewhere less decent. "Wondered some about that paint stuff."

"The book says Eleven is clever..." The Margraff-Elector had, naturally, never conversed with the creatures in his father's collection. He had barely even looked at them, and never commanded them directly.

The kennel-master grunted. It might have been agreement. "Clev'rest wild-caught's wuss'n a stupid captive-bred beast-born for dangerous: safest to point 'em at a target 'n' step back yerself." He cocked his head, considering. "Two an' seven... them's fine fer fancy work. Needs careful words, but the work'll get done t' match t' words. But eleven...?" He shook his head doubtfully.

"Which of the pack would you have chosen as a third tool? Not the captive-bred, I assume." The Margraff-Elector's tone was sarcastic, but the slave answered seriously.

"Nah. Beast-born'r bound by words, but they got to know t'words, like. Caprtive-bred get took fro t'mamas too young for fancy work. Words'r jus' noise. So that's nine o' the fifteen gone. So...fancy work... two an' seven's fine... 'leven an' fourteen need tight words: tight, tight words. Five's a hammer: no good fer needlework..."

"Leaving thirteen? The bitch?? For work that needs strength? Hardly!"

The slave shrugged. "T'Master knows best, o' course."

The Margraff-Elector struck the wooden box on his deck with the gavel, hard. When the guard stationed beyond ordinary hearing range arrived, he flicked a hand at the kennel-master. "Take that back where it belongs... and tell the kitchen it gets a lump of meat in its next bowl of swill."

When both men were gone and the study door was shut, he returned the book to the cupboard, still without looking at its contents. After locking the cupboard door he tested it twice.

Then he poured a third, even larger portion of the liqueur.

CHAPTER XVIII: The Pond and the Seas

Wherein Our Hero Learns Skills and Hears Tales of the World

Officially, the reason that Franz-Karl and Fritzel were doing all of their wandering around – aside from generally letting Franz-Karl learn about Traventi and the House on the Rock and letting his people see their newly Recognized Heir – was that they were looking for someone to teach them to swim. It had turned out to be quite hard to find such a person. Fritzel had not exaggerated the inhospitable reputation of the bodies of water available near the House on the Rock. There were rumors of a group of people who could swim over in the South Valley, near the road that led south toward the Mothersea, and possibly others in the North Valley, where there was a small lake that was easier to sail or row across than walk around, but swimmers were rare in and around the House on the Rock.

The teacher they finally found was a spice merchant called Argens. He had a small shop near the merchants' market by Saint Victoria and all the Saints, but the shop door opened into a quieter garden courtyard, not the main market square. His shop sign was a model ship fully rigged for ocean sailing, and his wares were rare and precious enough that customers sought him out, and did not haggle much.

Maestro Petros said that Argens' hair had been the same silvery white his whole life. He had mismatched cats' eyes – one blue and one green. One of his legs was missing below the knee, with the missing bit replaced by a clever wooden device of Traventine manufacture that would have been unavailable or fiercely expensive anywhere outside the Duchy's borders. He had been a sailor on the great salt oceans when he was young, and the amputated leg was his most dramatic scar, but not the only one. There was a scar on the left side of his face that barely missed the blue eye.

Franz-Karl thought that Argens was probably much older than him and Fritzel together: he was definitely a grownup and had traveled for enough time to acquire those scars. And he was almost certainly younger than Reverend Count Great Aunt Adrasteia. Beyond that, Franz-Karl was not willing to guess.

Argens agreed to go with them to one of the smaller – and therefore, hopefully, warmer – ponds on the next sunny afternoon. The pond had been made by damming a stream to regulate water flow to a mill, so the shape of the bottom was well known and included no sharp rocks or unexpected drop-offs. It was also too high on the mountainside to be reshaped much by the spring flood waters, or find itself stocked with unexpectedly fierce fish when the flood waters receded, so it was the safest place for swimming lessons convenient to the House on the Rock.

They set a pile of towels and blankets in a sunny spot safely away from the water's edge. Then Argens stripped completely and exchanged his complicated wooden foot in its boot for a simple peg. His remaining leg was complicated through the foot and ankle and rather furry from the toes to the knee, but aside from that and his cats' eyes he was shaped much like the Worldfolk men in the various wall paintings in the Karnburg Palace, though finer-boned than many – he carried his weight in muscle, not bone.

Fritzel also stripped quickly. He was not quite as human-shaped as Argens, but the differences were mostly subtle: more depth from spine to breastbone, less taper from shoulder to hip, bracing and buttressing in neck and shoulders and the heavy bones of his skull for the weight of heavy horns that were not there, more bracing in the hips and legs. His eyes were Elderkin cow-eyes: so dark the horizontal oblong pupils were not noticeable unless you knew to look, and he had much the same two-toed, hoof-nailed feet as those that ran in Franz-Karl's family. His short black pelt was as sparse against most of his fair skin as any Worldfolk man's, though the denser patches were arranged a bit oddly – and on his head and neck the barber had been able to sculpt borders that made it look like a human's hair and a fashionable, if close-cropped, beard.

Franz-Karl undressed slowly. He knew that it was not dangerous for people in Traventi to see his unclothed shape with its little goat's tail, but he knew it the way he knew the exports of the Isles or the list of Gallic Kings: facts in his head, not a certainty in his gut. The habit of caution was very strong. Being with a grownup who was also cow-eyed and cloven-footed made it a little easier. When he removed his loose shirt – it's long tails fell nearly to his knees – he stood looking across the pond, not at his companions, expecting... he did not know what he expected.

Fritzel said cheerfully, "Well, your Honor, we've shared rooms these past nights and I've truly not known you have a tail until this moment. If those Karnburg folk have trained you to such caution with your tail? It's as well I have none of my own, for I'd never manage it when we journey there."

Franz-Karl did not know how to answer that. Asking whether some of Fritzel's relatives had long tails like cows seemed too rude, even with no one but Elderkin to hear the answer.

Argens just began to explain the tricks he knew for surviving in and around water.

It turned out that Franz-Karl and Fritzel had both been partly right in their predictions about the swimming lessons. The water was cold, but swimming was fun after the shock of the first plunge. Fritzel preferred not to stay in the water very long at a stretch, but even though Franz-Karl was so much smaller, he found the water's chill less uncomfortable. Fritzel said after their third session, when they were beginning to travel through the water almost reliably, that it seemed unfair for Franz-Karl to take the chill less.

Argens was perched comfortably on a sun-warmed rock. He nodded in a satisfied way. "Not much surprise there. His Honor is in the Admiral's line to be sure: Corentin's much the same. Not a large man... but the water was always friendlier to him than the rest of us, even in the northern seas that carry blocks of ice as big as mountains."

Franz-Karl sat up abruptly where he was lying on the sun-warmed grass. He had a cloth draped across his midsection now that they were out of the water, so his tail was hidden. But his feet were bare for anyone to see – which still felt very daring – and his russet-brown hair was beginning to show anyone who cared to look even more green streaks than usual from sun-bleaching. Wearing his hat properly seemed to make little difference.

"Do you know my other grandfather, then, Maestro Argens?"

"I sailed with the Seadragon for nearly a decade." The old sailor's eyes looked into a distance that did not contain Traventi's mountains. "It would be false to say that we sailed a proper voyage around the world, for we never set out from a single port and went all of the way around and returned to the same port or one nearby. But we reached the great seaports of the Middle Kingdom more than once coming from the west, and at least once from the east, after making the Long Passage from the west coast of the Western Lands. So I think we can rightly claim to have been all around the world."

"Is Admiral Armorius a dragon himself, then?" Fritzel asked.

"Like Reverend Count Valens, d'ye mean?" Franz-Karl was surprised by that: no one had mentioned that the Reverend Count was a Dragon. But he kept quiet so as not interrupt Argens' memories.

"Nah." The former sailor continued cheerfully. "The Seadragon is the ship... or ships: the official Traventine Navy only ever has the one ship – unless himself has gotten shipwrecked again recently, so it's none – but it isn't always the same ship. But the name carries across whenever she's rebuilt, along with her figurehead if it can be managed." He shook his head slowly, smiling. "It usually can be managed. The Admiral himself carries a heavy weight of Watery Gifts and Manifest Heritage, of course: heavy as Her Grace. That's why he's out there beyond the coasts and not here." He swept a hand around from the House on the Rock on one side of them to the mountains on the other. "The Admiral has set a heavy weight of Bindings on that figurehead. And most of the crew carry some weight of Manifest heritage besides: those that die rarely drown."

Franz-Karl wondered whether that business with Philip-Augustus and the duck pond had been a hint of Watery Gifts and Heritage trying to come out in his generally stodgy brother. Trying to teach Philip-Augustus Hiding had been hopeless, and Sparks seemed unlikely. Watery Gifts – along with Papa's famous knack for languages – at least seemed not impossible.

From then on, whenever Argens was teaching them swimming, and rescuing people from drowning – and how to get the water out of the people once you got the people out of the water – he also told Franz-Karl and Fritzel wonderful stories about seafaring as a youth: stories full of pirates and storms and distant lands, spices and treasures and strange people and customs. He never claimed the stories were true – there were at least three versions of the story of what had happened to his leg – but it was fairly clear that many of the events he described had happened to someone, if not to him. There were other stories that Argens stated plainly were tales he had heard told in foreign places. Some of those stories were very strange indeed: telling of things like giant birds that could carry off full-grown elephants, and huge rabbits the size of deer that carried their young in pockets.

Argens never said that his Admiral was a shape-shifter, exactly, but he never said he was not. There were several stories where a wonderful golden water-beast appeared to aid members of the crew, with the famously golden-haired Admiral nowhere in sight until he turned up safely afterward.

When Franz-Karl and Fritzel discussed the stories during their walks through the city, they agreed that the hints about the water-beast were nearly as clear as plain speech. Shape-shifting was not common in Traventi, though it was said to be common in Manifest lineages elsewhere. But, of course, Corentin was not originally from Traventi, though he was now the landlocked domain's Admiral and had been the Duke's official consort.

One day when there was so much not-very-distant thunder that Argens judged that swimming would be unwise, Franz-Karl brought the spice-merchant into Her Grace's study, which held the finest globe in the Duchy, and asked him to point out some of the places he had visited. Franz-Karl agreed that Argens had been all around the watery parts of the world, north and south, east and west. There were even places Argens had visited that were not on the globe because the official map makers did not know about them. Fritzel took a pen and paper and drew maps of the landforms that Argens described that were not on the globe.

Her Grace Franz-Karl's Grandmother came in during the discussion. She showed them some gifts and trophies that Corentin had sent her from different foreign places and invited Argens to join their family dinner that evening, and talk with her about her wandering husband.

When they could not find other Elderkin things to say mean things about, gossipy people in the Imperial Palace argued about whether Franz-Karl's Mama's parents were divorced, which would be very scandalous, or the Admiral of Traventi had abandoned his wife and daughter, which would be even more scandalous. But the plaques for Corentin of the line of Armorius were still in their proper places both in Franz-Karl's Mama's Household Shrine in the Palace and in Her Grace his Grandmother's Household Shrine here in the House on the Rock. So Corentin Armorius was still to be counted as Family.

Franz-Karl thought Her Grace his Grandmother seemed quiet and sad rather than angry when she talked about her husband, off sailing around in the great oceans far away. The mountains around the House on the Rock made Franz-Karl happy – even just knowing they were there and thinking that someday he would be able to run around in them – but it would be horrible to be a sea creature stuck up in the mountains away from the ocean, as bad as being the cheetah in a Menagerie where there was no place to run. That cheetah was always sad and grumpy, and even hated the person who fed it.

It would be horrible to watch your home hurting someone you cared about, too.

Fritzel asked Argens a question about the Spice Islands that started a long and surprisingly funny story about a hunt for stolen treasure while protecting honest fisher-folk and villagers from reivers and slavers. Franz-Karl had heard some parts of the story before, but listened eagerly.

Her Grace his Grandmother cheered up enough to laugh at the funny parts, and to ask questions when Argens tried to slide past some things that had happened. The former sailor still glanced at Franz-Karl a few times and clearly changed some of the words he had been planning to say. There was one time Argens winked at Her Grace and she laughed that Franz-Karl did not understand at all. Fritzel laughed with them.

Grownups laughing together made him a little sad, because his Mama and Papa used to do that. But it was a warm kind of sad.

CHAPTER XIX: Summer Tax Day

Wherein Our Hero and His Companion
Make Themselves Useful

By the end of the month of Quintil, Franz-Karl was reaching the bottom of the larger pile of lesson papers that had come from Karnburg. All that were left were the most awful, messy puzzles: nothing plainly written.

Fritzel challenged some of the more senior Scholars and Archivists, to see what they could make of them. There were several quite fierce arguments about what a proper set of lessons ought to contain, that was missing from Franz-Karl's pile of results. Maestra Diotima from the Schola and Maestro Marcus the Chief Archivist became extremely sarcastic at each other. But eventually there were enough agreements that Franz-Karl was able to finish more of the assigned tasks and add their clean copies and results to the pile of finished lessons.

He was quite proud that once he knew what the lessons were supposed to be, he could usually manage to do them himself: no one asking him trick questions in Karnburg was going to benefit by doing it. But the part of the days set aside for working on lessons started to be emptier.

Summer Tax Day, on the first of Sextil, a full quarter of the year after May Day, provided a welcome change. That morning, Franz-Karl and Fritzel visited the tax office in the Tower for Looking at Stars, partly because Fritzel's family held some taxable property inside the House on the Rock's hedge and he had been sent a package of cash money to pay the amount due. Franz-Karl went with him because it promised a change from the Karnburg lessons, and he had been puzzling over a mention of Tax Day in an old story and hoped that seeing it would make more sense.

At first, after Fritzel's payment was handed over and the receipt had been created and handed back, they stood out of the way and watched the Chief Clerk Livia and the other clerks do their work. Franz-Karl tried not to interrupt when they were extremely busy, but he found that he had many questions and the clerks were very polite about answering them in between dealing with clumps of people paying taxes.

Then three ducks got loose from their basket, and soon Livia and the other clerks were letting Franz-Karl and Fritzel help count things and corral poultry and other livestock. Fritzel was very good at retrieving birds and animals that had escaped their cages or pens. Franz-Karl was less skilled at catching animals, but small enough to follow some of them into places where Fritzel would not fit. And he was nearly as good as Livia at counting things quickly and remembering numbers and summing them up.

Livia had been one of the scribes at the Council session where Franz-Karl became an official Notary. When she realized that Franz-Karl was carrying his Notarial signet, she asked him to sit at the counter and witness the receipts for people making payments. Notarial receipts were quicker and more trusted than clerk receipts, and having Franz-Karl sitting at that desk freed a pair of grownup hands for other tasks.

It was all quite noisy and chaotic, and Franz-Karl thought it was great deal of fun. It was all very well to read documents that talked about the amounts owed and the different ways the tax debt could be paid. Then you found yourself in a room where someone had paid his taxes with cabbages and someone else had paid with a live goat, and part of your time was spent making sure the cabbages did not get eaten by the goat, in between using the exchequer counters to add things up and signing and sealing receipts. It was a kind of fun that mattered, both to the Duchy and to its people.

He thought that it was probably a good thing that no one tried to pay their taxes with live wolves. Goats and cabbages were enough trouble. And the tax office did not have a boat.

At least... there were no live wolves at the House on the Rock this tax day. Franz-Karl would not be surprised if there was something in the Archives about paying taxes with live wolves. The way things seemed to work in Traventi, there was probably a case in the Archives where payment in live wolves was required for some specific fee. With at least two later amendments explaining what to do if there were no live wolves available.

Taxes in the Duchy seemed as complicated as jurisdictions and authority in the Karnburg Palace.

Some Traventine tax payments were classed as Gold, which included coined money and all sorts of material goods, but also work performed for the Duchy that did not require Gifts or Bindings. The other tax payments were classed as Favors, which included anything that required Gifts or Bindings. There were a few cases where the categories could be exchanged: there was a standard fee in Gold for Binding a contract that could be paid to a single Notary or Binder or divided among a group of lighter Elderkin. But most Favors had no fixed value either in Gold or other Favors. That was part of why saying 'Thank you' was tricky: people might decide that they were being taken advantage of in an exchange of Favors and get cranky.

The Duchy could not usually demand any particular Favors in payment because of the laws against enslavement of Elderkin, so arranging to get the Favors it needed sometimes got complicated. Being the installed Duke or a territorial Count was counted as paying taxes in Favors, because they were tangled in the Gates of Air and had some other tasks for Traventi that no one else could perform. The titles and ranks were partly compensation for being stuck with those tasks.

There was one grumpy old farmer named Gearoid – a large, stocky man with a hound's sad eyes and droopy ears – who was a Binder heavy enough to make the world twitchy, but not a Notary: he said Notaries carried too many Bindings. He insisted on paying all of his taxes in Gold even though there were plenty of reports that he had done lots of Favors during the Spring Floods that he could have claimed credit for. Livia handled his account herself. She seemed a bit embarrassed by the situation, and asked twice whether Gearoid was certain of his path.

Gearoid said firmly, "Unless the Law now requires Elderkin to pay in Favors – which if it does, some Councilors need to die, and I can't imagine Her Reverence standing for it – I'll pay my debts in the World's wares." But he did not sound angry, and he winked at Franz-Karl as he turned to leave.

Franz-Karl wondered whether paying Gold instead of Favors might be like the nineteen in twenty rule for the voting: a way of saying 'No' to prove that you could say 'No'.

Fritzel spent the entire afternoon carrying crates and lifting things, and being stern to livestock, and at the end of it he was brisk and cheerful, and almost annoyingly tidy, except for a few minor streaks of dust on his coat. Despite his very fair skin and pitch black hair, there was no shadow of stubble in the shaved places around his beard, even at the end of the long day.

Franz-Karl had sat in a chair on a cushion much of the time, reading receipts and signing his name and squishing wax with his signet, but by the time the tax office closed he was thirsty and feeling grimy, and his clothes were dusty with three colors of dust that managed to show even against the color-of-sorrow. And even more tendrils of his hair were escaping from his hair tie than usual at the end of a long, active day: green and russet-brown, both.

When he stood up, he went dizzy and his knees buckled. Fritzel caught him by the arm to stop him from falling over, and Livia sat him back down in the chair.

Livia sent her junior clerks to fetch bread and cheese and watered wine for everyone who had worked the day. She could not speak properly to Franz-Karl because he had his eyes closed waiting for things to stop spinning, so she said to Fritzel, "Well, young man, you'll need to have a better eye to his Honor when he's busy. Flesh doesn't rightly notice when the Manifest parts are working hard, so he'll likely surprise himself a time or two as he grows into being a full Notary."

"Oh, aye. It's a thing I've heard of but not seen, being youngest and least in my own line," Fritzel agreed readily, "and it seems open Favors are a rare thing at that Lowland Palace, so himself did not know to be cautious. I'll know to have a care, now... Here, your Honor, have some of this..."

A cold cup was placed in Franz-Karl's hand. He lifted it to his lips and drank without opening his eyes: it was a rich, sweet, red wine:

very good, and not watered nearly as much as he expected. After drinking about half of the cup, he opened his eyes. The world did a final shimmy, then settled down. He reached for some of the bread and cheese on the shared platter in front of him.

Livia watched him eat, probably to make sure the food stayed where it belonged, then stepped away to her work table. She returned with a small purse for Franz-Karl and one for Fritzel, and a paper record of account for each of them. Traventi did not use much gold coinage within its borders: sizable transactions were managed by careful record keeping, not heaps of metal.

Fritzel whistled when he saw Franz-Karl's record of account: the price in Gold of a Notary bearing witness was fixed, and a seven year old full Notary was still a full Notary, and Franz-Karl had been busy. "Dear Heaven and all the saints! It's no wonder your Honor went shaky. We'll need to see you pace yourself better."

Franz-Karl was more interested in the contents of his purse. This was the first time he had ever handled coins, which were a matter for servants and grownups. He was not even sure there were coins inside the Palace walls except locked in chests in some Treasury storeroom. And now these were his own coins. He could buy things for himself on market day without trying to explain what he wanted to some servant or clerk and accepting the wrong thing they gave him in response.

Traventi did not mint copper or silver coinage, no more than the gold. The brass coins in the purse had come south from Augsburg on the Daonas, much as Franz-Karl had himself. The silver coins had come north through the mountains from the fertile plains beyond, and the ports along the Mothersea. One silver piece was from Mistella, recently minted from good metal: Franz-Karl laughed a little when he turned it over and saw the Duke-Viceroy's Falkenburg device, differenced by a compass star like the one on his own signet. He stowed it in a waistcoat pocket as a luck-piece before he put the purse away in his coat.

CHAPTER XX: Weather and Preparations

*Wherein a Festival Draws Near
and the Mistress of Riddles Speaks Plainly*

As the summer was ending and the harvests began, Franz-Karl's cousins began to pay anxious attention to the sky and spent the breaks in their morning games and lessons discussing the weather. They also spent more time and attention on their dance lessons and games, so that Franz-Karl was very nearly late for some midday meals. Morgan had always been fussy about the precise details of how people did things – he reminded Franz-Karl a little of his brother in that, except that following Morgan's advice nearly always improved Franz-Karl's scores or performances – but as the days passed he got fussier about everything until he became very annoying.

Finally, on a day near mid-Sextil when the others were all looking at the sky during a pause in their dance lessons, Franz-Karl asked, "Does the weather matter so much more than it did last week?" He was getting quite bored with the frequent discussions about the color of the sky, and every tiny cloud that appeared in it, and whether the upper winds were blowing the same way as the ones near the ground.

Morgan just stared at him and said, "Of course!"

Andrea was the oldest of the cousins: teaching the dance, not learning it. She laughed. "Morgan, Franz-Karl is not from here. He doesn't know..." She sat down beside Franz-Karl and topped up his cup of watered cider. "The seventeenth of Sextil is the Feast Day of Saints Clement and Sophia, the patrons of the cathedral. There will be ceremonies at the Great Altar and the Stone Theater as well as at their cathedral, regardless of the weather. But if the weather is fine, there will be feasting or dancing or games or performances or contests in almost every courtyard in the House on the Rock, from end to end, not just the ones at the Great Altar and Stone Theater and the cathedral. If the weather is not fine... well ... they will try to move some things indoors or under cover..."

Fritzel had not been dancing in the Sun, he had been sitting in the shade of the colonnade, reading a text from the Schola. He looked up and said, "Our Saints' Days Across the Water fall in the spring, before the herds leave for the summer pastures, and in the autumn after they return. Too many folks are away at this season for a proper festival. But I heard tales there were some problems in the House on the Rock for last summer's feast."

Morgan's younger brother Dion said glumly, "Last year it rained. And thundered. And hailed. And the wind could not decide which way to blow. Even though the morning started fair as fair. It wasn't a proper Feast Day. At. All. They had to cancel most of the games and contests, and the dancers for things that could not be abandoned or move under roofs all caught colds. Some of them were bruised by the hail besides. Our neighbor Agathon was sick for weeks and weeks."

"The decorations and displays got broken and all the colors dripped." Helena agreed sadly. "Some of the damaged things were first built by people's grandparents. A few could not be repaired at all, but had to be remade entirely."

"But if the weather is fine this year, we need to be ready," Morgan said. "As the Duke's kin, we need to get things right: people notice our mistakes."

Helena rolled her eyes. "You just fret that Demetria will notice your mistakes. Do you think she even knows... that the rest of us walk the Living World?"

Morgan blushed and sputtered, but at least he fussed at Franz-Karl less, even though the great day was approaching rapidly. Things improved even more – in Franz-Karl's view – after Helena pointed out that the contest Morgan was most fussed about required all contestants to have at least one adult tooth. Even though he was a full Notary, Franz-Karl did not qualify yet – though one of his milk teeth was getting very wiggly – so they would need someone else for that contest. Morgan fussed at him less after that.

Preparations for the festival began to appear in various parts of the House on the Rock as the Saints' Day approached. Foods for the feast were gathered into larders and storerooms, and the beasts for the sacrifices were moved into consecrated pens and cosseted. Banners and wreaths and garlands were hung in the various courtyards. Statues in the market squares and courtyards were cleaned and had their bright paint touched up: even the flute player in the goats' fountain had his scuffs attended to. Arches and bowers and other shapes were constructed of wicker and decorated with flowers and set up in carefully chosen locations throughout the House on the Rock. And chairs and tables and small platforms popped up in unoccupied spaces like dandelions after a rain.

The large construction that Franz-Karl had noticed on his first morning in Traventi turned out to be a sort of puppet theater that would be performing scenes from the lives of the saints, especially the scenes with dragons and monsters and other excuses for wonders. Puppets could manage displays that living actors – even Elderkin actors – would fail at.

Reverend Count Great Aunt Adrasteia arrived at the House on the Rock at mid-afternoon on the day before the Saints' Feast Day, though her luggage train had arrived early in the morning. Her Grace the Duke, Franz-Karl's Grandmother greeted her with a kiss on the cheek, all of the tokens and oaths of hospitality suitable for a kinswoman and frequent guest, and a riddle whose answer was 'a welcome guest'. The Reverend Count stored a very large pile of small parcels in the Household Shrine, and assured all the anxious children that she had seen no signs of bad weather on her journey from the south.

The Sphinx spread and stretched her wings, then folded them neatly and asked Franz-Karl to walk through the House with her before dinner.

Reverend Count Great Aunt Adrasteia just Looked at Fritzel when he would have joined them. Franz-Karl's attendant politely decided that he needed to check the strings and tuning of his lira before the feast day, and finish some other preparations, more than he needed to join the walk.

Franz-Karl and the Winged Sphinx walked toward the Saint Victoria end of the House, where things were a little less busy than they were nearer the cathedral or the Ceremonial Gate and Great Altar, and for a while they just walked together. She let him choose their path through the courtyards and colonnades, and he tried to avoid places that might have a lot of goats or donkeys. Reverend Count Great Aunt Adrasteia made most four-footed animals nervous, even the hunters. People who walked on two feet were carefully polite. Poultry were unpredictable.

"How much do you know about the Manifest, and about Gifts and Bindings," she asked finally.

Franz-Karl did not hurry to answer. "Mostly what is told in old tales and chronicles," he said, "and what Her Grace My Grandmother the Duke told me the day I became a sworn Notary, after I saw the colors of the windows. But also…" He paused to think, then described the binding about food and oaths of fealty that his Mama had asked him to accept – which would not have been at all proper if he was already a Notary – and how the bad food had looked strange. Great Aunt Adrasteia frowned when he told about it, but he did not know if that was because of the Binding or because bad people tried to give them bad food, or for some other reason entirely.

They walked for a few steps, passing through one of the doorways between courtyards from a busy place into one that was empty of people. As the door closed behind them with a clunk, Franz-Karl took a deep breath, said "There is more…" and told her about the business of the thirteen true things and the Margraff-Elector, and the glove-bearer and his rod. The part about the rod had been in the papers Claudius brought from Karnburg along with Franz-Karl: it was part of the reason he had been sent. But he had not even told Her Grace his Grandmother about the thirteen true things, only Fritzel.

Thinking about telling Fritzel reminded him, so he also told about the tiny lightning bolt. He still was not sure whether to be excited or terrified by that tiny lightning bolt. Today he was leaning toward terrified. Walking with the Sphinx and feeling the World go strange around them tipped the scale a bit.

Reverend Count Great Aunt Adrasteia stopped walking, set all four feet on the ground, and looked directly at Franz-Karl. Her fur and feathers were all ruffled up, like a cat who wanted to look larger and fiercer. "Franz-Karl. You have been working Bindings out of half-remembered old tales. At six years old." The way she said it, the words were almost a question, but not quite. She closed her golden eyes and stretched her wings and tail in a way that probably meant something, but he did not think she was angry. She sighed and settled her feathers. The fur smoothed down, but not entirely: there was still a slight ridge along her spine. "Well, it has been a few centuries, so I suppose we were due. And you have no one to teach you in Karnburg." She turned to continue walking.

They passed through a fancy gate into the market square of Saint Victoria and All the Saints, which was as busy as a beehive some fool had stirred with a stick. (That was a saying of his Papa's.) She led him into a smithy they were passing – decorative ironwork and household goods, not farm implements and horseshoes: the smithy for those was on the other side of the square – and asked the blacksmith to heat a long black iron bar so that it was cold at one end and very hot at the other.

Then Great Aunt Adrasteia summoned a potter from next door who had human-looking eyes that did not even shine when the firelight caught them in the shadows of the smithy. The smith and the Sphinx and Franz-Karl and the potter all marked on the bar where the last place they saw color from the heat was. Great Aunt Adrasteia and Franz-Karl marked nearly the same place, much closer to the cool end of the bar than either the potter or the smith did, even though the smith had eyes that shone red as a dog's or fox's. The sphinx's eyes shone green as any cat's, naturally, while Franz-Karl knew he had shiny eyes that were pale greenish-yellow, like his Mama's when the lamplight caught them.

The smith and the potter both looked surprised when Franz-Karl marked the bar, and the smith said something quietly about baby-teeth.

Franz-Karl said, "Arg," and rolled his eyes like Helena (he had been practicing). When they were back out in the square he stopped, and turned, and looked at Great-Aunt Adrasteia, and said, "What do baby teeth have to do with anything?" Without her name or title or anything polite. He felt himself blushing a little. He knew people were trying teach him as much as he could learn about Traventi as fast as he could learn it –

sometimes he felt as stuffed as a festival goose – but he was not sure they were teaching him the right things. There were too many places where things did not connect yet, like a pile of colored tesserae that might someday be a mosaic, or might just be a pile of colored stones to fill the hollow space inside a wall. Everything was all too much and not enough, all at the same time, especially when you added in the Empire and the Kingdom and the Palace at Karnburg. And people fibbing about his Papa's death.

Count Great Aunt Adrasteia did not get angry at his rudeness, she smiled at him. "Have you heard of the Child Blessings?"

"Not really. Well... People here keep mentioning them. And perhaps Mama has said the words a few times. But I don't know what they are, or what they do."

She laid down next to a bench with a good view of Saint Victoria's Fountain, and arranged her wings. Franz-Karl sat on the bench, not so close to her that the World went too wobbly.

"Perhaps this is something your mother has not thought safe to speak of in the Palace, where there are always servants that belong to the Lowlanders, not to her, and listening ears that are often unfriendly."

"Of course not." The servants you least wanted to overhear things were always the ones who moved most quietly, too.

"This is what we have heard..." She was using the complicated verb forms that marked levels of expected truth. This was something that people believed without being able to test it. "The Manifest come from a place outside the Living World, where time and distance and meaning are all more jumbled together than they are here. We think from things some of them have said that while material beings start tiny and simple and grow in size and complexity, the beings in the greater world begin vast and tenuous and entangled and condense into individuals with edges: forms and boundaries."

"I suppose they do not have baby teeth." That conjugation of 'suppose' was not one of the neutral ones, but tended to contradict the word's plain meaning. That was very rude but he did not entirely care.

Count Great Aunt Adrasteia blinked slowly. "They seem not to have what we would consider bodies at all, there in the Greater World beyond the Threshold. The bodies that the Manifest wear in the Living World are not them, but more like clothing they create by pure will. The Manifest do not entirely follow the same rules as creatures that belong to the Living World. There are some extra rules that apply to them because they do not quite belong here, and other rules that apply to all things native to the Living World that do not entirely affect them. Children with one Manifest parent and one that is Worldfolk seem to largely exist by force of will in a way that draws out the physical form to suit the child's Manifest heritage. After that things become... complicated. In several ways."

Great Aunt Adrasteia waited with no signs of impatience while Franz-Karl sat quietly and thought about what she had said.

"Do the children of the Manifest have livers?" he asked finally. Butchers and sacrificers dealt with the larger animals, but he had seen cooks in the Palace deal with poultry and rabbits that started out with all of their feathers and fur. Livers were impressive. Goose livers were HUGE, even when people had not been mean to them.

Great Aunt Adrasteia laughed. "An excellent question, child... we believe that the children of the Manifest who are most ... lasting ...in their bodies commonly have full sets of vital organs. It decreases the labor of maintaining a bodily form if the body can largely maintain itself. And we have learned that the ones who are most sane in their minds do not have Manifest parts that awaken while they are in the womb, or Gifts and Bindings that become fully active before they are grown into enough strength and wit to manage them."

"Being born old and open-eyed is bad?" He shivered and wrapped his arms around himself.

"Being open-eyed in the womb is bad. It is dark in there, and said to be surprisingly noisy... Born old and open-eyed is a matter of elegantly successful timing." The Sphinx held up a paw and watched the sharp claws slide in and out when she flexed the digits sharply. "The Child Blessings used in Traventi include Bindings placed on parents so that their seeds will combine in ways most likely to create children that are healthy in their bodies and their wits. Children whose mothers will not die in bearing them. There are also Bindings placed on the Children so that they will grow ... human-like ... to start and will not awaken in the womb –"

Franz-Karl remembered some gossip from the Palace about a courtier from the western Falkenburg holdings. "Like Carlos Gonzalez y del Bosque? They say he woke early..."

"Very likely. El Gato del Bosque is young in these matters, and his line are still learning their way. The Child Blessings also try to block the children's use of Bindings and Gifts for a while. Growing into a human baby and then into a person who is whole in mind and body is a hard task even when there are no Gifts and Manifest pieces mixed in like lumps in the dough. The Blessings try to make things less lumpy and let the children grow up a little and learn some sense before they need to manage Gifts and Bindings on top of learning to walk and talk and everything else that humans need to do."

"And the Child Blessings use baby teeth somehow." A subtler, more polite truth marker.

"Yes." Plain truth, modulated only a bit in what followed. "The Blessings needed mileposts to mark where they should begin to unravel. It was found to be dangerous to try to anchor those parts of the Blessings to something outside the children, or expect some other person to manage unraveling things – people died inconveniently or misjudged the timing – so the progression of teeth came to be used as the clock. Usually, the Manifest part of a Traventine Elderkin begins to awaken at birth, largely finishing when the first baby tooth is in place. The limits on Gifts and Bindings are supposed to unwrap gradually beginning when you start losing your milk teeth and ending when you get your last wisdom teeth, so that you can learn to manage Gifts and Bindings a little at a time."

Franz-Karl looked away from her. "I'm already a full Notary. And starting to show Gifts, I believe. Am I broken?"

"You are not broken at all," Great Aunt Adrasteia answered very firmly. She moved around so that he was facing her and tapped his chin with a fuzzy paw so that he looked at her golden eyes. "The purpose of the Child Blessings is to keep the children and their mothers safer than otherwise. If the Living World decided that you were safer with some Gifts awakening than with the Blessings holding in full force? There is no way to argue with it." She shrugged her wings. "Telling the World the thirteen true things was a way of saying to it that you needed Bindings and Gifts in a hurry and were ready to use them."

"So the Living World was being polite and trying to protect me?" Franz-Karl was not entirely sure he believed all of this, but there was really no way to argue with it. Notary to Notary, she was telling what she thought she knew. He shifted a little on the hard stone bench and looked away from the golden cats-eyes again. "Her Grace my Grandmother said there is no way to know what Gifts I carry."

"Not in Traventi. Elderkin descended from a single one of the Manifest, like your Carlos and the other kin of El Gato del Bosque, or the Blessed Protector's Children in the Wald, can usually guess what Gifts and markers of Manifest heritage they are most likely to inherit, though there will still be some surprises. But the Duchy has been welcoming Elderkin – and especially Elderkin that had been slaves – for many generations... and then all marrying each other and making babies together. Some slaves don't know their Worldfolk kin, much less the Manifest ones. No one truly can say who all of Traventi's Manifest ancestors were or what Gifts might be hiding in some family Lineage, or what will happen when the Gifts of various Lineages combine."

"We should probably be happy we all mostly have livers." He thought for a moment, then offered, "I have a thing where people don't notice me – or Fritzel either, sometimes – and Maestro Argens thinks I have some Watery Gifts from my Grandfather the Admiral. And sometimes the World looks strange... not just different colors like the cathedral windows or the iron bar... I mean really very strange. Like when the food looked fake... and some other times..."

"You probably need not worry about strange sights. Or strange sounds or whatever, either. Your material body has the ordinary material senses looking at the World, while your Manifest part has other ways of knowing things. You have a very large and active Manifest part that will be trying to tell your body things..."

"Oh." There was no way to mark the single syllable for uncertainty... but what she had said almost made sense.

The Sphinx continued, "But as for seeing those colors and how that may be tied to the Gifts... I cannot say with certainty, but being able to see color far into the warm part of the bar, not just the hot part, suggests that you may very likely have the Sparks Gift when you are older, like my dear Grandfather Igniculo." She closed her eyes and looked away. "You should try to stay well away from anything involving gunpowder at least until the Gift has Manifested and settled, and you have had time to learn some control. I have heard of at least one with our Gift who died messily after sneezing too near a powder magazine, which I hold to be a sad and embarrassing way to die."

"I'll remember," Franz-Karl assured her. He did not bother saying it four times or using fancy conjugations because that was not the sort of warning he was likely to forget or ignore. He thought about those old tales about Igniculo and General Rano, which were some of his favorites. "The Remorans who came to fight against General Frog and your Grandfather did not have powder magazines, did they?"

"No. That was a very long time before gunpowder was commonly used, especially in this part of the world. So the Remoran Legions had no powder magazines." The Sphinx was amused enough that her paws started to make tiny kneading motions on the ground.

"Some of the old chronicles say there were things exploding loudly in the days before the Great Battle. That isn't quite the words they use, but that's what they mean."

Reverend Count Great Aunt Adrasteia smiled happily and flexed her front paws more, extending and retracting the sharp claws, pale as ivory and very pointy. "Ah, yes. That. The Remorans had no powder magazines, but they did have granaries. Exploding a granary is fiddly work compared to exploding a powder magazine. Gunpowder wants to burn the way a salmon wants to swim upstream. With a granary, you need to get the mix of air and grain dust juuust right, before you add the sparks. That's easier at some seasons of the year than others... but the Remorans chose an extremely poor season for their attack."

"Oh. Did we destroy very much food?" Her Grace His Grandmother had been discussing the stores of grain for the coming winter at dinner the night before with Livia and some other people. They had agreed that there was enough, provided that people were not stupidly wasteful.

"Not so very much as it might have been. Granaries here in the mountains are smaller than the ones on the plains, and the people are spread more thinly. And the campaign went quickly. At noon on the first day that the Legions marched from their provincial camp to attack us, a granary near the road between Traventi and Remora exploded. And two the next day, farther along the road toward Remora, and four the next, and so on. On the day of the Frog's Great Battle, thirty-two granaries exploded, sixteen at sunrise before the battle, and another sixteen at sunset while the Remoran officials were debating whether to sign the Frog's Treaty."

"Oh." He said again, adding numbers in his head. Sixty-three granaries still sounded like a lot, even if they were small. He remembered the small villages of hungry-looking people he had passed while traveling to Traventi earlier in the summer. Karnburg was mostly east and north of Traventi, while Remora was far to the south, but he did not think the people on the road to Remora would like to have their food exploded, any more than the Eastlanders would. "I expect that the threat of losing sixty-four granaries the next day made them more willing to sign the treaty."

"A few officers needed to be encouraged by their men," Great Aunt Adrasteia agreed calmly. "It helped that all of the food and water the Legions carried went bad when they were a three-day march from our border. Two full legions with their allied supporters was more soldiers than there were people in Traventi, and now they had no food and were being shown that they had no way to reach us to steal our stores of food or use our good water. Losing more granaries along their route home was... worrying."

"No wonder the chronicles say the Legions sort of fell apart..."

"And the treaty signing and Rano's Curse did not encourage them thereafter." Her tail twitched, like a cat stalking a mouse.

Franz-Karl shivered.

The Sphinx stood up and stretched all the way to the tips of her claws and the very tip of her tail, then spread her wings and stretched those as well. She turned to walk back toward the Ducal Residence, then stopped and turned back to face Franz-Karl. "Some soldiers caught a friend of mine ... about nine days before the trouble officially began... she did not survive them. There were a very great number of soldiers..."

"And very few of us," Franz-Karl finished for her. "I know." He let his shoulders droop. "There is a General in the Palace who likes to boast about the size and number of the armies that answer to him. I don't think the Stone Theater would fit even one of those armies."

After they walked a little way in silence, Great Aunt Adrasteia asked Franz-Karl how he was progressing with the lessons he had been set before he left the Palace.

Franz-Karl did not wonder how she knew about the lessons. This was Adrasteia the Sphinx, Mistress of Riddles, and the lessons had been a large enough part of his summer that it seemed everyone should know about them. He explained about finishing all of tasks he had been given except for finding the answers to three lessons that made no sense to him, or to Fritzel either.

"Have you shown your Grandmother these troublesome questions?"

He spread his hands. "There are still some weeks of the summer left, and I am done with all the rest of the tasks I was given, and much more besides. I expect that we will puzzle these last lessons out without needing to trouble Her Grace the Duke."

The Reverend Count Great Aunt Adrasteia smiled at him. "Perhaps. Did you see the book the questions were copied from?"

"No... and the copies I was given were very hard to read. Meister van Diesen's handwriting is... difficult...on a good day, and he was rushed and weary while things were being prepared. The pile of lessons was not arranged well." He blinked. "Oh! Do you think there were errors in copying?"

"I think that perhaps someone has made some errors." The Sphinx's tail-tip was twitching again, and she was walking like a cat that suspected a mouse behind the draperies: not quite crouching to pounce yet, but preparing to.

When Franz-Karl and her Reverence Count Great Aunt Adrasteia arrived back at Her Grace His Grandmother's study, Fritzel was sent to fetch the piles of lessons that had been given to Franz-Karl in Karnburg, both the original papers and the copies that Franz-Karl had made and used for his studies. He brought back all of the pages of answers that Franz-Karl had compiled along with the two sets of questions.

Great Aunt Adrasteia read the original list with a calm, polite face, even though she said 'tsk' at the writing. But her tail started twitching with annoyance along more and more of its length, especially when she saw the pages that were streaked with colors that had no Remoran names. She immediately guessed the three hard questions, and sent an attendant to ask Her Grace the Duke Franz-Karl's Grandmother to join them.

"Is there a problem?" Her Grace Duke Adriana asked when she arrived.

"Someone has been setting Franz-Karl problems using texts cribbed from old grimoires. He fortunately found them unreadable."

Franz-Karl shuddered.

Fritzel muttered something that might have been a prayer, or a curse.

Her Grace Duke Adriana did not look calm or polite while she read, she looked extremely angry. Her hair was braided and wrapped around her head so it could not spread out and go all crackly, like Franz-Karl's Mama's when she was upset, but crackly sparks began dripping from the end of the braid, like water off an icicle.

"Have... have I been very foolish?" Franz-Karl asked in a very quiet voice. Her Grace His Grandmother immediately set down the paper she was holding, came to kneel beside his chair and hugged him tightly. "Not foolish. Not foolish at all, dear child, but honest and clever. It is someone else who has been very foolish and very wicked."

The ancient Sphinx was examining the papers again. "These were... compiled by rote from some old spell-book, I think... and the maker of the book had no great knowledge of Traventi, but likely some knowledge of Elderkin elsewhere. The language of the spell-book was certainly not Elderic and likely not Remoran, though these questions are posed in mediocre Remoran."

"They seemed incomplete." The Duke said it as a question despite the shape of the words. One arm was still wrapped around Franz-Karl.

"Quite mangled," the Sphinx agreed. "The translator did not understand their purpose, so some of the words chosen are unfortunate. Even if they were whole, these three pieces together are not meant to entirely bind an Elderkin's power in themselves. Rather they will try to set the victim's feet firmly on a path into the trap leading to bondage to the will of some Lowland spell-master. There was likely meant to be a fourth puzzle, set in the presence of the intended slave-master..."

Franz-Karl shuddered again. He knew the Palace too well. He said in Allemanic, with a strong northern accent, "Oh Princess Silvia, your little son has grown so much while he was away. I wonder if he can solve this little riddle, now." He added in Elderic, "And then I would find myself tied to a lamp or ring or tinderbox owned by some fool, like some poor wretch in the old tales." He signed himself and added a vulgar gesture that was supposed to repel evil influences. He remembered the long list of rules he had written and signed and sealed, and his Mama's Binding even before that. Since fealty was barred, oaths of subordination were even less likely to hold. "The traps did not expect the Notary protections and rules about fealty?"

"Not the Defender's Oath," Adrasteia said. "That was well chosen."

Fritzel had gone even paler under his black hair and beard. "I am no Notary. And I've been helping his Honor puzzle at those things."

The Duke answered, "Even if these tatters were whole and met their intent... First, you are not a Binder, so not their target and also in some ways much harder to bind. Second, you are already freely contracted to a Notary's service, and will be difficult to lure elsewhere..."

"And third, how many wisdom teeth do you have yet?" Count Great Aunt Adrasteia finished.

"None now." Fritzel admitted. "Not really. Not yet. Maybe one in the near distance."

"You children both have better defenses than that clumsy Lowland spell-master knew could exist. Even if he could manage to write Remoran that is anything better than gibberish. Tscha."

The Duke said very precisely, "Great Aunt, I am not pleased that a trap was set for my grandson and guest under my own roof, however clumsy it was. Not pleased at all. How shall we answer this?"

The Sphinx eyed her directly. "Not without a Council vote, dear child, certainly. Tomorrow is the Feast Day, and dealing with such matters would be disrespectful. But most of the Council will be here for the Feast, and still here nursing sore heads the morning after. Until then, I shall consider the matter."

"And consider how you and Valens missed this attack?" Her Grace the Duke's hair was still dripping sparks, and they seemed to be dripping faster.

Spread wings made a shrug very impressive. "That, too. But fragments of something that might have been a trap if it was better constructed cast no great shadow on the world – not with the Childe protected from seeing the naked shapes of false words –" The Duke looked startled. The Sphinx finished, "We watch for tricks of policy, Valens and I, not hedge-wizardry."

"Do we need added precautions?" Fritzel asked.

"For a fully sworn Notary standing within the Duchy's borders?" Her Grace responded. "If a hazard remains here, now that the traps are known, I should resign my post."

"My Mama is a full Notary, but my brother and sister have fewer protections," Franz-Karl pointed out.

"We shall of course consider Franz-Karl's safety carefully before he goes back outside the Gates of Air, and the safety of all of the others in Childe Silvia's household as well," Count Great Aunt Adrasteia said, mostly to her Grace. Her claws were showing again as her paws flexed and released, flexed and released. Not kneading, this time. Too ready to hunt to be willing to settle.

CHAPTER XXI: Saints' Day Dawn

Wherein Sacrifices of Blood and Skill Are Witnessed

Olivia put out several sets of Franz-Karl's clothes on the evening before the festival. Despite the celebration, the festival was not an occasion when color-of-sorrow was forbidden – the Saints had been in the world and passed out of it – so she did not need to open the special chest. There were his very best color-of-sorrow clothes for the great feast at the end of the day. There were less fragile clothes in color-of-sorrow to start the day, and there were extra garments ready in case he got soaked by rain or mud, or whatever else, or something got torn. The hat she set out had a strand of ivy wrapped around the hatband: proper for the feast, but also a reminder of the Ivy and Iron.

She would be gone to the rites well before sunrise, but she told him that since he was not an Initiate, he could sleep late on the Feast Day if he wished. "The first sacrifice will occur when the Sun peeks over the mountains to the east. If you prefer to attend you should plan to arrive a bit earlier, and fasting..." She smiled and leaned toward him and tweaked a lock of his uncooperative hair. "So... little different than a usual morning for Your Honor." He smiled back. Olivia never fussed about his early morning restlessness.

He awakened at his usual time, let the orange cat claim the warm place in the bed, and dressed quickly.

Fritzel came out of his alcove barefoot and bareheaded, wrapped in a long cloak and carrying his lira. He had been invited to join one of the special contests held in honor of the Saints and the Gods and needed to arrive promptly, but he poured the water and combed Franz-Karl's hair and escorted him to the Great Altar at the Ceremonial Gateway before he went off to join the preparations for his own rite.

Franz-Karl stood quietly during the singing and the parts of the prayers and rites that were open to all comers, not just to Initiates. He was pleased that great care was taken so that the white bull that was paraded to the great Altar was proud and unfrightened until he was already dying in the first ray of the rising Sun. In Karnburg the rare sacrifices were as private as the preparations, and kept completely out of sight of the uninitiated, so he had not known what to expect.

With Fritzel and Olivia both busy elsewhere, Franz-Karl was jostled and ignored when he tried to approach the grills to get a share of the sacrificial meal. One short, stocky man shoved him so hard he nearly fell, but a woman standing beside him caught his shoulder. There was a deep sort of cough sound behind them.

The man looked around with an annoyed expression, but then looked surprised, bowed deeply, and stepped aside, saying "Your Reverence."

Reverend Count Great Aunt Adrasteia said cheerfully, "Stay close to me, Your Honor Franz-Karl. We don't want oblivious fools trampling you." The short man turned red and quickly backed away, after a hasty bow in Franz-Karl's direction. "And you, too, Iris," Adrasteia added to Franz-Karl's rescuer, who had rainbow colored hair under a gold colored cap, and a gown woven in a tapering swirl of white and gold.

"I did not notice Your Reverence at the sacrifice." Franz-Karl said, after bowing politely to the Reverend Count.

"I watched from the rooftop: no need to distress that fine Messenger in his great moment. And you? Where is your large shadow?"

"Some sort of ritual wrestling, Fritzel said." Franz-Karl answered. "Palae? I'm not sure where it is happening."

"Saint Victoria Square, between the Carters' Gate and the Fountain. Fill your hands with a few more skewers of holy meat and I'll show you the best path to get there without flying."

Since he was not sure of the rules of sacrificial meals in Traventi, nor how they applied to sphinxes, Franz-Karl paid more attention to the word 'fill' than the word 'few'. He was relieved when Iris did the same. They all ate as they walked, with Iris holding skewers at a convenient height for her Reverence Count Great Aunt Adrasteia to bite the bits of meat off them.

Adrasteia's 'best path' took them along the outside fringes of the House on the Rock, around paddocks and farmyards, and then into the market square by the entrance the farmers used for their carts on Saint Victoria's market day. They arrived at the wrestling ring – it was marked off by two concentric circles of rope as thick as a man's wrist laying on the ground an arm's length apart – just as three clusters of singers and a few soloists finished singing something complicated but catchy, and stepped out of the ring.

Fritzel and three other men dropped their cloaks and stepped into the ring. They were wearing nothing but olive oil, like heroes in a fresco. They were joined by a fifth man, clothed in a long robe the color of dark red wine and carrying a staff wreathed with grapevines.

The man with the staff walked over to stand by the inner rope. Her Reverence Count Great Aunt Adrasteia stood facing him from outside the outer rope. Together they began to decree the conditions for the bout, but it was a little difficult to follow because the choruses and soloists joined in and repeated things, and the counterpoint got fairly intense. The parts that Franz-Karl heard stated that no object would pass the boundary ropes until the barrier was opened or the matches were complete. No wish or will or Gift from outside, deliberate or otherwise, would weigh on the natural chances within the ring. No wish or will or Gift of any competitor within the ring would have effect beyond his own skin.

The ropes developed fuzzy colored outlines, not quite like the ones that marked fibbers. These were more like the rainbow ripples of light above the voting.

Iris said quietly, "I have heard that Lowlanders play at chance with dice and cards, but you will see no games of chance in Traventi, Your Honor. It is all games of strength and skill, for there is little enough that happens around Elderkin purely according to the chances of the World."

"That is not to say there is no wagering," the Sphinx added as she rejoined them, "and there are other styles of wrestling than this where the use of Gifts is encouraged more: but those are not part of these rites."

Someone standing behind them complained that a hornless boy would not last long in the ring. When Franz-Karl looked again he realized that the man was complaining about Fritzel. Fritzel was the tallest man in the ring if you ignored horns and antlers, but fully bareheaded as the others were not. And the other wrestlers looked solid rather than gawky and unfinished and... largely human.

There was a fighter half a head shorter than Fritzel but even broader through the shoulders and deeper through the chest, with heavy bull's horns, and a bull's long whippy tail, and hooves no cobbler would try to disguise below furred calves.

There was narrower man only a little shorter than Fritzel... until you considered the magnificent rack of antlers, just on the cusp of maturing past velvet, that extended high above everyone's heads. He had a deer's tail and hooves, and the tines of his antlers showed rainbow sparks at their tips. His hair was as white as Fritzel's was black.

The fourth man was ... might as well be honest and call him a faun... a full head shorter than Fritzel and narrowest of the four, but looking as tough as old vine wood: goat-horned and tailed and hoofed, and furred to mid-thigh, with a fair bit of gray-green in his hair and beard, but mostly brown-furred otherwise. He had familiar tawny goats' eyes, tan skin no darker than Franz-Karl's, and brown hair with green streaks, but if he was a cousin, he was not a cousin that Franz-Karl had met.

The man with the staff did not announce given names or names of calling, but assigned each fighter a title or role related to the seasons and harvests, and then set the matches accordingly.

The faun and the stag – Winter and Autumn, the next coming seasons – faced each other first, in a bout that went on long enough that no one would be embarrassed, but ended with a solid win for the faun. He looked about to lose, but managed a move that took advantage of his smaller size and more compact horns to get inside the reach of the stag and do something clever that felled and pinned his opponent.

The second match was Fritzel and the older bull-man as champions for Spring and Summer. Fritzel's opponent rushed him, then tried to grapple. They tangled together briefly, until Fritzel exclaimed, "Oh is that the way of it, then?"

It seemed like the next moment Fritzel was braced and holding the man above his own head: holding by the root of the man's long tail and the base of one heavy horn. Franz-Karl's own tail sort of winced in sympathy, and a few of the people watching said things like 'Oof" and "Ouch".

The Summer fighter twisted and kicked his feet to try to topple the pair of them with his weight, and pried at Fritzel's grips with his fingers, but it did him no good. One of the onlookers called "one", and others joined in to slowly count. At seven, Fritzel quickly put his foe on the ground and slapped the man's solar plexus to knock the wind out of him before moving back out of reach at 'eight'.

The man with the staff seemed to be more of an announcer or commentator than someone governing the contests, but he set himself and his staff between the two fighters and sarcastically asked the gasping bull-man whether he would prefer to be in the third match or the fourth.

The Summer fighter could not answer, so the third match was Fritzel against the stag-man: Spring against Autumn. Fritzel was declared the winner after a little while, but Franz-Karl was not entirely sure why. He was happy about the result, since the grownups watching seemed impressed by Fritzel's victory. There were no more comments about hornless boys from the people watching, and the odds wagered against the later bouts changed hastily and in ways that left some of the bettors unhappy.

The fourth match was the bull-man and the faun, who suddenly exclaimed, "That didn't work on a hornless boy, but you're still trying it with me?", twisted his opponent into a tangle, stuffed the furry tassel of the bull's tail into the man's own mouth, and pinned him while he was choking on it. There were some jeers and sarcastic remarks from the onlookers, including some very rude suggestions about what the Summer fighter should do when he had chewed his way down to the root of his own tail.

The fifth match ended when the stag put the bull onto the ground face down. That was not a proper pin, but he grabbed one of the bull's horns in each hand while kneeling on his shoulders and offered to twist his head off for him. He did not sound like he was joking. When the man with the staff separated them, the Autumn stag was bleeding from a deep cut near one eye. He was declared the winner very thoroughly because his Summer opponent was entirely disqualified from the rite for rule-breaking.

The man with the staff did something that closed the cut and stopped the bleeding, but left the injury looking stiff and strangely colored. The Summer bull could not go outside the ropes, but he huddled just inside them and did not look at anyone.

There was a sort of growling murmur in the watching crowd. Someone – not the man with the staff, someone outside the ropes – announced loudly that any wagers involving the Summer fighter in any bout were canceled and the stakes should be returned to the bettors. It was a very popular decree, but the noise in the crowd while the bets were changed stayed quieter than the growl had been. Some people made signs against evil influences.

Iris said, "Hmph. Finally misjudged the line."

Count Great Aunt Adrasteia's tail stopped twitching, and she settled her wings. "The man's a fool, and clumsy with it, which speaks ill for the coming year. If he had the sense Heaven gave a fish he would have been cautious after the boy caught him out."

"What just happened?" Franz-Karl asked.

"The ritual fight is supposed to be bloodless, and use of horns or antlers against flesh is entirely banned besides," Iris said. "Horns against horns is fine – and cursed impressive when the fighters are strong – but threatening an eye is far over the line. And that came after trying borderline nasty moves, time after time, and failing, time after time. The fellow would not recognize an honest bout if it bit him: he kept pushing things over the border from ritual to something grimmer but could not even seize the advantage before his opponents countered in the style he had chosen. Folk who concern themselves with omens will be fretting mightily after this."

The final match between Fritzel and the faun – Spring and Winter – was long and quiet and subtle. Everyone seemed relieved when it finally ended, even the bettors who had been getting more and more excited as the match continued. The man with the staff said that Winter had won because when the great clock rang the hour mark that ended the rite, he had almost managed to score against Fritzel, while Fritzel never came nearly as close. Fritzel bowed gracefully, accepting the verdict.

Reverend Count Great Aunt Adrasteia said something about old age and trickery against youth and strength that made Iris laugh, but Franz-Karl thought that Fritzel had shown plenty of trickiness in his bouts.

Reverend Count Great Aunt Adrasteia and the man with the staff needed to unbind the space for the rite before the results could be officially announced and the prizes given out. The singers came back to help with the unbinding: the music used was sort of swirly, and the ropes went dim, and then limp. The thick ropes that marked the boundaries were picked up and coiled and carried away so that people would not trip over them in the dancing that would use the space next.

With the ropes dimmed, Franz-Karl could see that the edges of the Summer wrestler were a little... wrong. Not badly wrong: probably three quarters of the people in the Palace in Karnburg were worse. But most people in Traventi were tricky differently, not fibbers, exactly. So here, strange edges showed more.

The wrestlers who had won matches were dressed in linen tunics with borders embroidered with seasonal emblems, with ornamented belts, and wreaths of leaves and flowers placed on their heads: the faun, who had won all of his bouts, was declared the winner over all and got the fanciest belt – the leather had been carved and then rubbed with gold to show the pattern – and the heaviest wreath, then Fritzel, who had won twice. The stag-man, who had won a single bout by default, got a fine tunic with a plain belt and no wreath, just a little skullcap that sat on his head behind his antlers.

Everyone looked at the bull-man, who had lost three times and been disqualified besides, but he just stood there without a stitch or a hat and scowled at the ground and did not look at anyone. The man with the staff pointed it at Fritzel. "Your victory was greatest."

"And there are none to argue with that," the faun agreed.

Fritzel sighed. "Right then." He turned to the Summer fighter. "You. Take yourself to Dancers' Hall at the Bull's Leap, naked as you stand, and beg the Masters there to teach you decent wrestling. Don't fight another public match until the Masters give you leave, Junio and Aldo both."

The man began to walk away very slowly, but some people in the crowd began to jeer at him, or jostle him. The sound of the crowd was getting growly again. He began to move faster and faster toward the Carters' Gate to get away from them, but he did not quite run.

The faun's eyes had widened. He said to Fritzel, "The Bull's Leap? You canna be Astolon, surely!"

"Not by a few years and no little weight of heritage. I am named Friedrich, called Fritzel."

"Saints! The years do flit like foam on a stream. I remember word of your birth... not so long ago that you'd be of age, surely?" He added hastily, "Not that I'm doubtin' the arrangers o' this rite took proper care."

Fritzel almost sighed. "I came of age these four months past." he said, very patiently. Helena would have rolled her eyes. Franz-Karl was proud that Fritzel managed not to.

"Corin Gwinbren," the old faun said with a polite bow.

Franz-Karl expected that might be the end of things but it turned out there was another layer of prizes: the stag-man, who owned a tavern that served meals, quickly offered a meal each to Corin the faun and Fritzel as his forfeits for the bouts he had lost.

Corin claimed that he was unable to choose an appropriate fee for a bout that had been so very close. "We'll talk further at Nestor's dinner, Fritzel, and settle a wee forfeit there." He looked at the antlered man. "Will tonight serve, d'you think?"

"Well enough for me... Fritzel? Man or maid, young fellow?"

Franz-Karl squeaked. Fritzel looked toward him worriedly but the Sphinx flicked a wingtip at him, so he answered the taverner, with a polite bow, "Both or either, and the night serves well enough." He stepped aside to gather up his cloak and the lira and its bow, then walked over to join Franz-Karl and Iris and Her Reverence Count Great Aunt Adrasteia.

"Your Honor? What was that?"

"They said the 'man or maid' thing: like in the books. So it's going to be a real grownups-only party for you." Franz-Karl was very happy that people were taking Fritzel seriously. That question about his friend's age had been annoying. Fritzel's birthday was a few weeks earlier in the season than Franz-Karl's, so he was already a grownup when Her

Grace the Duke hired him, and his contract to be in Franz-Karl's household was perfectly legal.

Fritzel blushed: one disadvantage of having such fair skin despite his black hair. Iris covered her mouth with her hand, but Franz-Karl could see that her eyes were laughing. The Sphinx raised an eyebrow. "Franz-Karl? What have you been reading that mentioned 'man or maid'? Was it Tullio ... or Nennius ... or... ?" Fritzel winced when Adrasteia mentioned Nennius.

Franz-Karl answered cheerfully, "Mostly Tullio, and Philemon of Syracuse. And some Ludovico Dionysio: the ones with the monsters and sea voyages and dancing girls. I opened a book by Nennius once, but the beginning was very boring. And either Nennius was a very bad poet or he was not writing in Remoran."

Iris sat down on a bench they were passing and laughed until she cried. When she caught her breath she managed to say, "You read very well for your age, Your Honor."

"And you are quite right about Nennius," the Sphinx agreed, nodding calmly, "He was both a mediocre poet and he wrote in a dialect much nearer Montani than proper Remoran."

"Then why do people keep his books in such fancy bindings? Her Grace doesn't have him in her library, but there are at least three sets in different rooms in the Palace."

Fritzel started coughing, and Iris snickered.

"Nennius goes into a great deal of detail about some grown up matters that some people find very amusing," Her Reverence said cheerfully. "But the poetry does not get any better, even if you look at it as Montani. If you want something else to read that is full of adventures, try Justinian Morro of Baiae, or any of his followers."

Franz-Karl almost slipped and thanked her outright, but remembered the rules in time, so he bowed very formally and said, "I will remember your advice, Great Aunt Adrasteia," instead.

CHAPTER XXII: Puzzles and Meetings

Wherein Our Hero Wins a Wooden Horse and Greets an Old Friend

Instead of going back out through the market gate the way they had come, Franz-Karl and his companions wound their way east through the ground level courtyards toward the center of the House on the Rock and then toward the cathedral beyond, sampling the festival fare and watching the festivities and occasionally joining in. They paused longest to watch the puppet show of "The Second Tale of Clement and Sophia": Elderkin puppet shows were *amazing*, and Reverend Count Great Aunt Adrasteia claimed that even she did not know how they managed some of the wonders.

Two courtyards later, Franz-Karl left the grownups to gossip with a vintner while his cousins Helena and Morgan pulled him into a children's dance wrapping ribbons around a tall pole.

In the courtyard after that, Maestro Petros was presiding over several challenges of skill. Franz-Karl won a prize by recognizing the number of beans in a glass jar. It was meant to be done by looking sideways in a way where it was the world that was sideways, not the direction of your eyes. The Maestro had been teaching him the trick of it, but Franz-Karl had only managed two brief glimpses before on market days.

When Maestro Petros congratulated him for his success with the jar, Franz-Karl said slowly, "I don't think I used the seeing thing... not exactly."

"That's no matter." The old man answered. "The jar has a Binding against the commonest way to see the count: anything else wins fair enough."

Franz-Karl felt confused. "I wasn't counting the *jar*."

"Well, you did not ask the beans: each bean only knows the number 'one'. Do you know what you did do?"

Franz-Karl considered. "It was a bit like Witnessing receipts on tax day. The guess before mine looked wrong and too high. The guess before that looked wrong and too low. The middle of the gap was still too high..." Formal Rhetoric had a gesture for 'and so forth'.

The people who had failed at guessing looked a lot less grumpy, and one even said "ooh".

Maestro Petros said, "Ah. His late Grace, Your Granny's Da, had a touch of the Truth-Seeing, but I never heard of it used for counting. Seems Your Honor has it stronger."

"Or His late Grace had less practice: people in the Lowlands fib a lot."

Maestro Petros laughed, and so did several of the people standing around the table. He pulled the jar out of sight and there were noises of beans going in and coming out before it was returned to the table for the next person to guess. Once the next contest was ready, he turned to the rack of prizes, thought for a moment, and gave Franz-Karl a brightly painted wooden horse nearly as long as Franz-Karl's forearm.

Franz-Karl thought the horse was the very best thing on the whole rack of prizes. Helena said that the horse was a good prize for someone who would be going on a journey at the end of the season. Morgan congratulated Franz-Karl for his skill: he himself had failed three times, and only succeeded at one of the other challenges.

The horse was simply carved and painted a shiny green, with his face and mane and harness added in other bright colors. Besides his painted features and harness, the horse was equipped with a leather saddle and bridle that came off, and a little woven blanket for under the saddle. Franz-Karl decided that his name was Harvest Prince.

Morgan spotted his ... friend ... Demetria through the open gate of an adjoining courtyard, and Helena was swept up into another dance that was all girls, so Franz-Karl made his way back to rejoin the grownups, carrying Harvest Prince carefully. It was helpful that Fritzel was so tall and the Sphinx tended to cause a sort of ripple in the crowd: it made them easy to find.

Iris had solved a puzzle fashioned of a tangled mass of sticks and string before some friends called her away to make up one of the sets in a dance that moved though complicated paths on the ground. Franz-Karl was glad no one asked him to join them. He liked watching that one, but he had never once danced it successfully with his cousins: there was one transition in the patterns that he always got wrong, as if his feet disagreed quite stubbornly with the instructors about how the dance should go. And then things always got worse and worse after that first false step. Maestro Argens was doing a better job of moving thorough the figures of the dance – despite his wooden foot – than Franz-Karl had ever managed on his best day of practice.

People who had not been at the wrestling recognized by the tunic and belt and wreath that Fritzel had been one of the wrestlers. They congratulated him, and bowed to him almost as respectfully as they did to her Reverence Count Great Aunt Adrasteia, and kept their distance almost as carefully, which was quite useful in the crowd: Franz-Karl found that people did not bump him when he stayed in the shadow of their respect. Fritzel also turned out to be very good at throwing bladed things – like knives and darts and axes – and won several small prizes.

When they reached the Square of Saints Clement and Sophia, the Sphinx settled on a couch in a shady spot by one of the fountains and began asking riddles. She set forfeits for those who gave the wrong answers and gave advice to those who gave the right ones. Some of the advice sounded very strange to Franz-Karl, but most people laughed at both the advice and the forfeits, so there were probably grownup Traventine jokes involved. Fritzel stood beside the couch, and laughed at the jokes, but he was watching a nearby knife-throwing challenge with a measuring eye: one of the prizes was a very nice earring, set with a topaz.

Franz-Karl perched on the foot of Adrasteia's long couch – it set him just barely far enough from the sphinx for the World to hold steady – and listened to the riddles game. He knew many of the answers and was surprised several times when people missed easy ones. He was listening to a rude sounding riddle that was really about a butter churn and wondering whether the challenger would know it when he heard a voice a short distance to one side that was surprising, and terribly familiar, and did not belong to the Traventine clothes the person was wearing.

He stood up, leaving Harvest Prince in the Sphinx's protection, and walked toward the woman who had spoken, speeding up as he went. "Nelia? Nelia, is that you?"

The woman turned to face him, and so did the man beside her. They were each carrying a child that looked about a year old as the Allemans counted age. She looked confused for a moment, then smiled beautifully. "Franz-Karl? How wonderful! How have you been, love?" Cornelia knelt and hugged him with the arm that was not full of a baby.

Franz-Karl hugged her back and buried his face in her shoulder and could not find words in any language or all of them. Cornelia had been one of his mother's Elderkin attendants, from before the wedding long before Franz-Karl was born until she went away a little after Sophie-Alexa was born. She had spoken Elderic to the children more than anyone except their mother, and played with them, and often looked after them even though it was not her official job.

Since he was absolutely, definitely not crying, Franz-Karl turned his head a little, so that his voice would not be muffled against her dress, and managed to say, "I am very well, Cornelia. I h-hope you are also. A-Are these your own children? And your h-husband?"

"Yes," she said. "My son here is another Franz, and my daughter is Silvia, after your mother. My husband is Melios. And we are all of us very well and quite happy."

When he pulled away from her to look at her carefully – just a little way, not so far that she needed to take her arm away from his shoulders – Franz-Karl was certain that it was very true. Cornelia was a little softer and plumper than he remembered, and there were smiles around her eyes instead of the tight, pinched, frightened look that he remembered from the end of her stay at the Palace. He took a deep breath. "I am very glad to see you prospering so well, Cornelia," he said carefully, hoping that the World would pay attention even though he did not use his signet. "I hope four times that things will continue to get better and better for you. And I am sure my Lady Mother would wish me to give you her best wishes as well."

"And mine to her and your brother and sister, of course. And my condolences to you all for the loss of your good Father. I burned candles for him the full seven days, even though the word of his death came slow."

"That was a kind thought." Franz-Karl found that he had nothing else to say, and too much. He kissed her cheek and each of the babies before he let go of her arm and turned away.

He held out his hand to Melios and was surprised when Cornelia's husband dropped to one knee and kissed his hand formally, with a polite murmur of "Your Honor."

After Cornelia and her family walked away, Her Reverence Count Great Aunt Adrasteia tucked Franz-Karl under one of her wings, even though that made the World go wobbly. When he was no longer not-crying she wiped his face and sent Fritzel to fetch them drinks to soothe his scratchy throat. He sat waiting and hugging Harvest Prince.

He was relieved that Count Great Aunt Adrasteia did not tell him that he had no reason to be sad, having just seen a friend prospering. He knew that perfectly well, but he was sad anyway: Cornelia going away was tangled up in his head with his Papa's death, and Sophie-Alexa crying and clinging to him at the Palace gate because everyone went away. He was suddenly afraid of what was happening at the Palace while he was so far away. Things did not stop in the Palace just because he was gone. Was Meister van Diesen giving Philip-Augustus lessons that were traps? Were people being mean to his Mama and Sophie-Alexa?

The Sphinx kissed his nose and asked him a very complicated riddle that he had never heard before. The answer turned out to be 'the Past Remembered', and the forfeit she set him was to tell her a story about the Palace... not his family, the Palace itself. He was still trying to decide what to tell her when Fritzel returned, bringing honey-cakes along with the drinks.

After they ate and drank, while Franz-Karl was still licking sticky sweetness off his fingers, Fritzel nodded sharply, set down the lira and its bow and walked over to the knife contest with the topaz-earring prize. Three more people had failed to win the prize since Franz-Karl recognized Cornelia. The target was a squishy ball hung from a string, so any throw that went the least bit to one side or the other made it dodge aside. Fritzel threw the knife underhand, with a snap of the wrist that sent the blade straight, without tumbling. It pierced the ball's center with such force that the knife's point went all of the way through the ball and stuck in the back-board behind the target. The people watching said "Ooh" and "Aah", and some of the men and women who had tried and failed to hit the target said ruder things.

When he claimed the earring, Fritzel also made a promise with the man in charge of the game to buy the knife he had thrown, after the festival was over and selling blades could properly happen again. Fritzel said that it was sharp and well-balanced and obviously blessed by the Saints, and the man running the contest seemed very pleased to hear that. He said loudly that he had others of similar make that might carry similar good fortune, and a few of the people watching moved closer to speak with him quietly.

The Sphinx asked Fritzel a riddle that sounded like the answer should be something about a blade, but the answer to the riddle turned out to be 'a riddle', which Franz-Karl thought was not entirely fair. But Fritzel knew that one, which made Reverend Count Great Aunt Adrasteia happy. She promised Fritzel a sheath for his blade with a long verse that referred to the evening's party and made him laugh, and blush a little.

Her Grace the Duke, Franz-Karl's Grandmother came through the square, walking toward the cathedral door with some of the other members of the Council of Traventi. They paused to gather the Reverend Count into their group, and congratulate Fritzel on how well he had done in the wrestling.

Tribune Ulrich chuckled. "I saw our youngest Notary there as well. Very intent on the wrestlers, he was. I daresay I know what he was thinking."

Franz-Karl stared at Harvest Prince's ears. He did not know what the man was talking about, but he knew when someone was making a joke about him in a mean way. He had lived in the Palace in Karnburg his whole life until a few months ago, and a lot of people had said mean things about him whether they thought he could hear them or not. He was still upset after meeting Cornelia, so it was probably a good thing for Tribune Ulrich that the Child Blessings stopped him from setting people on fire or turning them into newts. But it did not stop him from beginning a list for ten years from now.

He thought back to the wrestling. It was before he met Cornelia, and before Harvest Prince, so it felt like it had been a very long time ago...

but after a moment he remembered. "Oh, yes! I was trying to understand the rules of the contest and thinking that Meister DaCascio would like to paint the wrestlers: they were making interesting shapes and already being all allegorical and such. And it might make a change for him from painting regular naked people... In Karnburg cloven-footed men with horns and tails are always shown as demons or mockery, but the wrestlers looked fine: I won't mind being shaped like Corin Gwinbren when I'm older -- Oh!" He turned to the Sphinx and bowed and said, "Reverend Count Great Aunt Adrasteia, I have not forgotten that I owe you a story about the Palace..."

"Let us all move closer to the precinct gate and Saints' Altar, and you shall tell it," Her Grace the Duke his Grandmother said. She glanced at the position of the Sun since the cathedral tower had bells but no clock. "We have a while yet."

CHAPTER XXIII: Palace and Presents

Wherein We Hear of Old Customs and New Gifts

When Her Grace and the other Councilors and their guests paused near the cathedral's precinct Gate, people arrived almost immediately to bring seats, and cups, and little tables to set the cups on, and pitchers that were sweating because they held things to drink that were still cool from the wells and cellars.

Franz-Karl settled himself, waited for the others to settle, and took a few sips of well-watered wine before he began. "The inside of the Palace is a bit like the cathedral of Saints Clement and Sophia here," he waved toward the nearby tower, "the people who decorated the inside did not think their work was finished if there was a patch of plain wall or ceiling still showing. But the cathedral is mosaics and colored glass and frescoes, and the Palace is frescoes and oil paints, mostly... the only mosaics are some of the floors." He took another sip from his cup.

"There is an old custom... well, Her Reverence the Count will not think it is old, but the Kingship of the Allemans has been through at least five families since it started, and the old servant families in the Palaces that have followed the Crown from the beginning remember about it... People and animals painted on the walls and ceilings in the Palaces of the Allemanic Kings are called 'vesets' except by outsiders: not by name even if you know the person from a story or chronicle that the veset is supposed to be."

"It must get confusing if you need to talk about a room with many vesets," Her Grace said, as if she was thinking about it, not making fun.

"It does," Franz-Karl agreed seriously. "There is a joke about one third veset from the left that no one will explain to me until I am older, but I think it is about any third veset from the left..." The Praetor swallowed some of his drink wrong and started coughing. Franz-Karl waited for him to recover before continuing. "There are other customs about the vesets: they do not officially receive offerings as house guardians, but... that depends on the definition of an offering..." Someone snickered, but he was looking at Harvest Prince's ears, choosing his words, and did not see who it was. "New vesets have their eyes and mouths touched with feathers dipped in wine... to awaken them, I think. No one says why, and there are no special words: it is just always done."

He continued, "One very old custom is that the vesets in important rooms are not depicted with many clothes, but the vesets in lesser rooms are clothed more. If you ever go to the Palace to present a petition or ask a question, and the ushers show you into a waiting room with all fully clothed vesets, you might as well go home, because you are not likely to see anyone with the authority to give you an answer that you will like. And all the many vesets in the throne room in Karnburg have about two cloaks and three handkerchiefs between them." He shook his head. "People say it's all changed in the North provinces since the Sectarian Wars: old Palaces that were not wrecked outright in the fighting are all plain, clean plaster inside... and so are the public parts of Northern churches and cathedrals that were taken over by the Harfnerans and Pristinists."

Tribune Ursula said, "The Palace in Karnburg still has its vesets, though?"

"The Eastlands are not a Northern province, and in the Eastlands both the Falkenburgs and most of our people there are Ecclesialists who remain ... aligned: the word is always 'aligned' ... with their Holinesses in Remora." He sipped from his glass. "I have heard His Excellency My Grandfather say that the North won no battles that gave them command over Eastlands churches and palaces. Though speaking honestly, there seems to be a lot of whitewash in the cathedral in

Karnburg. The Arch-hierophant has a lot of Northern relatives, and complains about decorations that are 'too traditionally licentious'." Mimicking a Northern Allemanic accent while speaking Elderic was tricky, but he thought he managed: it was mostly in the Rs and Chs and a few of the vowels. And a sort of whine that sort of matched one particular voice. "There are petitions about the Palace – and the Cathedral, and some other places south of the Daonas – handed in to the Court a few times each year." He snickered.

Ulrich huffed. "You find that amusing, boy?" That 'boy' moved him at least a notch higher on the future-newt list, and the list only had one slot at the moment.

Franz-Karl waved his hands while he explained. "When people deliver petitions asking for vesets to be whitewashed over – or for clothes to be painted onto the work of famous artists in the Palace or the cathedral or other shrines, which is very rude to the artists, and not polite to the Gods in the cathedral and shrines – they usually get shown into rooms where the painted people are all very modestly clad and won't offend their propriety. His Royal Grace the acting Archduke my Uncle Helm-Friedrich told my Papa that it's a kindness, really..." He was imitating a voice again.

One of the listeners coughed: not the one who had snickered earlier.

Franz-Karl thought for a moment, then grinned. "His Royal Grace often holds his audiences in the room decorated with DaCascio's Procession of the Seasons. There are a few Northern Lords who try not to look straight at him during audiences even though protocol says they should: they have some odd beliefs regarding mortal authority, and also complain about dealing with His Royal Grace instead of directly with His Excellency. But the Chair of State is set so there is a veset on the wall by his Royal Grace's left shoulder and another veset by his right shoulder, and some vesets that look a bit like an allegory of the Night Sky embracing someone up on the wall just above his head. His Royal Grace says those Lords can choose to face him honestly, or look aside and blush, or retreat to their estates where they may trouble their tenants instead of their overlords." He took another sip of the watered wine. "Does that story about the Palace pay my forfeit, Reverend Count Great Aunt Adrasteia?"

"It does indeed, Your Honor Franz-Karl, and very thoroughly, too."

Someone said thoughtfully, ""I wonder how many factions there are in Karnburg."

"His Royal Grace says: at least two or three more than the number of highborn men," Franz-Karl answered promptly. "Her Royal Highness Aunt Queen Gertrude says, that's before you have considered the factions and guilds and societies among the lesser folk. *Or* the various religious sects."

The person who had asked said, "Oh dear Heaven and all the Saints!" but her Grace the Duke, Franz-Karl's Grandmother, started laughing as if she had just heard the best joke ever told. When she stopped, she said, "I believe I would get on well with your Aunt and Uncle."

"My Mama is friendly with both of them," Franz-Karl agreed.

The sunrise sacrifice at the Great Altar had been a pure white bull – many white bulls, actually, so there was no risk anyone one attending would go hungry, but there was one special one that was responsible for the formal bits and served as the official Messenger to the Gods – and the single morning feast was eaten by all under the sky.

The sunset sacrifice that closed the Feast Day took place at the Saints' Altar in front of the cathedral, and was a black bull (and various associates to make up the amount of meat needed). Once the consecrated meat had been shared out, people did not eat it under the sky, but took it home and gathered into smaller celebrations to feast with friends and families.

Corin and Nestor collected Fritzel for their wrestlers' dinner, while Franz-Karl accompanied Her Grace his Grandmother and Reverend Count Great Aunt Adrasteia and the other Councilors back to the Ducal Residence, accumulating Ducal cousins and Councilors' relatives as they went. He did not change into his best suit after all: it seemed rude when no one else was changing. But he paused on the way to the dining room to put his hat and Harvest Prince in his room.

After the evening meal was done, Her Reverence Count Great Aunt Adrasteia brought out gifts 'for the children': which was everyone in the room except herself. Even Tribune Ulrich. Franz-Karl remembered the way she had said 'after the first thousand years' during that meal earlier in the summer. Going by age, compared to Great Aunt Adrasteia, everyone living in Traventi was a child.

Franz-Karl was embarrassed to receive two parcels when the others got one, but when one of the smaller cousins started to complain, Morgan said, "Hush. He's missed a handful of years, and all the other gift days," and everyone seemed to agree with that, even the small cousin.

He opened the larger of his two parcels first, before anyone else opened theirs. He found a book, newly bound and freshly copied onto new vellum. There was no title or other identification on the outside of the book, just a frog tooled into the leather of the front cover, and little frog-shaped metal clasps holding it shut. He laughed, remembered at the last moment not to say 'thank you' and said, instead, "This is a wonderful gift, Great Aunt Adrasteia."

"I promised you stories of my Grandfather and his brother Rano and their friends," she said smiling. "But we are both too busy to meet often. With this, you will have my words ready to hand." She settled herself on the dining couch and he perched on the edge of it by her feet, where the world was not too wobbly, and they watched together as one by one the members of the household opened other parcels containing small wonders. The parcels for people like Fritzel, who were feasting elsewhere were set aside carefully.

"Is this customary here in Traventi? Gifts on Saints' Days are not customary in Karnburg."

"Do people in Karnburg give year-gifts on birthdays?"

"Yes, very often."

"Here, Year-gifts are given either at the settlement Saints' Day or at Harvest, or in some families on your own Saint's day, but not at birth anniversaries, which we hold of less importance. May Day and Midwinter are everyone's days for larger gifts. You were traveling this year at May-tide, and you will likely be traveling again at Harvest-tide, and no one with half a wit travels more than an hour's journey at Winter-tide if they can at all avoid it. So for this year, my Year Gifting to you falls at the Saints' Day."

Franz-Karl had received his signet on May Eve, which was generally counted as part of May-tide – and was also his birthday, for that matter – but that probably did not count as a proper gift, being an official matter.

When all of the other parcels had been opened, Franz-Karl opened his second package. It contained a long narrow wooden box which held a string of mourner's prayer beads, made of bone or ivory so they could be worn openly with color-of sorrow clothes as well as with regular clothes. They would suit well with the Crown of Ivy and Iron.

There was a pendant at one end and a hook at the other that could go between any of the beads: the string of ... he counted with a glance: they were too few to need a jar... thirteen ... thirteen long flat beads went nearly three times around Franz-Karl's small wrist, and a regular clasp would not have held them well. When he looked closer he saw that each bead was marked with a symbol matching one of the true things about the World. The pendant showed the tree-of-life with its protective dragon twined around it, or possibly a grapevine and a bunch of grapes: the carving was old and a bit worn.

The whole string of beads looked old. Franz-Karl had only told Great Aunt Adrasteia about naming the thirteen true things the previous day... but no one sensible would expect gifts from the Mistress of Riddles to be simple.

CHAPTER XXIV: Breakfast and Lessons

Wherein a Council Session Does Not Occur

That night Franz-Karl's sleep was troubled. He had dreams of following the sound of an unfamiliar crying woman through a series of rooms and corridors that were neither the Palace nor the House on the Rock. It was not his Mama's voice nor Cornelia nor Juliana nor Gwenlian nor Sophie-Alexa's Nurse Rosa, but it was a grownup woman crying. There were vesets on some of the walls that moved their mouths silently as he passed but were otherwise motionless. Some of them held scrolls that showed only jumbled swirls instead of readable words. Other walls bore interlaced animals whose heads turned to watch him pass. Some of them bared their teeth at him.

He awakened early as usual, but felt weary rather than refreshed. There was no sign of Fritzel yet, so he returned to bed until the Sun was well up and the morning meal should be ready. Olivia was yawning a little, but she helped him wash his face and hands before he said his prayers, and combed his hair for him, and waited at the Household Shrine while he greeted his Papa and the other guardians.

When Franz-Karl was ready, Olivia guided him to the room where the morning meal would be served. It was not the usual breakfast room, because of all of the guests who had come for the festival, but one of the larger dining rooms. It was very fancy, but in a properly hospitable way: the food was set out in abundance on tables along one wall so that anyone could take as much as they wanted of whatever dishes they preferred without waiting for things to be fetched from the kitchens.

There were covered platters and shallow pans set over candles and spirit lamps to keep some things nicely warm, and other platters and pans resting on beds of ice (Real ice! In Sextil!) to stay cold, and pitchers and kettles of things to drink that were hot and cold and everything between. The original bottles were displayed beside some of the pitchers. Franz-Karl automatically read all of the labels, at least the ones that were readable. There was a bottle that was labeled in strange symbols that he thought might be Naua, from the Western Lands.

Some of the tables nearer the center of the room were arranged for eating, while another larger table on the opposite side, as far as possible from the tables serving food, was scattered with books and papers and pens and inkwells. Her Reverence Count Great Aunt Adrasteia looked up from a text she was examining and absently wished Franz-Karl a blessed morning. "Choose whatever you like... and if you happen to like pickled eggs, that crock at the end of the serving table is nearly full of them. Or it was a while ago." She speared an egg with a claw from a small bowl beside her and ate it with a few quick bites. One of the servers tending the array of food platters took the empty bowl away, added a few more eggs from the crock, and set it back by her elbow.

The servers helped Franz-Karl fill his plate with small amounts of several dishes he recognized – including a pickled egg – and a few others that were new to him. Many of the platters and pans held things that had been left over from the previous day's feast before being sauced and decorated and remade into new dishes. There was even some meat of the sacrifice, carefully arranged and set out so that it would not insult the messenger by being wasted, but he was not sure of the rules for non-Initiates, so he did not take any.

He climbed up into one of the chairs at an eating table – there were no other Binders or Notaries besides Count Great Aunt Adrasteia in the room so it did not matter much which table he chose – and ate his morning meal, beginning with the egg.

Fritzel arrived before Franz-Karl had finished his meal, and wished the room a general 'blessed morning' with a yawn. His short hair was wet, and he was wearing one of his usual suits, not the victorious-wrestler's tunic Franz-Karl had last seen him wearing, but he looked tired. Fritzel filled three large plates with bits from the various pans and platters, including a few of the eggs and some meat of sacrifice. He was adding a scoop of the brine from the egg crock to a goblet when one of the servers pointed out the pitcher full of vinegary swichell lurking among the other beverages. Fritzel paused for a moment, swallowed the egg-brine, refilled his cup with the swichell, drank all of that, and refilled his cup once more before carrying his plates and cup to the table near Franz-Karl.

It was rude to interrupt someone who was hungry, so Franz-Karl waited until Fritzel had emptied the first two plates and begun to eat more slowly before he asked whether the party had gone well. It was not a very long wait.

Fritzel grinned cheerfully and reported that the party had gone very well indeed. He only blushed a little. He blushed more when one of the servers leaned toward him and said something quietly that Franz-Karl did not hear.

By the time Franz-Karl and Fritzel had finished their meals, the dining room was full of councilors and each of the various eating tables had at least one Notary or Binder. The Duke was there, and two of the three territorial Counts, both Hierophants, the Praetor, Archivist and Justice, and two Tribunes of the three. So they had ten of the thirteen Councilors – and five of the the six Notaries in their number – but it was just a meal, just a meal in dining room, not a council meeting. It was certainly not a council of war... even when the Council secretary Hieronymus arrived with one of his assistants. The secretaries were followed almost immediately by Count Valens' proxy, Cormac, so they were missing only the Guildsmaster, who lived in the North Valley, and Tribune Constans, who lived in the South Valley. Everyone had food and drink at their elbows, but some of the people at the tables had paper and ink at their other elbow. Most of the servers left the room, along with most other members of the household not attached to the Council.

Fritzel asked quietly, "Should I leave?"

"You were properly oath-bound for Council matters at the start of the summer." Franz-Karl answered. "And this is not even an official council meeting. Are you still willing to travel to Karnburg with me?"

"Certainly, your Honor." Fritzel looked honestly startled by the question.

"Then this matter concerns your safety as well as mine. You are my aide. Stay, if you please."

The Chief Archivist, Marcus, walked over to Count Great Aunt Adrasteia's table and poked warily at the pile of papers that had been carried from Karnburg. He had not seen them all together before. "These papers were like this when your Honor opened the parcel?" He poked them again, and half of them fell off the table and fluttered about, rearranging themselves.

"The papers were all jumbled when I opened the package, and there was no syllabus or inventory, just the number of pages written on the outer wrapper in Meister van Diesen's hand," Franz-Karl said carefully. "The papers and ink are no worse than they were then. But I had a thought, just now – I did not see the lesson papers packed, so they may not have come from Meister van Diesen's hand in that disordered state. They were certainly packed at least twice: there was a huge fuss and the loads of the mules needed to be rearranged."

"Dear heaven! Yet you completed the most of the assigned tasks. How did you decide your course of study?" Chief Justice Laurentina asked.

"I am not present during his lessons and did not hear the Meister's discourse, but I share a room with my brother. Beginning students have many things to memorize, which they are encouraged to do by repeating them aloud. Many, many times... " Franz-Karl walked over and picked the top pages off the messy pile. "After his first lesson, Philip-Augustus was instructed to learn the first declension of Remoran nouns, and a list of some nouns that used it, and a few verbs in the present tense. There were also some definitions in Logic to be memorized, and a short text to be memorized that would begin the foundations for Rhetoric." He handed the pages to the Justice.

"First declension. Nouns. Verbs. Definitions in logic. And a text... Your Honor had learned along with your brother?"

"Better to say that I became familiar with the tasks my brother was given. Learning formal Grammar is not really the same as learning a language, and we both already had some Remoran. Our parents speak... spoke... Remoran with each other more often than either Allemanic or Elderic, and sometimes to us. My brother and I speak some of all three languages to each other – sometimes in the same sentence – and we could read some of all three as well, even before the Meister came to us. "

"So the schoolmaster may not be entirely dishonest," Count Great Aunt Adrasteia said thoughtfully. "Since the page count was unchanged, it may be that the syllabus or inventory that was present, or intended, was replaced by these vile texts that we have identified. And without the inventory it will be difficult to tell what else might have been replaced – " Fritzel snickered, and the sphinx continued smoothly, "or apparently, not." She nodded toward Franz-Karl and raised an eyebrow. "Your Honor?"

Everyone turned. Everyone in the room was looking at him. If he tried to not be noticed, it probably would not work. He looked straight at Count Great Aunt Adrasteia, took a deep breath, and tried to ignore all the others. "Um. Explaining that is... messy? The Remoran in the Grammar lessons is not exactly like the Remoran they use in church, nor the Remoran used in diplomacy and official matters, nor the Remoran we speak at home. It is not even always the Remoran used in the Rhetoric lesson texts. There was a time Philip-Augustus became... notably stubborn, Mama called it... about being asked to memorize the parts of an irregular verb on the same day as memorizing a text that used the same verb with different parts. Our Papa – " He swallowed hard. "Our Papa finally said that Grammatical Remoran should be treated as its own thing."

"And those lessons were missing from the package you received?"

"Aye," Fritzel agreed. "The lesson with the parts of the verb. His Honor had transcribed about two parts in three of that pile by then. We wrote an inventory of what we were sure of, and what we guessed at in the remainder, and I asked at the Schola and the Archives what they thought was missing from the list compared to what they would expect for a beginning student."

"The answers helped us decipher that mess into a syllabus," Franz-Karl said, "and extend it."

"Extend it?" Tribune Ulrich seemed appalled.

Franz-Karl shrugged, the one-sided shrug people in Traventi used when talking about work. "When scholars outside Traventi say 'Grammar', they always mean Remoran grammar. But Remoran is not the only language with irregular verbs. And the Meister only knows fragments of some Remoran texts that the Archive here has in full. When we saw that this pile of lessons would not fill the summer we added a few of the less boring looking tasks from the lists the Scholas and Archive had provided: ones that needed full texts or Elderic documents. It seemed... wasteful? ... to live beside a wonder of the World and make no use of the Archive."

The Praetor laughed. "Fair enough."

The Archivist looked very satisfied. Almost gleeful. "I shall certainly write a letter to the University in Karnburg suggesting that they send Scholars to amend the inadequacies of their collections by copying some of our holdings."

Franz-Karl wondered who at the University in Karnburg had been rude to the Traventine Scholars, but he was sure that the Arch-Hierophant would gloat if Karnburg could claim to be honored before the founding seats of the Ecclesia. "Offer the collections to the Holy See and Alexandria and Clontarf first," he suggested. Archivist Marcus looked startled.

"An excellent thought!" Her Grace the Duke agreed, laughing a little. She took a breath and turned serious, "Great Aunt Adrasteia, have you discovered anything interesting about these spurious lesson texts?"

The sphinx waved a forelimb at one of the books piled on her table. "The paragraphs handed to our young Heir cover a Binding that was cribbed – badly – from a grimoire corruptly derived from the 'Silver Chain' of Philodorus Sextus. There are three or four possibilities for the fourth piece of the intended Binding that seem to be implied by the three we know, but they are very confused."

"Derived?" the Archivist asked. He was taking notes almost as quickly as Hieronymus the Secretary.

"Judging by the forms used... hmm... the 'Silver Chain' was written within the past thousand years. It was originally in reasonably good traditional Remoran, with not even any attempts at Elderic, so the few usable Binding formulas it records among the false ones are... brittle. The source used for the formulas in Franz-Karl's lessons in Remoran appears to be a 400 year old version in Allemanic. There are turns of phrase translated verbatim that were formerly common but are now forgotten. And the back translation was to the form of Remoran used for modern diplomacy, and done by someone whose grasp of the language seems as questionable as his handwriting."

Franz-Karl thought about Meister van Diesen, his brother's tutor. "Are the problems more Remoran or Allemanic?"

"Surely the scholar knew his own language," Tribune Ursula protested.

"Allemanic is like Remoran: more a family than a single tongue. Meister van Diesen comes from the north coast. Someone being mean said once that he would need webbed feet to come from any farther north. When he's tired or ... flustered ... he speaks in his native dialect and the local people in Karnburg and the Palace get confused trying to speak with him. Would a 400 year old Allemanic text be closer to Court speech or Coastal?"

"Possibly neither," the Archivist said, "depending on where the grimoire was written. The spelling changes two centuries ago would not help..." He looked toward Count Great Aunt Adrasteia. "I do not believe we have an Allemanic grimoire that age containing bindings from the Silver Chain but I shall have our agents try to locate one."

The Praetor asked, "Can we destroy the grimoire copy he used?"

But he was answered by his subordinate, the Borderer Notary who was serving as Count Valens' proxy, "Not safely or reliably, and probably not usefully. Working with translations rather than direct copies of the text would cloud our aim at the best of times, and he likely worked from notes or private copies, not the original book. Setting the Palace on fire in a handful of places might be convenient, but we are not presently at war."

Franz-Karl pointed out in the calmest tone he could manage, "I like some of the people and things in the Palace."

He was relieved when Cormac agreed cheerfully, "Of course, your Honor."

"We must do something," Ulrich snapped. "We cannot just let this pass unanswered."

"Of course, Ulrich," her Grace the Duke said. She sounded... tired. "But the shape of the world has not much changed, this past decade. If the Allemanic Kingdom or the Empire tries to devour Traventi they will break their teeth and worse. But while the Elderkin of Traventi could easily destroy the Kingdom or break the Empire – it's not for nothing that so many of the Notarial oaths concern ways of avoiding accidental damage – we are too few to conquer and rule anywhere large enough to be noticed among the nations. And we have no allies to speak of: not even some who logically should be our allies. We withdrew into our mountains for the past few mortal generations, and when the

Falkenburgs reached in to drag us out, there were none to stand beside us. The Empire and Kingdom may yet regret forcing the Elderkin to look outward again, but not this year, I think."

Ulrich half-stood and leaned forward across the table. "But... "

Fritzel interrupted. "Look ye, Councilor. The man who tried to write the traps is northern-born, and so is that useless Margraff-Elector that tried to snare his Honor with lies at his own father's funeral." Several people at the tables signed themselves. The Hierophants looked appalled and made more elaborate gestures accompanied by murmured prayers. Fritzel continued, "Traventi and the Falkenburgs may have a common foe... It strikes me that taking the bait set out by some Northern fool stirring trouble in Karnburg would be a stupid reason to have a war."

Count Severin nodded – his horns made that very impressive. "An excellent point. Is there a way to strike at the true culprits without unnecessary harm to the innocent?"

"Possibly." Count Great Aunt Adrasteia shuffled through some of the papers on her table. "Franz-Karl, will you kindly join me?"

She set out a pen and ink and a blank sheet of paper, and another paper that was very regrettably familiar. It was the tutor's copy of one of the trapped problems, except... "Some of the letters are more flickery than I remember."

"You are a full Notary and Heir, and aware now of the possible danger. Please copy all of the letters that are very clear, leaving gaps for the ones that are uncertain, and expand clear contractions and abbreviations on the line below. Don't stretch for the ones that are uncertain." She showed her teeth in a way that was not at all friendly to someone. "No, indeed. Do not stretch at all. Leave plenty of space. And don't handle the source paper more than you need: as much of the trap is in the paper itself, and the ink, as in the written words."

It was a harder task than it sounded. It was tricky to pay attention to what his eyes would show him of what was actually written instead of simply repeating what he had written before, expecting that he was copying a proper Remoran school text. It helped to think that by separating the words from the paper and ink, they might be chopping holes in the trap. When he finished the first text, she gave him the second, and then the third, to copy the clear portions while leaving gaps for the uncertain bits.

By the time Franz-Karl had finished the third page, Great Aunt Adrasteia had filled in letters and words in the blank spaces he had left on the first page. "Look at the tutor's original version," she suggested. Does anything that appears there completely contradict what I have written?"

He looked at her Reverence's version and had to be careful not to snicker: the new paragraph was much better Remoran than he had originally produced: real Remoran, not grammar-book Remoran. Everything was written out plainly without contractions or abbreviations, and none of the letters were flickering, though the whole text seemed to be... leaning or stretched, even without the shapes of the letters being changed ... in a direction he could not name. The text was taut. There was something waiting to recoil when it was released.

He read through it, comparing the texts carefully. The changes were small: a preposition here; a prefix there; a few verb forms that speakers would use that were outside the limits of beginning Grammar lessons, though one or two of those changed the intent more than a little. "No, nothing contradicts, exactly, but some of the readings are ones I would not guess for a grammar lesson."

"These originals do not pretend to be grammar," the sphinx suggested, "nearer rhetoric or logic, if they are claiming to be anything..."

"Yes," he agreed. "That fits better."

Looking at all three of the new question texts together made his eyes itch. Not the outsides of his eyes, where his eyelids were: somewhere deep inside the eyes, where they should not be able to itch at all. And the stretching was worse.

The sphinx smiled with teeth that were much pointier than usual. "Copy my versions of these three problems in your own hand, and decide on your answers. When you have written your answers to all three of these final problems, Her Grace the Duke's clerks will make a package of the tutor's texts, and the copies in your hand, and all of your answers, and send them back to Karnburg. Her Grace will also send a very strong complaint at the poor quality of the tutors given to her grandsons: children who have learned the Mother Tongue at the breast should not be taught false patterns by fools. Her Grace will insist on arranging for better tutors at Traventine expense and under Traventine control –"

"And someone to attend Sophie-Alexa who speaks Elderic," Franz-Karl inserted firmly.

"Indeed?" Her Grace the Duke said in an annoyed tone. "Have they bent the Contract so far?" She made a sharp gesture with her off hand. "As you say."

Count Adrasteia finished "And then... perhaps... we will see what happens when these pages return to the hand that wrote them and the will that devised them."

"You'll be sending the papers before His Honor himself leaves Traventi?" Fritzel asked.

"Oh, yes. I rather think so." The sphinx answered. The very tip of her tail was twitching. "Best to have Franz-Karl well away from whatever happens if they are careless and that trap is sprung thoroughly."

Franz-Karl asked, "What will happen to Meister van Diesen?"

"That depends on how deep he is in this tangle..." The tail twitched again and the great wings lifted slightly and refolded. "How much was he an author as well as a copyist. If it is his hand that wrote what was given to you, what happens will likely depend on what they were planning to use as the fourth wall of their trap. And whether they are stupid enough that they fail to take precautions when these three texts return to them in a shape they don't expect." She ate a pickled egg with teeth that were still far too pointy. "They planned Bindings, and Bindings there may yet be. But who will be Bound, and to what purpose, remains to be seen."

Franz-Karl shivered. People were Bound, in the North. Not just the Elderkin, that Pristinists thought should never be free and the Harfnerans mostly agreed. There were serfs Bound to the land, and slaves and indentured servants Bound to Masters. And that was just the men. Northern women were not so much Bound as tangled in a mess of ancient customs and Ecclesialist teachings and Harfneran rules and Pristinist strictures: his Mama said the rule that applied to a Northern woman in any time and place would be the one that made some man richer, the trouble was guessing which man.

And Highborn Northerners tried really hard to stop anything from getting unbound. Ever.

The laws in Traventi were arranged by former slaves: people, like Maximianus the Frog. They tried to keep people from being Bound so that they were stuck. Except, honestly, there were lots of stories about Traventine Elderkin arranging for slavers to get thoroughly stuck in their own traps. Or worse. It was scary to think about awful things happening to someone he knew. Even if they were not very nice.

Franz-Karl took a deep breath and let it out slowly.

The people in the Council of Traventi were angry, but there would not be open war, not yet: most of the council spoke against it. People mentioned the Marriage Contract, and it seemed to be blocking the war, but also making them angrier. Franz-Karl was glad that he could not see angry, the way he could see fibs: that would be scary.

CHAPTER XXV: Puzzles

Wherein the Trivia Are Rewoven into a Trap

Franz-Karl decided it would be better to be somewhere quiet. And away from the papers that Meister van Diesen had written: those had fallen off the table again, twice, without anyone touching them, and that was starting to be creepy. He took the question pages that Her Reverence Count Great Aunt Adrasteia had written, and Fritzel brought some clean paper and pens and some good strong ink, and they went back to Franz-Karl's room.

He wrote out the questions on three clean pages using his very best handwriting. He wanted the pages to be as different from messy ones Meister van Diesen had written as possible. Then he sat looking at them. They still looked stretched . And having sensible questions to answer was one thing. Having sensible answers to send back with them was quite another.

Franz-Karl climbed up onto the table in his room, because that made it easier to reach things than sitting or kneeling in a chair made for grownups. Having cushions on the chair helped in some ways, and made things worse in others: he could never quite reach far enough from the edge of the table, and the cushions had a Gift for slipping out of position at the worst possible moment. And then the ink made a mess, even if he managed to not spill the inkwell entirely.

On the table, besides himself, Franz-Karl had pens and ink and paper, the lesson sheets that Reverend Count Great Aunt Adrasteia had revised, and Harvest Prince. He also had a few of the books about Logic and Rhetoric that were considered most useful for beginners: it was not clear which bucket the false lessons had pretended to belong in before Count Great Aunt Adrasteia adjusted them. They were two logic puzzles and a rhetoric drill now.

He made sure the pens were well-trimmed and the ink was well-stirred. He wrote the clean copies of the Sphinx's versions, and then read the lessons again, and tried arranging the papers in different orders, to see if that made a difference.

The rhetoric problem looked like it wanted to be first, but it also wanted an essay written, and he was too angry to begin with that. That could go last, when he was certain the everything else was done. One of the logic puzzles was either the middle of the three: because the others connected to it but not to each other, or the last one: because it expected that things had been already decided in the others. It did not want to be first, but it was going to be first, no matter what it wanted.

Then he read the first puzzle aloud. Count Great Aunt Adrasteia had said that it was safe to do that, but he was still careful to warn the World that this reading was not any kind of agreement: he was just making noises to see how they sounded. It would be silly to get caught by something he already knew was trying to be a trap.

There were three arguments listed on the page. The task was to choose the true argument and name the classes of errors of the false ones, but none of the three arguments were jumping out as being preferable to the others. Franz-Karl was sure there was a trap in the puzzle but he could not see where the trap was. Her Grace His Grandma or Count Great Aunt Adrasteia could probably point to it, but when he became a Notary he had promised the World to make his own choices. Asking 'Where is the trap' seemed like more than asking advice... and maybe asking would be part of the trap. Or pull the person he asked into the trap with him.

He could almost see the fibs crawling on the page like caterpillars. But he still needed to pick one of the arguments to be the true one. He read the lesson instructions and texts again, silently. He galloped Harvest Prince around the desk top and across the lesson pages, thumpity, thumpity, thumpity, which was fun but not very useful. The pendant on his bracelet of thirteen true things was not looking much like either a bunch of grapes or a tree of life this morning: the angle of the light was striking its worn carvings oddly, so it just looked like a lumpy, unripe strawberry. It moved and bounced when he made the wooden horse prance, and the point of its shadow skittered across the words on the papers. He stilled the pendant and ran his finger along some of the beads, looking at the markings showing the thirteen true things that had broken the Trap of Lies.

Oh.

This was another Trap of Lies trying to fool him into agreeing with something that was not true.

The fibbers should try something different. But perhaps they thought that was the best way to capture an Elderkin. The others puzzles were likely to be traps of lies as well. Now he would know what to watch for.

One of the three arguments – it was in favor of trusting ones senses – left things out in a way that made the argument formally false, and the second – arguing against trusting authority – used different gaps that made it deliberately false in an opposite way. The third argument, in favor of obedience... was supposed to look very truthful compared to the first two. It had the shape of a truthful argument, but the statements did not connect the way they pretended to. The instructions were inviting him to look at the shapes of the arguments without thinking about their meanings. And part of the fib had tried to hide in the gaps of the grammar-lesson Remoran, before Count Great Aunt Adrasteia changed the words to real Remoran and stopped it from pretending things that were not there.

Don't trust your own eyes, because the argument in favor of trusting them was willfully broken.

Trust authority, because the argument against trust was broken.

Obey, because the argument in favor rested on rotten supports painted to look solid.

Franz-Karl dipped the pen into the ink and wrote in good Diplomatic Remoran, using large Remoran letters as clear as the Elderic ones Willy had taught him. 'There are no choices provided that are not false." And then he named the two clear kinds of falsehoods according to the rules and lists in the Logic book, without any mention of any other lessons. He described the third, more complicated falsehood, which did not seem to have a simple name in the beginning logic books: it said that things were connected that were not, then expected agreement with a statement that was also not really connected to them, but looked like it ought to be. Maybe it did not have a name because it was not really an argument.

His answer went onto a second page, but did not fill the space available. He signed his full name close to his answer, added the title Notary that still gave him a shiver of pride, and got Fritzel to sign and date the page, as he had with all of the other lessons.

But he did not feel ready to try the next trap yet. He looked at the half-empty page. One of Chief Justice Laurentina's stories had mentioned a time when someone sneaky added unexpected things to the blank part of a contract page, with terrible results because they got woven into the real things before anybody noticed. He did not want the trap to leak into the empty place. And no one could blame him for being careful, even if there was a fun way of being careful.

He filled the empty space with a picture that was supposed to be a goat in a boat with waves around it. Lots of waves. The goat seemed right, because he did not know where this puzzle belonged except probably not first, and the goat in the river crossing puzzle was first and last and in the middle. And because he was a goat, like Corin Gwinbren. And that was another true thing.

The second logic puzzle asked him to give the proper names for two kinds of true arguments. One was easy: it was an example of one of the very first things in the list of logic terms he had memorized, and now that Count Great Aunt Adrasteia had fixed the words, it really was true.

The other argument looked almost as clear in Remoran, but there was a fib crawling on it like a caterpillar, and it was talking about obedience, like the sneaky part of the other puzzle. When Franz-Karl tried to translate it into grownup Elderic using the fancy verb forms, it went strange because it was assuming things it should not. He spent almost an hour looking at the rhetoric and logic books before he found the name for the kind of false argument it was: way in the back with things most students learned a very long time after they started, which really was not fair. He wrote down the book and chapter where he found the name, and copied the words from the book describing it. He signed his name and title, and Fritzel signed and dated it.

He still did not want to write an essay. There was not much empty space at the bottom of the page below where he signed and Fritzel signed, but he drew a picture of the wolf anyway, and gave it lots of teeth so it could chase the fibs and bite them. It took him three tries to get the head the way he wanted it, and he could still see parts of the first two tries, charcoal shadows behind the inked head.

Franz-Karl finally had nothing left except the rhetoric essay. It was the last lesson of all the ones he had been given for the summer. Even if it was a trap. It was the last.

The instructions said they were giving him a piece of an ancient letter and he should write about it. But it was not really the letter: the words on the page were only ones from grammar lessons. When Count Great Aunt Adrasteia fixed and made it more like real Remoran, there was one sentence that was famous enough that even Franz-Karl knew it – it was a famous motto about obedience (again!) that got repeated a lot– and Fritzel knew what Letter it came from.

Franz-Karl sent Fritzel to ask the Archive for the oldest version of the Letter they had: and laid on his bed while he waited for it, thinking about the essay. The instructions said to write an essay about the text: they did not really say to write about what the text talked about. He was still angry about all the traps.

The copy of the letter the Archive sent was from the ancient writer's lifetime, but was possibly not the one written by his hand. They apologized. Franz-Karl looked at paragraph in the real letter, and saw how different it was from what Meister van Diesen had written, and laughed until he had hiccups. It was exactly what he wanted.

Franz-Karl copied the real words from the letter onto the lesson sheet below the fake version, with the name of the writer and the name of the Letter. He wrote his essay about teachers who used fake texts, and did not bother to pretend not to be angry about it. He did not skimp, either: the instructions said what the shortest the writing could be was, but said nothing about what would be too long, His essay continued onto a second sheet, and got a bit fierce at times. He even used phrases he remembered from three other old writings, and two lines from a hymn that talked about honesty. He knew what rhetoric was supposed to be, even if he was not very good at it yet, and he was very annoyed.

When Fritzel read the essay to sign it, he said, "Dear Heaven and all the saints!" and stared at Franz-Karl.

"Born old and open-eyed," Franz-Karl said in the calmest, butter would not melt voice he could manage: the voice that Philip-Augustus really truly hated..

Fritzel grinned. "Of course, your Honor." He signed and dated the page. Then he took up a pen and paper.

"What are you doing?"

"Making an extra copy of this essay for the Archive. There'll be someone wanting to see it, someday when your Honor is Duke."

While Fritzel wrote, Franz-Karl drew another picture below the signatures and date on the paper he had used. The goat and wolf had pictures, so it started out to be the cabbage, but it mostly just looked like a blob. He added a face – it seemed to need one, even though cabbages do not have faces – and it started looking a bit like a lion's head door pull. At least it filled the space, so the trap could not leak. He gave it a twig like a quill pen in its mouth instead of the usual ring.

They gathered up the pages that Franz-Karl had written, and Fritzel's copy, and the papers Count Great Aunt Adrasteia had written, in case she wanted them, and the letter from the Archive, because they would almost certainly want it, and returned to the dining room that was absolutely not being used as a council chamber. Some of the serving platters had been replaced by new ones holding different things to eat. That was good, because it was now mid-afternoon and breakfast – even a late, day-after-festival breakfast – had been a long time ago.

Fritzel carried the lesson papers to the Reverend Count's work table and presented the letter and the copy of Franz-Karl's essay to Marcus the Archivist. Then he joined Franz-Karl in loading plates with food.

The Sphinx laughed when she saw his pictures, but it was not a mean laugh. Or at least, not mean aimed at him. And she knew right away that the lion was really a cabbage, but Hieronymus the secretary said something approving about summoning the scholar's lion to defend truth and liberty. All of the Councilors read Franz-Karl's answers to the lessons before they left to return to their homes. They seemed a lot happier than they had been at breakfast.

Franz-Karl stood with Her Grace the Duke His Grandmother and Reverend Count Great Aunt Adrasteia to watch the lessons being packed for their journey back to the Palace. The pile of papers where he had written lessons and answers stacked neatly together in order and packed tidily into a leather case for the mules to carry. The papers written by Meister van Diesen that had come from Karnburg fell off the table – again – and landed in a shuffled, scattered heap, even though there was no wind in the room.

Her Grace the Duke, herself, picked up the papers, tapped them into a smooth pile and stuffed them into a pack. The paper that had ended up on top tried to crumple, but she glared at it, and it flattened out and went into the pack meekly. She sealed the pack shut with two colors of wax, and used both her own signet and the Great Seal of Traventi, and Reverend Count Great Aunt Adrasteia added a third seal using her own signet and a third color of wax on a strap that was wrapped around the package to hold it closed. The packages were starting to look a little like the ones that had traveled with Franz-Karl from Karnburg.

The letter from the Council to Their Excellencies and the acting Archduke had even more seals. There were all of the personal signets of the Council Notaries using different colors of wax, and seals for the offices of the other Councilors. The letter was enclosed in a protective wrapper that had an additional set of seals besides.

Heir of the Bindings

CHAPTER XXVI: A Message from the Duke and Council of Traventi

Wherein Karnburg Receives a Visit from the Wild Hunt

The messengers of Traventi passed in full array as the Wild Hunt. Once past the milestone three days march from Traventi Crossing, they passed unseen by dark and by day, with only a sound of pipes and hoof beats, always distant. The villages they passed summoned priests and priestesses to bless the wells, and looked worriedly at the fields, and gave thanks kneeling that this year's harvests were well advanced. Pigeon-masters they passed sent word ahead, and churches with long memories rang ancient tocsins unheard in living memory to warn their neighbors.

By dawn and by dusk, the Hunt were briefly glimpsed: cloaked and masked, surrounded by unnatural lights, and traveling at speed. North to the Daonas they rode, and then east on the ancient Trade Road where long ago the Legions had marched beside the river..

East of Augsburg, the Trade Road at dusk was blocked by unwary merchants traveling late. All of their mules shed harness and packs and fled away, and all of their axles broke, and a warning appeared carved into the door of their distant company storehouse. Their masters pondered apologetic gifts to send to Traventi Crossing and the Fishwatch, to be allowed to cross the Raenos and join in next year's trade.

At the walls of Karnburg at dusk, the outermost gate was shut against them, that in recent living memory had held three months against all the Sultan's generals might attempt. But the bars broke and the hinges failed, and the gate panels fell and later showed charred cloven hoof prints where the Hunt had passed across them. The inner gates were open, and so remained standing.

The Palace Gate was closed but not barred. It opened before the Riders as the gatekeepers scattered, with no man's hand seen to move it.

The doors of the Main Palace were tall enough for a mounted man and wide enough for two. The Old Palace Servants pushed aside the guards and opened the doors to the Riders' passage, and the polished floors took no mark nor mar from their passing.

The Hunt leaders rode up the stairs to the empty Great Audience Hall, cast down two bulky parcels and a document case, and were gone. None saw them go.

No one saw the Hunt leave, neither the Riders nor their Steeds, but the three packages remained. They flared with unnatural light at the approach of any hand but that of Friedrich-Augustus himself, but once the seals were broken they settled into apparent quiet.

INTERLUDE VI: Fire and Blood

Wherein a Trap is Sprung

When His Excellency summoned his vassals and councilors to the Audience Chamber, the response was less sparse that it had been earlier in the season. Nobles who had spent the summer at their estates had begun to return to the city and Palace. The North remained lightly represented: the Eastlands lords arrived sooner because their journeys were much shorter. The Falkenburg Privy Council would not resume its meetings until September, but there was a quorum of Eastlands councilors available. The Allemanic Privy Council remained fully adjourned in Karnburg, though the official meetings of the Diet in Konigsberg occurred monthly even in high summer.

The arriving Nobles could not crowd the dais too closely: the two chairs of state for His Excellency and the acting Archduke, with three lower chairs already placed between them, faced a table on the floor that bore three parcels with their seals broken. The Master of Protocol hastily began to assure His Excellency that he would find out who had broken the seals, but His Excellency interrupted calmly, "I opened those seals with my own hands, and the parcels have not been out of my sight since then."

The Master of Protocol subsided unhappily, only to bridle again when the Dowager Countess of Wolfsberg arrived with her two children, her two senior attendants, and her son's tutor. Invited by His Excellency and contrary to protocol, the Countess and her children took the seats between His Excellency and the acting Archduke, with their attendants standing behind them. The tutor remained on the main floor next to the table, carefully not looking at the parcels.

The Margraff-Elector stood at the opposite end of the table, insisting on his prerogative of standing close to His Excellency, looking at the dais, not at the table.

Commanded by the acting Archduke, the Master of Protocol – slowly – opened the smallest parcel and removed the three documents it contained. Two were from the Sovereign Duke herself, individually addressed to His Excellency and to the Duke's daughter, the Dowager Countess of Wolfsberg, Silvia, Childe of Traventi. The Master carefully handed them to their proper owners. The final document was larger than the other two together and among its seals it bore the Duchy's seal in unnaturally sparkling green wax. The Master of Protocol tried to read the superscription aloud twice, but his voice failed him.

The acting Archduke beckoned to the servant who had been announcing the arrival of various dignitaries. The man walked over to the table – the tutor hastily stepped aside – picked up the document, and read in a clear voice, "From the Duke and Council and People of Traventi to the Emperor of the Falkenburg Domains and King of the Allemans, the acting Archduke of the Falkenburg Eastlands, the Privy Council of the Falkenburgs and the Eastlands, and the Privy Council of the Allemans, Words."

His Excellency said quietly, "Oh dear." 'Words' rather than 'greetings' was not an encouraging beginning, especially after the visitation by the Wild Hunt.

The acting Archduke said cheerfully, "Well, a declaration of war would not need that much vellum." He waved a hand to the announcer. "Continue."

The man bowed an elegant acknowledgment, unfolded the document, and began to read. The text was written in something in the borderlands between Classical and Diplomatic Remoran, while the reader tended to use the Church pronunciations, but he did not stumble over the phrasing, reading with expressiveness, and even verve. The Eastlands

Lords were mostly Ecclesialists, so some may have found the announcer's performance easier to understand than the writer's own pronunciation would have been.

The text had been written by a master of rhetoric (and invective) and was very thorough. The gist was that the combined political entities of Traventi expected the Marriage Contract to continue to be enforced, to the letter, unless His Excellency gave formal notice of an intent to breach, when other measures would naturally become necessary.

Many of those listening winced. Arguments about how to repair the city Gate were still proceeding with considerable vigor. The broken hinges were not cooperating.

The document continued by explaining that at the moment the Powers of Traventi were specifically unhappy that his Honor, the Notary Franz-Karl of Traventi and Falkenburg, had been assigned lessons at the behest of the authorities in Karnburg without the courtesy of being also provided with a tutor. His Honor had managed well though his own efforts and the good advice of those at hand, but the Count of Wolfsberg, equally a child of Traventi and Falkenburg, reportedly remained afflicted with the tutelage of the unlettered savage from beyond the Limes who had set the lessons. The Karnburg authorities were invited to examine both Franz-Karl's work and the instructions he had been given, in the confident expectation that they would understand Traventi's insistence that the children of the Childe of Traventi should be provided more nearly adequate tutelage. The coffers of Traventi would naturally support the hiring of adequate instructors if the Falkenburgs found themselves unable to do so.

"Dear Heaven. Well, let's have a look. " His Royal Grace the acting Archduke got up and began to pull clean, elegantly written papers out of the larger package.

"Hardly written with his own hand," the Margraff-Elector commented.

"No, I believe they are," the acting Archduke answered. "The writing is larger than an adult's, and ... careful. Certainly this one... Here what do you think this is supposed to be?" He held out a page with a blobby round drawing.

The Margraff-Elector took it automatically, but flinched as if it stung him worse than any nettle. He handed it back quickly to the acting Archduke, who was looking at the partnered page.

Both pages were handed to the announcer. While he read out the rhetorical challenge, the mangled excerpt, the authentic excerpt and Franz-Karl's extremely emphatic response, the acting Archduke sorted through the rest of the pile of pages looking for more drawings. He invited the Margraff-Elector to view the three-headed dog... and the Margraff-Elector rubbed his fingers on his coat after handling the page before passing it to the announcer at Helm-Friedrich's gesture. His could not hide his flinch when he touched the third drawing, but claimed it was a picture of a demon among flames.

The Count of Wolfsberg shifted in his chair and cleared his throat, then flinched when his tutor glared at him. The acting Archduke looked at him. "Philip-Augustus?"

He said formally, "If your Royal grace pleases, I believe that's a goat in a boat crossing a river, and the other two are the wolf and the cabbage."

The acting Archduke studied the picture again, and nodded, "Very likely..." before he handed the pages to the announcer to be read, and opened the smaller parcel. Grubby, barely legible pages burst out and scattered themselves across the table top. They made an especially poor show when compared to Franz-Karl's clean pages with their clear handwriting stacked neatly on the other side of the table.

Trapped between the dais and table and the crowd who had gathered close to view the documents, the Margraff-Elector could not avoid helping to gather up the scattered papers. It took quite a bit of searching to find the originals of the pages with the drawings, and he was stung again by all three of the specially prepared pages. He began to hold his fingers half-curled to hide increasing blotchy redness.

His Royal Grace set the original pages written by the tutor on the table next to Franz-Karl's three responses.

The Chief Justice of the Eastlands said thoughtfully, "I wonder why those three lessons received drawings."

The acting Archduke looked toward the Count of Wolfsberg. "Does your brother often draw pictures on his lessons?"

Philip-Augustus answered indignantly, "What lessons? Franz-Karl doesn't have lessons. Franz-Karl is just a baby."

His Excellency was examining the three lessons: Franz-Karl's clean versions, not the illegible mess the tutor had provided. He said firmly, "All three involve baseless or specious arguments masked from the student, and none is fit for a young, beginning student. Franz-Karl is six." He waved at a pair of the guards waiting at the edge of the dais, and at the tutor still lurking by the table. "Escort the unlettered savage from beyond the Remoran Limes to the Palace Gate and do not let him re-enter. Someone see that he receives his personal belongings and any wages owed."

There was a gesture used for an emphatic 'Yes' in formal rhetoric, sometimes used after a victorious debate. Philip-Augustus had leaned it well, but not had much opportunity to use it before this.

When His Excellency left the Audience chamber, followed by his son, daughter-in-law and grandchildren, his attendants carried all of the various documents except the letter addressed to Childe Silvia.

The Margraff-Elector followed them out of the Audience Chamber, then strode toward the Palace Gate and the road to his own estate.

When the Margraff-Elector arrived home with his entourage, he was met at the gate by a stench of smoke and several of his servants, talking over each other in their distress. He walked quickly to his study and closed the door against all of his followers. The stench, accompanied by a few wisps of smoke, was managing to escape from the specially sealed, locked cupboard farthest from his desk.

He unlocked the cupboard with some difficulty: the lock was not quite glowing but it was hot enough that the mechanism jammed and the key – now stuck in the lock – quickly became too hot to hold with his already damaged bare hand. He splashed the cupboard door with the contents of his least expensive carafe of liqueur, which immediately caught fire and burned with a sickly green flame, not an honest red or yellow, or even the blue of spirits. The flames seemed to devour the stench, but smoke continued to leak through the cracks around the charred cupboard doorframe.

He finally used a handkerchief and the fireplace tongs to open the door, though it was not clear whether the key had turned in the lock or the lock had been wrenched loose within the door.

Opening the cupboard broke the lines of the protective patterns painted on the inside. For a moment there was nothing obviously amiss except the cloud of dark smoke that shrouded the dull red, glowing demon trap in place of its previous black silk wrapping. Almost immediately the trap began to brighten as if it had been plunged into a forge fire and someone was working hard at the bellows: red, orange, yellow...

There were no extraneous cloths in the room now that the handkerchief had been destroyed in the opening of the lock. The Margraff-Elector hastily took off his coat and used its skirts to sweep the talismans from the upper shelves. He dropped the talismans onto the top of his desk and tossed the coat into the fireplace just before the color of the demon trap reached a blinding blue-white and the cupboard completely burst into flame, followed almost immediately by the coat.

He unlocked a drawer and and pushed the talismans into it from the desktop before he opened the study door for the servants who were pounding on it. While they were distracted trying to deal with the conflagration in the corner of the room, he relocked the desk drawer.

With the study no longer demanding his immediate attention, the Margraff-Elector turned his attention to the shouting and metallic clashing at the back of the house. But silence had returned by the time he reached the area used as the kennels. In order, he encountered his hedge-wizard lying pale and dead with no outward sign of injury, the kennel-master dead of having his head twisted clean off,(there was surprisingly little blood: the vessels in the neck had been pinched shut by the twisting until after the heart had stopped), and kennel eleven standing empty with its door burst open outwards. The doors of kennels two and seven remained closed and locked, but when he thought to have them checked some hours later, both of those kennels were also empty.

There were three more dead servants scattered about the entrance of the kennels. The causes of their deaths were not apparent, but they had been armed with two boar spears and a battle ax taken from the ceremonial display in the mansion's foyer, and all of the weapons were bloodied.

When the Margraff-Elector was finally, privately, able to examine the desk drawer it contained only twelve talismans.

The Preacher attached to the White Hall of the Pristinists was present in the mansion after the tumult, but by the next morning he had vanished, along with his servant and all of their belongings. Some months later he was Preaching at what had once been a cathedral in the North. Notably, it was in the territory of Bremerhaven, not Ansbach. He politely declined an invitation to visit Ansbach. An invitation to return to Karnburg was declined with no politeness whatsoever.

CHAPTER XXVII: Invitation

Wherein Our Hero Is Invited to Travel Across the Water

Franz-Karl and the Councilors were not the only people who were busy in the House on the Rock on the day after the Festival. Most people from elsewhere began their journeys home before noon, while the local people were busy storing away the Festival until the next year. Saint Victoria's square was especially busy. Festivals followed the months and seasons, but markets rested on the endless eight-day cycle of the market week. The next day would be nondi, usually written 'VIIIIdi', and the Greater Market would happen in the square of Saint Victoria as it had for centuries, recent festival or no, so the space needed to be clear.

People in Traventi knew about seven-day weeks. They called them Lowlands weeks or astrologers' weeks and paid them less mind than birthdays. Franz-Karl had lost a day or two of his reckoning on the journey west and never found them again, so he never knew what day of the week it might be in Karnburg. It did not help that market weeks counted their days down instead of up, and there was a day written Idi and pronounced 'findi' that never happened: the count went from nine to two, then started over.

On the morning after the Great Market, very formal letters arrived at breakfast for Franz-Karl and Fritzel. They were written in three colors of ink on very fine vellum and sealed with honey-gold wax impressed with a sign of a bull's head.

Franz-Karl's letter formally invited him, as a Childe of Traventi, for a visit to the settlement and estate of the Bull's Leap for the time of a full market week, to end following the wedding of the Heir of the line of Boukolyos. Franz-Karl read the last bit carefully, twice, because Heirs were like Dukes and Counts: Elderic played tricky games with the genders compared to how they worked in Allemanic and Remoran. Finally, he asked, "Fritzel? Is the Heir of Boukolyos your brother? Or your sister?"

"Your Honor?" Fritzel looked up from frowning at his own letter. "Oh. Yes, Your Honor. My brother Astolon is the heir, being both eldest child of my parents and a full Notary, which I am not, nor ever will be. He will be marrying the younger daughter of our nearest neighbor the week after next: the families are kin, but not too close or recent, and Astolon and Imelda have been friends since they were your Honor's age, so it is no great surprise." He shook his head. "My Uncle Henk's wife Lavinia has argued against concluding the match since it was first suggested two years ago, for no reason that anyone has ever understood. I wonder whether she has finally agreed, or the families decided to seal the contract despite her complaints... Or perhaps she agreed and they are hurrying to have the wedding before she can change her mind. Has Your Honor been invited?"

"Yes, for a market week ending after the wedding." He turned to Her Grace his Grandmother, seated at the next table, who had also received a letter. "Will that cause any trouble, Your Grace?"

"Certainly not, Childe." She smiled. "You can leave the day after tomorrow, and then return here to the House with me after the wedding. Your guesting will give the Bull's Leap the advantage of a long Ducal visit without piling half the affairs of the Council onto the Boukolyos household on top of the wedding preparations. And you will become a guest-friend of the Boukolyos line and their allies." She smiled wider as she nodded to Fritzel. "And I have no doubt Junio and Margareta and Aldo have a long list of tasks and errands for the younger son of their House."

Fritzel groaned in a dramatic way and covered his face with his hands.

Franz-Karl turned to his attendant Olivia, eating, as usual, at a neighboring table where she was less surrounded by Notaries. "Olivia, will you join us on this small journey and attend the wedding with us?" He was not sure of Traventine protocol for this, but expected that someone would tell him if he got it wrong. A Tire-woman had authority over many kinds of woven things in a household, and she was not specifically contracted to his service the way Fritzel was, but she seemed concerned with Franz-Karl's clothing and quarters more than with the House as a whole. At least, an honest but mistaken invitation was not likely be a cause for insult.

Olivia answered, "That would be a fine thing, Your Honor. I'll see to the packing." She seemed pleased, and not very surprised, so he thought he had gotten it about right.

For all his wanderings within the House on the Rock's hedge, Franz-Karl had not yet seen much of the rest of Traventi except what could be viewed from the towers and windows of the ducal settlement. That was still much more than you could see from the Karnburg Palace, which was surrounded by gardens and walls that blocked most of whatever view there might have been of the city surrounding it. And there were tall walls around the city of Karnburg, with no tall mountains beyond them, just hills and some farmland, so there was not very much to look at from the Palace even when you managed to sneak up into a tower or onto a roof. In the House on the Rock he climbed to the top of one or another of the towers on almost every clear day. Franz-Karl had seen much more of the House on the Rock than he had ever seen of the city of Karnburg, where the Palace was, but it would be good to see even more of Traventi. Even if it meant riding a pony or donkey all the way to the Bull's Leap.

It turned out that Franz-Karl did not need to ride in a saddle to the Bull's Leap. All of the luggage – including some wedding gifts from Her Grace and other people in the Duke's Residence – were carefully packed into crates and parcels and piled into a cart pulled by two large mules wearing floppy straw hats with their ears sticking through. Franz-Karl and Olivia and Fritzel all rode in the cart, with Fritzel driving the mules. There were even cushions to soften the seats.

Traventi was a small place. That was part of why the Imperial officials were so annoyed that it remained free: if Traventi were larger, they might have been grumpy but resigned. The western border ran along a bit more than twenty-five miles of the Raenos river's central channel. The other borders ran along the peaks and faceted slopes of the ice-carved mountains in places frequented more by birds and ibex and chamois than by any creatures that had human speech. The eastern borders were drawn differently on Imperial and Traventine maps, but that did not matter much.

The Bull's Leap was the easternmost year-round settlement in the main valley of Traventi, but it was not really very far from the House on the Rock. It was a little farther by the roads, which avoided the Elde's meanders, than by the routes that birds might follow.

The travelers went out of the House on the Rock in the morning, through the Ceremonial Gate and across the Bridge over the Elde and then continued south to the edge of the flood plain, where they turned east onto the River Road. After all of the fuss about flood-damaged roads at the Council session earlier in the summer, Franz-Karl expected the ride to be slow and bumpy, but it was beautifully smooth. The Market Road from the bridge to the turnoff was even paved in the style of the old Remoran Roads. The country road that led east beyond the turnoff was well-packed, with very few ruts, and none that were likely to endanger a wheel or axle.

The few settlements they passed were set well back from the river and smaller streams. They looked very much like small pieces of the House on the Rock that had been broken off and set down in the countryside: brightly colored, thoroughly decorated, steep-roofed buildings that were linked by lower ranges of buildings instead of standing separated from each other by streets. At its nearest the Market Road ran beside the settlements, not through them, and the River Road eastward did the same.

Some of the larger settlements had altar plazas, and bell-towers with lamps on top, so they must be full villages with parish churches. Other settlements had the ceremonial gateways and altars of Lineage Houses separating them from the roads. Franz-Karl did not see any settlements that had an altar with both a shrine's bell tower and a lineage's gateway. It seemed to be one or the other, at least in this part of Traventi.

The fields around and between the settlements were well-filled with crops or showed signs of recent harvest, and the pastures were lush and not overcrowded by the sleek and sturdy beasts they fed. There were people working in the fields and orchards and tending the beasts, who waved to the cart as it passed. Franz-Karl was happy to wave back. On his journey from Karnburg most people working in the fields had pretended not to see the small caravan passing by them.

There was a village with a Shrine's bell-tower – the shrine was nearly as big as Saint Victoria and just as fancy – near where streams from the north and south joined to flow west as the Elde, but the cart turned south and continued past it. Franz-Karl signed himself as they passed, while the two Initiates made more complicated gestures of reverence that Franz-Karl politely ignored. The cart spent nearly half an hour moving south at the mules' slow pace before they turned east to cross a bridge. Like most bridges in Traventi it was huge compared to the late-season stream flowing beneath it.

Once they were a careful distance up-slope from the running water, they arrived at the Ceremonial Gateway of the Boukolyos Line at the Bull's Leap. It was large and well-decorated, and very impressive even though the consecrated Threshold and its lintel and doorposts were not attached to gate-panels or a fence. It looked odd and a bit unfinished to Franz-Karl, who had spent most of his life inside the walls and fortified gateways of the Palace in Karnburg. At least the Ceremonial Gateway at the House on the Rock had the hedge extending from its sides. This was just a little porch standing by the road.

The cart's arrival was clearly not a surprise to anyone. The party from the House on the Rock was met by a handful of musicians – two bagpipers, a drummer, a fiddler and a woman playing a large, complicated wooden flute – playing a traditional tune that was supposed to chase ill-luck away from arriving guests so that it could not sneak in behind them through the Gateway. Fritzel's family were gathered just on the House side of the Gateway, waiting to greet the travelers: there seemed to be quite a lot of people waiting. Some well-dressed attendants came out – around the outside of the Gateway: they did not bother to cross the Threshold – to take charge of the mules and the cart and the luggage.

A cart on smooth roads was still a cart. Fritzel got down, stretched to loosen his muscles and joints, then carefully lifted down first Franz-Karl, then Olivia, so that there would be no risk of an ill-omened stumble.

Franz-Karl walked carefully to a place midway between the Gateposts and just outside the line in the paving stones that marked the

Threshold. He had studied the formulas carefully to be sure that he knew the full Guest Rites for grownup Notaries and would not get them wrong: Notaries crossing Thresholds was important and scary, and part of him still expected that the grownups would change their minds about a small boy being a full Notary. Bearing a message from Her Grace his Grandmother made it even more important to get it right.

He took a deep breath and announced, "I am called Franz-Karl, Childe of the Elderkin of Traventi and a full Notary, and I come bearing messages of friendship from Her Reverend Grace Adriana, Duke of Traventi. I say three times that I come with peaceful intent toward this domain and this house and any within it that hold peace and friendship and good faith in their own hearts. So long as I rest here, your joys shall be mine, your enemies my foes, and my Gifts yours to call upon."

He held his breath for a moment after he finished. He hoped he had gotten the formula right and not left out anything: it had been a long morning in the cart and his head was aching a little. One of the pipers immediately blew a complicated fanfare, so he must have gotten it near enough to correct.

Baron-Notary Junio Boukolyos looked very much like Fritzel, but he was older, a bit larger and even more solid, and had large, dark bull's horns that made his face look more ... finished?... than Fritzel's. His features were better balanced and the muscles in his neck were doing what they were supposed to, which changed their shape. He stepped forward, stopping just on his side of the Threshold line, and bowed deeply. The horns made his bow especially impressive, though he was careful that they came nowhere near Franz-Karl. "I am called Junio Boukolyos, Notary and guardian of these lands and herds. Welcome to peace and safety and plenty under this roof! Welcome! Come freely and go freely and rest here in joy. Welcome! Any that pursue you shall be our enemies as much as they are yours. And Three Times Welcome also for the sake of Her Reverend Grace!" There was a different complicated fanfare answered by flurry of drumbeats.

Franz-Karl stepped across the Threshold line very carefully – this would be a terrible time to stumble –and bowed, not quite as deeply as the Baron-Notary. The two of them clasped hands, left to left and right to right. The people gathered behind the Baron-Notary came forward to demonstrate to Franz-Karl that all of the tokens of formal hospitality would be provided: fire and water and salt to dispel the dust and ill-luck of the road, water and wine to quench his thirst, and bread and meat and cheese and more salt, assembled into some clever and complicated aogreamana, to sustain life.

The aogreim Franz-Karl selected from the offered platter was a small crescent shape with large crystals of salt clinging to the pastry that enclosed the meat and cheese, and it had been prepared by a very clever cook who was not afraid of spices. He waited impatiently while the Baron-Notary drank and ate. Then he bowed to the company, quickly reckoned the numbers (including Fritzel and Olivia) and took two more aogreamana from the platter. They were extremely tasty, and there had been no convenient place to eat a mid-day meal on their slow journey from the House on the Rock.

The woman holding the platter – this must be Fritzel's Mother, Lady Margareta – smiled at Franz-Karl. "No fear of lack, Your Honor. There are plenty more in the Hall."

He bowed, not sure what reply would be polite.

Fritzel and Olivia were welcomed with all of the formal tokens, but simpler oaths of peaceful intent: neither of them was a Binder, though both of them were Gifted. Fritzel was a member of the Boukolyos Line returning home from business elsewhere, so there were different, even shorter formulas for him. But no one coming from outside crossed the consecrated Threshold without proper ceremonies.

The World went a bit strange once everyone was gathered inside the household boundary. Besides Fritzel's parents, the welcoming party included Fritzel's brother Astolon, and sister Hilda, both Notaries like their father. There was a Great Uncle introduced as Henk, with his wife Lavinia – they were also Notaries, and served as the priest and priestess of Saints Fortuna and Liber, the parish church over by the River Road. And there was Aldo Boukolyos, Junio's brother, who was introduced as a full Notary and Herdmaster of Traventi. The welcoming party at the Boukolyos Gate had as many Notaries as a full session of the Duke's Council, so it was no wonder the world went a bit squishy.

Every Notary in the group exchanged their own promises of peace and alliance with Franz-Karl. It took a long time, but the books warned having unconnected Notaries in a place might leave empty gaps where accidental Bindings could happen. That could be bad. Bindings that were not accidental could be worse. There were old stories about things that happened when Binders who were not peacefully connected were at the same wedding or child-naming. The only thing worse than inviting a lot of unconnected Binders to a big celebration was having a celebration and not inviting neighboring Binders. And Notaries were just Binders who were less likely to do things by accident and more likely to do them on purpose.

Franz-Karl was a new Notary and not connected yet to anyone but the Duke his Grandmother, and the Notaries at the Council session, and Maestro Petros: the Recognition vote did not count as enough of a connection. So he greeted each of the Notaries, and each one promised to be peaceful with him and he promised to be peaceful with them. And now he was connected to the Boukolyos Line.

All of the Boukolyos men except Fritzel were horned: Aldo's horns spread in elegant pale curves as wide as his broad shoulders, while Henk's were darker and heavier and swept forward. Astolon's horns were not yet long enough to show much personal style: they were not so small that they seemed like baby horns, they just had not had time for flourishes. Herdmaster Aldo's hair and beard were golden-red and his skin was almost ruddy, but the rest of the family were as dark-haired and pale-skinned as Fritzel.

Once the visitors entered the Hall – carefully avoiding stumbles – Olivia went off to find their luggage and make sure things were unpacked properly, while Fritzel divided his attention between looking after Franz-Karl and talking with his relatives. Franz-Karl sat quietly in the best guest-seat and listened to the conversation and nibbled on delicious things.

Inside the Bull Leap's Hall there were more platters of aogreamana – as promised – and various other small foods and drinks set out on small tables so that newly arrived guests need not go hungry or thirsty waiting for the evening's feast. There were enough different aogreamana that just trying them all made a meal for Franz-Karl. Fritzel ate what his Great Aunt Lavinia called a proper meal: it needed a large plate and a proper bowl to hold it.

One wall of the Hall was decorated with a large fresco showing several young people – young Elderkin people of varied Lineages – dancing with, and on, bulls. The other walls were painted with pictures of events in old tales. Not all of them involved bulls: there were also some goats, and wild ibexes from the mountains mixed in. The ornamentation around the frescoes and on the ceiling was done in many colors, but lacked gilding. There were interlaced patterns around the pictures, and many of the interlaced animals had bulls' horns. Some had udders.

Franz-Karl was given a bedroom that was much like the one he had in the House on the Rock, but one floor above the ground instead of two. The windows faced a different direction so the winds and light were strange. Olivia had her alcove at one end of the room. Fritzel would be staying in his own rooms elsewhere in his family's home, of course, so the second alcove was used to store the luggage. The cat that was in his bed when he awakened was gray and stripey instead of orange.

The next day, Astolon was very fidgety at breakfast. After the meal, he kept starting to help with some task or other, then getting distracted and turning his attention elsewhere. People teased him about it gently – Henk pointed out that it was nearly a week to the wedding and warned that at this rate Astolon (who was not a slender person) would fret himself to a mere shadow of himself that his bride would not recognize. Lady Margareta finally told her elder son to clear out of the way of the preparations, and make himself useful by giving Franz-Karl a tour of the estate.

Uncle Henk joined them. He leaned on his stick at first, but used it less as his legs stretched out.

Franz-Karl was happy to look around. Fritzel was busy helping with the wedding preparations, and it would have been rude to do lessons while he was a guest representing the Duke, even if he still had lessons to do. Without lessons, or his cousins, or the familiar spaces of the House on the Rock, he did not have much to do until the evening feasts, when he would need to be a proper Childe and Notary and Guest. And listen to more gossip about people he did not know and places he had never heard of before. He hoped that Baron-Notary Boukolyos had a good map he could look at before the feast to help figure things out.

The Bull's Leap was like a smaller version of the House on the Rock, with the lord's Residence behind the Ceremonial Gate, topped by a small lookout tower sort of thing, and with wings trailing outward in three directions away from the Gate and joining it to other Residences and dwellings and workshops. One of the open areas between the wings contained kitchen gardens and herb gardens, with fruit trees trained against stone walls to catch the Sun's heat, and a poultry run along one wall of a stable, and a pigpen at the far end of the outer wing beyond the places where people lived. The other open area was mostly paddocks and animal pens, and narrow fenced paths so that the animals would go where they were needed. That area was all rather crowded and very busy and noisy.

Astolon kept looking toward the Left Wing while they were walking around the settlement: people were shaking rugs and blankets out the windows. Because they were Notaries, Astolon and Imelda would not live as members of the main household at the Bull's Leap: they would have their own Household in the side wing, with their own small consecrated Threshold and Household Shrine and so forth. It made the needed preparations even more complicated than the usual ones for a Lineage Heir's wedding, since the rituals for creation of the Household needed to happen along with the wedding. The only way it could have been more complicated would be if Imelda was also an Heir of her Line, rather than a younger child.

Uncle Henk had told Franz-Karl the previous evening that marriages of two Lineage Heirs were very rare. Merging two Lineages into one was complicated and messy and seldom done except when one of the Lineages was running out of people. Keeping the Lineages separate despite the Heirs' marriage was even more complicated, and much messier.

The old man poked Astolon with his walking-stick: the head end, not the butt that had been in the dirt where animals were walking and such. Astolon sighed, and turned his back on the residential section of the wing.

He explained to Franz-Karl that the Boukolyos' estate raised food crops and wool-sheep for its own use. The Household's wealth came from goats and cattle, and the hay crops that fed them through the cold winters and flooded springs, and the cheeses and preserved meats that were carefully tended and stored in special buildings before finally being sent to market.

There were several carefully separated herds, each, of goats and cattle. Cattle for some important sacrifices needed to be pure white or pure black or red-gold, or a color called blue that was actually a sort of gray. And they needed to not have any other colored hairs mixed in, which was tricky to arrange since fur mostly did what it wanted, and the animals liked to mingle and did not care about fur colors. Suitable animals for sacrifices were more valuable than the others, so it was worth the trouble to keep the herds separate, even though the cow cheeses did not much care, and neither did the butchers and sausage makers and tanners who used the meat and hides.

Goats for sacrifice could be black or white, or just whatever – there was one sacrifice that was a prayer to break a drought that wanted either one goat each of several colors or one goat that was all colors, and most people did the one goat version unless it was a really bad drought or they wanted to show off.

But the goat cheeses did care about the different flocks of goats: the flavors and textures came out wrong if you used milk from the wrong flock, or mixed the milk together carelessly.

People at the Bull's Leap spent a lot of time building and repairing fences to keep the herds separated... Astolon sounded tired just talking about it.

There was a loud noise in the residence wing because someone had dropped something. Astolon jumped, then sort of drooped and looked miserable. "Go," Franz-Karl told him, and he hurried away.

Uncle Henk sat beside Franz-Karl on a shady bench in the kitchen garden. He was a lighter Binder than Her Grace, much less Her Reverence Count Great Aunt Adrasteia, so the two of them could sit close together without the world going wobbly while the old priest talked about the crops and the neighborhood. And the neighbors: if Uncle Henk was ever in a gossip contest with Maestro Petros, Franz-Karl would bet on Maestro Petros only because Uncle Henk often forgot to mention that a person he was describing had been dead for twenty years, or a landmark had been gone for thirty.

That evening Franz-Karl understood some of the conversations that were happening around him during and after the meal. At least, some of the names were familiar, and he knew why people were worried about that one stretch of river bank.

On the third morning before breakfast, Fritzel went out to carry a big pile of assorted stuff to the new home and Franz-Karl went with him to say 'blessed morning' to the goats after milking. The goats here were not the goats he knew from the House on the Rock, but that was no reason to ignore them. On their way back to breakfast after the delivery, they found Fritzel's Uncle Aldo leaning thoughtfully on a pen fence, looking at a small herd of goats inside. They were unusual goats, with long curly hair, and different shaped ears and noses than the goats in the other herds. They stood huddled together at the center of their pen, looking warily toward the goats in the other pens, and Franz-Karl thought they looked sad.

Fritzel leaned on the fence beside his Uncle. "Those are new."

"Aye. I sent east for them, to see if we can get them to thrive here. The sheared hair is supposed to be something special for spinning and weaving. Soft and silky, with a different feel than sheeps' wool."

Franz-Karl was shorter than the fence, so he was peeking through some of its openings. The openings were much, much smaller than the smallest goats (which might be why the smallest goats were still inside the fence) but they were a bit hard to see through. "They look sad."

"They have traveled a long way, Your Honor, and arrived at a strange place with new food. And there is no way to tell them that this is their new home. They will just need to learn it slowly."

He peeked through the fence again, a little farther along. "Do you have some treats that I can give them to cheer them up?"

Uncle Aldo smiled down at him. "I think we have something… give us a moment, Your Honor."

After a short wait, one of Aldo's underlings produced a bucket of kitchen scraps: mostly turnip peels and fruit peels and carrot tops and the tough outer leaves of cabbages. Fritzel and Uncle Aldo both went into the pen with Franz-Karl, in case the goats decided to be mean to him and kick or stomp or bite him. Some of them were large goats, and he was a small boy.

Franz-Karl was not worried about the goats being mean: animals were usually friendly to him, unless they were too hurt or scared or upset to know what they were doing. Even the big fierce dogs at the Palace Gates were usually friendlier to him than to most of the human guards that fed them. But grownups worried about those things.

These goats were not upset, they were just sad. The goats gathered around when they saw him with the bucket, because that was what you should do when someone brought a bucket into the pen, but most of them were more politely interested than excited. A few bossy ones tried to nudge the others away, but their hearts weren't in it. All of them together still ended up eating everything in the bucket, slowly, and one of the smaller goats tried to climb into the bucket to lick any morsels that were left. Franz-Karl laughed and skritched its curly head between its ears, behind where the horns were coming in. Then he and Fritzel went out of the pen and continued walking toward breakfast.

The following day, when Franz-Karl checked them before breakfast, the new goats seemed less sad and more eager for their treats, so that was good. He felt sorry for the sad goats, but at least, once they figured out that they were home, they would not need to pack up and go on another long journey. Franz-Karl was missing his family, a little, but not enough to look forward to the journey back to Karnburg.

As the wedding approached, more guests began to arrive. On sunny days Baron-Notary Boukolyos spent part of the day showing off his lands and the settlement. On rainy days, people sat and gossiped, and many of them did various kinds of hand-work.

Franz-Karl attended all the many formal greeting ceremonies at the Gate. Because he was Childe and a heavy Notary, and a Guest welcomed before the others arrived, he needed to be properly introduced to the newcomers and agree that, yes, he was not presently having feuds with any of them, and share promises of peacefulness. There were probably going to be a lot of Binders and Notaries at the wedding: the Boukolyos Line were ancient and respected and prosperous, and even more important now that they had a son attending an Heir. Some people might come to the wedding who would have decided the distance was too great without the added chance to exchange fellow-guest greetings with the new Notary and Childe.

Franz-Karl would need to promise peacefulness with all of them, but after a while he figured out that was why he was invited early. The other Binders and Notaries had been promising peace with each other at weddings and child-namings and festivals their whole lives, but he was new and needed to catch up.

Franz-Karl visited the sad goats in the mornings, though on rainy mornings he just looked out at them from the dry area under the nearest colonnade. He made sure they were getting their treats so that the rain would not make them sad again: Herdmaster Aldo smiled at him and made sure there were buckets of treats waiting.

Sheep that got rained on still looked like sheep, but the goats' long curls got sort of stretched out and drippy, which looked silly. They had a dry place to get out of the rain, but were taking turns instead of all staying inside, so they dripped a lot.

After breakfast and in between greeting ceremonies, Franz-Karl spent much of his time helping Lady Margareta and Hilda and Fritzel and Astolon make wreaths and garlands to decorate the Lineage Household Shrine and Altar for the wedding, and different wreaths and garlands for Astolon and Imelda's new house, especially the Kitchen and Threshold and the room that would become their new Household Shrine. There were plants in the wreaths that were included because they had fancy flowers, and plants that smelled nice, and plants that had meanings. Some of the meanings could only be explained to Initiates, of course, but Fritzel's Great Aunt Lavinia sat near them, hemming extra tablecloths, and told the stories that could be repeated publicly. They had so many flowers and branches in the buckets for garland making that they made some extra garlands for the Ceremonial Gateway and the Hall when they were done with the ones for the Shrines and Altars and the new house's Kitchen.

The plants in the wreaths and garlands stayed fresh instead of getting droopy while they waited for the wedding to happen.

CHAPTER XXVIII: Guest Rites

Wherein Our Hero Suffers a Malady

A big group of guests from the North Valley arrived the day after the rain, and were received with full Guest Rites for each and every one. Once everyone had been introduced to Franz-Karl and crossed the Threshold, the grownups spent most of the afternoon gossiping about people they knew and discussing the sorts of things – like roads and crops and wills and other weddings and the prices of trade goods – that had also been mentioned during the Council session that Franz-Karl had attended. It should have been interesting, but he found his attention wandering.

At dinner that evening, Franz-Karl was feeling hot and cold at the same time and sort of queasy and headache-y, though he ate a little try to be a polite guest and not cause a fuss. Fritzel hardly ate anything, which was so unusual that his mother felt his forehead and sent him to bed. Then she looked at Franz-Karl and felt his forehead and sent him to bed, too.

Olivia put Franz-Karl into his bed with an extra blanket and three whole bricks that had been warmed by a fire, and it was almost enough. He was still shivering a little when the Baron-Notary and Lady Margareta came to see how he was, and his words got all tangled up between Elderic and Remoran and Allemanic when he tried to apologize for the nuisance and promise he would be fine. Then he scared himself wondering if not being able to say that he would be fine was because it was not a true thing that he would be fine, and things got even more tangled in his head.

Lady Margareta said quietly, "Please do not worry, Your Honor. There are a few others also ill, but none seem dangerously so. I have warned the kitchens to take greater care about serving dishes that might have gone off in the summer heat. And we shall take very good care of you."

She scooped him up, still wrapped in both blankets, and sat in a chair by the fire with Franz-Karl in her arms. It was very kind of her, but with his head and throat hurting what he really wanted was his own Mama, not Fritzel's Mama, even though he knew that was rude and stupid. His own Mama was weeks of travel away, and Lady Margareta was being very nice to him. She began to rock him a little and sing to him – an old slow, sleepy tune – and he slid into sleep before he could put together something to say to her that would be polite instead of rude and stupid.

Franz-Karl spent two nights and the day between them dozing in bed and sipping broth – plain broth with herbs in it at first, and later, when his guts stopped shivering quite so much, broth with good bread soaking in it. The gray striped cat cuddled close, and occasionally kneaded his belly. That was not very helpful, but it felt like home.

On the second morning he ate breakfast that was actual food sitting in a chair at a little table in his room, and Olivia spent the morning reading to him from a book of old tales. He was too restless to do nothing, but still too tired to read old-style text himself: it was almost as bad as trying to read Meister van Diesen's handwriting. And he was going to miss the District market day – which was the least boring thing other than the actual wedding – because of getting sick.

He ate the midday meal properly, in company in the Hall. Fritzel was also at the table for that meal, but his Uncle Aldo was still keeping to his room and did not reappear until dinner that evening, and a few others did not appear that day at all. On the third morning after he got sick, Lady Margareta told Franz-Karl that everyone who had been ill was well again.

Guests had continued to arrive for the wedding all the time Franz-Karl was ill, and not just people from the House on the Rock or other settlements on Traventi's central plain. Some people arrived from the South Valley and a few more from the North Valley. None of the newly arrived Binders and Notaries came near Franz-Karl while he was ill, of course: startling a sick Binder was really stupid, even if he was a Notary. But once Franz-Karl was officially clear-headed and well again the Boukolyos Notaries escorted the new guests one at a time to exchange formal greetings with him. They were officially apologetic that Binders strange to him had been allowed to cross the Threshold during his 'inattention', even though these were all people who had exchanged oaths with Her Grace His Grandmother, and in most cases with his mother as well. A bench was set up near the Ceremonial Gateway so that he would not need to stand throughout the greeting ceremonies: but he usually stood up during the important bits that involved him, it seemed rude not to. Everyone was so serious about it.

There was no polite way to apologize for being a nuisance to a sworn host who had invited you to visit, but the greetings ceremonies seemed... excessive. Franz-Karl hinted at it to Uncle Henk and Aunt Lavinia, who were Boukolyos kin but also Guests, since their usual dwelling was not at the Bull's Leap. It was not something to say to a Host.

The old man looked at him seriously. "The guest rites are excessive when all is well," he agreed, "but do you remember how the World trembled at your Honor's Recognition?"

"Of course! How could I forget?"

"Gunners and archers and swordsmen can set aside their weapons. Elderkin, especially Binders, cannot. But our words Bind us, including words of peace and alliance. Traventi is a small place, but it holds more than two hundred adult Binders and thousands of heavy-Gifted Elderkin besides, and the lighter folk are mighty in their numbers. The connections we create during the better times – oaths binding kin to kin and host to guest and fellow-guest and colleague to colleague – carry us through the worse times without savaging each other – or the land, or the World – past all healing..." The old priest looked sad. "You should never exchange oaths across a Threshold with someone you do not trust, never give your oath to someone you distrust just to pass a Threshold, and never, ever allow anyone, Elderkin or not, to cross your own

Threshold without exchanging trustworthy oaths of some sort. It is precisely the times people think, 'Oh, this one time will cause no harm' that are most likely to lead to some dire outcome in a month or a year or a decade. Or an hour."

"I will not forget," Franz-Karl promised. He thought about the Palace, where doors were common and proper blessed Thresholds were rare, and servants went wherever they were sent. "What about if someone asks you to enter a place without offering any exchange of oaths at all?"

Uncle Henk's smile showed far too many teeth that did not match well with a bull's horns and eyes. "You may choose to grant mercy to fools, but it is not something that can be demanded of you."

"Ah." Franz-Karl shivered.

There was music and dancing in the evenings, besides the gossip and other entertainments. On the first evening after their sickness, Lady Margareta had chairs set up near a fireplace for Franz-Karl and Fritzel and Uncle Aldo and told them that they should watch and listen but not join the singing or dancing for at least another day.

Franz-Karl learned the rules for three table games that were different from the ones he had played in Karnburg. Uncle Aldo was a ferocious player of fox and geese – they called it wolf and sheep here – and very sneaky at nine men morris. Lesser Dragon's Teeth, which Uncle Aldo said could at least be played in an evening instead of a lifetime, had many sets of rules for both play and scoring: Franz-Karl limited himself to one simpler version called Sowing Dragon's Teeth, and occasionally won. Some of the other styles had rules as complicated as pattern dances or tax laws.

Besides the heavy Elderkin arriving from all over the Duchy, carts also came down from the summer pastures in the high valleys, full of cheeses to go into the storage rooms, and wedding gifts, and people who usually only lived in the Bull's Leap during the winters and springs. The long arms of the House got a lot less quiet with so many of their people returned briefly out of season. There were still people staying up in the summer pastures – someone needed to look after the cows and goats that needed to be milked every day, and start and tend the new cheeses – but they were going to be spread thin for a few days while the wedding was happening.

On the afternoon before the wedding, Her Grace the Duke Franz-Karl's Grandmother arrived, which caused a lot of busting and fanfares. Some of the fuss was because all three territorial Counts arrived at the same time: Count Great Aunt Adrasteia and Count Severin, whom Franz-Karl had met at the council sessions, and Count Valens from the North Valley, who had sent a proxy to the council, and Fritzel had heard was a dragon. The oaths of alliance exchanged at the ceremonial gate were complicated and impressive and thorough: Franz-Karl still thought it was funny to be asked, quite seriously, whether he was presently at feud with Her Grace His Grandmother, but managed to keep a straight face as he agreed that he was not. On second thought, there were enough family disagreements and dynastic squabbles described in the old chronicles of every nation he had heard of that the question was probably prudent. Exchanging promises of peacefulness with Count Severin was easy, because they officially knew each other. Exchanging promises with Count Valens involved three rounds of questions and answers back and forth, so it took a while.

Franz-Karl was still sitting in a chair on the inside of the gateway most of the time, because people still worried that standing too long might wear him out too much. He wondered how sick he had been: it was all a bit blurry. He was not the only one still recovering his strength: Fritzel and Uncle Aldo were standing near the Baron-Notary and Lady Margareta, but if you looked closely you could see that they were leaning against the wall of the house.

Reverend Count Valens was at least as unusual to look at as Reverend Count Great Aunt Adrasteia. He had huge peacock-blue-green eyes, and short arms and legs and a long twining serpentine body all covered with mother-of-pearl scales, and his mane and eyebrows and long mustaches were made of dark blue things like grapevine tendrils... except that they moved slowly as if they were feeling the air, or perhaps tasting it, or drifting under water

Franz-Karl thought the Count's hair was much more interesting than his own, even now that Fritzel had mostly convinced it to be ornamental instead of just messy.

When the formal greetings were finished, the Reverend Count bowed to Franz-Karl very politely, and said that he was glad to meet him at last. He explained that there was an ancient custom that all of the most heavily Manifest Elderkin in Traventi should not gather in the House on the Rock at the same time.

Franz-Karl thought about that. "If the Reverend Childe my Mother was in Traventi, instead of Karnburg, would she be here at this wedding with Her Grace and me? All three of us together?"

The Reverend Count's tendrils got very excited. "That is an excellent question, young lord."

The Reverend Count Adrasteia interrupted cheerfully. "And the answer is 'No'. Of course." She spread her wings to sort of scoop them up without coming too near either of them. "Come have a drink, Valens. Junio has some cider I think you will like. You, too, Franz-Karl. We need to build your strength back up again."

As they walked into the house together, Valens asked, with a nod toward Fritzel, whether Franz-Karl was getting along well with his Boukolyos attendant.

Franz-Karl laughed. "Oh yes, very well." He lowered his voice so that no one but the two Counts would hear. "I am smart for my age and even heavier Elderkin than people expect from my family tree, and Fritzel is smart for anyone's age and does a good imitation of an ox fresh from the plowing. Whichever court we end up at when I'm older won't know what hit it."

"Whichever court?"

He shrugged. "Younger sons of the Falkenburgs get sent as envoys to the courts that are too far away for the marriageable daughters. With some luck and making ourselves useful to the right people, it may be somewhere like Adenosani or the Middle Kingdom, not the Court of the Little Mountain..."

The dragon Count smiled and cocked his tendrils and asked, "What is wrong with the Court of the Little Mountain, do you think?"

"Life-hungry deities," Franz-Karl answered promptly. "My Papa told Aunt Queen Gertrude that it was hard to remain politely non-committal while conversing with a High Priest who had been cutting the hearts out of living people a few hours earlier."

"I can think of one Court that will most certainly be astonished by the pair of you," the Sphinx commented. She was looking at him as though he had said something very funny.

"Oh?" Franz-Karl said vaguely. Then he realized what the most important foreign court was for Traventi. "Oh, of course! I fear I'm not in the habit of thinking of Karnburg as a foreign court."

"Not a bad habit for a Childe of Traventi to learn," Count Valens suggested as he handed him a cup of cider. Franz-Karl replied with a bow that might have been acknowledgment of the cider, or the advice, or both.

Count Great Aunt Adrasteia smiled at him and lifted her cup in a small gesture that was almost a toast. "May your opponents never know what hit them, Childe."

The Counts bowed and turned away to talk with other Notaries and officials who were scattered around the room trying to avoid clumps that would make the World too squishy.

The conversations in the hall that evening carefully avoided Council matters. Really avoided: not like the breakfast after the festival. But toward the end of the evening Franz-Karl saw Fritzel discussing something with Count Valens and gesturing vigorously. He assumed that if it was something he needed to know, Fritzel would tell him about it.

The Priestess Lavinia paused beside Franz-Karl's chair to remind him that the next day would be a long one, and he should consider going to bed soon to save his strength. He smiled up at her. "That's a kind thought... and I will go soon. But first, if I may..." Sometimes it was useful to be very young and very high ranked. "I have heard that you were previously opposed to the marriage. Did something change?"

She smiled at him mischievously. "Yes. Traventi has a heavy new Notary, and Childe Silvia has a Recognized Heir."

He realized that his jaw had dropped, and shut his mouth.

She continued more seriously, "I must say that news was a great comfort. The portents were ever more emphatic that Silvia's Recognized Heir should attend the wedding of Astolon and Imelda, and I don't think those children would have been willing to wait another ten years for your brother to reach his majority and be Recognized."

"That would be much to ask of them," Franz-Karl agreed weakly, "like something out of an old story where the grownups are being completely unreasonable."

As he stood up to wander off toward his bed, Franz-Karl wondered how he was expected to sleep after learning that portents involving him had been disrupting people's lives. But once he was in his bed he slept well and soundly.

On the morning of the wedding, Franz-Karl dressed carefully. The color-of-sorrow was not worn at weddings if it could be avoided, so while his coat and waistcoat and breeches were still very plain and undecorated, and the quality of the cloth was no less, the garments were cut from cloth the color of dark red wine, not the color-of-sorrow. After wearing color-of-sorrow for all of the weeks and months since his father's death, it was strange to be wearing anything else. He kept being surprised when he glimpsed his own sleeves or coat-skirts in passing, and the cloth felt a little stiff because it had not ever been worn before.

After breakfast all of the guests who had slept at the Bull's Leap gathered in the space between the Ceremonial Gateway and the Residence itself, with the lighter Elderkin gathering around and between the heavier Notaries so that the World would not go too wobbly. They were joined by some people who had walked from the nearby villages, and needed to be formally greeted so that they could pass through the Ceremonial Gateway and be counted among the official Witnesses. Lady Margareta's mother – Fritzel's Gran – and some of her other relatives were in one of the groups.

And of course, Franz-Karl greeted all of them, especially the Notaries and other Binders.

Franz-Karl was pleased when the young Notary called Willy arrived. Willy lived in the large settlement on the Market Road that served as Count Severin's seat, but the Advocate he was apprenticed to had a sister – also a Notary, but a Priestess, not an Advocate – who lived nearer to the Bull's Leap. They had spent the night at her house instead of traveling with the Count's party for the end of the journey: the Bull's Leap was now too full of Notaries for anyone's comfort. Willy was the one person in all that crowd that Franz-Karl had greeted with the formula for a known ally – Her Grace the Duke and the Councilors and even the Advocates who had been at the Council session were all grownups, so the simple forms seemed wrong.

After a short wait, people began to arrive from Imelda's home settlement who were not very closely related to her but quite properly wanted to witness her wedding. They also needed to be properly greeted and added to the growing crowd of Witnesses.

The partly empty trays and pitchers from the welcoming ceremonies were taken away and replaced with fancy freshly filled ones. People began craning their necks to watch the road where the bride would be arriving. Baron Junio moved Franz-Karl's chair to the front row of Witnesses: he said cheerfully that leaning on the Ceremonial Gate would be unseemly and Franz-Karl falling on his face in the middle of the rites would be a horrible omen. Olivia stood behind the chair to make sure Franz-Karl spent most of his time in it, but really, he was glad to be sitting down. Willy stood beside him, since Fritzel was busy being a Boukolyos.

CHAPTER XXIX: Making a Threshold

Wherein Our Hero Witnesses a Wedding in the Traventine Style

Franz-Karl was embarrassed to be one of the handful of Witnesses who were seated instead of standing, but he had been warned that the ceremonies were starting early because they were likely to run very long. The wedding ceremonies themselves were the least of it. Both spouses were Notaries, which complicated some legal and practical matters. Both families were wealthy, which complicated the arrangements regarding transfers of property. Astolon was the Heir of the Boukolyos Lineage, which added another set of complications: Imelda would be joining the Boukolyos as an ally without entirely abandoning her native lineage, but her primary allegiance would change. Just announcing all of the arrangements and agreements so that they were Witnessed and Bound into the World was going to take a long time. Dealing with the wedding and agreements and arrangements was likely to take the better part of a day.

Besides all that, partly because the young couple were Notaries in their own right and the World went wobbly when too many Notaries crowded together for too long, they were going to consecrate a new

Household where they would be neighbors of the Baron's household rather than living together with Astolon's parents. And properly consecrating a new Household was also likely to take the better part of a day. A private household within a Lineage settlement would not have its own Ceremonial Gate and great Altar, but it needed a consecrated Threshold, a Household Shrine for the ancestral guardians with its own small altar and Lamp, and a consecrated Hearth and Oven for the provision of proper Hospitality.

There were also requirements for a proper Household that people who were not Initiated, like children Franz-Karl's age, were not supposed to know about. Grownup Initiates sort of signaled to each other with their eyes and hands when he was present, and Franz-Karl politely ignored the hints and clues that were spread before him. But he suspected that if he ever needed to create a Household, even without Initiates available and before he was Initiated himself, he might manage something useful by combining what he was seeing and things that were mentioned in the old stories and chronicles.

Weddings did not need to involve a making a new Household, and a Household creation did not need a married couple – at least not in the Traventine traditions. But once you got Notaries and Heirs involved, things got tangled so there were parts of the wedding that wanted parts of the Household to already exist, and parts of the Household making that wanted parts of the wedding to have already happened.

It was easier to organize the combined rite across two days and nights, but there were so many Binders and Notaries attending the Boukolyos wedding that it would be safer not to keep them gathered closely together for that long. Someone had figured out a way to fit everything into the time between one late summer dawn and the next day's noon, but it was going to be a busy day and a half, and there would be people fretting at anything that looked like a delay. Especially something as ill-omened as an honored guest falling over. Which was why Franz-Karl was sitting near the Boukolyos Ceremonial Gate in the early morning light, surrounded by other Witnesses and watching the road for the approach of the bride's party.

Finally, just long enough after the last Witnesses that their dust had time to fully settle, Imelda herself arrived, escorted by her parents and siblings and two of her grandparents. She formally bid them and her original Lineage farewell within the hearing of all of the witnesses.

Imelda's family held back a little while she stepped forward to the boundary line that marked the Threshold under the Ceremonial Gateway, while Astolon stepped forward to join his Mother and Father on the inner side of the boundary. The formulas of hospitality were repeated, but the wording was changed to speak of permanent alliance between Imelda and the Boukolyos Lineage, not just until an expected end of Imelda's stay at the Lineage House of the Boukolyos Line.

After Imelda had stepped across the boundary and tasted the wine and other tokens that joined her to their Lineage, Baron-Notary Junio asked Astolon and Imelda whether they wanted to be a family within the Bull's Leap. They answered by pledging to each other, using traditional verses, formally witnessed by Baron-Notary Junio as head of the community and witnessed by acclamation by everyone else there, including Imelda's relatives, who had moved closer to listen. Astolon was so nervous he almost forgot the third line of the quatrain he was supposed to recite, but one of the pipers played a three-note prompt to remind him.

Imelda's family stepped forward to the boundary, and were welcomed as kin of a member of the community of Bull's Leap, with her sponsorship. That was another slightly different set of formulas from the usual welcome.

When people were setting up a new Household there were complicated rites to establish the new Household Shrine and equip and consecrate it, and install memorial tokens for both dead kin and living ones. The memorial tokens might be sparse if the families disapproved of the new Household, or even were simply far away. But Baron-Notary Irena – Imelda's mother outranked her husband, though he was a Notary, too – exchanged some poetic speeches with Barron-Notary Junio in which they discovered (to their official surprise) that they had children who were establishing a new Household and would need to summon the Ancestors' attention to a new joint Household Shrine.

Lady Margareta and the ladies of the Boukolyos line produced some of the utensils that would be needed, and parcels of carefully wrapped memorial tokens, and Baron-Notary Irena and the women of her family provided more tokens and utensils. Everyone in the crowd of witnesses walked in a procession to the section of the Bull's Leap that would be Astolon and Imelda's new home, but only the close kin of the parent families entered the room that had been prepared to be the new

Shrine. The door was closed during the consecration, which ended with the door being opened so the doorposts and lintel could be anointed with scented oil.

Then everyone came out of the Shrine except Astolon and Imelda, and the Duke and Counts went in, and the door was closed again for the private part of the wedding ceremonies that told the Child Blessings about the marriage. Baron-Notary Junio led everyone to the main Hall, where the musicians were tuning up and the preliminaries for the feast were laid out on smaller tables around the one that held the Wedding Contract. Franz-Karl sat in a chair a careful distance from some of the other Notaries while they waited.

The young Notary Willy came to join him, not standing too close, and he and Franz-Karl spoke together, carefully not mentioning Council matters that were under seal. Franz-Karl felt very grown up, but waiting for the hidden part of the wedding ceremonies to finish was a little boring, even with Willy to talk to. Fritzel walked over to stand beside Franz-Karl's chair but he was not listening to the Notaries' conversation.

Fritzel was not acting worried, exactly, but he stood where he could see the door that Astolon and Imelda would arrive through. They were both children of Traventi, so they had carried the Child Blessings their whole lives, with roots extending back to the Blessings on their parents and grandparents. And the foundations of the Blessings for the future had been established when they reached puberty and strengthened when they were Initiated. Now that they were pledged, the Blessings needed to be harmonized so that their children with each other would be as healthy as possible, even if their Manifest Lineages were not especially similar. If the Blessings were not harmonized properly, there might never be children at all.

Since Astolon and Imelda were both Notaries, no one else could put Bindings on them or change the ones that were already there. They had to do that part themselves. But the heaviest available Elderkin were needed to support the tuning of the Child Blessings. There could be a sort of backlash when trying to make adjustments at the core of one's physical form if things got away from you. The Duke and Counts were present as anchors as well as Witnesses, and to provide useful prompts so that nothing tricky or important got forgotten, and that part of the wedding rite happened in the Household Shrine to provide more anchoring. And possibly to protect the neighborhood if things went terribly wrong.

There were only a few recorded occasions when adjustments to the Child Blessings had gone badly wrong – the Elderkin of Traventi had acquired strong opinions about arranged marriages where the spouses did not agree -- but the failures tended to be memorialized in the names of the new landmarks that had resulted.

The Blessings did not really take very long. The musicians played a complicated, joyful fanfare when the newly pledged couple arrived in the Hall along with the Duke and Counts of Traventi and were escorted to the table with the Wedding Contract laid out on it.

Fritzel took a deep breath and let it out slowly. "Glad that's over," he said quietly.

The Marriage Contract was written on one end of a very, very long roll of fine vellum sheets stitched together which was blank otherwise. It described the property that each spouse brought to the marriage and which parts of it would remain individual or be held as common, and how inheritance by any children should work. There were customary ways to handle all of these things, but there were generally exceptions, often involving heirlooms or tracts of land or both. In this case, the families were using the definitions of Imelda's dower lands to sort out some field boundaries that had been annoying people, probably since the last time there was a wedding between the two Lineages, so some of the contract terms were trickier than usual.

There were also some sections describing the expected future alliance between the two Lineages.

Willy said that when things were this complicated, the Advocates encouraged people to record their new wills along with the marriage contract, to make certain that everything would fit together. As an apprentice advocate in the Quarter Across the Water, he had worked on the wording of Imelda's new will, which would be signed after the Marriage Contract.

Astolon and Imelda took turns reading the Contract out loud. There were cheers at a couple of places and laughter at a couple of others. When they had finished, they each signed the Contract, and sealed it with their signets as Notaries. Then all of the other Notaries present signed and sealed it, from Her Reverend Grace Duke Adriana down to Willy and Franz-Karl. When the Notaries were done, all of the other Witnesses, including the servants and musicians, added signatures or marks to the vellum. It was no wonder they had to write the contract on such a long roll. Even small children and tiny babies had a drop of ink put on a finger or thumb, or even a toe, so that their witnessing could be recorded.

Some young men took lanterns – even though it was full daylight – and searched all of the connected courtyards and buildings and barns of the Bull's Leap to make certain that no one was left out. They found two people: one in the stables and one in the kitchens (Franz-Karl was almost certain that was on purpose: the search felt ceremonial, not serious), and both the finders and the people that were found got special rewards after they had signed the contract.

Fritzel announced the total number of Witnesses, and everyone agreed that was a very fortunate number of Witnesses to have, and would surely bring good luck to both the new family and the Witnesses. Willy told Franz-Karl quietly that any number of witnesses greater than 'none' was praised as a fortunate number, and Franz-Karl managed to keep a very serious expression on his face.

And then the Contract was taken away and the platters of food for the feast were brought out to fill the table where the contract had been. The platters always filled the table even at some weddings where each platter contained only a small dollop of something: filling the table left no room for bad luck. These platters were piled high with food, in addition to filling every bit of space on the table and sticking out over the edges.

The musicians started playing dance tunes.

Franz-Karl had been taken to a few important weddings in the Palace, and remembered the Arch-Hierophants making a huge fuss, even at weddings that did not happen at the cathedral, with incense and choirs and lesser clergy chanting responses. He was a little surprised that there were no sacrifices, not even of incense, at the public parts of a Traventine wedding, nor any other rites to invite the attention of the Powers beyond the World.

Willy seemed horrified at the idea of a wedding that involved any Shrine except the Household one. He said asking the High Gods to notice a wedding just asking for trouble. Even the meat served at weddings was usually hidden in things like casseroles or pies or complicated subtleties, not sitting naked under the sky being itself, so there would be no mistaking it for consecrated meat from a sacrifice.

All of the Witnesses watched while Astolon and Imelda selected bits of food from different platters set out for the feast and poured wine into special cups and then gave the plates and cups to each other to eat and drink. Then they invited the Witnesses to eat and drink their fill. Everyone watching cheered, and then selected their own food and drink and the proper feasting began.

People ate and drank, and danced in the Hall, and danced in the courtyards outside, and played various games indoors and out. When midnight approached, some grown up but unmarried people, including Fritzel, escorted Astolon and Imelda to their new home with a song about saying farewell to singleness that was partly improvised and caused a lot of laughter. That was almost the end of the wedding ceremonies. There was still a bit to be done beginning when the couple rose from their bed in the morning, and the wedding would be completely finished at noon.

Before then, the Household needed to be established.

Once they were within their own walls, the escorts gave Astolon and Imelda clean salt and wine and cheese and bread and 'meat' in the broader sense that included food from plants as well as from beasts. Water was fetched from their new Household's well and spilled twice, once at the doorway that was not yet a Threshold and once on the floor beside the Hearth. The third time water was fetched it was shared between the font in the Household Shrine and the pitcher that would be offered to guests during the rites of Hospitality. A new fire was kindled in the kitchen Hearth using a spark carried from the Lamp in the Household Shrine, and carefully fed and banked so that it would last until sunrise and beyond. A bowl of dough was set to rise in the warmth near the Hearth: where the dough came from was one of the things that Franz-Karl was politely ignoring.

Even if guests arrived at daybreak, the new Household would be able to greet them properly with all seven of the holy tokens.

A few guests who would not be sleeping at the Bull's Leap – not even in the tents that had been set up in the pasture – said formal farewells to Baron-Notary Junio and Lady Margareta and began their journeys toward their beds by torchlight and lantern light. Some of them were accompanied by musicians, so they carried the party along with them. Most of the remaining guests continued eating and dancing and talking until well after midnight. Some people even decided that it would be easier to stay up celebrating than to get up early to see the rites at dawn.

Franz-Karl went to his bed in the guest room not long after midnight. He was almost too tired to undress properly and say his evening prayers, but he managed to rise before dawn despite the short time he slept.

Just before sunrise, a richly dressed man carrying two unlit torches pounded on Astolon and Imelda's door. He was wearing a mask that had a smiling face on the front of his head and an angry face on the back of his head. When Astolon and Imelda answered the door, they exchanged verses with the masked man, who offered treasure for them to let him in and serve him but refused to give his name or any promises of peace and fair dealing. After the third refusal he handed over the torches and declaimed a couplet that was either a blessing or a praise of steadfastness, depending on how you viewed the phrasing. Then he went away. Astolon stirred up the fire in the Hearth and added wood to it, lit the torches from it and set them in holders on the wall by the outsides of the doorposts. Imelda set a fire to begin heating the Oven and did things to the dough that had been rising all night.

When the first drop of true sunlight began to spread from the eastern horizon, a woman approached the doorway and exchanged verses with the Householders. She was cloaked and hooded in darkness and wearing a mask that was a mirror – so people looking at her saw only themselves – and carried a pack that was overflowing with... things. She offered wares for purchase at what she claimed were good prices, but the name she gave was false (she literally said 'I am False' in an old style of Elderic) and she offered no promises of peace or fair dealing, so they refused her. After the third refusal, she turned away, declaiming about caution, and dropping something from her pack as she went. The token that had fallen from her pack was picked up and mounted above the lintel inside the door. The dough in the kitchen was shaped into loaves and set out for a final rise.

Franz-Karl shivered a little and not just because of the chilly early morning air. Witnessing this was like having an old story break its banks and flow around you like a river in flood. First the Guardian of Gates, and now... Her... Weddings went by threes, not fours, and Households were probably the same. He almost held his breath, waiting to see who would be the third.

Finally, when more than half of the Sun showed above the eastern mountains, a pair of people masked with youthful faces approached the door. They were dressed in what looked like dull tatters, but when the breeze stirred the bits of cloth, the undersides were as bright and richly decorated as butterfly wings. When The Twins offered true names ('We are called True': the allegory was a bit heavy-handed) and recited the full formulas of peaceful guesting, they were welcomed to cross what was now plainly named as a Threshold, and provided with the seven tokens of Hospitality. The Holy Guests handed over a wreath of holy herbs to bless the kitchen and another one for the doorway that was the Threshold.

Franz-Karl felt a bit stunned: Traventi had no sacrifices for the wedding, but summoned blessings from the mighty for a new Household, and even the High Gods were turned away if they arrived without proper courtesies. Some old stories suddenly looked different, especially the Elderic versions. The Arch-hierophant in Karnburg would have an apoplexy if he heard of such a thing, and might not survive seeing it.

While they waited for the bread to rise and bake, people breakfasted at Baron Junio's table, and spent the morning napping or packing for their journeys homeward, or both. The carts that had come down from the summer pastures were preparing for their return journeys. Franz-Karl went to visit the goats one last time.

Just before noon the wedding guests gathered again to Witness outside Astolon and Imelda's Threshold. Baron Junio and Lady Margareta, and Baron Irena and her husband, arrived at the door. They spoke the Guest formulas and were greeted with the Host formulas by Imelda and Astolon, and welcomed in to enjoy tokens of Hospitality that included bread from the first loaves baked in the new Oven. All of the Witnesses were given watered wine and aogreamana – prepared in every kitchen at the Bull's Leap – in return for reciting two formulas that greeted Astolon and Imelda as truly married and the shared authorities of their Household. Those were the final pieces of the wedding and the Household creation.

When he returned to the bedroom he was using, Franz-Karl found Olivia closing and fastening the last few packs and Fritzel carrying the finished packs out to the mule cart. Since the House on the Rock was a half-day's journey away, most of the guests from the capital were planning to leave the Bull's Leap after a midday snack and eat a late dinner in their own homes that evening: Her Grace would be traveling back with Franz-Karl and his attendants, but riding a horse, not sitting in the cart.

Count Severin would be leaving at the same time, but arriving home sooner: his home was somewhere just beyond the village where Willy lived.

Counts Adrasteia and Valens would leave the following morning, with other guests from the North and South Valleys.

INTERLUDE VII: Winged News

Wherein Childe Silvia Gives Thanks and Some Do Not

G ossip and news swirled through the city and Palace like flocking birds disturbed in some plaza: wings feathered with truth, falsehood, speculation, denial, witness.

Pigeons flew from Traventi to Karnburg. More pigeons flew from Karnburg to Traventi. Pigeons from other lofts flew North, East, West, South. Pigeons from the provinces sought Karnburg lofts like compass needles seeking the Pole Star.

Nobles returned from their season in the provinces. There were new faces in the retinues and households, and familiar faces with new titles. Gossip flew: which reliable face was gone, which face to look for at need?

Regiments returned from summer maneuvers to unfamiliar camps. There were new faces in the staff meetings, and familiar faces with new ranks and titles.

The missing faces were mentioned to warn that they were gone, to complain about gaps in service or influence. Why or where they had gone? The swallows might tell you, before they leave. The Highborn will not. Others will give five answers before breakfast.

The Generals post announcements of staff changes. Who does the work that goes with a title? Good question.

There was a deadly fire at Ansbach House. No, there was not: the house still stands for any to see. There are new faces among the servants, yes, but there are always new faces. Ansbach never hires from the City, he summons dependents from the North, or he buys... and his slaves do not last well.

The acting Archduke has another grandchild on the way. Their Excellencies ordered a thanks offering in every parish.

Ansbach is breaking in a new Glove-Bearer. This one is more... decorative... than the previous ones. Perhaps he will keep this one.

The Dowager Countess of Wolfsberg paid for a thank offering at the Cathedral. The Changeling Heir of Traventi was at death's door, but the wizards pulled him back.

Ansbach is wearing gloves in public at all times. The new fashion sloshes through the Court and begins to drip down into the lower orders. The Dowager Queen of the Magyars appears barehanded, and Her Excellency takes her hand to greet her. Bremerhaven appears un-gloved. Gloves at Court become scarcer .

The Pristinists are seeking a new Preacher.

Wolfsberg is seeking a new tutor and other new staff.

There is sickness in the regiments, but no worse than usual for the season

CHAPTER XXX: The Marriage Contract

Wherein Our Hero Reviews a matter of History

After seeing and signing Astolon and Imelda's Marriage Contract – he had read it all before signing, as he was sworn to do – Franz-Karl found that he was curious about the Contract that had shaped his own life and family. He had heard it mentioned, even partially quoted, many times, but never seen it himself. People did not show Marriage Contracts to small children...

But he was not just a small child. Franz-Karl was a sworn Notary – and nearly an apprentice advocate – with an interest in the matter.

The day after they all returned to the House on the Rock, Franz-Karl went to the Archive to look at the original copies of his parents' Marriage Contract. He was surprised by some of the things he found, and sadly unsurprised by others.

He had not known that the marriage had received a public vote, like this own Heirship, but with some surprising differences. It had been formally proposed in Council by the Duke and referred to the populace by something recorded as a unanimous vote of the Councilors present, but the list of those present and voting included no Notaries other than the Duke herself. The populace vote was similarly grudging: two voters more than needed for the quorum, two votes more than needed for passage within the quorum – so only about a third of the population had agreed – and the only Notaries mentioned as voting at all were the Duke and her daughter. Traventi assembled had officially consented to the marriage of their Heir to the Emperor's younger son, but they had not pretended to be very happy about it.

And the Notaries... oh, dear. Out of all of the Notaries in Traventi, only the Duke and her daughter were directly connected to the Marriage Contract. Franz-Karl was not certain whether being a product of the Contract counted as connecting him to it. He would need to ask Maestro Petros and Chief Justice Laurentina about that. But if the Imperial officials in Karnburg and Konigsberg pushed Traventi too hard, they might be surprised at what pushed back. With or without Franz-Karl.

The clauses in the Marriage Contract itself had been phrased very carefully in the Remoran copy and even more carefully in the Elderic version, and again there were no Notarial Witnesses. There were Traventine witnesses to Bind the Contract but no Notaries at all except the Heir had signed or Witnessed the contract, not even her mother the Duke.

The reported numbers were almost shocking compared to the votes on Franz-Karl's heirship. But, the Allemanic and Falkenburg negotiators would not know or care – or know to care – about the populace vote, even though it shook the earth and the sky.

The Falkenburgs had acquired their best territories by marriage, not war – there were famous jokes about it in three languages, not including Elderic – but Franz-Karl wondered how openly the Allemanic Kingdom and Falkenburg Empire had threatened a war to arrange the marriage that provided their desired claim to the monarchy of Traventi. And then the Margraff-Elector had started to spoil things by pushing so hard that Franz-Karl became ducal heir to Silvia of Traventi instead of Philip-Augustus.

Turning to the actual text of the contract, Franz-Karl found that the first clause, identifying the new spouses looked almost exactly like Astolon and Imelda's.

The second clause stated flatly that, "Contrary to the recommendations of the Traventine negotiators, this contract makes no provision for any special process for future amendments". Franz-Karl read it three times – twice in Remoran and once in the Elderic copy – to be completely sure he was not somehow misreading it. He could almost hear the annoyed voice of Chief Justice Laurentina in the phrasing, and he was quite sure that even though the head judicial Notary had neither voted for the contract nor signed it, she had been deeply involved in the bargaining that created it.

Laurentina was an honorable person. She would have warned the Allemanic negotiators about the curse of Rano setting pitfalls in the way of amending contracts. But they had no doubt followed their usual habit of ignoring any Elderkin matter they found inconvenient. Half of them had probably been Reformists, besides, and outraged at being addressed by a woman, much less one that dared to give them advice.

The Contract could not be amended now that Franz-Karl's Papa was dead and could not agree to the changes. But even before that, with Rano's Binding in full force, the same need for agreement had applied to all of the people who had signed, either as parties or as witnesses, whether or not they were Notaries. The Contract was locked past changing as soon as any of the signers and witnesses died. The quorum was two thirds of the voting adults of both sexes among the twenty-five thousand folk of Traventi, and passage was just over half of that... and all of those who voted for approval counted as witnesses. What were the chances all of the people who voted for the contract were still alive even a year after the wedding? Considering the way Traventines managed elections, what were the chances the voters had all lasted a month? Theodore the Potter had not lasted through the night after Franz-Karl's Recognition before his death bound the votes and Franz-Karl's oath into the foundation of the World.

The next clause of the Wedding Contract was even harder to believe. The third clause of the marriage contract required Silvia to bear Falkenburg children during the first ten years of the marriage, with penalties for failure. That was not a clause for a marriage contract. It was a clause fit for a transfer of livestock. Or for slaves, maybe, outside the borders of Traventi. It was insulting and immoral to use it in a wedding contract. Franz-Karl wondered what they would have done if his Papa had died in the first year of the marriage instead of the ninth. With this stupid, wicked, unchangeably Binding contract in force, the Living World would not allow them to do nothing. No wonder barely two years separated him from his older brother and younger sister.

The fourth clause established strict rules of primogeniture for Leon-Alexander's titles and property. There were provisions for the widow, any daughters and any younger sons, but the wording assumed the heir would be grown before his father's death, and probably the younger children, too, so things were going to be a mess until Philip-Augustus was reached his majority, if not until Sophie-Alexa was grown.

The fifth clause, read strictly, was the one that had led to Franz-Karl becoming an Heir of the Duke of Traventi in line ahead of his older brother – proposed as an heir as soon as he became a Notary – at least when combined with the sixth clause, which held Traventi responsible for dealing with any unexpected eruptions of Manifest or Elderkin ... 'matters' within Falkenburg territories.

Franz-Karl had heard his Papa discussing privy council meetings with acting Archduke Uncle Helm-Friedrich, and understood more than they realized: though less about what was decided and more about how the discussions worked. He dearly hoped that Hieronymus the Traventine Council Secretary had not burned his notes of the debate that had led to that word 'matters' in the Contract. He was beginning to be surprised that there were no reports of people being set on fire or turned into newts during the negotiations, and he was only up to the sixth clause out of twenty-five.

Even considering that it was a marriage contract – Astolon and Imelda's had contained some odd clauses – the remaining clauses of Silvia and Leon-Alexander's contract were an odd mix of promises between families, promises between monarchs, and promises between polities, sometimes combined in odd ways: the clause that promised ritually correct food for the Heir of Traventi while resident in the Falkenburg Household included the scaffold of a trade agreement between a pair of parentheses. And the clause about the organization of the Heir's Household mentioned at least three unrelated topics... it made no sense...

Oh. He was thinking like Worldfolk.

In the Palace, agreements among Worldfolk sometimes meant very little. Powerful men changed their minds about the terms of a deal and lesser folk had little recourse but to pray the terms would not change further.

Among Elderkin... The will of a single Elderkin Binder could inscribe a request for changes onto the walls of the World and the World might respond. But the combined consent of thousands of lesser Elderkin had woven the Contract into the fabric of what was real, and without any process for amendment the Curse of Rano had sealed the fabric past any hazard of fraying. Any agreement or advantage wedged into the Contract, for either side, was now part of the legal and metaphysical terrain, and formed landmarks that must be accommodated in any future agreement. There were ways, of course: Traventi had not lived with Rano's Binding for upwards of thirteen centuries without learning a few things... Being careful to specify the means of amending an agreement was one of the things they had learned, and it seemed that their fellow negotiators had ignored that warning.

Franz-Karl read the Marriage contract again from the beginning – the Elderic version – and began to see how the thorough, vivid nastiness of the third clause and some quirks within the later clauses served as distractions, like sticks and leaves strewn over the top of a pit trap created by the unyielding reality of the Contract as a whole.

The Privy Councils or the Diet or His Excellency could send a message to Traventi saying, "From now on things will work this new way..." and it would not matter. The World would not let it matter.

The final clause of the Contract was as simple as the second: a promise by the Falkenburgs that messengers from Traventi would have access to any Heir of the Ducal line at any hour of the day or night whenever she or he was in a Falkenburg Holding. Oddly, simple though it was, that paragraph flickered on the page when Franz-Karl looked at it, as if it was as uncertain of its place in reality as an Allemanic chamberlain. He wondered how or why someone had broken such a simple law.

The Contract concluded with a final section that acknowledged a possible future need to heal breaches of the terms, but like the processes for amendments, it simply stated that there was no way to do it. If the flickering that Franz-Karl could see in the promise of access was because some idiot had blocked a messenger from reaching the Childe of Traventi, the contract had been breached and there was no way to properly repair it.

Franz-Karl was certain that his parents had read the Contract in full and in detail before they signed it. The entire Traventine Council would have read it, and all of the fully sworn Notaries at the time – Maestro Petros would have gotten someone to read it to him , or discussed it with Justice Laurentina over dinner – and a fraction of the voters that would seem surprisingly large to anyone outside of Traventi. Hence the very pointed voting results.

Considering the way the Kingdom and Empire handled negotiations, the people negotiating the details and the people signing the agreement would have been different. He wondered how many of the signers for the Allemanic and Falkenburg side had read all of what they signed. Or any of it: Allemanic Lords did not follow the customs of Notaries, and expected that agreements were breakable. He was quite sure that His Excellency had not read more than just enough to be sure which document he was signing. The acting Archduke had very likely read the whole thing.

Aunt Queen Gertrude was not a signer for the Falkenburgs: the Allemanic lords never let women sign, the Falkenburg domains rarely did, and she might have still been in the Szekely Kingdom at the time.

Franz-Karl arranged to visit the Archive again, to write his own copy in his own hand of the original Elderic copy of the Contract: not all of the thousands of names of voting Witnesses, but all of the rest of it. He made a copy of the official Remoran version as well, just in case there were problems getting at an unedited version of the Palace's copy.

He noticed that several of the Allemanic Nobles had signed the official copies with their titles and domain names and their seals but omitted their personal names. If that was an attempt to avoid validity or culpability, they would have failed: Franz-Karl had clear memories of an afternoon that Maestro Petros had spent discussing similar tricks. Signing as their positions would make the contract apply almost as strictly to their successors in office as to themselves, and stick tighter to both than if they had signed as their own persons.

The Margraff-Elector of Ansbach was one of the signers whose personal name was missing. Franz-Karl wondered whether the youthful Margraff-Elector he knew was the same man that had signed the contract: his parents' wedding seemed a long time ago to him, but the grownups who remembered it would not agree. It did not really matter: if the Margraff-Elector was involved in deliberately ignoring or breaking the Marriage Contract – especially that twenty-fifth clause – his luck was going to be terrible.

CHAPTER XXXI: Lists

Wherein There Are Too Many Discussions and Plans Begin to be Devised

It seemed that almost as soon as they finished unpacking after returning from the Boukolyos wedding, people began to plan Franz-Karl's journey from the House on the Rock back to the Imperial Palace in Karnburg.

There were a lot of lists.

There was a long list of the things Franz-Karl had brought from Karnburg and needed to take back with him or at least know what had happened to them. Some things were broken or used up. Some things were gifts that had been brought from Karnburg to be given to people and were expected to stay behind in the House on the Rock.

Some clothes were intact but so thoroughly outgrown that it made no sense to carry them all the way back to Karnburg. It was not just that he had grown taller, as would be expected in a child his age: a long season of swimming, and dancing practice, and games with his cousins, and walking all through the House on the Rock had changed his shape since he had arrived. And the seam allowances so that his clothes could be let out as he grew were not all in the right places, so there was little to be done. Falkenburg children did not wear patched clothing.

There was a list of new things that belonged to Franz-Karl; and a list of all of Fritzel's things that needed to go to Karnburg; and a list of things Her Grace was sending to Karnburg as gifts for people or supplies for what people kept referring to as the notional embassy. And a long list of books, recommended by the Schola and the Archive, that Franz-Karl and Fritzel were taking to Karnburg so that they would have good copies available.

On the second day of planning, when Olivia was describing the clothes and things she planned to pack for Franz-Karl and how the packs would be arranged to ride in carts or on animals without needing repacking, Franz-Karl began to cry – not noisy crying that people would notice, but there were tears running down his face. He could not wipe his eyes or people would notice, so it was itchy.

Finally, when Olivia started to list her own luggage, he managed to gasp out, "N-no. I'm sorry. You c-can't. You can't come."

Her Grace the Duke his Grandmother pulled him into her lap and wiped his face with her own handkerchief.

Praetor Aurelian, who was there to explain the plans for guards for the journey, said quietly, "Your Honor, the Marriage Contract allows..."

Franz-Karl interrupted him because he had spent all day listening to plans to carry him away from Traventi, and grownups trying to be sensible but talking about fake things just made it worse. "Allows and real are different! The Marriage C-contract says that Mama should have five Elderkin ladies in waiting, but she only has Gwenlian because the mean people in the Palace were so awful. 'Nelia cried for days and days before she went away, and now Sophie-Alexa only has Nurse Rosa, who only speaks Allemanic – no Elderic and not even any Remoran. Except a few church words." He choked and sniffled. "I don't want the bad people to be mean to Olivia, and I don't know how to stop them. Papa couldn't stop them, even though he tried. And Papa was the Emperor's son. And now he won't be there to be able to try."

Olivia had been happy, talking about plans for traveling, but now she looked scared, or angry. Maybe both.

"Would your Honor prefer to stay in Traventi?" Fritzel asked. He sounded worried.

"I p-promised Mama and Sophie-Alexa that I would come back, and Sophie-Alexa is so little she might forget me if I stay away too long."

The Praetor made an angry, growly noise that was not a word. "With Grand Duke Leon-Alexander dead, we should bring Her Highness and all her children back here."

Her Grace the Duke, Franz-Karl's Grandmother hugged him tighter. "By Heaven and all the saints, I wish that we could. This needs to be reconsidered, now that my son-in-law is dead."

Franz-Karl knew that would not work. It was like a big rock that had fallen into a road so there was no way to pass.

It was very surprising to not be ignored or laughed at or yelled at for being troublesome, but that made it a little easier to stop crying and discuss things. Franz-Karl wiped his eyes and nose again with her Grace's handkerchief, thinking about how to explain. It made him tired just thinking about it. "That won't work," he said, not hiding the tiredness, but trying not to whine too much. "Philip-Augustus is a noble Allemanic lord now that Papa is dead. They won't want to let him come. And Mama won't leave him alone with the mean people –"

"Nor should she," Olivia said angrily.

"Not with who they are likely to give him as a trustee and guardian," Her Grace agreed. "Silvia is spending half her time arguing against the most foolish suggestions, since they won't accept her for the position."

"We shall see about that," the Praetor said.

Franz-Karl had heard discussions of the size of Traventi in Her Grace His Grandmother's council meetings, and the boasts of generals and officials in the Palace. He rolled his eyes and made sure the Praetor saw him do it. "There are more soldiers in camps just near Karnburg than the whole population of Traventi unless you add in some of the goats. Maybe a lot of the goats. And there are plenty of soldiers in other parts of the Allemanic Kingdom and the Falkenburg Domains. Mama said once that the Marriage Contract was instead of having a war... has the Council changed their minds? Or will you make a Desolation, like General Rano, only bigger?" Franz-Karl was sad just thinking about it. Newts sounded like a better idea all the time, but, of course, turning lots of people in newts would just be another kind of war.

Now all the grownups were looking as upset as Franz-Karl felt, which did not help anything or make him feel better. Except that at least now they were thinking about the real shape of the world.

Fritzel had been quiet during most of the discussion of the journey, just listening and writing occasional notes on a wax tablet. He was like Franz-Karl, someone who was going to be transported, not someone who organized the transportation. He shifted in his seat, and said, "Whatever else we do, unless we decide there's a need to be hasty, we need to bring plenty of pigeons from here to Karnburg, and arrange for plenty of Karnburg birds to be brought here. Best not to be shut inside city walls with no way to send messages."

"Better not to be trapped at all," the Praetor grumbled.

Fritzel cocked his head in a way that would aim the horns he did not have yet at an opponent's eye. It was a Boukolyos gesture, not really a threat: not even when Baron Junio and Uncle Aldo did it with real horns. It was more like thinking about possibilities than planning to use them. "We have been playing hiding games all summer, His Honor and I, and we are both strong swimmers now. If it comes to it, I will undertake to bring him – and very likely the little girl as well – clear of the city despite all the walls and guards of the Worldfolk. Her Highness, being a full Notary herself, will of course do as she pleases. Where we would go next after passing the city walls and gate? That I have no thought for."

Her Grace the Duke said, "For matters outside the Karnburg walls, I have a few thoughts... which I must consult with the Reverend Counts Adrasteia and Valens about."

The grownups began adjusting their plans to expect enemies as well as allies. And they agreed that Olivia should stay safe in Traventi. Franz-Karl felt a bit better, even though he did not really understand some of the plans. Besides the pigeons, and arranging for horses waiting outside the city walls, there seemed to be a lot of talk about gold and letters of credit. There was no mention at all of Gifts or Bindings, unless they were tangled up with the Gold.

One of the Borderers in the discussion had a cousin he carefully described as not-female, who very likely had the skills needed to perform a Tire-woman's duties. So the discussion turned to questions of what people could be safely included in Franz-Karl's household, or added to Childe Silvia's. Which resulted in more lists.

Franz-Karl was a little worried that Olivia might think he was angry with her, so the next day – it was market day again in Saint Victoria – he left Fritzel to sit in the planning meeting, got out his purse and record of account, and went to look for a special present for her.

He walked all around the square looking at the booths and shops, but did not find anything special enough. He sat for a while with Maestro Petros, who was directing an odd spoken contract about a transfer of fish. That was interesting for itself, and also reminded him of someone else to talk to.

Franz-Karl left the square by the inner doorway that led deeper into the House on the Rock and followed the colonnade to the doorway whose shop sign was a fully rigged model of an ocean-going ship. He entered, then paused to take a few deep breaths. The Spice Shop was probably the best-smelling place anywhere, because it was full of all the best smelling things from everywhere. From the east: tea and dozens of spices – ginger and cinnamon and cloves and nutmeg and black pepper were just the beginning of the list, which also included myrrh and several kinds of incense. From the south: coffee (which tasted horrible but smelled amazing) and sugar and dates and figs and other dried and preserved fruits and flowers. From the west: cacao and vanilla and chili-pepper-fruit and sweet pimenta and dried tomatl and maple sugar and more kinds of preserved fruits, some sweet, some savory.

He opened his eyes – which had closed almost without his noticing – when Argens said, "Blessed day."

"Blessed day, Argens. I am seeking a special present for Olivia, so that she will know I am not being mean because I am angry."

Argens' eyes widened. "I've not seen Your Honor being mean to those that serve you at all. What did you do that needs a special gift?"

Franz-Karl waved both hands in a frustrated gesture. "I said that she cannot come to Karnburg." He sighed. "I think some of the grownups are listening now, as well as hearing, but not all of them... not yet."

"Ah." Argens nodded seriously. "The lady has never crossed the border, I take it? Well, come and sit and drink, while we consider this."

Argens kept a small brazier and a kettle filled with the best spring water available so that he could serve samples to prospective customers for the most expensive foreign drinks. Franz-Karl sat in the honored-patron seat, which would have been too big, but Argens immediately tucked a cushion behind his back and a footrest beneath his feet.

"Tea or cacao?"

"Cacao, if that is easy."

"Chile powder?"

"Just a tiny bit to wake up the cacao?"

"An excellent choice, Your Honor... and a touch of sugar to blunt the bitterness just a little..."

Before he took his own seat, the merchant offered a tray with two cups then picked up the one Franz-Karl had not chosen. They both sipped their drinks a few times before either spoke again.

"So, Your Honor, things are bad in Karnburg City?"

Franz-Karl shrugged, "I don't know Karnburg City worth mentioning. The Palace is horrible..."

"Truly as bad as that?"

"The Marriage Contract says Mama should have five Elderkin ladies and five gentlemen to attend her, but when I left she only had Roland, and two young men, and Gwenlian, who is old and good at being ferocious and scary. I don't want Olivia to learn to be scary, or cry all the time. Or both."

"Ah... hearing that is a sorrow. Even with all of its faults, this town here on the Rock must seem like the Fields of the Blessed after such a snake-pit." Argens finished his drink and set the cup aside, then leaned forward a little in his seat. "May I ask, will this be paid from the household or the Ducal funds?"

"I hope, neither." Franz-Karl took his purse and the record of account out of his pockets, weighed them briefly, one in each hand, then put away the purse and handed the paper to Argens. "Is this enough for something very nice?" He had done enough small Favors for people in the markets and Scholas that the balance had risen, not dropped, since Tax Day. He hoped it was enough.

Argens looked at the record and grinned, "Your Honor, this is enough for a season's lease in a fashionable district, most places."

Franz-Karl smiled back at him. "I don't think I have been so mean that it warrants the gift of a house, altogether. You know the world – better than me – and you know your stock... what do you suggest?"

Argens seemed struck by a sudden thought: "A house!" The mismatched cats' eyes blinked. "My apologies, Your Honor: a thought I'll explain later, if it bears fruit... as for your lady Olivia, I think I have something that will serve, if your Honor will bide a moment?" He set the record of account down on the small table beside the empty cups and walked though the door marked with torches to the private space behind the shop.

The merchant returned with a beautifully fashioned and inlaid wooden box, equipped with a small lock and a key. It opened to reveal compartments – suitable for the storage of jewelry or small packages of spices or other small items – and two instruction cards. One card explained to a Binder how to link the lock's Binding to the box's proper owner so that no other could open it. The second card explained to the owner how to designate a deputy who was also allowed to open the box.

"I'll confess I don't know why they bothered with that deputy business," Argens said.

That seemed perfectly plain to Franz-Karl. "When the first person stored a will in one of these, and the heirs needed to fetch a hatchet?"

"Heh. I can believe that."

"This is lovely work: the woodcraft and the Binding, both. Shall we choose some gifts to fill it?"

Olivia liked tea, and Argens naturally knew her tastes, but Franz-Karl did not only choose tea to fill the compartments, he added sweets and spices. When they were all filled, Argens wrapped the box in paper that had strange printing on it because it had originally wrapped a bundle of stuff from far away on the other side of the world.

When they were settling up, Franz-Karl looked at the record of account and realized how much was left. He could buy gifts from Traventi for many people besides Olivia, like a grownup traveler. He asked, "Does the box maker also make boxes sized to hold documents?"

"I believe so... if your Honor has need?"

"I have a Grandfather who is King of the Allemans by Election, and Overlord of the Domains of the Falkenburg Empire by birth, but if his treasures include a document safe with a magical lock, I have not heard it mentioned... and it would be."

"Ah. Of course. Well, Finn Locker will be busy about the market today. Shall I arrange a meeting?"

"That would be helpful... and be sure you are well stocked with these small treasure boxes, also. Besides my Mother and sister and Itron Gwenlian, I have a Grandmother and two aunts and a great-aunt in Karnburg. And a brother and an uncle and various other kin to be thought of besides my grandfather."

"Do you, indeed?" Argens looked very cheerful at that. "May Heaven prosper them all."

He looked even more cheerful when Franz-Karl added. "My Aunt Gertrude and her companion are known artists in thread and dye: they have stitched cloths for half the altars in the cathedral, and raiment for the holy images. We should plan at least one of the treasure boxes accordingly." Dyes and pigments were famously more costly than gold or jewels, being scarcer outside Traventi.

The merchant bowed formally. "I shall be very glad to make arrangements, Your Honor."

Franz-Karl thought that Olivia seemed very happy when he gave her the treasure box and set the lock to answer to her.

In the end, he bought treasure boxes and document boxes and small keepsake boxes for everyone he could think of in Karnburg, some to give as gifts on his return to the city, some to save to be given as Midwinter gifts.

He gave Fritzel both a document box and a treasure box full of tea and spices, but those two boxes did not have locks with Bindings by Finn Locker. Franz-Karl set those two locks himself, after carefully watching how Finn did all of the others. He thought that if something went wrong after a while, he would be with Fritzel and available to fix his own work without needing to send for a hatchet. Though it was really not so different from telling the strongbox under Fritzel's bed to make itself unnoticeable.

When he was very certain that locks he made himself had the Bindings set correctly, Franz-Karl made a document box for Her Grace the Duke his Grandmother with a lock that he had set entirely by himself.

Finn Locker laughed at his worries. "Truly, Your Honor, your lock workings are as well-made as anyone could ask for. My only worry is what the tax people will say when they hear I've finally found an apprentice, but one that's leaving the Duchy almost at once. The bounty they've named for anyone that can learn my tricks will make your eyes water." The old man was heavy-Gifted, not a Binder, and had faded scars on his face and showing at the cuffs of his sleeves. Gifts were often trickier to match than Bindings because they did not need thinking about: they just happened. That would have increased the bounty.

"Hmm." Franz-Karl... 'consulted with himself', was the best description he had found for trying to look at the World with his whole self, not just the bodily senses. "People in the Duchy trust those around them," he suggested. "They do not seem to exercise the 'Don't Notice Me' Gift much. And talk about it less."

The scarred old craftsman looked thoughtful as he took his leave.

CHAPTER XXXII: Contingencies

Wherein News Arrives at the House on the Rock

The Harvest-Tide session of the Council of Traventi had no fixed date: the law books said that the date should be set sometime in September according to the state of the crops and the mountain passes and various other concerns. It was decided that Franz-Karl's journey back to Karnburg was a various other concern, so the date was moved up so that Franz-Karl could attend the session before before he went away, and so that the Councilors could discuss the complications around Franz-Karl going away to the Palace in Karnburg and his Mama and brother and sister being there already. Thinking about both Heirs: Franz-Karl and his Mama, being in Karnburg at the same time made people worry.

The first morning of the Council session was about wills and contracts, and plans to make sure that everyone in Traventi had enough food to last through the winter and until after the spring floods. Franz-Karl was fascinated by the ways all of the different pieces of government fit together, but somehow that did not stop him from being edgy and distracted. It was hard to sit still properly. Part of him felt like he was already two steps down the road toward the Palace and missing the House on the Rock.

After the pause for the mid-day meal, Her Grace the Duke his Grandmother asked Franz-Karl to sit in a chair next to her at the Council table. That was more than a little scary: the councilors all had serious expressions.

Her Reverence Count Great Aunt Adrasteia stood in the opening of the U made by the tables, stretched her wings, folded them, and said quietly, "We have news from Karnburg regarding the lessons that were set as a trap for His Honor Franz-Karl."

Tribune Ulrich said, "So soon?" Franz-Karl had thought it, and was glad someone else said it, though he thought he would have used a more polite tone.

"The package of lessons went with a demand for an explanation. As agreed by the council, they were carried by couriers riding fast horses and changing at the posting stations, arrayed as the Wild Hunt. The initial reports in response came by pigeon, but the first return courier arrived this morning. I believe he killed at least one horse, pushing farther and faster than was wise."

Franz-Karl felt bad about the horse.

Someone said, "Oof."

Hieronymus the Secretary read out three letters. There was a short letter in fluent diplomatic Remoran from His Excellency Franz-Karl's Grandfather and the acting Archduke Uncle Helm-Friedrich that stated plainly that they were furious, taking appropriate steps, and were not entirely certain of what all of those steps were going to be: there was a final note in Helm-Friedrich's own hand asking for suggestions.

The second letter was longer and written in Elderic by Franz-Karl's Mama. In various places she wrote as Heir of Traventi, Leon-Alexander's widow, the Duke's kinswoman, the mother of the child who had been endangered, the mother of other children possibly at risk, and the acting ambassador from Traventi to the combined Allemanic and Falkenburg court. And she did it using one of the spikier verse forms.

People winced. There was no place in which she stated plainly that she would not leave Karnburg, but after Hieronymus reported that the letter had been signed by Silvia, Childe of Traventi, without Lineage names, and sealed with her signet, Tribune Ursula smiled and shook her head, "There speaks our Silvia, right enough. I assume we have no plans to arrange for a large herd of elephants and a quantity of blasting powder to try to shift her?"

Franz-Karl was proud of his Mama for standing her ground, but he thought it would be easier for most people if she had just berated the Palace authorities for false dealing and invoked some punishments on them before bringing Philip-Augustus and Sophie-Alexa to Traventi to join Franz-Karl. But someone with a high rank would use that as an excuse for a war to come get Philip-Augustus back. Of course. That would be very stupid, but grownups – especially the grownups in the Palace – did a lot of stupid things.

The third letter was written in stiff, awkward, diplomatic Remoran, and seemed to come from one or more of the Privy Councils, or possibly a bunch of individual Privy Councilors. In between polite formulas, it assured the Duke that the teacher responsible for the lessons had been removed from the household of the Count of Wolfsberg, and a better teacher would be provided.

Franz-Karl shifted in his chair at the end of that letter. The sphinx looked straight at him. "Your Honor Franz-Karl?"

"Three things. First, the Councilors never said 'children of Leon-Alexander'. It was always 'children of the household of Leon-Alexander', which does not mean the same thing. There will be legal problems if that is allowed to stand unchallenged: some of them tried it with a Waldense inheritance last year and my Papa was very angry about it. I learned a lot of new swears in Naua and Adenosani. And second, they speak as if Meister van Diesen is the only one who might be at fault at all, and the Councilors are responsible for arranging for the tutor."

Chief Justice Laurentina made an annoyed sound that would have been less surprising coming from the sphinx. "And the teacher who was responsible for the lessons may not be the true culprit. We shall review that letter carefully, Your Honor, and more carefully with your warning. What is your third point?"

"That letter comes from the Margraff-Elector or his people."

"May I ask how you know?" That was Tribune Constans, and it was curiosity, not a challenge. With Ulrich, it would have been a challenge.

Franz-Karl repeated a section of the Remoran letter Hieronymus had read, then repeated it in much smoother Northern Allemanic, before adding in Elderic, "I have been memorizing a great deal of Grammar this summer." Several people chuckled at that understatement. "The Margraff-Elector and his people need to learn better Remoran, even if they don't like their Holinesses in Remora. Or else they should hire a better translator: some of that bad Remoran is word by word translations of phrases used in the Ansbach provinces and elsewhere in the North, but seldom in the Eastlands."

The Chief Archivist stood up and bowed to Franz-Karl. "Elegantly done, Your Honor." He sat back down.

"I agree," Count Great Aunt Adrasteia said, nodding to Franz-Karl. "And I believe I will make some effort to modernize my own knowledge of the Allemanic dialects. It seems they will matter, this next while." She held up another document, but did not give it to anyone else to read. "There are reports that on the day His Honor Franz-Karl's lessons were delivered to the Karnburg Palace, the home of the Margraff-Elector of Ansbach in Karnburg suffered from a fire and some sort of disturbance involving bloodshed. Von Neumark and his household completely deny that anything of note occurred, which is foolish since some of the servants displayed fresh wounds the following day. There are also reports that at least one corpse was removed from the premises that I judge unlikely to be false: I have three reporters unconnected to one another who saw similar things." She dropped the paper so that her forelimbs could be paws and flex their claws, and smiled terribly. "Corpses are difficult to hide, even for the wealthy and mighty. Even in Karnburg."

There was once a Sphinx on a road that ate people: the Count looked... hungry.

The Council was pleased by that last news. The Sphinx was not the only one that looked hungry.

Franz-Karl felt a little sick to his stomach. He hoped if someone was dead, it was someone who was trying to trap him, not just some unlucky servant. He would not be sad that somebody had died because they tried to trap him, not exactly. But it was still a horrible thing.

The discussion of how to reply to the letters from the Palace went on so long that the people in the Council session were all late to the evening meal. Franz-Karl had answered a lot of questions about the Imperial and Royal Court. There were some he could not answer, but between things he knew himself and things he had heard grownups say, he surprised himself with how much he could answer. It was a quiet dinner: Karnburg was too many layers of traps hiding other traps, and people were thinking about ways to deal with them.

The second morning of the Council began with petitioners, and the last of the petitioners was Argens. He was dressed as an important merchant, not as a former sailor: the cloth of his suit was very finely woven, and dyed with expensive dyes, and the silhouette and cut of the lapels matched the latest fashions in the wealthy port cities on the Mothersea – or at least, the latest fashions that anyone in Traventi had heard of. He carried a walkingstick that was so very fine and thoroughly decorated that it would have looked purely ornamental to anyone who did not know one boot had no meat in it. It was stronger looking and more elegantly decorated than the Margraff-Elector's Glove-bearer's rod.

After a magnificent bow to the Duke and the other Councilors, Argens said, "I have two items for the council. First, the Line of Armorius is originally Karnburger, not Traventine, and still owns property both inside and outside the walls of Karnburg City. I hold Corentin's keys, but it is... inconvenient... to manage the various tenants and caretakers from this distance. Therefore I propose to designate Tiarna Friedrich Boukolyos as Deputy Steward of the Armorius holdings at Karnburg, to manage them for the benefit of Corentin and his daughter and grandchildren."

The Duke said, "I see nothing wrong with this Deputy Stewardship, and I will gladly Witness it. Is there a reason this needed to be a Council matter?" That seemed like a very reasonable question to Franz-Karl.

"The reason is my second item, which I raise in part on behalf of an alliance of merchants. As a venue for the Embassy from Traventi to the Imperial Courts, a widow's apartments within the Palace Gates do not suit the Duchy's dignity nor the convenience of the merchants who need the Embassy to serve properly as an intermediary with the offices of the Falkenburg Domains and the Allemanic Kingdom. The Armorius House at Greenoak Square in Karnburg is untenanted, conveniently close to the Palace Gates but outside them, and presents many advantages as a possible site of the Traventine Embassy. I offer it for your consideration."

Count Adrasteia purred, which was an odd sound to come from a human-shaped head and neck.

Argens bowed slightly and continued. "A removal of Her Highness the Childe Silvia and her children from the Palace precincts to Greenoak Square might properly be viewed as a young widow returning to her father's roof. The various councils among the Worldfolk might find it difficult to publicly oppose such a move, if it seems prudent."

Several of the members of the Council looked very thoughtful. Franz-Karl managed not to snicker openly. One of General Frog's maxims was: when offered two clear paths, find a third... and now Argens was offering one on a platter.

That afternoon, there was a discussion of the exact terms of the Marriage Contract and how things had changed since Leon-Alexander's death, and which terms were likely to be in breach already, or might be after the weeks of Franz-Karl's journey. Maestro Petros joined the session as an Observer and was very sarcastic about some of the contract clauses. Hieronymus wrote a list of sneaky things that Franz-Karl should watch for.

There were rules that some of the Palace authorities tried to enforce to avoid having Binders in the Palace and limit the Gifts that were available in Childe Silvia's household. But those were not part of any written law or treaty, and if the things that were written and signed and Witnessed were being breached, the Elderkin would have plenty of reasons to stop cooperating with less formal requests. Some people might be about to break their noses by walking into the wall of Rano's Curse.

Beyond all of that, the wicked paragraph of the Marriage Contract required Silvia to produce children, but there was nothing else in writing anywhere about those children or their households, or who, in the absence of Binders and Gifted Elderkin, was supposed to teach the children to be civilized Elderkin instead of feral ones. They had demanded children? Well, one of those children was now a full Notary and an Heir of Traventi, as well as the King and Emperor's grandson, and there was nothing in writing anywhere to stop him from returning and settling into the Palace with a full Century of Borderers and a Schola of Sorcerers. At least not in principle: Traventi did not really want to send a Century of Borderers and a Schola of Sorcerers to a place where 'those people' in the Palace were running things. And they did not really have a spare Century and Schola to send: Traventi was too small.

In the end it was decided that the party that traveled to Karnburg to stay would include several people to be Embassy staff – clerks and guards, for now – besides Franz-Karl and his aide Fritzel and a few additional members of the households for both Childe Silvia and Childe Franz-Karl. Whether the Embassy and its new staff would officially reside in the Palace or the House in Greenoak Square would depend on the situation they found when they reached Karnburg after the weeks of their journey. Childe Silvia, being officially the Ambassador, would decide. They would need to carry luggage and supplies sufficient for either case.

Fritzel spent time in discussions with Argens, and the Praetor and other Borderers, and the various offices supplying the embassy clerks. Livia was not happy at losing her best tax office clerk: she warned Philemon several times to watch his back among the Lowlanders, and his front and sides as well.

Olivia spent time discussing household matters with a person called Tam, who would be taking care of that part of Franz-Karl's household in Karnburg. The title Tire-woman was as genderless in Elderic as Duke, or Count or Heir, but that would not work at the Palace – Argens suggested that 'Valet', while too narrow, would annoy the Allemanic lords, and Tam found that amusing.

Tam was a tall narrow person, with very smooth pale golden-tan skin and golden eyes whose pupils narrowed to vertical slits in bright light. The stuff on Tam's head was as red as fresh blood and more like the fluffy parts of ostrich feathers than it was like fur or hair. The valet had no facial hair except eyelashes and eyebrows. Franz-Karl found a private moment to warn quietly, "In the Palace... some people may think you are a eunuch, which might be bad. Some people may pretend they think you are a eunuch, which might be worse."

The valet answered quietly, but smiling, "Some people may be in for a surprise, which might be amusing... Your Honor need not concern himself," and bowed, and returned to folding clothes. Franz-Karl did not entirely stop worrying about his new valet, but he worried less.

Franz-Karl spent as much time as he could manage with his cousins, now that their time together was coming to an end. He still had not successfully performed that one tricky pattern dance, which remained annoying. On the other hand, he was becoming almost useful at five-a-side court hockey, which was annoying in a different way: there would be no one to play with in Karnburg Palace, since he was too highborn to play with the servant children, and too Elderkin to play with the few Noble children who occasionally dwelt in the Palace or passed through its gates to visit their kin.

Two days before they were planning to leave the House on the Rock, Her Grace the Duke called Franz-Karl and Fritzel into her study and gave them a set of maps. One showed the city of Karnburg and some of the area around it and further west. The map showed the walls and gates of both the city itself, and the Palace inside it, and it showed some of the minor roads and streams, not just the Old Road and the great Daonas River. There were patches of Elderkin green: one outside the Palace but within the city, and three more green patches at increasing distances west of the city walls, near, but not exactly on, the main trade routes. She tapped the patch inside the city with a finger. "This is the house in Greenoak Square that we expect will serve as part of our embassy in Karnburg. These outer estates will have horses and other necessities ready at need."

Fritzel's shoulders softened and he let out a breath much longer than the one he had taken in. "That is good to know, Your Grace." He showed Franz-Karl, on another map, where to find some other Armorius holdings that were too far from the main roads to be useful for quick travel, but might be useful as places to hide.

Franz-Karl looked at the maps carefully and counted the road turnings within the city, and the crossroads and streams outside it, so that he would know the paths if he needed them.

When they were packing the maps, Her Grace picked up a wooden box sealed with her signet in dark wax. "Franz-Karl, this package will be useful to whoever awakens the Household Shrine at Greenoak Square. That task should properly belong your Mother, as an adult child of the Armorius line. But in case you cannot reach her, or she is captive in the Palace and cannot go to the House, Adrasteia has enclosed instructions that should allow an Uninitiated Notary of the Armorius Line to awaken the House without further damage to the Child Blessings. Follow the instructions exactly, if it comes to that, and try not to think about what you are doing too much."

Franz-Karl accepted the box with both hands: it was heavy for its size and oddly squirmy for something made of wood. It did not have a lock, but probably did not need one. "I will remember," he promised her. "I'll try to do it right if I have to open it."

Her Grace suddenly knelt beside him and hugged him hard, so the box was pressed awkwardly between them. She kissed his forehead and said softly, "Franz-Karl, I am sorry that you are tangled in all this and we don't know a good way to keep you and the others safe. People who summon children into the world should do better." She continued, louder, "May Heaven and the Living World curse those who would choose to turn children into weapons for their hands. May their goals slip through their fingers like sand and their lives be shadowed, and the scales measure their deaths with exactitude."

Fritzel signed himself and said, "May it be."

Franz-Karl said the words, but his arms were full and also tangled with his Grandmother, so he did not make the sign.

INTERLUDE VIII: More Contingencies

Wherein Traventi is Not the Only Place
Where Plans are Progressing

The Inner Hall of the Pristinists remained polished and free of dust, but it also remained empty. Only the Teacher presided in the White Hall. Preachers from across the North had declined invitations to serve the Karnburg community, but there was no sign the former Preacher had revealed anything untoward. But the Margraff-Elector was. Not. Pleased. His servants walked softly whenever a letter arrived from the North.

The laws of the Eastlands did not allow free men to be kidnapped off the street and enslaved, but the Margraff-Elector ignored non-Pristinist laws that were inconvenient. If he said that someone under his roof was a slave there were few who would dare claim otherwise.

Once the former tutor van Diesen had been ejected from the Palace, he had been easy to gather in. Slaves in Pristinist communities had no family names, and their personal names changed at their owners' whim, so with careful management enslavement could be made to be nearly as silent and as anonymous as an unmarked grave. The man named van Diesen no longer existed, but his knowledge remained conveniently under Horst-Konrad's hand.

The Ansbach Estate's master was missing a hedge-wizard, a kennel-master, and a Glove-Bearer, among others. The new slave, once trained to his state, might fill one of the gaps

Pristinist officials had not yet inserted their own candidates for Wolfsberg's new tutor and the female brat's nurse into the Traventine household, but they were successfully blocking the candidates proposed by others. Funds and servants intended for the household were being successfully diverted to more virtuous uses.

The General and Prince-Elector von Bremerhaven worried, but lacked a Preacher to back them, and detailed knowledge of the Margraff-Elector's failed gambit. Von Ansbach retained enough status, barely, that they fell silent rather than speak against him. And they had no better course to recommend.

CHAPTER XXXIII: Journey to the East

Wherein Our Hero is Not a Parcel

By the morning before they were due to leave the House on the Rock, everything was packed and ready to go except a few things that Franz-Karl and Fritzel would use or carry with them on the journey. The wooden horse called Harvest Prince was one of the exceptions: it was an awkward size and shape to put into the packs and Franz-Karl became certain that it would be crushed or all the bright paint would be scraped and ruined, so he decided to look after his prize himself.

The embassy people were ready as well. The loads for the mules were carefully balanced and ready, and all of the packs had official seals, though not nearly as many seals as the packs carried on the trip from Karnburg.

Everything was as ready as they could make it. They could have left a day early if the weather had looked threatening, but the advice of those who knew about such things was: 'wait', and everyone in the House on the Rock seemed to be extremely busy.

Unlike the rest of the household – the rest of the town – Franz-Karl had nothing that mattered to do after breakfast, that last day, except wait for the Farewell dinner that evening. He found that he could not settle himself to read, or play chess or other games with Fritzel. He kept jumping up to see to some bit of packing, or some other task in the House on the Rock, only to remember that the task was already done. Or required some item that was packed and ready for the mules. Or no longer mattered, since he would be gone.

After watching him fidget for a while, Fritzel said, "D'ye know, Your Honor, that today is Harvest Tax Day? Shall we see whether Livia and her tax clerks need a bit of aid?"

"Do you think they will want us?" The way this day was going, Franz-Karl had doubts.

Fritzel shrugged easily, the one shouldered shrug used by Traventine country people talking about work. "Tax Day is like hay harvest for clerks and bookkeepers: no one sensible turns down the aid of an extra pair of hands. Don't spend too long Witnessing at a stretch and things should go well enough."

"I'll be careful," Franz-Karl assured him fervently. Doing something useful that needed attention and care would feel good...

There were goats, this tax day, but no cabbages. Quite a lot of grain, and several kinds of cheeses, and wines from last year's pressing. More payments in coinage than there had been at the Summer Tax Day, and about the same number of payments as Favors, but some of the Favors were very strange indeed. Quite a number of people Franz-Karl knew from the market days wished him 'Farewell' while he was counting their goods or signing and sealing their records.

When the hour for the Farewell dinner was approaching, Livia stopped them from working even though it was not yet time to close the office. She gave them each purses that were quite full of copper, and some silver. Besides the records of accounts within Traventi, she also gave them letters of credit at three different foreign banks, with a stern warning against carrying all of the papers in a single pocket while they traveled.

Franz-Karl had been in no doubt at all that he was leaving Traventi and the House on the Rock, but somehow being given money to spend elsewhere felt like a door closing, even more than the people saying 'Farewell'.

Their guide on the journey back to Karnburg was Claudius, the same courier who had brought Franz-Karl to the House on the Rock at the start of summer, but the two journeys were not very similar. For one thing, Claudius was the guide, but this time there were grownups in the party who outranked him. Even Franz-Karl outranked Claudius this time: he was officially a Notary now, not an 'Elderkin problem' to be transported.

They traveled more by the rivers, which were less direct than the ancient Legion roads, but the aid of the downstream currents made up for that. The river boats were also more comfortable than donkeys and mules, especially when it rained and the travelers could take shelter under roofs of canvas, or occasionally even wood, without interrupting their progress. Franz-Karl was not sure whether there was less rain on the journey east, or it was just less annoying traveling with his own people instead of being transported as a package for delivery.

Despite everything, during the whole time of their journey from Traventi to Karnburg, Franz-Karl was afflicted by unrestful dreams. They did not come every night, or rather every morning, but they came often enough to be thoroughly annoying. Over and over he would find himself holding some necessary or useful object, set it down, and then not be able to find it again no matter how he searched through a series of rooms that might be part of the Palace, or the House on the Rock, or both, or neither, and became stranger and stranger as he searched. These searching dreams were certainly preferable to dreaming of being pursued or attacked by enemies or monsters, but that was the most that could be said for them.

He took to sleeping with his signet, and the prayer bracelet, and his father's memorial token, and his sheathed penknife, and his purse. That did not stop him from losing them in the dreams, but he felt better when he woke if they were ready to hand. Setting Harvest Prince at the head of his bed by his pillow seemed to help a little to keep the dreams away.

When they were awake, there was conversation and music. Fritzel had his lira, and Damian, the leader of the embassy Borderers, traveled with two wooden recorders and a metal pipe that was a bit like a penny-whistle with ambitions. Franz-Karl answered questions about the Palace and about what little he knew about the city outside the Palace walls.

The biggest difference between the two journeys was that some of the grownups he was traveling with asked for his opinions and listened to his answers.

CHAPTER XXXIV: The Palace Threshold

Wherein Things Fall Apart

The travelers from Traventi arrived at Karnburg late on an afternoon that was soggy but no longer actually raining. By the time they had dealt with the authorities at the city's water gate and their river boat had found its place at the wharf, there was still weak sunshine gilding the wet rooftops, but the narrow streets between the tall houses inside the city walls were deeply shadowed.

They were met at the riverside by ostlers with mules and carts for the baggage and a group of horses: one very large one for Fritzel and one very small one for Franz-Karl, and several middling ones for the embassy clerks and guards. Franz-Karl was glad that his mount was not another donkey. City people had strange ideas about donkeys.

Claudius went off with a few of the mule carts to deliver some items from Traventi to various banks and merchants before they closed for business for the day. He was happier dealing with the hazards of the countryside than guarding things inside city walls, and wanted to hand things over to their custodians as soon as possible.

Franz-Karl and his companions took the streets that led most directly from the river wharf to the main Palace Gate.

The broader streets around the Palace wall were not as generally dark as the ones in the River District, but there were dark shadows around the gatehouse. Someone was being stingy about torches and lanterns: not lighting them until the evening bells rang. But even though the bells had not rung and it was not officially night yet, it was growing difficult to see clearly.

Franz-Karl wondered who was pocketing the savings: he doubted the darkness was commanded by the acting Archduke his Uncle, who preferred light. Not a question that small princes were expected to worry about, but after a summer of Traventine Notarized contracts and Council sessions and Tax days, his thoughts tended to run in those directions.

Fritzel swung down from his horse and walked toward the most ornately dressed Gate Guard, saying, "Good afternoon," politely in his least accented Court Allemanic.

The guard, more than a head shorter, looked up at Fritzel and snorted. "Looking to visit your bitch of a lady are you, beastie? Well, you can forget about that."

Fritzel went very still and one of the Borderers said something too softly for Franz-Karl to hear.

Franz-Karl felt very cold. The man's accent was strongly Northern and 'beastie' was not the worst slur he might have used, but 'bitch' for His Excellency's daughter-in-law should get the man executed. But only if someone in authority bothered to listen to the complaint, so it was frightening that the man should be so openly... insolent.

There was a runner moving away behind the Gate Captain. Franz-Karl realized that he knew the man's face, and he was the wrong runner, and moving in the wrong direction.

This was bad. This was very bad. The Contract was broken, and broken again in this very moment, so the Living World would be pushing the situation toward disaster, especially for the breakers, but the World's aim was notoriously bad. If soldiers came, it would be the wrong soldiers, and there were enough Gifted Elderkin in their party, even if Franz-Karl himself managed to stay out of it...

Fritzel took a stride forward, and Franz-Karl remembered the bull-man – taller and heavier than the Guard Captain – being lifted so quickly above his aide's head at the Saints' Day Match. He nudged his little horse forward out of the shadows of the carts and said, "Tiarna

Boukolyos," projecting his voice as well as he could. He felt very small and shrill.

Fritzel pivoted into a graceful bow that left him on one knee facing Franz-Karl.

Franz-Karl spoke in Allemanic so that the guards would have no excuse for not taking notice. "Give this... fellow... the letters for his Highness my Uncle the acting Archduke and for His Excellency my Grandfather and the rest, so that he may carry the blame for any delay in delivery of official matters. And then come away. 'Elderkin lords do not thrust themselves in where they are not welcomed, unless they come arrayed for war.'"

The Guard turned pale, and looked worried, which was probably not for the part about the Elderkin: delaying an official message to His Excellency carried dire penalties that were harder to evade than the ones for having a vile tongue in his mouth or delaying messages to his Excellency's guests. Delaying Imperial messages had been officially treason ever since some problems a few years earlier. There were no body parts displayed outside the Palace Gate at the moment, but that could change if acting Archduke Uncle Helm-Friedrich decided someone needed reminding of their duty.

Fritzel, with his back to the guard, now looked like he was trying not to laugh, which was also not surprising: Franz-Karl had finished by translating a line from a famous old story that sounded even more sarcastic in their current situation. Franz-Karl felt his own muscles loosen a little: Fritzel wanting to laugh was much better than Fritzel wanting to tie some foolish guard into a bow-knot when they had been in the city less than an hour.

Fritzel made a great elaborate business of moving from one cart to another and piling several large packets and a rather unwieldy basket of scrolls into the arms of various guards. He added an apple with a bite taken out to the top of the basket, and spat the other piece of the apple at the Gate Captain's feet.

Franz-Karl winced. Fritzel had not entirely given up on tying the bow-knot: that apple thing – refusing to share food -- had started a war once, according to the chronicles. But Fritzel mounted his horse, and led the way through the streets away from the Palace.

Fritzel did not use the shortest route to Greenoak Square. He used the route that followed the widest roads with the best sight-lines.

Franz-Karl approved: there was movement in the distant shadows, and he was worried that the answer to that runner might be arriving before they were well away.

The house in Greenoak Square looked dark and silent when they arrived at its gate, but when Fritzel knocked they were greeted with all the proper words and formulas and the seven tokens of hospitality. The travelers entered and the gates were locked, and barred behind them. They had been locked but not barred before the newcomers arrived.

Franz-Karl took his bath in the laundry copper and was reminded of his first arrival at the House on the Rock. When he was clean, he put on a clean linen shirt and clean house-shoes and gathered his pen-knife and water and salt and a lit candle and Adrasteia's sealed box, and walked to the door of the dark room that had been the Household Shrine when the House was awake and in use by its family.

He did not expect to be able to awaken the shrine: he was not a grown man, nor a woman, nor an Initiate, and he was alone. But he had to try. With the Marriage Contract broken, his people would need every remaining legal advantage they could arrange. A local property – well-rooted in history and clearly theirs – would be very helpful. And if the dispute moved beyond legalities, the estate's walls and consecrated Threshold would be helpful in a different way.

Franz-Karl opened the door of the Shrine and lit a new candle with fire brought from outside. He made sure the offering bowls contained clean water and salt. Then he closed the door, and broke the seal on the box that he had been given.

He performed the required acts as much as possible exactly as they were written, without reading ahead or planning. It was all just: do this, do that, do the next thing. It was hard not to think or plan, not to wonder why, but he nearly managed it.

He thought he felt something shift in the World when he finished: there was a sort of distant thud, more felt in the bones than heard. Three wax candles with white wicks never touched by fire began to burn.

"I guess it worked," he said aloud. He knelt and bowed very deeply to the Shrine's tiny Altar. "Thank you," he said in Elderic. It was one of the few times when it was proper to say those words.

The candle flames turned pale green, like the newest leaves in spring. That was not a thing he had ever heard of or read about, but the prayer beads of his bracelet showed glowing traces of the same color deep in the carved symbols of the thirteen true things.

When he opened the door, Fritzel was waiting to lift him up to anoint the shrine door's lintel with scented oil, and to help and guard him when he marked the front door: posts and lintel and sill.

And then the same for the estate's front gate. There were carved stone torches on each side on the wall outside of the gate, invoking the Guardian of Gateways. Franz-Karl thought that they did not look much like real torches, but they were a shape that everyone knew meant 'torch'. When the gate lintel and sill were anointed, the stone shapes at the tops of the torches that were supposed to be flames began to shine that same pale green, like the earliest spring leaves that look like fog in the distance on a sunny day.

The evening bells rang just as they closed and barred the gate and the front door. Awakening the Shrine had taken more than an hour, though Franz-Karl had no particular memory of the time passing.

Franz-Karl put on proper clothes before they went into the main room of the house and sat down to eat a proper household meal together with the few servants who had been staying in the house and looking after it, as well as all of the men that had come with them from the House on the Rock. The gatekeeper took his choice from the platters and pitchers out to his seat by the gate, while the rest of the diners finished their meals in peace.

Franz-Karl was very tired after the long day of travel followed by worry and Binding work, almost too tired to eat. As soon as the formal meal was done he changed into a clean nightshirt – he was sure the linen he had worn in the Shrine had weird... stuff... on it, even though it had started clean and nothing had spilled – and climbed into the bed that had been prepared for him.

CHAPTER XXXV: Across the Threshold

Wherein Our Hero Returns Home at Last?

Franz-Karl was awakened far too soon. "Whattime...?" he mumbled, shielding his eyes from a candle that seemed far too bright.

"Not yet gone midnight," Fritzel answered quietly. "I am sorry to awaken you, Your Honor, but there are people at the gate Your Honor may recognize."

Clean clothes again: from the skin out... Franz-Karl thought wearily that it was a good thing this house had a well-equipped laundry: he seemed to be using clothes at a prodigious rate since they had arrived. He forced tired feet into his human-shaped boots, made sure his needful things were in his pockets and Harvest Prince was safe at the head of his bed, and followed Fritzel downstairs toward the front gate.

He was glad to see that some of the household had picked up weapons, while others gathered water and wine and fire and the platter of aogreamana in case their lord was disposed toward hospitality rather than battle.

The gatekeeper open the small challenge-hatch in the gate and looked out. A familiar voice said loudly in Allemanic, "I am Helm-Friedrich, Heir of the line of Falkenburg, acting Arch-Duke of these lands, and I have come in search of a kinsman. I say three times that I come with peaceful intent toward this house and any within it that hold peace and friendship and good faith in their own hearts."

The gatekeeper said loudly, "His Royal Highness and companions," in Elderic.

Someone set a block so that Franz-Karl could stand on it to look out through the hatch. There were two rows of men facing the gate. The five in the back row were men wearing the badges of Falkenburger guards. The front row – between a pair of torchbearers – were His Royal Highness Prince Otto of Karnburg, His Royal Grace the acting Archduke Uncle Helm-Friedrich, and a richly dressed fibber whose face was so distorted in Franz-Karl's vision that he was unrecognizable. To be fair, the continuing pale green glow of the stone torches mixed oddly with the firelight from the torches the attendants carried, and the uncertain light did not make anyone's features clear.

Franz-Karl raised his voice, in the purest diplomatic Remoran he could manage, not Allemanic. "I am named Franz-Karl of the lines of Falkenburg and Armorius, presently residing here in my Armorius Grandfather's house by the courtesy of his Deputy Steward. I am Recognized Childe of the Elderkin of Traventi and a fully sworn Notary, and I stand witness that the Marriage Contract of Leon-Alexander von Falkenburg and the Childe Silvia di Armorius stands in breach." He paused for one long breath. "Where are my Mother and my Brother and my Sister?"

The unrecognizable man's jaw dropped. Prince Otto took a half step back and bowed politely.

Archduke Uncle Helm-Friedrich looked up at the sky for a moment, then back down. He said carefully in Remoran, "If your Honor will come out to us, we will conduct you to them. I swear by my life and hope of judgment before Heaven and all of the Holy Gods that no harm will come to you or your companions in my care."

Franz-Karl turned his back on the gate to look at his people. Because of the block his eyes were at their shoulder level (except Fritzel) instead of belt level, which was a nice change. "I shall need Fritzel, of course... and ... Damian?"

The Traventine Borderer bowed, and his eyes flared gold in the changing light. "Of course, your Honor." His bare legs and knee-length tunic might not look like a military costume to the people of the Kingdom and Empire, and the silver penny-whistle that hung from a chain around his neck would surely not look like a weapon unless they gave him a reason to use it as one. But Damian was very likely the most dangerous fighter within a half-day's journey from where they stood, even though he lacked a Binder's Manifest weight.

Franz-Karl hopped down from the block so that they could move it aside to open the gate a little way, just enough for two men and a boy to exit. Tam bowed to Franz-Karl before he stepped through the house gate. "We will bring the baggage along when Your Honor calls for it," the Valet said in Elderic.

Franz-Karl nodded acknowledgment of the well-wishing before he crossed the threshold. He heard the locks and bars go back into place as he and and Fritzel and Damian walked toward His Royal Grace the acting Arch-Duke Uncle Helm-Friedrich and his companions. He had wondered whether the acting Arch-Duke would be angry at not being allowed to cross the threshold, but his Uncle just tipped his head subtly toward the fibber and said quietly in Remoran, "Thank you for joining us, Your Honor."

Franz-Karl felt chilled. He was sure the acting Archduke knew the rule about not saying 'Thank you': he had joked about it during gift-giving last Midwinter. He wished he knew what was going on in Karnburg and the Palace.

Franz-Karl and his Uncle bowed to each other and turned to walk toward the main Gate of the Palace, with their companions and the Falkenburg guards taking their positions around them. Franz-Karl gestured. "The Tiarna Friedrich Boukolyos, my personal aide and the Deputy Steward of the Armorius holdings in the Karnburg lands." One did not introduce guards and attendants, so Damian's name was safely hidden.

Prince Otto managed an elegant sort of walking bow, "Welcome to my city, Tiarna. It will be good to have those holdings tended more closely." Fritzel returned the bow. Prince Otto's Remoran was very fluent, for an Allemanic lord: Franz-Karl thought using the language of diplomacy even when speaking of local matters was a nice touch.

The richly dressed man made a disgusted noise in his throat. His face kept shifting in Franz-Karl's vision so that he sometimes looked like he had a long pointy snout like a caricature of a rat or a weasel. The acting Archduke gestured, much as Franz-Karl had, and said, "Prince-Elector Heinrich of Bremerhaven."

Franz-Karl's walking bow was not as elegant as Prince Otto's but it was not a disgrace. He murmured, "Prince-Elector," and left it at that. Bremerhaven was as far north as Ansbach and disliked Elderkin nearly as much. At least the Prince-Elector spent more time in his home territory and less time in Karnburg than the Margraff-Elector.

His Royal Highness Archduke Uncle Helm-Friedrich walked on for a few steps before he asked quietly, in Remoran, "May I ask why your Honor did not enter the Palace after arriving at the Gate this afternoon?"

"The Guards at the Palace Gate declared a policy of not admitting Elderkin to the presence of the Childe Silvia," Franz-Karl said, in the most neutral tone he could manage, "It seemed... rude ... to press the matter."

His Royal Highness pressed his lips tightly together and pinched the bridge of his nose. "Philip."

"I shall look into the matter tomorrow morning, Highness," one of the Falkenburger guards answered with a slight bow. Judging by his pronunciation, he had learned Remoran in a church school.

Franz-Karl pointed out, still in the neutral tone of a judge or a Schola lecturer, "That will not make the Contract less broken. Since the document that was signed defines no methods for repairing breaches of the twenty-fifth clause, the Marriage Contract stands irreparably in breach at the hands of the Falkenburgs."

Helm-Friedrich looked at the sky again, then looked back at Franz-Karl. "Their Excellencies are holding audiences this evening, if Your Honor would care to accompany me? They are very eager to see you."

"No." Flatly. "Before I left the Palace I promised Sophie-Alexa and my Lady Mother that I would see them when I returned. Your Royal Grace said that you would conduct me to them. How many promises will you break, Uncle?"

His Royal Highness Prince Otto said, "Dear Heaven" very softly.

"Naturally, then, we shall visit the Count of Wolfsberg's Residence before we proceed to the audience chamber." The acting Archduke sounded as if he might have rolled his eyes.

The night guards at the Palace Gate were different from the ones that had been there in the afternoon. These guards seemed to flinch from His Royal Grace's gaze, and they were not much calmer about meeting Franz-Karl's eyes, which were probably all shiny in the torchlight.

Though not really so much shinier than His Royal Grace's eyes, which reflected a rather feline green when the light caught them just right.

No one offered hospitality or asked for an oath of peace when the party crossed the threshold, not even the acting Archduke, who had used some of the proper forms at the Armorius Gate and even knew to say 'three', not 'four'. The threshold was probably not consecrated, anyway.

Franz-Karl remembered Astolon insisting on guest-oaths from the High Gods, and Uncle Henk's warnings, and wondered whether the Worldfolk of the Palace should regret their sloppiness. Perhaps they thought a child Binder was not dangerous. Perhaps they would learn that was wrong.

They were a smaller party after they passed through the gate: one of the torch-bearers and most of the Falkenburg guards left them once they were inside the Palace walls. Prince Otto and the Prince-Elector waited inside the main door of the West Palace: the building where Franz-Karl's family had their apartments. There was no offer of hospitality or exchange of oaths at the building's threshold either.

When Roland, his mother's attendant, met them at the Threshold of the family apartments, he bowed to Franz-Karl and welcomed him home as a son of the house in formal Elderic. He welcomed the acting Arch-Duke as a guest and kinsman of the house in Remoran. Franz-Karl murmured the proper response for a return from a journey, and His Royal Grace had visited the Household often enough to use the short form of the proper reply. Fritzel and Damian received the proper welcome for Elderkin less weighty than Notaries. The aogreamana were a bit stale, and the wine had been an unimpressive vintage even before it was watered, but at least the tokens were offered. The candle was tallow, not wax, and flickering.

His Royal Grace looked around as they walked through the apartment, and frowned deeply, but said nothing. The state of the less used parts of the rooms would have been disgraceful at Greenoak Square, which had been shut up and mostly empty for a decade: here, there was dust in the corners and the woodwork and furnishings were in dire need of polish. Greenoak Square, though understaffed, had been very well tended by comparison to this suite of Palace rooms: the house was clean, though not completely tidy, and had dust sheets over some of the furniture.

Franz-Karl turned to Fritzel and asked in Elderic, "Do you have the copy of the Marriage Contract, Tiarna Boukolyos?"

Fritzel held up the bundle of parchments. "Only the short versions, Your Honor... without all of the long list of signatures. There's a copy of the long one not yet unpacked."

Helm-Friedrich winced. 'Marriage Contract' was probably one the few Elderic phrases that he was familiar with.

Roland led them to Franz-Karl's Mama and he ran to her and hugged her as hard as he could. She hugged him back, then tipped his head up so that she could kiss his forehead. "Let me look at you, Child," she said. His eyes fill up with tears at the familiar words, and she hugged him again while he cried.

When Franz-Karl stopped crying long enough to look around for his sister, he found that she was being held by a stranger: a pale, narrow-faced woman with a sour expression. He held out his arms, and Sophie-Alexa struggled free of the clutching hands that held her. She ran to him and grabbed his coat in tight fists. "You came back! You came back!"

"I promised I would come back. So I came." He wrapped her in his arms, but turned his head to look at his Mama and sort of nodded his head toward the sour woman.

His Mama said sharply, "You may leave us, Doutzen."

Franz-Karl thought for a moment that the pale woman would actually disobey his Mama and refuse to leave them. But His Royal Grace set down the guest cup he still held and cleared his throat, and when she realized who was standing there, she turned even paler and almost ran out of the room.

"Where is Nurse Rosa?" Franz-Karl asked. In the reply to the protests about the lessons, Traventi had been promised someone to speak Elderic to Sophie-Alexa, but he greatly doubted this Doutzen person would fill their need. He wondered whether she even spoke Remoran, much less Elderic. Proper Court Alemannic might also be a stretch, since her features and style of dress looked very Northern.

"Gone," Sophie-Alexa said miserably. "Gone away. Like you. Like Papa. Like everyone. Gone." Her fists were still twisting in his coat.

"Where is Philip-Augustus?" Speaking Elderic in front of His Royal Grace was a bit rude, but this was properly Traventine territory, according to the contract, so using other languages here was pure courtesy, not a requirement, no matter who was standing there listening. Franz-Karl was not much in the mood for courtesy. Everything was wrong, and worse than he had expected.

"Somewhere with his new tutor, Meister Grawert," his Mama answered in Remoran, sounding sad and tired. "I have not seen him since two days ago, but I am assured he will be well protected and cared for." Her tone was much less certain than her words.

"That's probably true," Franz-Karl judged, also speaking Remoran. "If anything happens to him, they'll get me as next heir to Papa's estates and titles, and I don't look nearly as much like plain Worldfolk as Philip-Augustus." Helm-Friedrich made a noise as if he wanted to disagree, but would not say those words in front of a Notary – Franz-Karl had learned to recognize those kinds of swallowed words since he got his signet.

Sophie-Alexa kept holding onto his coat, but he managed to bow to his mother and wave Fritzel forward. His memory would not tell him how to address her as anything but 'Mama', which was not at all proper for a formal introduction. The Traventine and Palace protocols were having fights in his head. He finally gave up and said in Elderic, "Mama, Sophie-Alexa, this is Tiarna Friedrich Boukolyos, called Fritzel, whom Her Grace has sent to be one of my attendants now that I am a fully sworn Notary and an acknowledged Heir to the Duchy." He repeated everything in Allemanic, in case Sophie-Alexa was too upset – call it too upset – to understand the Elderic: he was sure Remoran would be hopeless for his sister. He looked more directly at his mother and continued in Allemanic so that His Royal Grace would have no excuse for not understanding, "Is there room for my aide and other attendants to be housed within these apartments?" He would be vastly surprised if there was no space, but it was proper to ask. He was glad to see His Royal Grace wince again.

His Mama formally welcomed Fritzel to her son's household – in Allemanic – and said that there were plenty of empty rooms for attendants. She offered another round of guest cups and aogreamana to both Fritzel and Damian... and she did not ask Damian's name in front of their Royal guest. Franz-Karl felt a shiver again: that was... not quite wrong.

These guest offerings were of better quality than the ones Roland had offered at the door, but not by much.

Sophie-Alexa managed a sort of curtsy without letting go of Franz-Karl's coat. She started sobbing when His Royal Grace said that they needed to go to His Excellency's audience, and held on tighter.

Fritzel sat on the floor beside them and said quietly, in Allemanic, "Little lady?" She did not stop sobbing but got a little quieter. "Little lady, I belong with your brother Franz-Karl, so if I carry you, it will be the same as Franz-Karl carrying you. He's been away a long time, and their Excellencies want to see him, same as you. Shall we all go together to see them?"

She took a long moment to decide, but finally turned to him and held out her arms. One hand kept hold of Franz-Karl's coat as long as she could reach it.

Fritzel shifted the bundle of the Marriage Contract to one arm, scooped Sophie-Alexa up with the other, and stood up, carrying her on his hip. She looked even tinier than usual cradled against his bulk.

Turning to His Royal Highness Helm-Friedrich, Fritzel said calmly, "You'll need to guide us, Your Royal Grace. I don't know this place yet."

Damian did not take the Marriage Contract from Fritzel: there was still a chance he might need his hands free.

CHAPTER XXXVI: The Main Palace

Wherein the Situation Curdles

Unlike the House on the Rock, moving from one part of the Palace to another often required walking under the open sky. They were met at the outer door of the West Palace by Prince Otto and the Prince-Elector and the guards and torch-man they had left waiting, and escorted along the garden walkway to the central block of the Palace buildings. They left the guards and torch at the outer door again and were passed to the guidance of an assortment of increasingly magnificent functionaries as they moved up the great staircase and toward the Reception Hall. Not one of them offered formal welcome or asked for oaths of peace.

Considering some old stories, Franz-Karl thought that a grandson of the house – coming with an honest grievance and not sworn to peace – could do a great deal of harm in this place.

Franz-Karl saw Fritzel noticing the vesets on the walls. Damian noticed them, too: he gave a little hint of a salute to one, and snickered very softly at least twice.

His Royal Grace spoke to some of their guides quietly but with great ferocity that left them a bit wide-eyed, and when the party reached the Reception Hall, Franz-Karl's Mama's name and titles were announced with an exquisite care and precision that matched the announcement of His Royal Grace himself. Children and attendants were not announced, being generally considered accessories, not people deserving attention. But the announcer finished, "His Honor the Notary Grand Duke Franz-Karl von Falkenburg, Heir of Traventi."

People in the crowded room turned to bow as His Royal Grace's party walked up the long room, and people around the edges of the room who were talking quietly, stopped, so the room became much quieter. Walking with so many people staring at them, it seemed to take a long time to reach the dais. The small platform was two steps up, so the people sitting in the two ornate chairs – the only seats in the room – did not look up to see the faces of most people who faced them.

When they were in easy speaking distance of Their Excellencies, Franz-Karl and his Uncle and their noble companions bowed, and his Mama curtsied very formally. Fritzel, who was still carrying Sophie-Alexa, took a knee and stayed down. So did Damian, who was nearly as tall.

His Excellency's sister Sophia-Augusta was standing on the platform beside Her Excellency's chair, with the Chief Justice of the Eastlands standing beside her as he generally did on all but the most formal occasions. Prince Otto, her Excellency's brother, moved to join them.

His Excellency's side of the platform was crowded by Ministers and Secretaries. Philip-Augustus was standing near the group of officials, just at the edge of the the platform, with the Margraff-Elector standing on the floor beside him, resting his gloved hand on Philip-Augustus's shoulder... or perhaps grasping him by the shoulder. Franz-Karl thought that the Margraff-Elector was hurting him: his brother was standing too stiffly and trying a little too hard to keep his expression neutral.

There was a glove-bearer with a fancy new rod of office standing near the Margraff-Elector, not the same man who had been at the funeral. He was holding a fancy pair of gloves even though the Margraff-Elector was wearing gloves on his hands. Franz-Karl wondered whether there would be more gloves underneath if the Margraff-Elector took off the ones that were touching Philip-Augustus.

Maybe it was all layers of gloves until you reached the bones... That was silly. Franz-Karl blinked his eyes a couple of times. After all the travel, he should not be here without sleeping first.

The Prince-Elector that had accompanied them from Greenoak Square walked over to the group of men attending on the Margraff-Elector and the two Electors exchanged bows and subtle hand gestures. But the Margraff-Elector only used one hand: he did not let go of Philip-Augustus.

There was an unfamiliar, scrawny man in scholar's robes standing behind the important people close to the Electors. He had a moderate amount of fibber's flicker and was probably the new tutor, Grawert.

The familiar form of the old tutor, van Diesen, was lurking in the background behind people like the Margraff-Elector's glove-bearer. He was not in robes, and had the edge of an iron collar showing behind the linen at his throat: that meant slave or serf, by northern practice, but the cloth masked the details. His hair had been cut and his face was oddly blank, but he still stood like himself. There were fewer fibs marking him than Franz-Karl was used to seeing.

Their Excellencies finished exchanging formal greetings – but not hospitable Elderkin welcomes or guest oaths – with Franz-Karl's Mama and His Royal Grace. Sophie-Alexa was mentioned but not spoken to.

There was a pause while their Excellencies looked at Franz-Karl without greeting him, so he said loudly, "Margraff-Elector von Ansbach, remove your hand from my brother and let him join our Lady Mother." He managed not to squeak.

The whole room went even quieter and the Margraff-Elector said, "What?" He was too shocked to speak loudly, which might be the first time that had happened in ages.

His Excellency said sharply, "Franz-Karl, this gentleman is a guest here."

"Which I am not, being neither sworn to peace nor welcomed here," Franz-Karl agreed, almost cheerfully. There was a scholar at the University who was said to speak Remoran with a clarity that would cut glass: Franz-Karl was trying for that clarity in the diplomatic rather than the scholarly version of the old Imperial language. He was too angry to be really cheerful. His Mama, the Childe of Traventi, living under His Excellency's protection, had only stale morsels and cheap wine to offer as tokens of hospitality, but this ... big, mean FIBBER... who was hurting her child was accounted a guest under this roof.

Franz-Karl continued, pulling phrases from old stories. "Since I arrived in Karnburg this afternoon I have been offered hospitable welcome, and a bath, and a meal, and slept under my Grandfather's roof... but it was not this Grandfather, nor this roof. I was not invited to this... place... but conducted across Your Excellency's Threshold without any exchange of pledges nor the offer of cup nor morsel. Since I have not been offered welcome in this place as either kinsman or guest, I am merely ... present. Therefore –"

He took a deep breath and hoped he was translating the formulas into Remoran correctly. He felt his hair pulling out of its tie, and hoped people would think it was scary. He hoped very much that he was doing the right thing, but he looked up at the King of the Allemans and Emperor of the Falkenburg Domains and said firmly, "I, Franz-Karl, of the lines of Falkenburg, Armorius, Leonstein and Capradaventi, stand here as a fully sworn Notary of Traventi – and one Recognized in the succession for the position of Duke – to bear Witness before Heaven and the Living World that the Marriage Contract between Childe Silvia Armorius of Traventi and Leon-Alexander von Falkenburg stands in breach – irreparable breach – in defiance of Heaven and the Living World and not by any choice or act of Traventi."

His Excellency said, "Franz-Karl, my boy?" uncertainly.

"Why is this changeling brat allowed to speak among his betters?" the Margraff-Elector demanded. The line was unrehearsed so his Remoran was abysmal: both the grammar and the pronunciation were... off.

Franz-Karl looked at him, looked him up and down, and shrugged. It was the one-shouldered shrug of a Traventine at his work, though the Allemanic Lords would not know that. "Horst-Konrad, I think I see my parents' faces in every mirror. If I am who I seem, I owe thee nothing. If I am not, I owe thee less." He shrugged again and felt the heavy purse in his coat pocket bump against his leg. "Ah!" he said, surprised, remembering the Tax Office. "And who my parents are does not matter for this, in any case."

"Does... not... matter...?" the Margraff-Elector seemed to be having trouble understanding the formal Remoran, or perhaps it was the thought that birth did not matter in something. Or being addressed familiarly as 'thee' and by his given name.

Franz-Karl stood as tall as six years growth in the Living World would allow. "I am not a Notary because of who my parents were: I am a fully sworn Notary because I was born an Elderkin Binder and I have taken the required oaths," Franz-Karl was actually cheerful this time. "It would not matter if I was a former slave without a family name at all... I have the Binding Gift and have taken the oaths, so I am a Notary, regardless, and qualified to bear formal Witness about any contractual matter." He thought the light and shadows in the chamber were doing something strange, but suspected that no one else would notice, as usual.

He continued, "The Heirship is similar: the topic of the vote that was taken in the Stone Theater was not 'Will you have Franz-Karl the son of so-and-so in the Succession for the position of Duke', the topic was 'Will you have this Notary, Franz-Karl, standing here before you, in the Succession for the Duchy'... and I assure you, having thousands and thousands of Elderkin decide that you are theirs and they are yours is not an experience to be doubted or forgotten."

His Excellency suggested, "But surely, any other Notary would not have faced the vote?"

Franz-Karl shrugged again. "The fifth section of the Marriage Contract requires that any child of Silvia and Leon-Alexander who attains the status of Notary must be presented for the Succession vote as soon as possible. And a number of people who are very, very hard to lie to successfully believe that I am a Notary who is the child of Silvia and Leon-Alexander. Therefore I was Recommended for Recognition as properly in the line of Succession. Traventi, unlike certain other parties, has been scrupulously careful to fulfill the terms of the Contract. But the Succession has no requirement for ancestry, just Notarial status and the consent of the populace." He paused then added in what he hoped was a very neutral tone, "I have heard that the Kingship of the Allemans is similar: depending on a vote, not ancestry, but that is not a thing that I have Witnessed.."

The Margraff-Elector looked a bit stunned. He raised one hand in a formal rhetorical gesture and opened his mouth to say something, but the Chief Justice of the Eastlands said hastily, "Your Honor said that there was an irreparable breach to the Contract. Can you explain the breach?"

Franz-Karl's heart stopped pounding quite so hard. They would listen, and this was a very public gathering: nothing said here could usefully be hidden. He hoped he would not forget the things Justice Laurentina and Maestro Petros had told him. He took the sheaf of parchments from Fritzel and sorted through them to find the page he wanted in the Remoran version. "The twenty-fifth section of the Contract says..." He read it aloud in the Remoran, then continued in Allemanic, "... that section says that 'Elderkin messengers will have immediate access to the Childe Silvia or any Heir in the Ducal line of Traventi at any hour of the day or night while the Heir is resident in any Household in Falkenburg territory.' It does not say 'if possible' or 'The Falkenburgs will give orders that...' or include any other phrase that would add flexibility. It also does not say that it is talking about a Falkenburg Household, which would limit the scope."

He shuffled the pages back into order, then continued. "Both of my parents and two of my grandparents," he bowed to each of their Excellencies, "together with all of the College of Electors of the Allemans and all of the members of the College of Princes of the Allemans, and a number of other Falkenburg vassals, and a majority of the Council of Traventi, and more than half of a quorum of the voting populace of Traventi, all agreed and swore to Heaven and the Living World by their lives and souls and hope of reaching the Halls of Judgment that this thing would be: that messengers will have immediate access at any time..."

He held out a hand and turned it palm up. "This afternoon, nearly two hours before the evening bells, I was present when an Elderkin carrying messages approached the Main Gate of the Palace and I heard the guard there say to him, 'Looking to visit your bitch of a lady are you, beastie? Well, you can forget about that'." Franz-Karl missed the guard's growl by more than an octave, but he mimicked the man's phrasing and accent precisely.

"So the Elderkin messenger handed over the messages for His Excellency and His Royal Grace – in accordance with the rules about delaying Imperial messages – and took the others away again." He paused, thought of something Count Great Aunt Adrasteia would care about, and added thoughtfully, "It does seem that there were still delays in the messages in the Palace, since I was roused from sleep with a summons to this Audience instead of receiving one that was better timed."

Several people winced. His Excellency looked furious, possibly at the suggestion that official messages were still going astray or being delayed, and gestured sharply to one of the Guard officers that was standing nearby. The officer hurried away, collecting companions on his way out of the room.

The Margraff-Elector said nastily, "If you are so mighty, I'm surprised... Your Honor... did not turn the fellow into a newt."

Franz-Karl looked at him calmly. "I am six years old, as Allemans count age. I am not allowed to turn people into things or set them on fire until I reach my majority. There are exceptions for emergencies – the College of Notaries are generally quite careful about that sort of thing when formulating rules – but a puffed up oaf with a vile tongue on him does not qualify... Of course, there is a wide space between doing nothing –" Franz-Karl spread his arms wide and wiggled the fingers of his right hand, "and turning people into newts –" he wiggled the fingers of his other hand, then brought his hands together and looked the lord of Ansbach up and down. "The Notary Count Great Aunt Adrasteia says that the Living World is wide, and full of possibilities. If your lordship values the use and sensation in your own hand, I suggest, again, removing it from my brother's shoulder... this is twice."

The Margraff-Elector's jaw dropped, but he did not move. His hand remained grasping Philip-Augustus. In fact, Franz-Karl thought he gripped tighter: he saw his brother try to hide a wince. He caught the eye of Philip-Augustus. "Count Wolfsberg, come join our mother."

His Excellency snapped, "Neumark" as if he was chiding a servant: no title or dominion name, not even a 'von'. At least it was the family name not the personal one Franz-Karl had used.

The Margraff-Elector did not appear to move, but Philip-Augustus pulled away from the man, hopped down from the platform, and hurried to their Mama's side. Franz-Karl's Mama hugged Philip-Augustus, then held him close. The Margraff-Elector waited a beat, then let his arm drop to his side.

The Justice asked curiously, "Would being a Notary affect Your Honor's ability to turn people into newts? I refer to after Your Honor's majority, of course..." His Remoran was slightly accented – so was his Court Allemanic, though it was still better than most of the Northerners at Court: he came from somewhere out east along the Daonas in the Falkenburg domains where no one claimed to speak Allemanic as a birth tongue.

Franz-Karl eyed him calmly. "It has been said that if an ordinary Binder does something appalling to you, it may very well be inadvertent, but if a Notary does it, it is almost certainly deliberate." He was feeling a vast temptation to do something... demonstrative... here, where he was not sworn to peace. He repeated the maxim in Allemanic, and the open space around him became a bit larger, as people stopped crowding him.

"Ah."

"I was considering whether a glover might find crab-claws difficult to fit: I'm not certain the transformation rule applies to parts that are not vital. Or, of course, warts are also very traditional. Lots and lots of warts..."

The open space got a lot larger. Franz-Karl stopped feeling a sort of twitch between his shoulder blades as the area around him became emptier.

Franz-Karl held up the Contract and bowed slightly to the Justice, switching back to Remoran. "If the Marriage Contract is examined carefully, I think you will find no mention of any way of curing that twenty-fifth section of it: once the thing that must happen has failed, the fault cannot be undone, though additional failures in the future may be and should be prevented. But I believe the other sections that are either questionable or in breach may be curable." He bowed slightly toward their Excellencies. "While the Marriage Contract of Silvia and Leon-Alexander remains extensively in breach this is no proper abode for those most nearly bound by the Contract. My attendants can assist Her Highness Silvia and her household in relocating from this ill-omened and inhospitable edifice to the household of her fathers at Greenoak Square... preferably before this accursèd roof falls on the lot of us." He carefully did not look at the acting Archduke his Uncle.

Her Excellency asked gently, "Childe Silvia, my dear, would it help at all if I sent for the formal offings of hospitality?"

Franz-Karl's Mama sighed and shook her head, "Not for His Honor Franz-Karl. Not before the next sunrise, and some notable progress toward curing the parts of the Contract that can be cured." She still sounded tired, though she had smiled at the suggested move to Greenoak Square.

His Excellency said, "Franz-Karl can you provide a list of the problems with the Marriage Contract?" He sounded like he expected, or hoped, that the answer would be 'No'.

Franz-Karl snorted, and rolled his eyes for good measure – his cousin Helena would have been proud of him. "Your Excellency, I have only been back in Karnburg for a few hours, and I was asleep for part of that. There has hardly been time for an audit."

"At least make a start, so that we can plan to offer you proper hospitality..." His Excellency was eager. And probably hoping an unprepared list would be neither lengthy nor severe.

Franz-Karl thought that saying nothing would give them all an excuse to do nothing. He walked over and sat on the edge of the platform in front of the chairs of state so that His Excellency could see the contract over his shoulder if he cared to. It was a horrible breach of protocol but it had been a long day and he was too tired to care. Did protocol even apply to someone who was merely present? If he was going to do a bunch of grownups' jobs for them, he was at least going to sit down to do it. He sorted through the pages of the Remoran copy of the contract.

"Well. The twenty-fifth section of the twenty-five has already been discussed. The first and third sections of the contract have been fulfilled and are sealed by the death of Leon-Alexander, and the second is a null statement that cannot be breached... However, the fourth section concerns the inheritance of the Wolfsberg titles and estates... Count Wolfsberg? Have you received your inheritance in full?"

Philip-Augustus was at least as tired as Franz-Karl, but woke up enough to say, "Uh, no. Not entirely. Not yet. They have been arguing about trustees." He closed his eyes again and leaned against their Mama.

"So, the fourth section needs investigation – I do hope someone is taking proper notes..." Count Great Aunt Adrasteia had said that in one of the council sessions. There were scuttling noises off to one side of the Audience Chamber, but Franz-Karl did not bother to look. "The fifth section has been fulfilled as much as it can be until Philip-Augustus or Sophie-Alexa become Notaries. The College of Notaries claims that they have dealt with all the matters referred to them according to the sixth section of the contract, but there are rumors that not all problems are being referred, so that is another section for investigation..." He worked his way quickly through the rest of the contract.

In all? Of the twenty-five sections of the contract, even without a proper audit, it was clear that there were three sections that needed investigation (which meant they were almost certainly in breach), four that were definitely in breach but with minor, easily remedied faults, the twenty-fifth which was incurable, and three that combined serious breaches with the more ingenious provisions by the negotiators (some of which were also in breach).

Franz-Karl was privately certain that the sections discussing the children's education and guaranteeing ritually proper food for the Traventine household could be cured almost completely if the Palace authorities stopped playing stupid games and did what they had agreed to... but he was not quite tired enough to say that out loud.

The long section about the Childe Silvia's household – the one that included the three different unrelated agreements – was amazing. Between the authorities in the Palace playing stupid games with household matters, and people abusing the Elderkin ladies, and the Landgraff across the river from Traventi playing stupid games with the border rules, almost every phrase in the section was in breach, one way or another. And Franz-Karl planned to warn the real auditors to look carefully at the punctuation that joined the phrases... in case someone had found a way to breach that as well as the words.

The Justice shook his head as he ended, "Franz-Karl... Your Honor? Do these later sections of this Contract seem sensible to you? At all?"

Franz-Karl smiled at him tiredly. "Not really." He stood up. "I suspect... well, there is an old curse on Traventi, so that contracts and agreements become an unchangeable part of the landscape once any of the signers die, whether parties or witnesses. The most usual thing people do is to make sure there are explicit rules stated in the contract for how to amend it, or how to cure it if there is a breach, even after someone involved dies. The other thing people sometimes do is make sure the new landscape will be as useful as possible, and then make sure someone very sick or very old or both is one of the signers..."

He waggled the Contract slightly. "I think the second section of the Contract says plainly that some fool blocked the first option." The Justice winced.

Franz-Karl continued, "For the rest? Well, if someone told me the negotiators had a contest to see who could shovel in the most stuff into some of the later sections...? " He held out the Contract. "Most of it looks balanced: I mean, there's none of that 'give me your first born child and half your kingdom in return for three peas and a cup of water' stuff that you see in some of the old stories. That trade agreement thing seems … elegant? And doesn't feel like only one side built it."

The Justice flipped through the pages of the contract, then once more, slowly. "I agree." He said slowly. "People were building foundations for the future, and some on both sides were doing it…"

"And some of those odder bits would be very useful if someone built on them instead of trying to wreck them," acting Archduke Uncle Helm-Friedrich said. He had been writing orders raining down thunder and lightning on various departments and offices within the Palace while Franz-Karl was summarizing the Contract problems, and he looked almost as tired as Franz-Karl felt. A lot of the other people standing in the Reception Hall were looking worried, which Franz-Karl thought was only fair.

Franz-Karl began to walk toward his Mama and Fritzel and Damian, then he stopped, turned back toward the chairs of state and made a slight bow. "A small warning, Your Excellency, for kinship's sake and no other price: do not house anyone you care about in the north end of the East Palace." He turned back again and continued to walk toward his Mama and their attendants.

Franz-Karl went back to Greenoak Square with Fritzel and Damian for the night.

His Mama and Philip-Augustus and Sophie-Alexa stayed in their usual apartments in the West Palace – but without the new tutor and nursemaid. No one said it out loud, but Franz-Karl thought that it was pretty clear that if his Mama ever got well out of the custody and trusteeship of the Allemanic and Falkenburg authorities, they were going to have a terrible time getting her back in, and everyone knew it. That was why offering to move her to Greenoak Square gave them some leverage. People being nervous about Binders had leaned on the lever a bit, too.

Crab claws… he poked at the World a little. Crab claws seemed doable, if the time came for them.

CHAPTER XXXVII: Household Arrangements

Wherein a Fragile Balance Is Established

The next morning, when they were at breakfast in the Greenoak Square house, Fritzel asked Franz-Karl when he had learned so much about contracts. "Did you somehow spend a lot of time with Her Honor Laurentina when I wasn't looking?"

Franz-Karl snickered. "No. But on some of the market days when you were busy chatting with girls and scholars, I was chatting with Maestro Petros. Especially after the first time I took a good look at the Marriage Contract." He ate a few bites of his breakfast. "Things in the Palace got a lot worse over the summer – I think my uncle was too busy managing supplies for a war or famine or something to pay enough attention at home – but the roots and sprouts were there before I left. I asked enough of the right questions, it seems."

"What was that about the East Palace? There at the end..."

""What? Oh, that." Franz-Karl sighed. "After talking about accurséd roofs, I thought I'd better warn them, or I'll get blamed when the roof does fall in or someone falls through a floor. I think the builders of the East Palace were corrupt. Or the timber merchants? Or both. You don't want to look at the beams in the cellars and attics at the north end too closely: it will turn even your hair white, and leave you treading as lightly as possible."

Damian settled beside them with his own breakfast. "Heaven and the saints, what a snake-pit that place is! Can we keep your Honor out of there?"

"No." Franz-Karl pressed his fingertips against the places where his horns would someday grow: they got itchy, or tender, sometimes. "Is it possible to get a hangover from too much stupid?" He sighed. "No, we can't really not be in the Palace unless we somehow manage to go all the way to Traventi. I'm not a grownup, and Philip-Augustus is not a grownup, and my Mama is a woman. Even aside from all of us being Elderkin. The written laws here about women and children and property are stupid, and the unwritten ways things actually work are even stupider. It's the Palace or Traventi for me, yet a while."

"That is not good."

"I think there are some cousins on the Admiral's side still in Traventi. Perhaps someone can come in the spring to play host or hostess at Greenoak Square... then I might live here at least part time. And we might manage Sophie-Alexa, but probably not my Mama or Philip-Augustus."

"Spring seems very far away."

"But at least not getting farther –" that was a Traventine saying. "For the moment? We keep to Count Adrasteia's plan: you live here, and keep the house safe, and make it safer if you can devise ways to do it. And you choose among those who traveled with us which ones stay here and which join my Mama's household. Fritzel will have rooms here as Deputy Steward, and rooms in the Palace as my aide, and should move between often enough it that the Palace guards learn to see his coming and going as commonplace. I live in the West Palace in my Mama's apartments – which at least has a proper Threshold – with conditions... and visit here more than the Worldfolk know."

"And if things go badly sour, I'll take His Honor and the little lass and run for Traventi," Fritzel added.

"Ah, is that the way of it? Well, I suppose we'll bide 'til spring..." Damian was still not happy about the situation – no one was, probably not even the Palace officials, at least not after last night – but there was nothing more to be done.

"Remember that I am a Binder, and not sworn to peace except in my Mama's apartments," Franz-Karl warned them. "People outside of Traventi have stopped listening to the tales their Grannies tell them, but... I suspect there may come a time when they are reminded. It is a long time until I reach my majority... nearly twice as long as I've yet lived... "

Damian's eyes widened and Franz-Karl realized that he had been 'born old and open-eyed' too much lately, so people were forgetting that he was young as well as short. One more problem. But things would be in a greater mess if he hadn't leaned on his Manifest side.

When Franz-Karl returned to the Palace, he was accompanied by Fritzel and his Valet Tam, who was pleasant enough, but nowhere near as comfortable to have around as Olivia, not yet. There were also two of the men who had come with them from Traventi: apparent footmen to be added to his mother's household. Largish footmen.

None of them were asked for pledges of peace at the gates, nor offered proper hospitality, except in his Mama's apartments, and the Elderkin began to exchange thoughtful glances. Franz-Karl decided that if his warnings the previous evening had fallen on deaf ears, he was not going to lessen his own freedom to act by reminding the Palace authorities again about prudent conduct when dealing with Elderkin. They should have paid better attention to the stories their Grannies told them, instead of pretending that Elderkin customs were just... manners.

When the Chamberlain's office balked at the new household arrangement, Franz-Karl refused to allow his luggage to be sent for until Fritzel and Tam were acknowledged to be part of his own personal staff, not directly under his mother's authority. That would leave her with the five men promised by the Contract, and only the one Elderkin lady-in-waiting, so she still had fewer people than the contracted number. And the crew of house servants assigned to their apartments were more than a bit sparse.

Compared to his Mama's staff, Fritzel and Tam both looked... not so much less human as more Elderkin. It was as much a matter of the way they stood and moved as of their appearances, though neither looked at all local. He thought that any future additions to his personal household should probably be at least equally exotic, if they could manage it without causing riots.

The Chamberlains complained about the new arrangements in the West Palace. When Franz-Karl and Fritzel asked to look at the accounts for the apartments, they were handed a jumbled pile of records, which they sorted into clarity according to the rules of the Tax Office in Traventi. While sitting in the Chamberlain's office.

Franz-Karl did most of the reading – Meister van Diesen's lessons had given him him plenty of practice with the style of writing – and Fritzel did most of the ciphering. They found that the household of her Grace the Reverend Childe of the Elderkin Franz-Karl's Mama had become smaller and smaller since her husband's death.

Somehow rearrangements in the Palace in her husband's absence had also meant that servants were reassigned and not replaced, even though the people who handled the money claimed the household had not decreased in size. Whoever was pocketing some of the funds that should have supported Childe Silvia in proper style did not want an investigation, so when Franz-Karl sent for paper and ink to draft a report to his Uncle and Grandfather, Fritzel and Tam were suddenly added to the list of Palace residents and Franz-Karl's household was provided with suitable allowances. And the servants who did the cleaning and tended the fires and such in Childe Silvia's Residence mysteriously became more numerous and quite busy.

Franz-Karl sent the report to His Excellency and the acting Archduke anyway.

One of the more annoying junior Chamberlains who reported to Ritter von und zu Ostwald was given the task of arranging for Fritzel's quarters. When the man asked nastily what kind of quarters he was supposed to give some jumped up peasant. Franz-Karl answered pointedly, "Titles work a bit differently in the Duchy, so Tiarna is difficult to translate, but I suppose you should provide whatever you think would be appropriate for a younger son of a major Baron. Or perhaps a son of a minor Count."

The Junior Chamberlain was the younger son of a man who was holding onto the status of minor baron by his fingernails, so he winced. Fritzel was assigned a room that had been used by Franz-Karl's Papa's secretary, Ernst, who had retired after Leon-Alexander's death. It had plenty of bookshelves, which would be helpful.

Tam was preparing to move Franz-Karl's luggage into his old room to unpack it when Philip-Augustus stepped in front of the door and announced in Allemanic that as Count of Wolfsberg it was inappropriate for him to share his sleeping quarters. Half the phrases were pronounced with more than a hint of the North: Franz-Karl thought he must be repeating things that had been said to him many times by Meister van Diesen or the new tutor, or others.

Franz-Karl looked at him for a long moment, long enough that Philip-Augustus' face reddened and he began to squirm. Finally, Franz-Karl said quietly, in Elderic, "Very well, but I'll have my own possessions out of the rooms that are now only yours. And the presents our Papa gave to both of us will remain shared in ownership, though you may have the keeping of them." He looked at his Mama. "Are there still two beds for children in the nursery?"

Sophie-Alexa gave a delighted squeal. Franz-Karl's Mama said quietly, "There are."

There was another long pause, then Philip-Augustus gave a jerky nod and disappeared through the door for a very short time. He returned with a handful of trinkets which he dropped on the table where Franz-Karl was seated.

Franz-Karl sorted them and said calmly, "It seems that between the two of us, I am not the forgetful one." Yelling at Philip-Augustus would just give him an excuse to start a fight, and his brother was still two years older, and larger... though he looked oddly small and fragile after Franz-Karl's summer of playing with the larger cousins.

And everyone outside the Bull's Leap looked small beside Fritzel.

Philip-Augustus blushed again and looked away. "Well, fetch them yourself, then, if you remember where they are. But only you. No one else."

Their Mama started to protest, but Franz-Karl just shrugged and went through the door into the large room they had shared.

The Count of Wolfsberg's rooms were as shabby and untended as the rest of the apartments. Franz-Karl judged from some of the undisturbed dust that his brother had been unable to find some of the treasures he had not taken with him to Traventi. Or perhaps Philip-Augustus had known where they were but been unable to lay his hands on them: Finn Locker's trick had been oddly familiar once he figured out how it worked. He left the dusty places undisturbed at first, while he investigated the hidey-holes the two of them had shared in the months before their father's death.

The first time Franz-Karl returned to the outer rooms, he carried several small precious things he thought belonged to their Papa and Mama, which he paced in her lap so that she could judge where they belonged. There were also two of his own best pieces of jewelry, set aside when he donned mourning after their Papa's death, and Sophie-Alexa's most precious doll, with imported porcelain hands and face and feet and exquisite garments stitched by Aunt Queen Gertrude and her companion Lady Lenke, as fine as any of their work for the cathedral.

Sophie-Alexa shouted "Mina!" and gathered the doll into her arms, hugging her tightly. Then she stomped over to Philip-Augustus and kicked him in the shins. Twice. Hard.

Franz-Karl handed his own jewelry to Tam and returned to the Count's rooms to retrieve the rest of his belongings and avoid the impending argument.

There was less free space in the nursery than in the room the boys had shared, so in the end about a quarter of the luggage that had come from Traventi and – pointedly – half the items Franz-Karl had retrieved from his brother's rooms, were sent back to the house at Greenoak Square for safekeeping. There were still empty rooms where his Mama's ladies should live, but using those for storage would be admitting that there were not going to be any more ladies. Most of the stored luggage contained items that were destined to be given as Midwinter gifts, or had other limited uses, but Franz-Karl saw no great reason to mention that. He and Philip-Augustus were not saying much to each other.

Sophie-Alexa was very glad to have company in the nursery, though a little shy at first when dealing with Tam and Fritzel. She offered all of the best places for Franz-Karl's possessions, even places that were occupied by her own things. She even offered Franz-Karl the bed she had been sleeping in, but he took the empty one instead, which was in the end of the room that got the best morning sunlight.

CHAPTER XXXVIII: Gifts

Wherein Our Hero Is Present and Gives Presents

Once he was sure that he was staying in the Palace, Franz-Karl asked his Mama's staff (that was Roland, but there were rules about these things) to inform the Palace's Master of Protocol that his proper style was now Franz-Karl von Falkenburg, Notary and Honorable Childe of the Elderkin of Traventi. At the next formal event he attended, tagging along behind his mother and brother, he was announced as His Highness, Grand Duke Franz-Karl, Honorable Childe of the Elderkin. With Highness, and the Grand Duke courtesy title, but without his dynastic name or the Duchy's name. Or Notary. He decided that was close enough. For the moment. Since he was merely present, and neither a guest nor a member of the court, it did not matter much what they chose to call him. He had no need to respond to names other than his own.

On that first occasion, two days after his return to the city, he was accompanied by Fritzel and by two footmen carrying armloads of parcels. Before he approached the chairs of state, he removed the cloth that was draped around the gift for His Excellency, and opened it so that it was clear that it was empty. Approaching the King and Emperor with a wrapped parcel that had not been inspected by the Guards was not quite a certain way to end up dead or in shackles, but it would be very reckless and might frighten Her Excellency His Grandmother. The parcel would very likely be damaged or destroyed by the Palace Guards, which would be a great pity since the box was beautifully joined and carved, and inlaid with His Excellency's arms and personal badges.

When His Excellency beckoned to him, Franz-Karl stepped forward and bowed, carrying the box in his own hands. "I have brought this gift from Traventi for Your Excellency. The lock has the special property that it will open only for you and for one other person you designate, even when the proper key is used." He made sure that he touched his grandfather hand when giving him the keys, to ensure the the Binding was set correctly.

At first, Franz-Karl was disappointed that his Grandfather's response seemed stilted and impersonal. Then he realized that he was receiving the usual formal acknowledgment of an exorbitant gift from a foreign ruler. It was the most effusive response His Excellency could give in public without giving offense to an Elderkin by saying 'Thank you'. From the murmurs and a few sour expressions, there were at least some people in the crowded room who also understood that.

Franz-Karl gave their gifts, carefully unwrapped, to Her Excellency and to his Uncle and both Aunts that were at Court but left the rest of the presents for other occasions. It would not do to take up too much time and attention at His Excellency's Audience: there were always more people who needed His Excellency's notice than the hours of a day had room for. But this way, when more treasure boxes began to appear around the Palace, the highest-ranked people would have received their gifts first.

He stepped aside so that others in the crowded room could approach their Excellencies and looked around at the crowd of Worldfolk, who looked very boring after his season among the Elderkin. There was not a single decent set of horns or feathers or antlers in the room, nor any truly interesting variations of hair color or eyes. He said very softly in Elderic, "Will you have problems telling them apart?"

Fritzel answered just as softly, "No worse than a flock of sheep the month before shearing, but I'll warn the lads to have a care."

The announcer at the entrance to the room declaimed "His Serene Highness Horst-Konrad von Neumark, Margraff-Elector of Ansbach..." and continued, listing two duchies, a county and a couple of baronies that were properties and titles of the same man, before continuing with "His Serene Highness Heinrich von Nordenham, Prince-Elector of Bremerhaven", followed by a list of his titles, and then by two other poor souls in their party – merely Nobles rather than Electors – who only had a half dozen titles between them. The group of nobles had a bevy of at least a dozen attendants trailing behind them.

"We're going to need a list to memorize, Your Honor," Fritzel observed. "Likely more than one."

"Don't trust the Master of Protocol for it, considering what he does to my style, and Mama's," Franz-Karl warned.

"Fair enough... Dear Heaven and all the saints!" Fritzel had just gotten a good look at the Margraff-Elector's clothes: white silk that was as thoroughly covered with graffiti as the black suit he had worn to Franz-Karl's Papa's funeral. Fortunately, the exclamation had been spoken very softly and in Elderic.

The Margraff-Elector and his companions paused very, very briefly to pay their respects to their Excellencies, then began a sort of procession around the room, forcing people to step out of their way and deliberately disrupting quiet conversations happening around the edges of things. They were such a large group that most people had to step aside... and then the Margraff-Elector's people spread out and trailed behind and ... lingered ... blocking people from rejoining their companions. Their wandering was not quite contrary to protocol, but did an excellent job of causing people to pay attention to His Serene Highness the Margraff-Elector instead of to his Excellency, who should have had their attention.

Franz-Karl's willingness to be bullied had not increased over the summer. He said, "Stay close, and still," to his companions quietly and set himself as the Margraff-Elector stopped for a moment, then turned toward them. The feeling of being watched was so familiar that he hardly noticed it any more.

Franz-Karl kept facing quite properly toward their Excellencies while Fritzel and the two footmen backed him. He also watched the Margraff-Elector and his party approach from the side in the wider field of view provided by Elderkin eyes. He decided that if he was addressed by his proper name or title he would step aside, but not allow them to separate him from his attendants.

Fritzel shifted his position very slightly so that he would be a rock that the oncoming stream of men would strike against, rather than immediately trampling Franz-Karl. Then he ignored them, looking toward their Excellencies as Franz-Karl was doing. Franz-Karl heard one of the footmen shift position behind him.

Franz-Karl thought very hard about how he was the grandson of their Excellencies and the chosen spear-point of the will of thousands of Elderkin, and the Worldfolk rabble stampeding toward him were led by a scrawny man wearing clothes that were scribbled all over with rude things that were looking ruder as they got closer. It made it easier not to flinch. The watching was getting stronger.

The Margraff-Elector took just a little too long to realize that the Elderkin party was not going to move out of his way. He managed to stop before he 'polluted' himself by touching an Elderkin, at first. Two of the people following closest behind him were less attentive or less agile and did not stop quite so promptly. They collided with each other, and then with the Margraff-Elector, who was shoved forward into Fritzel. Dress swords and rods of office got tangled with legs, and occasionally heads, and half of the people with the Margraff-Elector landed on the floor. Fritzel was as immovable as one of the pillars that supported the Palace, so the Margraff-Elector staggered back, tripped over someone, and landed on his back on top of the pile with someone's dress sword sticking up between his legs in a way that was almost as rude as some of the scribbles on his clothes. Something broke with a crack.

It was clear to everyone watching that Franz-Karl and his Elderkin companions had not so much as raised a hand against the Margraff-Elector and his companions. In fact, they had barely twitched: people nearby watching very closely might have noticed Fritzel's muscles flexing as he braced himself, but probably not. He was not a poor man wearing tight clothes to save cloth.

Franz-Karl turned to look after the people fell, of course. He thought that some of the vesets on the walls might be turning to look. Everyone in the room could see that what had happened to the Margraff-Elector and his companions had been completely their own doing, not the result of any Elderkin spookiness.

The laughter began on the far side of the room, beyond Their Excellencies, so that could not be blamed on Franz-Karl, either.

Fritzel held out a friendly hand to help the fallen get up. The Margraff-Elector took the offered hand before he realized who it was, then tried to push Fritzel away so hard that he himself nearly fell again: Fritzel was being immovable. He stripped the glove off the hand that had grasped an Elderkin's.

Franz-Karl was disappointed that it revealed skin, not another layer of gloves. But the skin was reddened and blotchy, which probably explained the gloves.

The Margraff-Elector looked around for his glove-bearer, but the rod was what had broken, and the fancy gloves had been trampled underfoot in the scrum. He stuck his bare hand into a coat pocket.

Franz-Karl had stepped politely aside with his companions so that the fallen could untangle themselves. He was joined by Prince Otto, who asked a polite question about the organization of road repairs in Traventi. Franz-Karl answered politely while he listened to the thrashing that accompanied the untangling of the fallen.

The Margraff-Elector turned away and stalked out of the Audience Chamber before all of his companions had been untangled. He should not have done that, properly speaking. There were official announcements planned for later in the evening and people were not supposed to leave until his Excellency dismissed everyone.

Franz-Karl stood quietly facing Their Excellencies. He could not see his own shadow: the lights were arranged so that the faces of Their Excellencies would be clearly visible to the gathering, but also so that Their Excellencies could clearly see those who addressed them. But he could tell that his hair had pulled itself out of its tie and gathered itself into tendrils, and there were shuffling noises behind him that suggested his shadow was also doing something untoward and people were trying to avoid standing in it. It had been getting frisky since his return from Traventi, which was possibly just as well.

Someone in the crowd – nowhere near the front row – snarled something in what was nearly Remoran that ended, "... should be Bound."

Franz-Karl, properly, continued to face their Excellencies. He knew his voice would be high and thin in the room, but he was careful not to shout, and to keep his Diplomatic Remoran very pure. "In Elderic, contract and oath, and promise and Binding are all the same word. When the authorities in Traventi say that I am a fully sworn Notary, they are literally saying that I am fully Bound. As a sworn Notary, the Bindings of my heritage are Bound to me. But they are always present. And so the things I Witness may be Bound. Those in my presence should have a care which of their words or actions might be bound before Heaven and the Living World." His bow was Justice to Petitioner, which was... not quite beyond his proper status.

Her Excellency his Grandmother smiled at him. His Excellency gave a nod so deep it was almost a seated bow and said, "Of course, Your Honor. We are certain all those here present find the reminder helpful." He gestured sharply to the announcer holding the paper with the agenda.

The announcements were anticlimactic after the earlier fuss, but Franz-Karl made a point of congratulating each of the people who received promotions or commendations, and politely ignoring two others involved in less happy announcements.

At the end of the evening, Franz-Karl thought His Excellency's Audience had been quite satisfactory. His enemy had made a fool of himself. Franz-Karl had not. And he had been summoned for a second conversation with His Excellency just before the end of the gathering, and quietly asked for advice.

The next morning he wrote a letter to Her Grace the Reverend Duke of the Elderkin of Traventi, his Grandmother, describing his return to the Palace in Karnburg and many of the events that followed, to be sent by express courier. His second letter, to Reverend Count Great Aunt Adrasteia, had things written between the lines in colors that Worldfolk could not see, and some of the things he wrote were built of riddles, besides being hidden. Other messages had been sent by pigeon when he first arrived, and some of those were answered by pigeon even before the express riders set out. But there were things happening that needed more explanation than would fit in a pigeon's message capsule. And he thought the Duke and Count would enjoy hearing about the Margraff-Elector in some detail.

EPILOGUE: The Margraff-Elector of Ansbach

Wherein Horst-Konrad von Neumark is Not Content

Horst-Konrad von Neumark, Margraff-Elector of Ansbach walked steadily out of the Royal Audience Chamber, and down the Great Staircase, with the disheveled remnants of his entourage trailing behind him. He was not really watching his steps, but he had walked that path – out the Door of Honor in the Palace facade and down the path to the main Palace Gate – so many times that he did not need to look. He had left Friedrich-Augustus and his degenerated progeny including that changeling brat back in the Audience Chamber, so he was fully confident that no other lesser being would dare to cross his path.

The distance between the Palace Gate and the entrance of his own Ansbach Residence was shorter than the distance from the Door of Honor to the Palace Gate, but in the tumult of the city street it always seemed much longer.

Once inside his own place, with the city chaos shut out, he did not hasten as he walked his usual route through all of the plainly but richly decorated reception rooms and other public spaces. He did not enter the area that served as the White Hall in Karnburg.

The silent servants scattered before him, careful not to meet his eyes, but he found no flaws worthy of punishment.

That seemed unlikely and he admitted it was mildly annoying.

As one of the Purified Select, he was born and shaped to be an instrument of Providence. His plans should naturally succeed unless there was some deep corruption among the tools that were set ready to his hand. His first course of action needed to be rooting out that corruption.

Horst-Konrad passed through the doorway into the private section of the house... Here in his own place he never needed to touch a doorknob to open a door or close it behind him, not if the servants were properly attentive, which those serving nearest him always were. In this part of the house, away from prying, fashionable eyes, everything was meant to be restful to the spirit. The floors were polished but very plain, the walls and ceilings were pure and white and spotless, and the furnishings were sparse but elegant and made of materials so precious that decadent fool wearing the crown would be envious if he ever heard a hint of them.

He walked past the closed door of the empty women's quarters.

He walked past the door that led to the kennels, with the demon-cages waiting for the Traventine monsters he had expected to summon to heel by now, all these months since the nuisance of Leon-Alexander was cleared from his path.

When he reached his personal quarters he dropped the clothes he had worn to Court on the floor and dressed in unpolluted garments. But he was sure he could still smell the warm stench of the Elderkin he had collided with, and the herbs and spices in which the beast's clothes had been stored, so he ordered the servants to burn every stitch he had worn to Court and cleanse the leather thoroughly. Better to waste the expensive goods than to let them contaminate his other possessions.

When he left his dressing room he found a messenger waiting: kneeling with its eyes lowered decently and a folded paper in its raised, trembling hands. When he read the message, Horst-Konrad's own hand trembled, though he quickly controlled the unseemliness: his recent glove-bearer had evaded proper discipline by taking his own life. He ordered disciplinary measures for the guards who had been sloppy, but it was unsatisfactory. This day continued to be a desecrated mess.

As he walked toward his study, he wondered briefly whether anyone more useful than the past failures remained among his staff. The few with special skills had not yet been replaced, and a new Preacher for the White Hall remained elusive.

He made a mental note to increase the rigors of his own discipline: Heaven would support the designs of the Purified Elect, as it provided those designs. Doubt was unworthy.

After he reached his study and sat in the un-cushioned chair behind the bare wooden table that served as his desk, the Master of Ansbach consulted passages in a few old books retrieved from locked cabinets. Then he spoke the number, 87, that was engraved on the collar of the former tutor in the house of Leon-Alexander, and followed it with the single word 'Beer'.

The drink arrived before the man, unsurprisingly. By Pristinist custom the servile were washed and installed in clothing that covered them decently from neck to wrists and ankles before they were brought to kneel, barefoot and bareheaded, in the presence of the wellborn, especially the Select. He sipped while he waited, and reviewed a few more passages from the books.

When 87 arrived, he looked terrified, not entirely without cause. Horst-Konrad was certain that his plans had failed to turn out as he expected because of some failure of obedience or diligence during the time 87 was installed in Leon-Alexander's household. Until he knew what that failure had been, his plans were likely to be incomplete and the results of his followers' efforts might be less than his ambitions demanded.

The End of Volume I of the Elderkin Chronicles
to be continued in
Childe of Sorrows: Elderkin Chronicles Volume II.

Heir of the Bindings

Solution to the Puzzle

The man with the wolf, goat and cabbage should put the goat into the boat and take it across the river, leaving the wolf and cabbage safely together on the original river bank.

He should leave the goat and go back across the river alone.

He should put the cabbage into the boat and take it across the river. Then, leaving, the cabbage, but taking the goat with him, he must return across the river.

Once he reaches the first side of the river, he should put the wolf into the boat and leave the goat on the original river bank.

Taking the wolf across the river, he can leave it safely with the cabbage on the far river bank.

Finally he can travel across the river again, alone. He can put the goat in the boat so they cross the river to rejoin the wolf and cabbage.

The wolf and cabbage cross the river once each.

The goat crosses the river three times.

The man and boat cross the river seven times.

Acknowledgments

Early and ongoing inspiration, builders of worlds and characters: Andre Norton, Zenna Henderson, Poul Anderson, CJ Cherryh, Chris Claremont, J. R. R. Tolkien, Tanith Lee

Half a century ago Jacqueline Lichtenberg pulled me into the world of SF fandom and conventions, and changed my life.

More recently, useful information and encouragement have come from the participants of the WordWeavers and WritersCoffeClub hashtag discussion groups on Mastodon

Flint Dibble's YouTube channel and Bret Devereaux's blog at https://acoup.blog provided many useful research rabbit holes.

Melissa Ann Singer (former senior editor at Tor/Forge) read an early draft of this book.

So did Anna McDonough.

Mary Robinette Kowal's Live Virtual Workshop on Avoiding Infodumps was extremely helpful.

Finally and most importantly, Nanette Furman has been reading my stuff for decades and served as an alpha and beta reader in addition to reading an amazing number of earlier drafts and fragments. I am profoundly grateful for her encouragement.

Colophon

The image on the cover was created by the author in Krita, based on the Sphinx of Naxos, as modeled by a figurine purchased from an Etsy shop, *GreekRomanArt*, that no longer seems to be active.

The title font used is Black Chancery, which has been released into the public domain. The body fonts are EB Garamond and the font in the Superior Magpie logo is Essays1743, which are both covered by the SIL Open Font License (OFL).